A Soufflé of Suspicion

Also by Daryl Wood Gerber

French Bistro Mysteries

A Deadly Éclair

Cookbook Nook Mysteries

Pressing the Issue

Grilling the Subject

Fudging the Books

Stirring the Plot

Inherit the Word

Final Sentence

Cheese Shop Mysteries (writing as Avery Aames)

For Cheddar or Worse

As Gouda as Dead

Days of Wine and Roquefort

To Brie or Not To Brie

Clobbered by Camembert

Lost and Fondue

The Long Quiche Goodbye

A Soufflé of Suspicion

A FRENCH BISTRO MYSTERY

Daryl Wood Gerber

NEW YORK

Published in the United States by Crooked Lane Books, an imprint of The Quick Brown Fox & Company LLC.

Library of Congress Catalog-in-Publication data available upon request.

ISBN (hardcover): 978-1-68331-586-5
ISBN (ePub): 978-1-68331-587-2
ISBN (ePDF): 978-1-68331-588-9

Cover illustration by Teresa Fasolino.
Book design by Jennifer Canzone.

Printed in the United States.

www.crookedlanebooks.com

Crooked Lane Books
34 West 27th St., 10th Floor
New York, NY 10001

First Edition: July 2018

10 9 8 7 6 5 4 3 2 1

To my sister, Kimberley Greene.
Thank you for all your loving support.

The only time to eat diet food is while you're waiting for the steak to cook.

—Julia Child

Chapter 1

"Mimi, whoa!" Stefan, my sous-chef, reeled back as I pushed through the swinging doors leading to the kitchen. "Hot stuff!" he yelled. He wasn't referring to me, sorry to say. He was commenting on the preparations for crème brûlée with caramel flambé that he was carting into the main dining room. The delicious aroma of burnt sugar permeated the air. As if reading my thoughts, he said, "Though you do look good."

"Kiss up," I said.

Stefan let out one of his rollicking laughs. "I'm not stupid."

I looked the same as I always did, clad in my work uniform of khaki pants, white shirt, and clogs, my toffee-colored hair slung into a bun. It wasn't a *hot* look but not unattractive, I'd been told. And I was always ready for whatever the day might bring. The only fashion statement I wore was the pink tourmaline necklace my father had given me when I turned sixteen and the matching tourmaline studs I had recently purchased to go with it. A little sparkle did a girl good.

I said, "Thank heaven you have young legs or I'd have been toast."

"Your legs are almost as young," he said. "*Almost.*"

At thirty-five, I was ten years his senior. "Go!" I chuckled. "Someone is expecting a delectable dessert after their lunch."

"*After* lunch? This *is* lunch." Stefan winked. "You know the Friday crowd. People splurge!"

Humming, he pushed the cart into the main dining room. As he deftly wove between tables, I glimpsed multiple images of him in the mirrors that adorned the bistro's walls, and I couldn't help thinking how much he resembled Johnny Mathis in his heyday. His father did, too, right down to his espresso-colored skin and chocolate brown eyes. Did Stefan's twin sister look like Johnny, as well? I'd never met her. Last week was the first time I'd heard of her. Stefan could be secretive, and for good reason. He had wanted to follow his own path without his influential father's help. Fortunately, my gifted sous-chef oozed talent in the kitchen; he had never wanted for a job. When I was his age, I'd been equally precocious.

"Chef C!" I called as I reentered the kitchen and moved past the white farmhouse-style table where I ate most of my meals. "Chef!" I zigzagged through the busy kitchen crew.

Camille Chabot, or Chef C as she liked to be called by the staff, was standing by the eight-burner stove. She twirled a wooden spoon, acknowledging that she'd heard me, but she didn't take her focus off her task. How I adored her. She was a talented French-born woman with a lust for food as well as a hunger for excellence. Lucky me; I had discovered her a year ago after a statewide search in California for someone to head up the kitchen in my new bistro.

I said, "A birdie told me—"

She shook her head, indicating she couldn't catch all of what I was saying.

I knew how she felt. I'd once been a full-time executive chef. The cacophony in the kitchen could be daunting. I drew nearer.

"What is up, Mimi?" she asked with a hint of a French accent.

She had worked hard to get rid of it after moving to America as a child. She tilted her head to make eye contact. I wasn't that tall, but she was a cube of a woman. Her toque teetered on her head. I steadied it for her. "*Merci*," she said. Although she was in her forties, her hair was snow white. She claimed it was because her daughter—now a sous-chef in New York—had been a hellion in her teens.

"A birdie told me your sister Renee is doing a bang-up job setting up the Sweet Treats Festival at Maison Rousseau."

"*Oui*. I have been told the same."

After I'd given up my career as a chef—long story, not so short—I'd moved home and caught a break. A generous benefactor was willing to sponsor my dream of owning a restaurant. With wings on my feet, I tossed aside my toque and chef's coat and set to work. Soon after, I owned Bistro Rousseau. Rousseau was my maiden name and I was proud of it. My family had produced quality wine in Napa Valley—specifically in Nouvelle Vie, an unincorporated enclave in Napa between Yountville and St. Helena—for six decades. In addition to the bistro, I owned the neighboring and growing-in-popularity inn, Maison Rousseau.

"Renee is having the best time. She is on cloud nine." Camille cranked off the burners for the three huge pots of boiling water—a large pan filled with pasta that had been cooked al dente sat on the nearby counter—and redirected her attention to the four skillets in which she was sautéing fresh herbs, oil, and garlic. The aroma made my mouth water. "Renee has not told me much about it, and I will not ask. She does not need my two cents."

I usually served as chef on Fridays so Camille could relax before the weekend rush, but a few days ago she'd advised me that she was too excited to sit still. Now I understood why. If she had taken the day off, she might have been tempted to butt into her sister's business.

"Help, please," Camille said to me rather than to a sous-chef. She directed me to finish making the pasta appetizers. "And make it snappy, missy." At times she could be gruff. None of the staff seemed to mind. They had soon come to realize, as I had, that she was all bark and no bite and had a wicked sense of humor.

I saluted. "Yes, Chef." I plated four servings of pasta and topped them with the fresh herbs, oil, and garlic sauce. I added a basil leaf and a slice of *chabichou*, a traditional non-rind French goat cheese. "Ready," I said.

One of the waitstaff loaded the dishes onto a serving tray and hurried out of the kitchen. A sous-chef removed the skillets and replaced them with fresh ones plus the fixings for another batch of pasta toppings.

Camille went right to work. "Setting the festival at Maison Rousseau was a coup for Renee. Thank you for allowing her to do so. This is the first of many such events for her."

"I heard she acquired the rights to the festival from another woman."

"That is correct. The woman could not make a go of it. She could not get advertisers on board. She did not have the—what is the word—*knack*." Camille punctuated the word with a wave of her spoon. "Renee is a dynamo. To spread the word about the festival, she came up with the brilliant idea to donate ten percent of the proceeds to a local charity that helps promote education. Plus, she is going to include a bake-off competition."

"She sounds industrious."

"She is." Camille beamed. "Both the fundraiser and the bake-off helped her secure five prominent sponsors. The rest is history."

"The festival is going to be a huge draw for us," I said. Most festivals in the valley ran Thursday to Sunday, but Renee had decided a weeklong Saturday-to-Saturday event might really get people talking. The event, which would open tomorrow, would feature bakers, ice cream makers, and dessert beverage mixologists. Businesses from all over the valley had signed on to sell their wares. And hopeful amateurs had entered the bake-off. "Festival employees and volunteers are busy setting up tents, tables, and demonstration areas in the inn's gardens right now," I said. "I'm going over after lunch to take a peek."

Camille clacked her spoon on the rim. "Renee has told me each festival area will match the gardens' color schemes."

"How lovely."

With my benefactor's help, we had built the inn in the style of Monet's Giverny, each wing of the two-story building boasting a pink crushed-rock façade with green windowsills and shutters. There were three primary gardens, which we had named after Monet's family and artistic friends. Behind the inn, there was an idyllic lily pond and a walkway covered by arches of climbing plants.

I said, "Before the festival gets under way, you should stop by and take a peek, too."

"I will if I can. We have been packed with customers."

Every year in October, Napa Valley was busy. But this year, in particular, it was going to be busier than all get-out. In addition to the festival, people were flocking to the area to attend Crush Week—the time when grapes were pressed at the vineyards. There were going to be hoedowns, hayrides, and farm tours. At some vineyards, they celebrated the fall release with wine and food tastings. I loved how the heady scent of ripening fruit mixed with the excitement of those who grew the grapes as well as those who came to participate made the valley brim with energy. A walk through a vineyard preparing for a crush could be intoxicating.

"Renee has spoken highly of the inn's staff," Chef C went on. "She says they are very cooperative."

"That's great to hear."

"Plate," she ordered.

I set to work, preparing the pasta again as I had moments before. "You know, I have yet to meet her."

"You cannot miss her when you do. She is nothing like me. She is taller, for one thing, and she is colorful and tells the best jokes."

"You tell pretty good jokes."

"She is also a slob." Chef C slid the skillets aside and fetched six petit filets from a nearby platter. "Perhaps she is not . . ." She laughed as she prepared the filets for *steak au poivre* by rolling them in cracked pepper. "Perhaps I am a solitary person who prefers everything in its place."

"Like your kitchen."

"*Exactement*," she said in a full French accent.

Renee hadn't always been a festival operator. Up until two weeks ago, she had managed a chicken-and-egg farm with her husband. Mid-September, she had announced to her husband that she had tired of the life and had secured the rights to the festival with savings she had amassed over the years. She'd also informed him that she had grown weary of their marriage and needed a breather. That afternoon, she'd moved into her sister's house. Talk about major life changes!

"I also heard she's touring a few more places this morning, looking for her next festival site." According to my source, Renee hoped to grow the festival business. She wanted to put on one a month.

"Yes. She went with Donovan." Camille's eyes glistened with excitement. Donovan Coleman, the son of a local vintner, was her new boyfriend. Well, sort of. I knew she had fallen for him; I wasn't sure how he felt about her. He was quite a bit younger and a tad impetuous. At the ripe age of thirty—he was all of thirty-five now—Donovan had shunned the family wine business to become a baker. Camille raved about his cookies, especially his bite-sized French *macarons*, a meringue and almond flour sandwich cookie filled with icing. "Renee and Donovan have gone to Calistoga."

"What's there?" I asked.

"The Bookery. Do you know it?"

"Indeed, I do." The Bookery was a charming bed-and-breakfast that held literary events. In my spare time, I loved to read, and I enjoyed attending book fairs and meeting authors. I'd visited The Bookery at least a dozen times. One of my favorite mystery authors, Kate Carlisle, who'd written a series set in San Francisco as well as the wine country, had appeared at a book event there a few months ago.

"Donovan is checking out the bakery," Camille said.

The Bookery boasted a thriving bakery and café. The owner's motto was "Nestle in and get comfortable." She believed one couldn't read a book without a cup of tea and something sweet in hand.

Chef C said, "*Shh*—it is a secret—but I believe Donovan is hoping to steal some ideas. He wants to open his own bakery. He does not wish to teach cooking classes forever, although the position has provided him a steady income." She sighed. "Men. They dream big, do they not?"

Yep, I thought. *The man had won her heart.* "I hope he gets what he wants."

"Me, too."

"Mimi!" Heather, my hostess and right-hand woman, breezed in via the kitchen's rear door. Her curly blonde tresses bounced on her shoulders. Her cornflower-blue dress clung to her lithesome frame. "You'll never guess what I did all day yesterday."

Dare I ask? I thought, suppressing a giggle. Heather had taken the day off. Who knew where she might have gone? When she'd first started working for me, she'd claimed that she had been abducted on numerous occasions by aliens—*Glonkirks*, she'd called them. Soon after, however, she disabused me of that notion, saying that talking about aliens was her way of pulling people's legs. The truth saddened me. I had enjoyed the stories, as fanciful as they were. I'd often fantasized about her visiting Mars and soaring outside the Milky Way. *Yoo-hoo, Scotty, beam me up.*

"Let me guess," I said. "Did you trip the light fandango? Or take tango classes? Maybe you've been typing your husband's latest manuscript." Henry wrote science fiction novels. For a long time, I hadn't believed he was real, either, until one day when she had finally brought him to the bistro. He was a dumpling of a guy.

Her bright eyes crinkled with amusement. "No, silly. I was playing with my babies."

"Your furry babies?"

"Yes!"

A few months ago we'd found out that Scoundrel—a gray-and-white mouser that dwelled in the neighboring vineyards and visited the bistro for real cat food and affection—was female, not male, and pregnant to boot. It wasn't my fault for the error. Heather had been the primary caretaker. I hadn't thought to, um, look. Six weeks ago, Scoundrel had given birth to a litter of kittens.

"You'll be pleased to know I've found them all homes." Heather rattled off the names of the new owners. A former math teacher, she was terrific with facts and figures. "Do you have a minute? Come see them. I'm not needed in the dining room at the moment."

"They're here?"

"Henry had a meeting with an attorney in the city. When he's done, he'll drop by and pick them up. It's okay, isn't it? I hate leaving them home alone. They're in the shed."

After completing the construction of the bistro, we'd realized we needed more storage. We'd added a small air-conditioned space where we kept staples like flour, sugar, and spices.

"It's fine."

"The kittens are so much cuter now."

"I hope so." When I'd first seen them, they'd looked like pinch-faced, furless rats. Growing up, I hadn't owned cats—my mother was a dog person. As a chef, I hadn't acquired any animals for fear of transporting their hair to my cooking area. Since then, fellow chefs had advised me that I needn't worry. Bobby Flay was a huge cat lover; if he could own a cat, so could I. Nowadays, Scoundrel often made her way to my cottage at the rear of Maison Rousseau—it had once been the caretaker's unit. She would meow a hello, as if she was there to visit me, but I believed she was more interested in getting to know my resident goldfish—intimately. *Yum.*

"Come on." Heather beckoned me.

She exited the kitchen, and I followed her to the shed. In the corner, inside a wire crate, huddled six mewing kittens.

"Ooh," I murmured. "They're adorable." One with gray-and-white markings reminded me of Scoundrel. Another was black with white paws. Three were charcoal gray. The sixth was black with a white stripe down its nose. "And each of them has a new home?"

"Yep." She buffed her nails on her dress. "I'll turn them over to their new owners in a couple of weeks. One couple is taking three of them, one for each of their little girls. How sweet is that?"

As I bent to unlatch the door, a flash of black whizzed between me and the crate. I started. "What the heck?"

Heather steadied me. "Bad Scooter!" She wagged a finger at a retreating feline.

"Who's Scooter?"

"Sorry, Mimi. I forgot to close the door to the shed."

"Who is Scooter?" I repeated.

"Scoundrel's significant other."

"He's a black cat," I murmured, my heart chugging from the fright.

"As black as lava and faster than a bullet train."

A shiver ran down my spine. I was not superstitious by nature. Fantasies and folk tales didn't suck me in, but I had to admit, a black cat crossing my path unnerved me. Black cats signified imminent danger, didn't they?

Chapter 2

Needing a moment after the lunch crowd departed to collect myself—I was still thrown by the black cat incident—I tossed on a pink scarf and light jacket and headed to Maison Rousseau to introduce myself to Renee. I wanted to see how she was getting along with the preparations for the festival. As I strode down the path toward the entrance, a crisp breeze swept through. I was glad I'd donned the extra clothing.

"Hey, Mimi!" Jo met me halfway.

Jorianne "Jo" James, the little birdie who had told me about Renee, was my best friend and the manager of Maison Rousseau. She was also the brilliant woman who had come up with the idea of introducing me to my benefactor, Bryan Baker. I would be forever grateful to her for that. How I missed him. He would be so proud of our successful venture. Thinking of the way he'd been killed last June continued to jar me. I pushed the horrid memory to the recesses of my mind—dwelling on the negative was never fruitful—and powered on.

"Love the look." I drew a finger up and down, indicating her outfit. Jo usually dressed in tailored blue suits, but today she was wearing a peach-toned floral silk combination that showed off her shapely figure. She had even dusted her spiky ebony hair with peach-toned hair color. "Peach suits your coloring."

"Tyson said the same."

Wow! Dating Tyson Daly was apparently taking Jo out of her *blue period*, as artists might have called her devotion to the color.

I grinned. "I bet he likes you in any color."

"You might be right."

Tyson, Jo, and I had grown up together. For years, he'd had a crush on her. Three months ago, he had finally found the courage to ask her out. I'd never seen her happier.

"But aren't you cold?" I asked.

"Not a bit. I'm moving at warp speed. And the breeze will die down. It always does."

Napa Valley's climate was mild and akin to that in the Mediterranean.

We hugged and strolled toward the entrance. As we drew near, I gaped. The Sweet Treats Festival banner at the entrance to the inn was huge and packed with words, all in capital letters:

CRAZY ABOUT MUFFINS? PASSIONATE ABOUT PIES? ZEALOUS FOR SOUFFLÉ? THE HUNT IS ON FOR AMATEUR BAKERS TO TAKE PART IN THE FIRST SWEET TREATS FESTIVAL BAKE-OFF. IF YOU DREAM ABOUT PUTTING YOUR SKILLS TO THE TEST, ENTER NOW AND PROVE YOUR METTLE. IF YOU KNOW FRIENDS UP FOR THE CHALLENGE, GIVE THEM A BUTTERY PAT ON THE BACK AND ENCOURAGE THEM TO COMPETE. THE MORE THE MERRIER!

"Renee sure put effort into the sign." I giggled. "Will festival attendees take the time to read it?"

"You did." Jo squeezed my arm. "If you think that's an eyeful, wait until you see the rest of the festival. It's popping with color and energy. The Renoir Retreat is packed with red tents and red balloons." The Renoir Retreat featured chili-red bougainvillea, a variety of red tea roses, and a beautiful marble fountain. "The Sisley Garden is under way, too. We'll tackle the Bazille Garden after that."

The Renoir Retreat and Sisley Garden lay to the left of the inn; the larger Bazille Garden was situated to the right.

Jo hooked her arm through mine. "Come this way."

"You're sure in an upbeat mood. What's going on? It can't simply be the festival. Are you going on a date with Tyson tonight, hence the pretty dress?"

"No, we're not going on a date, and for your information, I decided to give myself a makeover *because*." She planted a hand on her hip.

"*Because*?" I echoed.

"Okay, fine, Renee Wells suggested the idea."

I balked and cleared my throat. "Ahem. Since when do you let someone else dictate your clothes? You've never let me."

"There's a reason for that." She poked me in the ribs.

Jo and I were opposites in almost every way. She was dark to my light. She towered above me; I felt petite around her and I was five feet five. She almost always thought with her head, not her heart. She'd graduated UC Berkeley with an MBA; I'd never gone to college. The family couldn't afford it—every penny went into the vineyard—so I'd skipped off to San Francisco to follow my dream of becoming a chef. But Jo and I did have the same sense of humor, and that was where we bonded. Plus, she loved my cooking. She had been my childhood guinea pig when I'd attempted recipes from every French cookbook I could find.

As we sauntered through the inn, Jo righted a few of the Monet-style paintings that were askew. Thanks to Bryan, who'd owned a huge art collection and had donated a couple of works to our enterprise, some were the real thing.

"By the way, the inn is booked up," Jo said. "The festival plus Crush Week are drawing huge crowds." She rubbed her fingertips together. "I can't wait to tell my sister and lord it over her. I dare her to say something derogatory about my career switch. We are going to be rolling in dough." After their mother had walked out on the family, Jo's older sister had become Jo's staunchest supporter—until Jo had given up her profitable CPA job to help me in my venture; she had been on track to becoming partner. Her sister had called her an idiot, and, truthfully, maybe Jo hadn't made the wisest choice. I was paying her a good salary, but I didn't have the funds for sizable yearly bonuses yet. But Jo enjoyed a challenge.

"By the way," Jo said, "you can tell who the festival employees are. They're all dressed in the same khaki outfit."

She steered me left, past the green-and-pink mosaic fountain in the middle of the inn's foyer and through the archway into the Sisley Garden. Sunlight flickered through the trees and made the beds of white roses and crushed-quartz gravel pathways glisten. Volunteers had constructed five white tents with white poles. Festive white bells hung from the tassels. The breeze, as Jo had predicted, had died down, but there was enough to make the bells jingle.

Near a refreshments table that was set with beverages and cookies, a skinny man in a khaki shirt and shorts was filling white balloons with helium. Jazzy instrumental music emanated from gigantic speakers.

"Hold it! Not so fast. Whoa!" A curvy woman in tight jeans, fashionable red boots, and a tight long-sleeved T-shirt bedazzled with the words SWEET TREATS FESTIVAL darted into the area and motioned to a quartet of festival employees who were trying to erect a display tent. "Hey, you four, stop!"

The woman flipped her beribboned blonde pigtails over her shoulders and marched toward the problem. One of the four, a freckle-faced female volunteer, was teetering and couldn't manage her tent pole.

I said to Jo, "The woman in the red boots is Renee, I assume?"

"Yep."

"Stop! Do not move!" Renee looked nothing like Camille, and she didn't have a French accent like hers, either, but she had the same commanding voice. She scuttled to the crewwoman and helped insert the pole into the cement base. "Whew. That was close." She circled the tent and made sure all the anchors were tight. "Okay, let's put up the next one, everybody."

Across the way, our gardener, Raymond Cruz—who had also grown up with Tyson, Jo, and me—was working alongside Nash Hawke, the former wine representative who had, as of July, taken on the responsibility of running my mother's vineyard. Raymond and Nash were quite a handsome pair with their dark hair and muscular physiques. Nash was wearing jeans and a blue T-shirt. Raymond was dressed like the festival employees. In addition to his normal job, he would head up the physical labor for the festival. He and Nash were pounding tent pegs into the ground.

Nash caught sight of me and waved. My heart did a little skip. I offered an inconspicuous wave. I refused to let him know how much I liked him. Not yet. We went on a date every few weeks, but I was wary of his, um, *appeal* to the opposite sex. Truth? There wasn't a woman who didn't flirt with him. Granted, when he was with me, he gave me his undivided attention, so I had scrubbed the notion that he was a playboy from my mind—a devious rumor his ex-wife had fostered—but I was still reluctant to open my heart. What if I wasn't enough for him? What if another woman knocked his socks off? Perhaps my deceased husband's duplicity about our finances was the reason I questioned a man's undying love. I mean, c'mon, Derrick had lied to me for years about how flush he was. How could he do that if he'd cherished me?

Nash beckoned me. I mouthed, *Business*. He nodded that he understood.

I headed to Renee, hand extended. "Renee, hello! I'm Mimi Rousseau."

A big grin spread across her face. "I'm so embarrassed." She pumped my hand. "I should've stopped by yesterday and introduced myself, but I was too eager to get started. Jorianne has been amazing."

"Pshaw," Jo said, though she was drinking in the compliment.

I gestured to the tents. "It looks like you've got this whole thing under control, Renee."

"I'm doing my best. Wait until you see the crowds." She rubbed her hands together with glee. "We've sold all of the week's presale tickets. That was the number needed to cover initial expenses. More people will purchase at the gate. Ooh, think of the press you'll get for the inn and your restaurant."

I smiled. "Reservations at both places are spiking. It's a win-win."

Renee beckoned us to join her as she made the rounds. Jo begged off. She had to help out at the reception desk. A large party was checking in. I kept pace with Renee.

"We're a tad behind," she said. "It's my fault. I was out all morning. I couldn't oversee everything. We have a number of tents left to put up."

It did my heart proud that Nash had finished the chore he and Raymond had been doing and had already started in on another. He was that way about life, jumping in with both feet. Was I wrong to keep him at bay? Would he run the opposite direction if I said we needed to talk?

"Mimi?" Renee said. "Are you with me?"

I blushed. "I sure am."

"Speaking of tents . . ." She stopped and faced me. "A man goes to the shrink complaining of an identity crisis. 'You have to help me,' he says. 'Sometimes I'm a yurt. Other times I'm a tepee. A yurt. A tepee. A yurt.'" She gestured with her hands, weighing her options. "The guy goes on. 'It's too much, doc. Help me.' The doctor says, 'Calm down. You're two tents.'" Renee paused. "Get it? *Too tense.*" She roared and slapped her thigh. "I told that to Donovan Coleman. That's who I was with this morning. Do you know him?"

"I do."

"He didn't get it." Renee tittered. "How could he not get it? It's a camping joke, for heaven's sake."

"Camping joke?" I racked my brain and a light dawned. "Got it. His name is Coleman. Like a lantern. Cute." I chuckled. "I heard you two went to The Bookery."

"We did, indeed. What a terrific place. Your inn is much prettier, but it was so festive. They were having a ten-year anniversary celebration with confetti and balloons, and it was such a treat." She spoke to me out of the side of her mouth. "While we were there, I pitched them a festival and Donovan learned all sorts of baking tips. He is so talented."

"Camille told me he wants to open his own bakery."

"He does. He—" Clucking her tongue in a dismissive way, she approached a display table set with mason jars filled with goodies for do-it-yourself cookies. "Some people don't have an eye for display, you know?" She rearranged the taller jars behind the shorter jars and pressed on. "Where was I? Right." She snapped her fingers. "Donovan has a great head for business. He'd like to start his own line of cookies, like Famous Amos. He's calling them Donovan's

Delights. Catchy, don't you think? He's rented a tent and is going to sell them over there."

She pointed to the spot next to the COLORFUL COOKIES tent. DONOVAN'S DELIGHTS was written in pink script on a white banner. A table was set with pink bakery boxes.

I scanned the crowd for Donovan, who because of his height would have stood out, but he was nowhere in sight. "He's not here?"

"Not yet. He's teaching a cooking class. Today, his cookies are free for the volunteers. Hey"—Renee tapped my arm—"while we were out, I learned that, in addition to cookies, Donovan loves soufflé. Camille makes a killer chocolate one. She's going to teach me how."

"Wonderful. So will The Bookery host your next festival?" I asked.

"Yep! I landed it. We're calling it the Read for Life Festival." She grabbed a handful of Sweet Treats Festival flyers off a table and directed me to follow her. "And thanks to a very influential friend, I've got two more booked—a folk music festival and a wine-and-chocolate festival."

"An influential friend as in the councilman's wife?" I asked. Nouvelle Vie, though unincorporated, had a town council that was quite active on the town's behalf.

Renee glanced at me. "How did you know?"

"Word gets around." I'd overheard a couple of customers talking at the bistro. The restaurant wasn't huge. Gossip was hard to miss. Plus, people liked to chat about the councilman's wife. If people would describe Renee as colorful, then they might describe Felicity Price as garish.

"She's been so helpful," Renee said. "So informative. I've gotten a real education from her. With her help, I plan to produce nine more festivals over the next few months." She flashed nine fingers.

"All of them will donate ten percent of their proceeds to educational causes throughout Napa Valley. Isn't that great?"

When I'd learned that a portion of the festival's sales would be donated to bringing local schools new tables and chairs and trailer-style classrooms, I'd cheered. The fundraising aspect of the festival was one of the reasons it was drawing such enormous crowds. People could donate more if they chose.

"If everything goes as expected," Renee continued, "I'll be riding high in less than a year. Crossing my fingers."

"Is your husband embracing your new venture yet?" I asked.

Renee scrunched her nose. "He doesn't have a say in it. He and his chicken feathers can go to—"

"Renee Wells!" a woman bellowed. Storming toward us was a doughy-faced, tawny-haired woman in her thirties. She was stuffed into a tight white blouse and frothy pink skirt that made her hips look rather large. Her short hair framed her face like a lion's mane. "We need to chat."

"Not now, Allie," Renee said. "I'm too busy."

"Now!" Allie demanded. She flailed an envelope. "What is this?"

"Mail," Renee quipped.

"Don't make fun. You lied."

"Go back to being a short-order cook, Miss O'Malley," Renee said with saccharine sweetness. "I hear you're great at it."

Allie sneered. "I sold this festival to you with the agreement that I would earn a percentage. You call this a contract?"

"No, I said it was *mail*."

Allie stared daggers at Renee; Renee didn't flinch. Her ski jump–style nose scrunched up and her eyes sparkled, as if she found Allie entertaining.

"This is not a contract. It's a single page of nonsense," Allie sputtered. "You're thumbing your nose at me."

"I told you to have an attorney look it over. You opted not to."

"How could you?" Allie's voice skated up an octave. "I trusted you."

Renee frowned, then yelled to the volunteers, "Everyone, take five! Grab something to drink and snack on a Donovan's Delights cookie! Mimi, don't move. I'll be back." She dumped the festival flyers on a nearby table and clasped Allie's hand. "Let's go." She ushered her toward the rear of the garden.

Allie continued her rant at full volume. "You also promised that I could buy the business back at any time. Well, I want to do so now."

"I'm sorry, but I never promised that." Renee matched Allie's tone.

"Yes, you did."

"Where is it written, and where would you get the funds? Did you rob a bank or kill your father to get your inheritance?"

Allie stomped a foot. Renee guided her to a wrought-iron bench and forced her to sit. Renee said something I couldn't make out and didn't care to. This was a private matter. Allie covered her face with her hands.

I strolled to the refreshments table, where Nash was pouring tea into a plastic cup filled with ice. Raymond and two volunteers stood at the end of the table. Raymond was telling them about the next master gardener chat he would be giving at a local nursery. He was the most talented gardener in the valley, and I was lucky to have snagged him.

"Hey." Nash sidled up to me and ran a finger down my arm. I shivered with pleasure. Knowing the effect he was having, he grinned and said, "Fancy seeing you here."

"I do own the place."

"Huh." He cocked his head, a twinkle in his eye. "I heard the owner was a real bear."

"Goldilocks, at your service." I roared in the cutest way I knew how.

"I also heard she's a pretty good cook."

"She might know a thing or two."

"Enough to toss together a meal for a beleaguered soul like me on her next day off?"

"I think she could swing it. How about *jambon-beurre*?"

"Sounds exotic. What is it?"

"A ham sandwich with the best ham and the creamiest butter on the freshest baguette I can find."

"Perfect. I'll take you wine tasting. Afterward, we'll go to your place for a ham sandwich"—he added in a whisper—"and I can kiss you properly. I know you don't like public displays of affection."

It wasn't that I didn't like PDAs; I just wasn't ready. But then he winked, and something inside me went *snap*, and I felt like having a major public display of affection—right here, right now.

"You big tease," I said.

"That's me." He hitched his head toward Renee and Allie. "What's going on with those two?"

"The former festival owner—the shorter one with the wild hair—is upset with the deal she made with Renee. There's something in the fine print of her contract."

"No fun. I've learned the hard way that it pays to have an attorney look over everything." Nash had divorced his ex-wife over the summer. The settlement was amicable, but he'd lost a few prized possessions because he hadn't hired a lawyer. He hadn't wanted to make waves. "Why, I've learned so well that I've engaged an attorney to read over a lease-option to purchase a vineyard, even though everyone in town knows that I could trust the seller with my firstborn child."

I grinned. The vineyard owner was my mother. After meeting Nash and learning he hoped to own a vineyard one day, she had offered him the chance to do so in the form of a lease-option to buy Nouvelle Vie Vineyards. Though my mother was only in her sixties and could continue to pour every ounce of herself into the family business, she wanted to gallivant while she could. She and my father had never traveled. When he'd died three years ago, she'd had no desire to strike out on her own. Now, with a dashing new man by her side—Stefan's father—she hoped to see the world. Nash was deliberating on whether he liked the challenge of running a vineyard. So far, so good. He continued to pitch the vineyard's wine at the bistro, which meant I was able to relish those weekly moments of taste-testing wine at the bar with him in addition to our occasional date.

"The contract dispute seems to have calmed," Nash said.

Renee was on her feet doing all the talking. Allie sat hunched forward on the bench. She bobbed her head, as if in agreement with whatever Renee was explaining. Renee stopped talking and patted Allie's shoulder. Then she held out her hand. Allie delivered the envelope holding the offensive contract. Renee pulled out the single sheet of paper, scribbled something on it using a pen she plucked from her rear pocket, slotted the contract into the envelope, and handed it to Allie. Maybe she had agreed to honor whatever deal Allie had assumed was their verbal contract—or maybe not. Renee blew Allie a kiss, but Allie didn't smile. She rose to her feet, swiped tears off her cheeks, and slinked out of the garden through the rear archway.

"Renee, we have to talk!" A tan, ginger-haired man marched toward her, the lapels of his denim jacket flicking as he walked.

The plaid shirt he had on beneath the jacket was partially tucked into his jeans. He wore his baseball cap backward, a look I'd never understood. Per the description Chef C had provided, I guessed he was Rusty Wells, Renee's husband. He reminded me of a rooster—beady eyes, beak nose, and a small pointy mouth.

Nash leaned into me. "Do you know who that is?"

"Renee's husband."

"This is turning into a soap opera."

"You're telling me."

Renee met Rusty halfway.

He grasped her by the shoulders. "I love you." An actor overplaying his part couldn't have emoted better. "I want you to give up this baloney and come home."

"Rusty, sweetie, you know I can't do that. I'm done with you and farming and chicken feed and the stench." She flapped her hand in front of her nose.

"You didn't mind it before."

"I do now."

"But I love you. Didn't you hear me?"

We could all hear him.

Renee wrenched free. "I don't love you anymore. I'm moving on. I'm sorry, Rusty. We're through. I am not cut out to be a farmer's wife. I never was. Please leave. I've got work to do." She strode past him and clapped her hands. "Listen up, everyone. Back to work. I have to make a few phone calls and check on the bake-off contestant entries. I'll be back in twenty. As you know, the vendors are arriving in shifts. The last wave will be here in an hour to set up their sites. Let's show them we're on top of things!"

She walked toward the inn while her husband stood immobile, his face as red as a coxcomb.

Chapter 3

Friday night's first seating at the bistro was boisterous. Usually I could roam my intimate restaurant and talk to patrons, but I couldn't get a word in edgewise because every stool at the hand-carved, pub-style mahogany bar and every chair at the white cloth-covered tables was filled. The second seating wasn't any quieter. Each conversation concerned Crush Week or the Sweet Treats Festival. Some diners were discussing the bake-off. Others were planning which foods or beverages they would sample at the festival. Two groups were chatting nonstop about taking vineyard tours at midnight. In total, the kitchen served over one hundred appetizers or salads, plus an equal amount of dinners. The salted caramel soufflé—one of my favorites—was the most popular dessert. When we closed at eleven, my voice was hoarse, but I didn't head home until I'd eaten a bowl of the night's special soup, a savory French lentil soup—French because of the added splash of champagne. Heavenly.

Near midnight I slogged into the cottage and fed my goldfish. Cagney was orange in tone and bug-eyed and Lacey was a slim matte, meaning she lacked any reflective pigments and the pink of her muscle showed through her white scales. I'd given them those names because, although I wasn't much of a TV watcher, hunkering down with popcorn and watching reruns of *Cagney and Lacey* had gotten me through a dark time after my husband's death. Right before I retreated to my bedroom, I sang two verses of "Rock-a-Bye Baby" to them—yes, I spoiled them. They wiggled their fins with joy.

Throughout the night, I struggled to sleep. I worried about how our first festival would go. Would there be any snags? Would Renee be, as she promised, on top of things? Would a festival give us the press and word-of-mouth marketing we needed to expand our clientele? We were doing fine, but we could do better. We served lunch and dinner six days a week, taking Tuesdays off because that seemed to work well with the tourist crowd. Dinners performed the best; we could use a boost with the lunch crowds.

When my alarm chimed, I awoke shaking because my last dream had involved a black cat chasing Rusty Wells, who looked as mad as a wet rooster.

I threw on my chenille robe and Ugg slippers, fixed myself a rich cup of black coffee, and made a quickie breakfast of an English muffin with toasted Brie and homemade blackberry jam. I took my meal to the patio behind the cottage and nestled into my bent-wood hickory rocker. I donned a ski hat that I kept at the ready—the breeze had kicked up again—and enjoyed the flavors of my breakfast while drinking in the view of the vineyard and fruit tree orchard that abutted my place. I noticed that workers at the neighboring vineyard had recently planted evergreen wisteria as well as pale pink roses at the ends of each row. Both were intended to lure bugs away from the grapes.

Around seven AM, I threw on my work outfit, said good-bye to my aquatic pets, and hurried to the bistro to attend to the menus for lunch and dinner. After confirming we had all the provisions, I tossed on my jacket and pink scarf and hustled to the inn to take in the first hour of the festival.

Renee had designated day one as Family Day. The Sisley Garden was packed with parents accompanied by children of all ages, from infants in ergonomic baby carriers and strollers to teenagers who didn't seem upset to have to accompany their parents. Would wonders never cease? Sweets were a unifying force.

I checked out the names of the various vendors: TUTTI FRUTTI was dishing up homemade ice cream; SHAKE YOUR BOOTY was serving malts and milkshakes; RAMEKIN was offering pudding, custard, and soufflés; SWEETLY SORBET was doling out exactly what it advertised. I made a mental note to stop by. It didn't matter what time of the day it was—I could always eat sorbet.

"Mimi!" a woman called.

Felicity Price, the councilman's wife, hurried up the gravel pathway toward me. Felicity's teenage daughter, Philomena—accent on the second-to-last syllable—trailed behind. I knew the girl's name because a month ago, when Felicity had visited the bistro, she had told me its origin. In Greek myth, Philomena was a princess transformed by the gods into a nightingale. It was a mouthful of a name for a kid, I thought, vowing never to name my children hard-to-pronounce or hard-to-spell names—if I had kids. Time was ticking, and my career demanded my full-time attention.

"Mimi, darling." Felicity's lily-of-the-valley perfume reached me first. She threw her arms around me like we were old friends; we weren't. Truth be told, she wanted everyone to adore her and to tell her she was hotter than hot. To her credit, she did have perfectly dyed blonde hair, which she must have spent a fortune on, and she had becoming features—big eyes, full lips—but she invariably wore clothing that made her look like she was trying too hard. The cherry-red, low-cut and backless sweater dress she was wearing clung to her pear-shaped frame. If I'd attempted that style, I would always have been tugging up the neckline. I imagined she donned revealing dresses so everyone could see the exquisite infinity sign tattoo inked at the nape of her neck. "You remember my daughter."

"Of course. Hi, Philomena."

The girl, a gawky freshman who even in flats stood a head taller than her mother in heels, stopped a few feet behind Felicity. She toyed with her lackluster hair and tugged on the hem of her short-shorts. Her bare legs were dimpled with goose bumps. The pink sequined words THEATER JUNKIE on her T-shirt caught the sunlight and sparkled.

If only her sad eyes would glisten half as much, I mused.

"Mimi, isn't this luscious?" Felicity gushed. "I don't eat anything but paleo, of course. In fact, that's what I'll be entering in the muffin competition."

There were to be three separate competitions: muffins, pies, and soufflés. The semifinals were being run off-site in the kitchen of the twin judges. The muffin and pie final competitions would take place on Thursday. The soufflé battle would occur on Saturday morning. Saturday evening, the finalists from all three contests would vie for the big prize—a Sweet Treats Festival personalized wine trip hosted by a tour guide.

"Paleo gluten-free chocolate zucchini muffins," Felicity went on.

"Wow," I said, trying not to grimace. Not that I didn't like gluten-free muffins or chocolate muffins or even zucchini muffins, but all three in one? And paleo to boot? Why bother?

"I'll indulge today, though," Felicity went on. "One must sacrifice for the betterment of our beautiful valley's educational facilities, don't you think?"

I nodded. *Let's hear it for people who like to give, give, give.*

"I almost forgot." Felicity reached into her red patent leather tote bag and withdrew a cream-colored envelope. "For you." She handed it to me. "I painted pictures of flowers in my garden and imprinted notecards with the art."

I removed the notecard from the envelope and opened it. It was a thank-you note. "Um, what's this for?"

"For sponsoring the festival."

"I'm not the sponsor. I'm getting paid."

"Yes, of course, darling, but you provided the property when no other hotel would. You're golden in my book." Felicity wiggled her red fingernails at the note. "Read it and bask in the glow."

In sprawling handwriting, Felicity thanked me for being an open-minded and forward-thinking individual. I acknowledged her with a smile, murmured, "Lovely," and turned to her daughter. "Philomena, I heard you've taken up guitar."

She hummed a yes.

"And you got a cat. A big calico."

She hummed a second yes.

Giving up trying to engage the girl in conversation, I said to Felicity, "Renee Wells has done a bang-up job, don't you think? All three of the gardens are filled with tents and bustling with activity. Frozen desserts, puddings, soufflés, and beverages here. Cookies, cakes, and pies in the Renoir Retreat. And all the demonstration and souvenir tents are in the Bazille Garden."

"Renee does have energy and enthusiasm," Felicity said, but I could see she was distracted because her eyes widened at something she spied over my shoulder. "Philomena, go tell your father I need to see him. Immediately."

Parker Price, a former pro football player and our current councilman—which was why he was wearing a suit and tie to a casual event—was standing near TUTTI FRUTTI with a flashy brunette and a distinguished gentleman I recognized from last year's political posters. He had run against Parker and lost. An overcoat hung over Parker's arm and a duck hunter–style cap dangled from his finger. The trio were enjoying ice cream cones and laughing at some joke Parker must have just told. He had a great sense of humor, which for some unknown reason ticked off Felicity, his bride of twenty-two years. I also happened to know that he trimmed his salt-and-pepper hair just to rile her. One night at the bistro, Heather had overheard Felicity griping about the fact that the back of Parker's hair looked like he'd used pinking shears to trim it.

"Hey, sweetie!" Renee bounded up to us in a candy-apple red–striped dress and white espadrilles. She embraced Felicity and gave her a warm hug, making the white bakery bag she was holding crackle. "Thanks so much for making me tea yesterday afternoon. Boy, did I get an education looking at your book collection."

Felicity shrugged her off. Her gaze wasn't filled with warmth. Didn't she like to be hugged and appreciated? Maybe she was concerned that Parker was still talking to his pals and Philomena had vanished.

"I've got to say, Felicity, I had no idea how government worked." Renee turned to me. "You might not know this, Mimi, but Parker Price is the absolute best at raising funds for our public schools, and Felicity is right there by his side, generous to a fault with her time." She pulled an oversized Oreo-style cookie from the bakery bag and thrust it at Felicity. "Have one. These are scrumptious."

Felicity wrinkled her nose. "I don't eat sweets."

"I beg to differ," Renee said in singsong fashion. "I happen to know you love dipping your cookies into skim milk. But I understand if you want to pass. We've got to watch our figures, don't we?"

Felicity swiveled to take in the crowd. Her foot tapped a *rat-a-tat* on the gravel.

"Hey, girlfriend." Renee flicked a finger. "I didn't know you had that tattoo."

How could she not? Felicity was brazen about making sure everyone saw it. Maybe that was why she had turned her back on Renee, to flaunt her art.

"What does it represent?" Renee bit into a cookie and hummed her approval.

Felicity spun around. "My endless bond with my husband. I had it inked the day after we met in high school."

"Hmm." Renee cocked a hip. "Does Parker have a matching infinity tattoo?"

"No, I don't," Parker said, walking up to us with a distinctive limp, which I'd heard was due to an old sports injury. He was using a napkin to mop melted ice cream off his hand. "I didn't need to tattoo myself to show the world I loved you. Right, hon?" When he smiled, his crooked nose looked even more crooked.

"He has a tattoo of a football," Felicity said.

"Well, sure." His laugh reminded me of a truck trying to rev up. "Here, you look cold." Clumsily, trying not to topple his ice cream, he offered his overcoat to Felicity. The hem scraped the ground.

"You keep it." Felicity shoved it at him, playfully swatted his arm, and took a lick of his ice cream cone.

So much for eating paleo, I mused. Maybe it was her contribution to the cause. Maybe the Oreo she'd shunned had whet her appetite for sugar.

Renee said, "Mr. Price—"

"Call me Parker. Everybody does."

"Parker"—Renee smiled—"I was telling Felicity how nice it was to have tea with her and receive a personal tour of your home. She's so proud of everything you do. She says you're a whiz of a councilman."

Parker beamed. "She should have been the one to run for office. She's so bright."

"She sure is," Renee said. "Wicked smart."

"She's wicked all right." Parker grinned, his eyes filled with mischief. I would have bet that devilish look had flustered many a defensive linesman. "Hey, hon, let's chat for a second." He looped a hand around his wife's elbow and guided her to a spot near the archway leading into the inn. Felicity, who seconds ago had bid her daughter to fetch her husband, now tried to wrench free from his grasp. Parker held on, his impish gaze replaced with outright annoyance. They stopped ten feet from us, their voices hushed.

"Well, that was, um, awkward," Renee wisecracked.

"I agree."

"Time for me to make the rounds," she said. "Make sure you taste the sorbet. Jorianne told me it's your favorite."

How well my pal knew me.

Philomena, who reappeared with a paper cup of ice cream, drew near to her parents. Parker waved for her to skedaddle. She tripped over her feet as she hastened away. I beckoned her to rejoin me. She seemed relieved to have someplace to go.

"Is the ice cream good?" I asked.

She hummed a yes.

"You're into theater, right?" I pointed to her T-shirt.

"Mm-hm." She twisted so I could see the words on the back of her shirt: St. Mary's HS Loves the Arts.

"I hear St. Mary's is excellent. What play are you doing?" *That should require more than a single-syllable answer*, I mused.

"*Cats*."

"Are you playing a calico cat?" I made the reference because of her new pet.

"No. I'm the Glamour Cat."

"You're Grizabella?" I gawped. "That means you must have a terrific voice." Grizabella was the cat that crooned the spectacular song "Memory."

She mumbled, "Yeah, I guess," then added, "It's tech week."

"That's fun." I remembered doing a few plays and looking forward to tech week, which was the week before the show opened when the technical crew had to hammer out any problems with the lights, sound, and props. We had treated it as goof-off time because we stopped and started so often. I hadn't starred in the plays; I liked being in the chorus. "Do you—"

"Why do they argue about love all the time?" Philomena asked.

"Cats?"

"My parents."

I eyed her folks, who continued to go at it.

"Love this and love that," she intoned. "And money. They're always arguing about money."

"Parents quarrel sometimes," I said, wondering, more to the point, why they were hashing it out in public. Renee had taken on Allie in public. Maybe the prevailing winds were triggering emotional friction. "That doesn't mean they aren't in love," I went on. "They have different opinions on certain subjects."

"I will never argue. Ever. I have a boyfriend and we're going to be nice to each other forever. We've made a pinky pact not to fight."

A pinky pact. How sweet.

She lifted her lackluster hair with one hand and let it drop. "Money isn't everything, you know?" She scooped some ice cream into her mouth and double-licked the spoon.

"I do know that fighting about money can put a crimp in relationships." I wouldn't tell her how my adventuresome husband had snowed me into believing in his dreams. When he fell from that peak in Nepal and died, he'd left me with a ton of climbing equipment and a mountain of debt. Bankrupt and bereft, I had returned to Nouvelle Vie to start my life over. I was glad I had. "You and your boyfriend will have to see where life takes you. One day at a time."

"Life isn't always fair," Philomena muttered.

"True that," I said in teenlike fashion.

A blur of black darted between us.

I whooped with shock. "Scooter!"

"Was that a kitty?" Philomena asked, pure innocence returning to her tone.

"A cat that is trouble with a capital T."

"Some people say black cats bring bad luck. I don't believe it. I think they're beautiful and exciting." Philomena's eyes shimmered with enthusiasm for an instant, but the light quickly dimmed. "But what do I know? My parents tell me I'm too young to know anything."

Poor girl. At least I'd had the total support of my parents as a teen. I patted her slim arm. She brightened at my touch.

"Come with me," I said. "I need to track down some raspberry sorbet."

* * *

Later, I returned to the bistro to find the place hopping. Every table was filled, and there was a line of customers waiting outside. None of the diners inside seemed to mind how packed it was, maybe because the mirrors on the walls made the area feel larger. I loved how they reflected the warm twinkle from the lights in the bronze-finished, candelabra-style chandeliers. I also appreciated that I could see pretty much every angle of the bistro via the mirrors and know in an instant when a customer needed something.

Heather, in a black sheath with her hair swooped into an updo with dangling tendrils, beckoned me to the hostess podium. "You're late," she said with a grin.

"You're early. What's going on? Are we having a sale?"

"Didn't you get the text I sent?" She consulted her cell phone that was tucked into a pocket of the podium. "Ooh, it never transmitted. Anyway, we had to set up two seatings for lunch because so many people wanted reservations, plus we have two full seatings booked for dinner. It's the festival and Crush Week's fault. Do you mind?"

"Mind? No." *The more the merrier.* I did a quick head count to make sure we had enough supplies to feed the crowd. If we ran low, I could always raid the pantry at Maison Rousseau. We only served breakfast there. "How is Chef C holding up?" I asked.

"She's in her element. You know she loves a challenge."

"I smell rosemary and cloves."

"Yes, you do. One of today's specials is beef bourguignon."

Since the festival was focusing on sweets, we had decided the bistro should focus on savory dishes. To compliment the choices, I had stocked up on Pinot Noirs, Merlots, Zinfandels, and Cabernets, not that a white wine couldn't go with piquant meals, but I'd noticed that diners perused the red wine side of the menu whenever heartier entrées were offered.

"I'm going to nab a serving of today's special before it disappears," I said.

After locking my purse in my office desk, I strolled to the kitchen. I dished up a plate of the beef bourguignon, settled on a stool at the farmhouse-style table, and lit into my meal. Every bite was delightful, the cloves offering an added depth to the sauce.

The lunch hour zipped by. The afternoon, too. By the time the second round of dinner guests were peering at menus, I was spent. I covered my mouth to stifle a yawn and spotted a woman across the room waving at me. I recognized her from the festival—Allie O'Malley, the doughy-faced woman with the lion's mane of hair. She had changed into a mocha-brown long-sleeved dress and was dining alone. A book rested to the left of her plate. Was it a primer on how to wage a court battle? She beckoned me with a finger and offered a bright smile. How could I refuse?

I drew near and said, "Nice to see you. Enjoying your meal?"

"Mm-hm." She sopped up the rest of her beef bourguignon sauce with a wedge of bread, popped it into her mouth, and swallowed. "What's not to like? The seasonings are perfectly balanced. The sauce has exactly the right texture. It's superb."

"The chef will be pleased to hear that."

Upon closer inspection, I noted the book on the table was a cookbook—to be specific, a cookie and muffin cookbook with an exceedingly long name. An envelope marked a section in the book. Was it *the* envelope containing the disputed contract? I was curious what Renee had written on it.

"Are you entering the muffin competition?" I indicated the book.

"Me? No." Her cheeks flushed. "I can't read a novel when I'm in a restaurant. There are too many delicious distractions. So I bone up on food." She frowned—not at me. She was looking past me.

I spun to see what had turned her happy face upside-down. Renee, in her sporty red-striped dress, was exiting the kitchen. Muted choruses of "There she is" and "She's the one" resounded from the customers.

Chef C emerged from the kitchen, too. Her chin was dusted with flour. Her eyes gleamed with energy. She hugged Renee. "See you later."

"You bet." Renee kissed her sister on both cheeks and weaved through the tables toward the exit. She caught sight of me and headed my way. She hesitated when she realized I was conversing with Allie, but she forced a smile and continued toward us. "Mimi," she said, snubbing Allie. "Aren't you thrilled with the turnout?"

I nodded. "The festival has been a boon to our business."

"It's all about getting the word out and enticing the right mix of people to attend." Renee shot a triumphant look at Allie. "Some people have a gift for that sort of thing; others don't."

I didn't peek at Allie, but I could feel her seething. Waves of angry heat wafted my way. *Why is Renee being so rude?* I wondered. She had won. *Be gracious*, I telegraphed to her. She missed or ignored the message.

"I am dying for a sweet," Renee said, "so I'm going home to try my hand at something new."

"Home to the farm?" Allie asked. "Where you belong?"

"To my sister's place."

"I'll bet Chef C doesn't know what she's in for," Allie sniped.

Oho. Two can play the rudeness game, I thought.

"Renee," I said, trying to deflect the tension, "didn't you like what our kitchen had to offer?"

"It's not that. It's . . ." A curious look crossed her face. "I've got something special in mind." She did her best to suppress a smile.

Allie snorted. "Good luck with that!" To me she said, "Renee isn't a cook."

"I will be. I'm learning." Renee jutted her chin and added as she retreated, "See you tomorrow."

"Not if I can help it," Allie muttered.

I cut her a look. She offered a tart smile, then pulled her wallet from her purse. I signaled her waitress for the check and made a tour of the bistro, making sure the rest of the customers were satisfied.

An hour later, I headed home. Since I was craving something sweet, too, the moment I entered the cottage I switched on the oven. Once a month, I made a batch of vanilla bean sugar cookie batter, which I portioned into small containers and stored in the freezer. That way, whenever I had a hunger for a quickie dessert, I could pull a container from the freezer, let the dough thaw for a few minutes, drop one to two cookies onto a cookie sheet, and *voilà*, enjoy fresh cookies without the fuss.

As I waited for the cookies to bake—the aroma of vanilla permeating my kitchen was blissful—I toured the cottage and took note of chores I needed to do: mop the bathroom floor, dust under the sofa in the living room, scour the sink. A maid from the inn usually came in once a week to do a cursory cleaning, although she'd missed this week, but in twenty minutes, how much could she really do? I had decorated my tiny abode in wine country colors: stylish taupe with burgundy and moss-green accents. I loved the gas fireplace, which was spotless because I hadn't used it since I'd cleaned it at the end of the previous winter. Next week, when the temperatures dropped, I would find time to nestle into my comfy sofa with a good book and enjoy a toasty fire.

I paused at the living room window and glimpsed outside. The goldfish ogled me as they often did, noses pressed to the glass of their tank. I imagined their conversation: *What is our silly human doing? Beats me.* I was making sure there were no intruders—not because Napa Valley was a high-crime location (it wasn't) but because living in San Francisco had taught me to keep one eye and one ear open at all times. Plus, the encounter with a killer last June had made me wary.

Something scratched the front door. I glanced out the peephole. No one was there. I bent down and peeked through the cat's-height peephole that I'd installed after the encounter in June. Scooter was standing there, tail rigid. Was he checking up on me? That was Scoundrel's job. I opened the door. Scooter bolted inside. I scanned the area for his ladylove, but she was nowhere in sight. She wasn't with Heather because the kittens had been weaned. Where was she?

"Well, hello, fella. Want to introduce yourself?" I crouched and held my arms open. He didn't move into them. He eyeballed the goldfish, gave them a haughty swish of his tail, and continued deeper into the cottage. He scoped out the bedroom. Seconds later, he toured the small living room. After a long moment, he peered at me with wide eyes.

"Hungry?" I asked. Heather fed the cats outside the bistro's kitchen, but I had a few kibble treats on hand. I gathered some and set them on the floor. Scooter ignored them and scampered to a spot beneath the table in the dining nook of the kitchen. He curled into a ball and instantly fell asleep.

"Well, I'll be," I said. Scoundrel had never settled down in my place. Ever. Maybe Scooter wasn't a mouser. Maybe he was a stray that had lost his family. Poor guy.

The timer on the stove buzzed. A split second later, my cell phone jangled. Scooter raised his head, alert for danger.

"It's okay, fella." I donned an oven mitt, whisked open the oven door, and removed the tray of cookies. Then I nabbed my cell phone and answered it. "Hello?"

"Mimi!" Chef C cried. "It is horrible. *Tragique!*"

"What's wrong?" My heart chug-a-lugged. She never panicked.

"It is Renee. She is . . ." She sucked back a sob. "She is dead. She has been murdered. In my kitchen. Come quickly. Please!"

Chapter 4

Twenty minutes later, I stood in the living room of my chef's Victorian house waiting for the sheriff's department to show up. Since I'd arrived, I hadn't stopped staring into the kitchen with its white Corian counters and white kitchen table and chairs. I didn't want to enter, afraid of disturbing evidence. The moment I'd seen Renee lying facedown on the hardwood floor, one arm stretched toward the cabinets, the skirt of her red-striped dress bunched around her legs, her head bashed with a countertop mixer, I'd telephoned the sheriff.

"Camille, I'm so sorry," I murmured.

"*Merci.*"

She was perched on the front of an oak rocking chair in her living room, wearing what she typically wore to work—a collared white shirt, black pants, and black clogs. She was hugging herself. Her hair was askew. Beside the chair stood a reading lamp and an end table stacked with cookbooks with titles I recognized. Forties-style music was playing on a CD player. A lit candle sat in the middle of the coffee table in front of the all-white sofa.

After I'd contacted the sheriff, Camille had filled me in on her exact movements. She had entered the house, seen her sister, and dropped the groceries she was carrying. The bag lay on the floor near the front door. Goop from broken eggs oozed out of it. She telephoned me. When I asked her why she hadn't dialed 911 first, she said she had automatically clicked speed-dial on her cell phone, seen my name, and stabbed it.

"What's all that?" I indicated the debris on the kitchen and living room floors, which included seeds, a feather or two, and snippets of paper.

"I told you my sister was a slob," Camille replied. "She tracked gunk home from the festival as well as from The Bookery, I imagine. If you recall, the inn was having a celebration."

"I remember."

"I have a Swiffer mop, which works best on hardwood, but would Renee think to . . ." Camille covered her mouth. Between parted fingers, she mumbled, "I am a monster. Speaking ill of my poor sweet sister." She lowered her hand. Her eyes grew misty.

"Tell me about her," I said, trying to get her mind onto happier thoughts.

A soft smile graced Camille's lips. "Renee was always a prankster. When we were children, she liked to hide things in my bed to scare me. Creatures and bird nests and ticklish toys."

"Sounds like something Scoundrel would do."

"Renee short-sheeted my bed one time. I remember getting so angry. I thought"—she hesitated and gestured to the crime scene—"she was fooling me tonight. I thought she had staged this. The mixer. The mess. She liked horror movies. I do not." Camille shook her head.

"It appears she was getting ready to bake something." I recalled Renee telling Allie and me that she intended to try her hand at making something sweet. Allie had implied that she would fail before Renee strutted out.

A variety of items sat on the counter: a recipe card, bittersweet chocolate, a cube of butter, a canister of sugar, and espresso coffee. "Soufflé, perhaps?" I asked.

"*Oui*. I was going to teach her when I got home."

"She mentioned that."

There was also a tipped-over canister. A couple of tablespoons of flour dusted the floor by the cabinet. Had Renee reached for the container to use as a weapon?

"I gave her the recipe card. I told her I would pick up eggs right after work. You saw how she hurried out of the bistro. She was so excited." Camille sighed. "Alas, she did not wait for me to get started." She rubbed her arms up and down.

"Are you cold?"

"No. I am miserable." She stopped rubbing.

"You left work when I did, an hour ago."

"Yes, but I went to the store, and—"

A siren whooped outside. A second higher-pitched siren bleated. Whirling red lights flashed through the windows. Two cars pulled to a stop, the sirens ceased, and doors slammed.

Camille rose to her feet. I drew near and slung an arm around her.

Seconds later, Sergeant Tyson Daly rapped on the screen door and, without invitation, entered the house. Tyson, who was dating Jo, was a Napa County sheriff contracted by the town of Yountville, but he wasn't in uniform tonight. He was wearing a Pendleton shirt, jeans, and boots. His Buffalo Bill Cody–style goatee and mustache were trimmed and neat, but his flaxen hair with its distinctive gray streak was as unruly as if he'd driven with the windows wide open. A female Asian deputy in an official uniform, her black hair secured in a hairband, followed him inside. She let the screen door close with a bang.

"Good evening, ladies," Tyson said, finger-combing his hair. "Chef C, I'm sorry for your loss."

"Thank you, Sergeant," Camille said.

"EMTs are on their way. Crush Week traffic is a bear."

"My sister . . . Renee . . . was like that when I . . ." Camille pointed at the body. "I have not touched anything. Neither has Mimi. We—"

Tyson held up a hand. "I'll ask questions in a moment." He concentrated his attention on the crime scene. With great care, he took off his boots, slipped sterile booties over his black socks, and strode into the kitchen.

Doing his best not to disturb anything, he checked Renee's pulse. He released her wrist, retraced his steps to the living room, and suggested that the deputy, who had donned sterile booties as well, take photographs of the crime scene.

She entered the kitchen and, using a digital Nikon camera, started taking pictures from every angle.

"Why would someone kill her?" Fresh tears pooled in Camille's eyes. She blotted them with her fingertips before they could fall. "Who did this?"

"We're going to find out. I promise."

"Allie O'Malley fought with Renee earlier," I blurted. "She owned the festival before Renee—"

"Got it." Tyson pulled a notepad fitted with a pen from his rear pocket and jotted a note.

"She can't have been dead for long, Sergeant," I said. Although Tyson and I were friends, whenever he was serving in his official capacity, I addressed him by his title. "She left the bistro during the second dinner seating. Is her body warm?"

Tyson stroked his goatee. "Is Chef Mimi, with her keen eye for detail, going to recap the scene for me?"

"*Keen eye . . .*" I glowered at him. "You know that's not what I . . ." I jammed my lips together. A few months ago, I'd told Tyson that chefs were natural-born sleuths. We naturally broke apart recipes flavor by flavor. I hadn't expected him to throw my own words in my face.

He offered a *gotcha* wink. "Let's go through the timeline. You first, Chef." Tyson faced Camille. "Tell me when you last saw your sister."

"She visited me at the bistro. She left . . ." Camille silently implored me for help.

"During the dinner service, around eight thirty or so," I said. "She was on her way home to make a new dessert. Right after she argued with Allie O'Malley."

"She called me when she arrived," Camille added.

Tyson wrote more notes on the pad. "What happened next?"

Camille repeated what she had said to me, about going to the grocery store and returning home at eleven thirty. That was when she found Renee on the floor. She added that her sister could be an imp, so she believed Renee was playing a trick on her. "But she was not."

"You left the bistro at what time?" Tyson asked.

"Around ten thirty," I answered for her. "The same time as I did."

"I needed to buy eggs."

"Why didn't you grab a couple of eggs from the bistro?" Tyson asked.

She gasped. "That would be stealing."

"Why did it take you an hour to purchase eggs?" Tyson asked. "Was the store packed with Crush Week fans suffering the munchies?" He pocketed his notepad and moved farther into the living room. He inspected the lit candle on the coffee table. It looked brand-new. The wax had melted about two hours' worth. He pressed on. What was he looking for?

The two end table lamps flanking the all-white sofa were switched on. Only now did I realize that the music that was playing was all Sinatra. He was singing "That Old Black Magic." Renee must have put on the music. Camille wouldn't have done so after what she had seen.

Tyson ambled to the bookshelves behind the sofa and picked up a CD case. He flipped it over, perused the backside, and returned it to where he'd found it.

"I asked you a question, Camille," Tyson said. "Was the grocery store busy?"

"No." Camille pushed away from me, her face suffused with fear.

"So where were you for the remainder of the time?"

"I took a walk in the woods."

"At night?"

"I often walk at night. I like the sounds of the creatures. I am indoors all day at the bistro. I carry a flashlight with me."

"She does take walks," I said. "At Yountville Crossroads. It's an easy hiking route—"

"I didn't ask you, Mimi." Tyson threw me a cautionary look. "Is that where you walked, Chef?"

"Yes."

"Did anyone see you?"

"I do not know. I did not happen to see anyone." Camille hugged herself again. She started rubbing her arms and cut a worried look at me.

Tyson ran his hand along the two-seater sofa. He jostled a throw pillow and dug deeper, between the seat cushion and the back of the sofa. "What's this?" He pulled out a piece of white stationary and unfolded it. "Well, well." His eyes widened. "It seems I'm holding a declaration of love from your sister to Donovan Coleman."

Camille sucked in air. She turned milk white.

"Aren't you and Donovan an item, Chef?" Tyson asked.

"No," she said, her answer clipped.

"I think you are. I dine at the bistro often enough to hear the gossip."

"We have been on a date or two."

"Why would your sister have hidden this love letter?" Tyson withdrew a plastic baggie from his pocket, slipped the note into it, and set it on the stack of cookbooks.

"Maybe she felt it was fanciful and did not want me to see it," Camille offered.

I stared at the kitchen and recalled my encounter with Renee at the festival and how she had raved about the splendid morning she and Donovan had spent in Calistoga. How had I not picked up on her infatuation? Talk about dense! I glanced at the sprinkling of flour on the floor and noticed a squiggle in it. Had Renee tried to draw a heart before she died?

Tyson said, "What are you looking at, Mimi?"

"Me?" My voice cracked. "No footprints."

"I noticed that. I also see the makings for soufflé on the counter," he said. Jo had told me Tyson was a whiz at fixing deli sandwiches. Was he also a baker? "Why were you gawking at them?"

Camille cleared her throat. "I will answer, Mimi. Sergeant, I was going to teach my sister how to make chocolate soufflé. She was not a cook." She shifted feet. "She must have learned soufflé was Donovan's favorite dessert."

"You knew that?" I asked.

"*Oui*. I suppose, by the words in that note—"

"She had a crush on him. How did that make you feel?" Tyson asked.

She thrust her hand at the note. "I did not know until you read that."

"Are you sure? Maybe you were the one who stuffed this note behind the pillow."

"I did no such thing."

"Maybe you hid it before you called Mimi, knowing it would be incriminating."

"No."

Tyson tossed the bagged note on top of the cookbooks on the end table. "Were you jealous of your sister, Camille? Did you think she might steal Donovan away from you?"

"She is"—she faltered—"*was* married."

"Married people do all sorts of silly things when it comes to love."

Camille sniffed. "That is a jaded view of life, *monsieur*," she said, reverting to her native tongue. She mumbled something else in French that I couldn't make out. I did pick up the word *beast*.

Tyson ran a hand along the sides of his hair, smoothing it off his face. "Did anyone see you walking in the woods, Camille?"

"I told you, no. At least I do not think so. I did not see a flare from another flashlight."

He grimaced. "I hate to say it, but your alibi is weak."

Camille hurried to me and clutched my hand. "Mimi." She was shivering like an aspen. Her hands were cold as ice.

"Is there something you're not revealing?" I asked her.

Her shoulders sagged. "Yes, all right. I knew about her infatuation. I admit it. She told me tonight as I was icing a dozen *mille-feuille*."

"Napoleons," I explained to Tyson.

"Did others in the kitchen hear her?" he asked.

"No. I do not know. I—"

Tyson made a clucking sound.

"Stop!" Camille demanded. "Do not mock me. I did not kill my sister."

I threw Tyson a scathing glance, begging him to be patient. "Go on, Camille."

"Renee wanted to know if I was in love with him. I could not say that I was, you see, because Donovan and I do not know each other that well. We have dated a few times. When does one know one is in love?" She placed a hand on her chest. "The matters of the heart take time. One must not be impulsive." When we first met, Camille had confided that she'd been in love before, with her daughter's father, but the loser had run off when Chantalle was born.

"Renee asked me to consider whether I could give him up," Camille went on. "I said I would think about it. Of course, I could not think at the bistro. We were so busy." She smoothed the collar of her shirt. "When I left and purchased the eggs, I realized I could not face her without clearing my head. I needed to know what to say, what to do. That is why I went to the woods." She squeezed my hand. "It is not like Donovan and I are, what is the word—" She searched for it and landed on "*exclusive*. We have not even . . ." She halted and worried her upper lip with her teeth. "We have kissed once. That is all. But I had hoped—"

"You were jealous," Tyson said, cutting her off.

"No."

"You didn't want her horning in on the love of your life."

"No!"

"Tyson," I said, "Chef C isn't like that."

"Isn't she? She's flesh and blood. Two sisters in love with the same man? Murder has happened over less."

"Renee was not in love with him," Camille yelled. "She was infatuated. That is not love. She was angry with her husband. She was changing her life's course. She did not know what she wanted. Perhaps she hid the letter because she had second thoughts after writing it and did not want me to see it."

"She was younger," Tyson said. "Isn't Donovan younger than you?"

Camille's face flushed the color of rhubarb. She released me. "I told her that she should return to her husband. I told her she needed to try and make the marriage a success. Love is not easy. Love takes work. Rusty loves her."

"When did you say all this?" Tyson said. "Right before you hit her in the head with the mixer?"

"I spoke with her in the kitchen. At the bistro. I did not do this. I did not kill her. Mimi, please"—she pleaded with her eyes—"you have to believe me."

"Let me in!" a man with a squeaky voice yelled from the front porch.

The door opened an inch and *thwapped* closed.

"Sir, this is a crime scene," a second man with a gruff voice said.

"Out of my way, dang it!" the first man bellowed.

Through the screen door, I saw Rusty Wells wrestling with a sizable, squash-faced deputy. Where had he come from? Had he carpooled with the technician?

"It is Rusty," Camille said. "He is Renee's husband."

"Deputy, allow him to enter," Tyson ordered.

The deputy stepped aside. Rusty tramped in. He hadn't shaved recently, and a heavy stubble of ginger hair covered his chin. He was wearing the same dirty denim jacket and jeans he'd worn the day before, although he had thrown on a turtleneck sweater and he was carrying a single red rose—not the store-bought kind, one he had plucked off a bush.

Tyson held up his hand. "Stop right there. I'm Sergeant Daly. Why are you here?"

"I've been calling Renee all day. She hasn't returned my calls. I know she's here. I want to speak to her." Rusty's gaze darted left and right, which made his beady eyes look even beadier. Perspiration peppered his face. "Please. I need to talk to her."

"Sir," Tyson said, "that won't be possible."

"Why in heck not?"

"Because"—Tyson swallowed hard—"she's dead."

"What?" Rusty recoiled. He dropped the rose. "What happened? Did she have a heart attack? Is that why you're here? Ah, man, I knew this festival thing was too much for her. She's been on medication for anxiety. She—"

"She was murdered," Tyson said, no preamble.

Rusty staggered. Tears sprang to his eyes. He batted them away with his weathered fingers. "When? How?"

"Someone"—Camille pointed—"hit her with the mixer."

Rusty peeked around Tyson. His face trembled with shock.

Camille glowered at Tyson. "The sheriff thinks I had something to do with it. I did not."

"Why would you have killed her?" Rusty asked.

"The sergeant believes I was jealous."

"Aw, heck, you found out, didn't you?" He ran his hand over his face.

"Found out what?" Tyson asked.

"Renee told me she had a thing for a baker named Donovan." Rusty's voice caught in his throat. "I asked around and found out that you like him, too, Camille."

"It is not like that, Rusty. I swear." Camille put a hand to her chest. "I did not do this. I loved her."

"Camille couldn't have killed her," I said. "She wasn't here. She was walking in the woods near the Yountville Crossroads."

Tyson coughed, his skepticism obvious.

I added, "Someone else must have attacked Renee."

"Who?" Rusty pleaded. "Maybe this Donovan person made a move on her and she rejected him."

"Or Allie O'Malley killed her," I said, feeling like Johnny One Note. "Allie and Renee exchanged barbs at the bistro. When Renee said, 'See you tomorrow,' Allie replied, 'Not if I can help it.' "

"Duly noted." Tyson inserted his hands into his pockets, striking a casual Mr. Nice Guy pose, but he didn't fool me. He was after facts and lies. "Where were you tonight, Mr. Wells?"

"Me? You don't think—" He jammed a thumb into his chest. "I didn't kill her."

"Answer the question, sir."

"First, I went to the county clerk's office. I wanted to reverse the divorce proceeding."

"Divorce?" Tyson raised an eyebrow.

"Renee filed papers," Camille said.

"I told her I objected." Rusty glanced in the direction of the kitchen. "I don't . . ." He hesitated. "*Didn't* want a divorce."

I said, "The clerk isn't open this late."

"Yeah, I know that now." Rusty sank into one hip like a sluggish teenager.

Tyson's forehead pinched. He wasn't buying Rusty's story. Neither was I. "Sir, you said *first.* What did you do next?"

"I went to that coffee place near the bistro, the one with the coffee cup–shaped chairs."

"Chocolate?" I asked.

"They have Internet," Rusty said. "I wanted to go online and learn how to sell my farm by myself. I figured if I could find someone to buy it, I might win Renee back." He heaved a sigh. "She hated that farm. With the money, I hoped maybe I could buy into her new venture and we could run it together. Be a team."

"How'd that go?" Tyson asked.

Rusty shifted feet. "Not so good. I didn't learn squat."

"So you left there and came here?" Tyson regarded Rusty. Were the wheels in his head going as fast as mine were, trying to establish a timeline?

"No, I . . . I took a drive."

"Hoo-boy," the deputy in the kitchen said.

We all looked in her direction. She wasn't responding to something she had found. She was on her knees, listening to our conversation. Her response must have been a flippant reaction to Rusty's *took a drive* response.

Tyson bit back a smile. "Where did you drive, sir?"

"Around. But I think I saw Camille. At the bridge between Highway 29 and the Silverado Trail. That's the spot, right? She was holding a torch. I mean a flashlight."

Rusty's gaze flitted from Tyson, to Camille, to the deputy, and then to me. Was he checking to see if any of us were buying his alibi? He cut another look at the crime scene.

"Let's go outside, Mr. Wells." Tyson motioned to the front door.

Feet dragging, Rusty followed him to the porch.

I edged in that direction, wishing I could hear everything they said, but I couldn't. Tyson steered Rusty under the crime scene tape that was now in place—the deputy must have strung it up—toward a stand of bushes far enough away that I couldn't pick up a word either of them said. I couldn't read their lips, either, because there were no streetlamps in the area and the light from the moon, though bright, was of no help. *Rats.*

A crowd had gathered on the street. Was the killer among them? A couple of women were pointing at a battered green Ford Truck with the license WELS EGS that was parked across the street. I loved the game of figuring out cryptic license plates' meanings, but this one was a no-brainer; it had to be Rusty's vehicle.

I refocused on Tyson and Rusty. Tyson was talking. Rusty shifted his feet; his right hand was rubbing his thigh. Tyson aimed a finger at him.

"No way!" Rusty jutted both hands. "Renee had her heart set on the festival being a success. Who's going to manage the dang thing if I don't? I can't let those people flounder. She would be devastated."

"Sir!" Tyson shouted. He immediately lowered his voice and continued. I would imagine he was telling Rusty to calm down.

Observing the two of them, I wondered whether Rusty's indignation was a put-on. Was he a master liar? What if he had confirmed seeing Camille on her outing not to exonerate her, but to make sure he had a credible alibi?

Chapter 5

Close to midnight, I begged Tyson to allow Camille to come home with me. Her house was a crime scene. She couldn't stay there. Seeing as he didn't have enough to hold her on—his tech didn't find any fingerprints on the mixer; it had been wiped clean—he allowed it. I assured him she wasn't guilty. I promised that I would keep a close eye on her.

Needless to say, I didn't sleep well. I heard Camille pacing and crying and blaming herself for not being there for her sister. When Sunday morning rolled around, I awoke bleary-eyed. Camille was passed out on the sofa, one arm dangling over the edge. I tried to wake her but she didn't rouse, so I did the only thing I could think of—called my mother.

An early bird like me, Mom arrived in less than ten minutes with her adorable Goldendoodle, Riesling, in tow. He gave me a bounty of kisses.

"Shh," I said as I closed the door and signaled that Camille was sleeping.

"Riesling, sit. Stay." My mother wrapped her arms around me. "Sweetheart, I'm so sorry. What a horror."

Though my mother and I were thirty years apart, we looked similar—same height, same weight—but she appeared worlds better than I did. Her toffee-colored hair was washed and blown dry, and her eyes were bright and alert. Her smile was easy, too. Mine wasn't. She sported a burgundy lipstick that matched her cabernet-colored Bohemian dress. She enjoyed wearing romantic clothing at any time of the day.

"I hope Camille likes dogs," my mother added. "I couldn't leave him home alone."

"Growing up, she had two French Briards. I'm sure she'll be fine."

Mom petted my cheek. "How are you holding up? Can you tell me what happened? Who did it?"

"We aren't sure yet." I gave her the basics: Renee bashed by the mixer and dead the moment she hit the floor, the love note found in the sofa, Camille's flimsy alibi, my misgivings about Allie O'Malley, and Tyson's suspicion of Rusty Wells.

"Poor Camille." My mother shook her head. "Have you contacted her daughter?"

"Not yet. It was too late last night. I'll let Camille decide when is the right time." Would Chantalle beg to fly across country to be at her mother's side? Would she say hurtful things about Renee to console her mother? She hadn't been close to her aunt, Camille had revealed on the drive to the cottage. "I've got to leave. I need to be in charge of the kitchen at the bistro."

"Don't worry. I will watch over her and make sure she eats." She petted my cheek again. "Go."

When I arrived at the bistro, the staff asked why Camille wasn't there. Not knowing how much Tyson would allow me to say but certain I could share a few things, I told them the basics. A pall settled over everyone. Heather grew teary. Stefan was the glummest of the bunch. With all the oomph I could muster, I begged everyone to buck up. Chef C would be furious if we let her down by turning out a day of bad meals.

Around ten AM, Jo stopped in, responding to a text message I'd sent telling her to "see me." She looked fresh in a pineapple-yellow dress. Her disposition matched the cheery color. "Hey," she said as she sauntered toward the bar, where I was polishing the chrome features. "What's new, pussycat?"

Heather was helping the waitstaff place crane-shaped napkins on tables. She peered at us, concern in her gaze.

I set aside my cleaning tools. "Jo—"

"Everything is lively at the festival," she continued. "Sunday crowds are ebullient. I haven't seen Renee yet, but her husband seems to be managing things quite well. He's making nice with all the vendors."

"Rusty?" I faltered. So he had gotten his way after all. Tyson had let him take the helm for his late wife. "Listen, Jo, there's something I need to tell you . . ."

"What's wrong?" She perched on a stool and patted the one beside her.

I sat and folded my hands in my lap. "Renee . . ." My voice caught in my throat. "Renee was murdered last night."

Jo's mouth dropped open. "Are you kidding me? When? How?"

I shared the same details I'd given the staff. "I can't believe Rusty didn't tell you."

"He didn't mention a thing," Jo said. "What a poker face he has. How can he be holding it together?"

"I'm shocked Tyson is allowing him to oversee things. I thought he would have—" I faltered. "Tyson didn't tell you, either."

"You know him. He holds his cards close to the vest."

Tears pressed at the corners of my eyes. I hadn't cried last night.

I hadn't known Renee that well. But now the awfulness of the situation for Camille pierced me like a skewer. All I could recall was her grief and her plea for me to help her.

Jo hugged me. "Let it out. You know if you don't—"

I wept. My shoulders heaved. After a long minute, a horrible notion hit me. I said through jagged breaths, "If Tyson told Rusty he was free to supervise his wife's proceedings, then he must think Camille is guilty."

"That's not true. You don't know that. You said a second ago that Rusty provided Camille with an alibi. Tyson might think they're both innocent."

I broke free of her. "Do you really think so?"

"Yes, I do." She handed me a cocktail napkin. "If only we had another suspect."

"I suggested the former owner of the festival to Tyson."

"Allie O'Malley? I heard festivalgoers gossiping about the way she and Renee went at each other on Friday."

I bobbed my head. "I witnessed the fight."

"As my sister would say, Allie's got claws and sharp teeth." Jo bared hers.

"According to Allie, she wasn't pleased with the way Renee handled their contract. Renee blamed Allie, who didn't have a lawyer review the agreement."

"Oops."

"As much as I don't like speaking ill of the dead . . ." I really didn't. Rumors could spread like wildfires.

Jo motioned for me to continue. "My lips are sealed."

"I'm pretty sure Renee took advantage of Allie. She was downright condescending when Allie claimed she'd hoodwinked her."

"Getting duped is a pretty good motive for murder."

"I agree. I'll talk to Tyson about her again." Jo cuffed me on the arm and headed off. She stopped short of the exit, spun around, and waggled her cell phone. "I almost forgot. *You* texted *me*."

"To tell you the news about Renee and to tell you I'm on duty. Chef C needs the day off."

"Of course she does. Gosh, where is she? At home? Do you want to pack a meal and take it over?"

"She's staying at my cottage. Her place is off-limits."

Jo groaned.

"She's exhausted," I went on. "My mother is with her. She'll feed her. I can handle lunch, but we're so booked because of the festival crowd and Crush Week that I'll need an assistant at dinner. Do you think Yves can help out?" Yves was the breakfast chef at Maison Rousseau.

"He can, but only for tonight. He's going out of town tomorrow. Family business. We've arranged for a temp for a week, a female chef. She's a genius with French toast."

"Tonight would be great. Thanks."

"I'll arrange it." Jo told me to stay strong and hurried off.

By noon, we were so busy that none of the bistro's staff had time to breathe. Over the course of the next two hours we made no less than twelve orders of beef stew, six orders of ratatouille, seven orders of *côte de porc*—savory pork chops served with shallots and cornichons—twenty French onion soups, ten servings of *salade Niçoise*, and two dozen chocolate soufflés with *crème anglaise*, and that wasn't counting all the chicken dishes and appetizers. We worked nonstop.

When the crowd dwindled to two or three tables, I called my mother. She said Camille had roused for a moment and then fallen back to sleep. She urged me not to worry. Sleep was a great healer.

By three PM, I was exhausted. The emotions roiling through me were raw. Thinking of Renee lying dead on Camille's kitchen floor made me nauseous. What was the world coming to? Napa Valley was supposed to be a gentle, loving place.

I walked to the vegetable garden between the bistro and the inn and sat on a bench. I closed my eyes and took deep, restorative breaths. The sun warmed my face. The sound of the gentle breeze cleared my head. I could even hear bees buzzing as they flitted from fading sunflower to fading sunflower.

When Yves showed up at four PM to help with dinner, I rallied. He was a tall man with a simple face and easy demeanor, and he was quite capable with food presentation. He wasn't as clever or as independent as Camille, but I couldn't worry about that now.

We concocted the prix fixe menu. Diners would have their choice of lobster bisque—my grandmother's recipe—or a baby-greens salad with fresh figs, goat cheese, and raspberry vinaigrette. They could then choose between a three-cheese plate or *pâté du jour*. The main course would be chicken *au jus* with steak frites—a mouth-watering way to quick-cook chicken and top with pan juices and fries. For dessert, I settled on a selection of *petit fours*. Two would be filled with apricot glaze; the other two would be filled with blueberry jam. I loved making them; Stefan enjoyed decorating them.

Six hours later, I pecked Yves on both cheeks, thanked him for his devoted service, wished him luck with his family business—whatever that entailed—and slogged home. Camille didn't stir when I entered. Riesling did. He bounded to me. My mother followed him and strapped on his leash.

"I've set a therapist appointment for Camille in the morning," she said. "I'll return bright and early to escort her. Also, I fed your fish, and I provided treats for your cat."

"Cat?"

"The black one. Fast as all get-out. He has come and gone. I don't think he appreciated seeing Riesling here. Cats can be territorial." She kissed me *la bise*—on both cheeks—and gave my arm a quick squeeze. "Go to bed. You look beat."

I crashed onto the mattress, thinking how lucky I was to have the best mother in the world. I hoped sleep might make me look half as good as she did tomorrow.

* * *

Monday morning I awoke before dawn. By the time I'd downed two cups of French press coffee and washed my cup, my mother had shown up looking fresh in an aqua tunic, leggings, and lacy sandals. She eyed my work outfit with displeasure. She thought it was odd that I didn't change it up daily. She would have preferred that I wear more colorful ensembles.

"Will a pretty scarf turn that frown upside down?" I joked.

"Yes, please."

I chose a pink chiffon circle scarf and looped it fashionably around my neck. My mother patted my cheek.

"Do we have company?" Camille asked as she exited the bathroom in a chenille robe, her face glistening with moisturizer, her hair damp.

"Good morning," my mother said.

"*Bonjour*, Ginette. Thank you for coming." After sleeping all day Sunday, Camille had paced through the night. I'd heard her talking on and off to Cagney and Lacey, spilling out her concern for Renee's soul. "I don't know what I would do without you and your daughter."

"Think nothing of it," my mother said. "Let's get you fed and on the road."

"I am not hungry."

"I know, but you're going to eat."

"Let me change clothes first." Camille retreated to my bedroom and shut the door.

My mother shooed me out of the cottage. "Go. She'll be fine."

I hadn't been sitting at my desk in the bistro office more than two minutes when Donovan Coleman rushed in.

Heather was trying to stop him. "Sir, you'll have to wait outside." Though she was no slouch in the height department, she appeared quite diminutive next to him. "Sir, please."

Donovan pulled free and plowed inside.

"I'm sorry, Mimi," Heather murmured and shot him a disparaging look.

"No worries," I said. "I have a minute. Donovan, come in."

"Thank you." Donovan was as lanky and sinewy as a long-distance runner. His arm muscles pressed at the seams of his short-sleeved shirt. His trousers hung on his lean legs. With his oat-colored hair and hyper-alert eyes, he reminded me of a puma ready to spring at a moment's notice—a very attractive puma.

"Have a seat," I said.

The office was decorated with a French flair: cream-colored rustic file cabinets, a couple of green-tinted industrial barn wood side tables, a weathered gray kidney-shaped French desk with scrolled legs, and—my favorite—a pair of ecru shabby chic chairs.

Donovan didn't sit. He shifted feet.

"Okay, stand." I forced a smile. "What can I do for you?"

"I'm looking for Camille." His voice was young-sounding for a man in his thirties. "She's not at home. She's not here, according to *her*." He jerked a thumb at Heather.

"I have a name. It's Heather."

"Sorry." Donovan acknowledged her with a flick of his hand, which seemed to placate her. "Heather."

"Camille is at the doctor's office," I said.

"Is she ill?" His voice scudded upward.

"She's suffering."

"Because her sister died."

"She was murdered," Heather said, clipping off the words.

"Yes, of course. I heard. I didn't mean to diminish . . ." Donovan staggered into one of the chairs and swooped a hank of hair off his forehead. "I am so sorry for Camille."

"And not Renee?" Heather hissed. Gee, she was acting crusty.

"Of course, I'm sorry for *her*. All I meant was—"

"Renee was making soufflé," Heather said.

"Soufflé?" Donovan repeated.

I shot my sweet assistant an annoyed look. She blanched. I had shared that tidbit with her and sworn her to secrecy. But since the truth was out, I said, "Do you like soufflé, Donovan?"

"I do."

"We believe Renee was making it for you."

"Me?" he squawked.

"Mimi!" a man called from the main dining room. I recognized his voice. Nash. The front door closed with a clack. Seconds later he appeared at the office door and rapped on it. He hesitated when he saw I had company.

"Have a seat at the bar, Nash. I'll be right out." Mmm, he looked good in his white shirt, jeans, and leather jacket. He was carrying a two-pack of Nouvelle Vie Vineyards Chardonnay. "Heather, please get Nash a cup of tea or coffee. Thanks."

Nash eyed Donovan with outright disdain. What was that about? Without a word, he spun on his heel. Heather followed him, pausing to align one of the paintings on the wall before she exited.

"Donovan," I said in a reassuring tone, "I believe Renee might have been in love with you."

"With me?"

"That's why she was making soufflé, so she could impress you."

"But"—he sputtered—"I'm dating Camille. I gave Renee no indication . . ." He scrubbed his tousled hair with his fingertips. "Shoot. Do you think when we went to The Bookery that she might have gotten the wrong impression? She flirted with me, but I didn't encourage it. She wanted to pitch an event to the place. I went there to study the cookies."

"So you could start your own bakery."

"Yes. The Bookery has a great café. I wanted to analyze its model and see the selection of baked goods and meet the staff." He splayed his hands. "As you know, all it takes is one wrong move, and a reputation can be ruined. When I take the big leap, I want my business to be an instant success."

"Success doesn't always come in an instant."

"I know that." He pursed his lips. "But I've got to make it big and fast; otherwise my father will stick it to me. See, he doesn't think I have it in me to be successful, but I do." He sat taller and squared his shoulders. "And I will be. I . . ." He shook his head. "I'm sorry. This isn't about me."

"In a way it is."

"No, I mean it's not about my success or my relationship with my father or . . ." He fanned the air with his enormous hands. "When I went to Camille's house this morning, a neighbor told me what happened. She said you saw the crime scene, Mimi. You were there. Is that true?"

"Yes." How much of the story had leaked at this point? Was he testing me to see if I would reveal details? A fleeting notion ran through my mind. Was there any reason for him to have killed Renee? Had he made a move on her, but she rebuffed him, as Rusty had suggested? Or had Renee learned something nefarious about him on their outing that he might want kept quiet? I recalled the finger drawing she had started in the flour. Had she meant to implicate him by drawing a heart?

Donovan tilted his head. "What? You're looking at me funny."

"I was wondering where you were Saturday night."

"You don't think I had anything to do with Renee's murder, do you?" His eyes widened. "You do."

"No, I—"

"Why?" he cut in. "I have no motive. No cause to wish her ill. She was a friend. She was Camille's sister. The sheriff already questioned me."

"Sergeant Daly?"

"Uh-huh. He didn't say why, but I know it's because of the love letter that was found."

My mental antenna went on high alert. I tilted forward in my chair. "How do you know about that if the sheriff didn't mention it?"

"Camille's neighbor—a caterer—told me. She said . . ." He twirled a hand. "The whole neighborhood is talking, Mimi. Everyone has a theory."

So much for secrets staying secret.

"Since you asked, I was teaching a cooking class that night." Donovan rose to his feet and removed a business card from his wallet. He placed it on my desk. "You can call the school like the sheriff did, if that'll convince you. I taught six students. We made pavlova, meringue nests filled with fresh fruit and whipped cream. It's named after the ballerina—"

"Anna Pavlova. It's delicious."

Donovan lowered his chin and exhaled. "When you see Camille, please tell her I came looking for her. When she's up to seeing me, I'm here for her." He shuffled out.

A minute later, I joined Nash at the bar and perched on the stool next to his. He smelled like a tasty mixture of honey and lemon. I leaned closer to drink in more of his scent as I set Donovan's business card on the countertop.

"I like the scarf," he said, twirling his finger in my direction.

"My mother's idea. What do you have on tap today?"

"The newest Chardonnay release from your mother's vineyard. We're calling it *Live Fully*." He had opened the wine and poured two tasting samples. He pushed a glass by the stem toward me. "It's great, if you ask me, with a vigorous acidity and nice balance of tropical fruit."

I loved how he explained wine. His word choices were accessible and unpretentious.

He hitched his chin toward the exit. "Why was Donovan Coleman here?"

"He came looking for Camille." I swirled the wine. "Why don't you like him?"

"Is it that obvious?"

"It is. Could it be because he's younger than you?" I asked, goading him.

Nash threw me a mock-scornful look. "Hardly."

"At least you're better-looking, old man."

"Bet your sweet booty I am."

Playfully he tapped my hand. A shiver of desire ran up my arm.

I took a sip of the wine and swirled it around my tongue. "Yum. This will pair perfectly with shellfish." I set the glass aside. I didn't want to drink any more before lunch. I needed my wits about me. "Care to tell me why you don't like Donovan?"

"He's a flake."

"How so?"

"He had a run-in with my ex." Nash's ex-wife, Willow, owned Fruit of the Vine Artworks in Yountville. The shop featured local artists' works. Every piece was unique. I'd found two of the mirrors that were hanging on the bistro walls at her shop.

"What was the run-in about?"

"He was purchasing some blown-glass platters and asked for discounts because of imperfections."

"Okay." I wasn't ready to jump to conclusions. I'd have done the same. "Go on."

"He was nasty about it. Willow felt threatened and called me."

Had she really felt intimidated? I wasn't convinced she was ready to let Nash go, even though she'd signed the divorce papers. Don't get me wrong. I liked Willow. But she wasn't your typical damsel-in-distress type. Maybe she had called Nash to make him think she needed him so he could feel manly and act as her protector.

"I was in the area and dropped by," Nash said. "He cooled his heels and paid full price, but I've never liked him."

"Is it possible Willow brought out the worst in him?"

Nash's mouth quirked up in a smile. "You mean, like she did in me?"

I knuckled his arm. "She is a tough negotiator." On a few occasions when I'd visited the store, I'd seen her be curt to customers. I understood why and cut her some slack. She cared about her artists and wanted them to get top dollar. "Suffice it to say, for someone as gorgeous and polished as she can be in social settings, her business *bedside* manner could use a little refinement."

"That's an understatement."

"As for Donovan, Chef C adores him, so I'm going to trust her opinion for now. Deal?"

"Deal. Speaking of which, I heard what happened to her sister. How is she doing?"

"She's managing."

"What's this?" Using a fingertip, he twirled the card I'd set down.

"Donovan's business card."

It was a vertical-style card with a gorgeous picture of French macaron cookies at the top. Beneath the picture, in rows, were Donovan's name, cell phone number, and the telephone number for the Yountville Cooking School.

"Why did he give it to you?" Nash asked.

"I sort of asked him for his alibi on Saturday night."

"Sort of?" Nash tipped his head. "Do you think he might be guilty?"

"I'm not sure."

"Don't kid a kidder." He chucked my chin.

I glanced over my shoulder. "Between you, me, and the lamppost, and you have to swear on your mother's Bible that you won't reveal this . . ."

He mimed twisting a lock on his mouth.

"Renee wrote a love letter to Donovan. Tyson found it hidden in the sofa. Donovan claimed he heard about the letter from someone in the neighborhood when he went to check on Camille, which could be true. Or not."

Nash whistled. "You're wondering who hid it."

"Renee is my first guess, hoping Camille wouldn't stumble upon it. But what if Donovan killed Renee and, seeing the note, hid it to throw suspicion on Camille?"

I pulled my cell phone from my pants pocket.

"What are you doing?" Nash asked.

"Calling the cooking school. Donovan says he was there that night. I want to double-check."

A female receptionist with a Valley Girl–style inflection

answered. I asked her whether Donovan had taught a class Saturday night.

"Yeah, like, uh-huh," she said. "He's, like, the best! The pavlova thing with meringue and fruit and whipped cream was, like, one of the yummiest desserts I've ever eaten." As she spoke, I imagined her twirling her hair and flicking her ankle to and fro. "Every class member was as enthusiastic as I was."

"What time did class end?"

"We all stayed until midnight. Everyone was begging Donovan for tips like, you know, how to pipe meringue and stuff." She added that she, in particular, had needed more hands-on experience. Piping was difficult to learn. She said she didn't quite grasp how to keep the meringue toward the tip. Hers was always squishing out the top end and oozing all over her hand. "What a mess."

Piping is difficult, I thought, but I would have bet that wasn't why the bubbly receptionist had asked for extra help. Donovan was dishy.

"The sheriff asked me this already, FYI," she said, using texting shorthand.

I thanked her and ended the call.

"Is Donovan innocent?" Nash asked.

"Yes."

"Back to square one."

Frustration ate at me as I tucked my cell phone away and fingered the stem of my wine glass. Camille was family. And I had to figure out how to clear her name.

Chapter 6

On Monday mornings, Chef C and I invariably spent a few hours concocting specialties for the week. We would then invite the staff to taste-test them. Without Camille's presence, everyone was off-kilter. The sous-chefs, cooks, waitstaff, and even the busboys were asking questions like: *When will she be back? Is she okay? How will she cope?* I had answers because, right as I was saying goodbye to Nash, my mother called and informed me that the therapist had suggested Camille take some time off. The sheriff's department hadn't removed the crime scene tape from her house yet, so Mom and Camille had swung by my mother's place to fetch Riesling, and she and the dog had accompanied Camille to my cottage. They would stay with her until I returned.

All I told the staff was that, at present, Camille was sedated and sleeping.

For the next hour, I threw together the weekly specials menu: *brochette d'agneau à la Grecque*, which was lamb brochettes with sweet peppers, zucchini, and onions with a Greek citrus sauce of fresh rosemary, orange, lime, and grapefruit juice; *pâtés aux fruits de mer*, which included bay scallops, prawns, snow peas, and wild mushrooms over egg linguini with a garlic vermouth sauce; *porc à l'orange*, a sautéed pork tenderloin medallion with an orange sauce; and a very simple grass-fed steak topped with bleu cheese. For the appetizers, we would serve mussels in wine sauce or asparagus with hollandaise sauce. For dessert we'd go simple with *profiteroles*, which were chilled cream puffs drizzled with warm chocolate sauce. As always, we would offer my specialty dessert—crème brûlèe with vanilla sugar.

As I jotted the menu on a dry-erase board, Heather sidled up to me.

"How are you?" she asked.

I blotted my forehead with a clean napkin. "Sweating bullets. I haven't had to do the week's specials by myself in ages."

"Maybe you should throw in tuna tartare. The simple one with sesame seeds and wasabi powder."

"Good idea."

Over the past few months Heather had felt more comfortable offering suggestions. When I'd first hired her, she had been tentative to voice an opinion. After all, she wasn't a cook. She rarely set foot in her own kitchen. I was pretty sure her husband feasted on salt-free frozen dinners. On the other hand, she was an admitted foodie. She enjoyed dishes with a French Polynesian flavor, like *poisson cru*, a raw fish marinated in lime juice and soaked in coconut milk.

I scribbled the tuna tartare suggestion on the board with the other appetizers.

"You know, maybe Chef should see a hypnotherapist," Heather said. Her non sequiturs never surprised me. She could change subjects quicker than a politician.

"The guy you work for?" I asked.

On Heather's days off, when she wasn't typing her husband's latest novel—he wrote everything on a legal pad; he hated computers—Heather put in hours at a hypnotherapist's office in Calistoga. She said she admired him and enjoyed drinking in his insightful nature. Call me cynical, but I believed the guy had planted the initial belief that Glonkirks had abducted her.

"He's brilliant," she gushed. If I didn't know how much she adored her husband, I'd have said she had a crush on the guy. "Maybe he could even get Camille to remember more about what happened."

"Camille knows what happened," I said. "She came home and found her sister dead."

"That's not what I mean. Maybe she knows who did it, you know"—she twirled a finger by her head—"psychically."

"ESP?" I chuckled. "Honestly?"

"Don't you believe in ESP?"

"Let's table that discussion for now. We've got to get a move on." I brandished a spatula like Chef C would. "Pair some wines with this menu. The Nouvelle Vie Vineyards Chardonnay will go well with the seafood appetizer."

"You're biased because Nash hawks it. Oh, ha-ha." She choked back a laugh. "I made a joke. Nash's last name is *Hawke*."

"You're a hoot. Just do it."

She grinned and saluted.

"Stefan," I called. He was standing at the stove filling industrial-sized pots on the burners with water. "The menu is ready. I'll make two entrées and you make the other two. Then let's meet in the dining room. Skip the desserts and appetizers. We're pressed for time."

"On it," he said and spun to his right, running smack dab into Yukiko, a petite Asian cook who'd come to us after quitting her job at a restaurant in Japantown, an enclave of San Francisco. In a high-end restaurant, the cooks—we had three—did the bidding of the executive chef and sous-chef.

"Out of my way," she said. Usually Yukiko had the most endearing smile and was quick to tell a story about her ancestors.

Not now. She was gritting her teeth tightly. Her coal-black eyes were smoldering.

"Out of *my* way," Stefan retorted.

"Now children!" I shouted like Chef C would have. "Play nice."

Both apologized to the other and yelled, "Sorry," to me.

Without Camille, things were getting heated in the kitchen. Due to Renee's murder and the furious activity at the inn for the festival, everyone was on tenterhooks.

As I was fetching the lamb and pork from the refrigerator, Jo scuttled into the kitchen. "Mimi, I'm here and ready to help."

"How did you know I needed it?"

"Your mother called me and told me to hurry over."

"But you can't cook."

"I can taste-test and give my two cents, and I'm pretty good at peeling potatoes and veggies, not to mention I've got a good shoulder to cry on in a pinch."

"You'll get dirty," I said. "I don't want to mess up your dress." She was wearing a raspberry-red scoop-neck dress.

"This old thing?"

"*Old* as in brand-new?" I quipped. "I've never seen it." I set a selection of lamb and pork on the counter, unwrapped it, and set the pieces on platters. "I would remember it with all those details."

She plucked the flounce to freshen it and centered the thin black belt.

"It looks great on you," I said. "Did you just buy it?"

"Yes." She fetched a chef's jacket from the closet at the rear of the kitchen and donned it over her outfit.

"To impress Tyson?"

"No. I bought it for me. I needed a pick-me-up. As for Tyson"—Jo marched to me, her nose wrinkled with distaste—"we're not talking about *him* today."

"Uh-oh, what did he do? Did he get mad when you told him you thought Allie might be a suspect? Did he think you were butting into his case?"

"No, he took that in stride. He said she was already on his radar."

Hooray, I thought. Apparently a whole slew of people were on his radar, including Donovan.

"Then what?" I asked.

Jo lifted a potato peeler from a drawer and wielded it like a sword. "He wants to settle down."

I gasped. "He asked you to marry him?"

"Not exactly."

I titled my head. "Either he did or he didn't."

"He didn't."

"Then what's your problem?" I edged around her and fetched a knife to trim the fat from the meat. "What did he say? Be specific."

"You know him. He sort of hemmed and hawed."

Around anyone else, Tyson Daly was forthright. Around my pal, he could be as shy as a wallflower. He loved her so much that he wanted to defer to her wishes at all times. Maybe he was the one who needed to visit Heather's hypnotherapist.

"He was talking long-term, though," Jo went on. "He chattered about expanding the house he just bought and fixing up rooms for future children." She threw me a sour look. "You know me and kids. I never even babysat growing up. I don't think kids like me."

I laughed out loud. "How would you know if you haven't tried? And it's not like once you get married you jump right in and start a family."

"Yes, it is. You and I are the same age and our biological clocks are ticking." She made *tick-tock* sounds with her tongue.

"Speak for yourself." I pushed the lamb aside and started in on the pork tenderloin, trimming the fat and silver skin away. Next, I cut it into twelve inch-thick slices. After that, I whipped up a bowl of flour and spices that I would use to dredge the meat. I heated a skillet and added a couple of tablespoons of safflower oil and quick-fried the slices. They sizzled and spit.

"I want a long courtship. Lo-o-ong." Jo selected a cucumber from a pile at the cooks' station and perched on a stool nearby. "Want this peeled?"

"Sure." I would use it to adorn appetizer portions of tuna tartare. "You'll have to be honest with Tyson."

"I am. I have been. He doesn't listen. He—"

"Whoa, Nellie!" Stefan shouted.

I swung around and gasped. Water and white foam were boiling over the two industrial-sized pots on the stove.

Without taking the time to don mitts, Stefan tried to move the pots off the burners. "Ow, ow! Dumb, dumb, dumb. I forgot to set a timer."

Yukiko threw him a pair of mitts. He put them on, shimmied the pots to safety, and ratcheted down the heat. A busboy swooped in with a mop and started to swab the floor. Another helper tossed microfiber cloths to Stefan.

Heather hurried into the kitchen. "What's going on?"

I said, "Everyone's on edge without Camille. We all want resolution. We want her sister's killer brought to justice, and we want her to find her smile again. Most of all, we want calm. A kitchen requires calm."

Jo said, "I'm sorry Yves couldn't help out longer. How about hiring a temporary chef?"

I shook my head. "What if whoever we choose is bad? What might that do to the reputation of the bistro?"

"What will happen if you don't? War might break out." Jo grinned.

"Then I'd better become a general and delegate. Yukiko, take over this entrée." I ceded my position.

"Yes, Chef."

I handed Heather and Jo clean towels and moved to Stefan to help him reorganize his area.

Heather followed me. "I heard Allie O'Malley was a chef before."

"You've got to be kidding," Jo trailed her. "For all we know, she killed Renee."

Heather's eyes widened. "Really? What's her motive?"

"Money," Jo said.

"They argued about a contract." I wiped down spoons and sauté pans that were wet from the boiling water.

"O-o-oh," Heather dragged out the word. "Follow the money."

I replayed the confrontation between them in my mind. Allie had begged Renee to cede control of the festival. Did she believe that she might regain ownership if Renee was dead? She had been at the bistro when Renee left that night. She'd paid quickly and split. Had she followed Renee to Camille's house, barged in, and clobbered her with the countertop mixer? Though she had been the first suspect to come to mind, I didn't sense Allie was evil at her core. However, as history had proven, I wasn't an expert at determining a person's character. I thought of their last exchange again: Renee had said, "See you soon"; Allie had responded, "Not if I can help it."

"Knock-knock," a woman said from the entrance to the kitchen. "Am I interrupting?"

Nash's ex-wife Willow strutted toward us. I could have sworn she'd been a siren in a prior life. Not only did she look incredible, with her flowing red hair and her shapely body wrapped in an apple-red dress, but she also came across as the warmest, most alluring human being on the planet. Anyone who met her instantly wanted to be her best friend, including me—that is, until I'd learned she was Nash's wife, at the time.

"Jorianne, I was hoping I'd find you here." Willow had a melodious voice. "I'm almost finished setting up."

"Setting up what?" I whispered to Jo.

"I forgot to tell you," she said. "Willow asked if she could place a display from her store at the inn. She thought festival people might want to invest in arty plates and baskets for the sweets they purchase. She said she'll donate ten percent of her proceeds to the educational fund, too."

"It's a very good cause," Willow said, moving farther into the kitchen. "I know how much I've valued my education." She and Nash had gone to UC Davis together. She for art, he initially to become a veterinarian. "Come with me, Mimi." She beckoned me with a finger. "I want you to meet somebody."

"I can't. We're taste-testing the week's menu soon."

"Please."

Knowing she wouldn't relent—like a siren, she always got her way—and knowing I needed a breather from the chaos if I wanted to serve up a good lunch, I asked Stefan to take command, instructed Heather, Jo, and the rest of the staff to obey him, and allowed Willow to steer me through the dining room, across the parking lot, and up the front path to Maison Rousseau.

"You'll be so surprised to see what we've done," she said. "It's a gem of a store."

A thickset couple wearing colorful T-shirts approached us and waved. "Hello, Mimi! We're off to see a crush!" they said in unison.

"Have fun," I said. "Did you secure a tour like I told you?" They had come into town a month ago and dined at Bistro Rousseau.

"You bet." The woman's voice was as jolly as her apple-cheeked face. "We're going to Frog's Leap Vineyards."

"That'll be fun. It's an old frog farm, you know."

The man said, "I wanted to do the Cakebread Cellars tour."

"That's a good one, too," I said. "It's one of my favorites. They're all done in small groups so you won't get caught in the crush of people during the, um, *crush*."

"Told you." He poked his companion.

"We purchased wine passes," she said.

"Terrific. It's such a good deal," I said. Many wineries honored the pass and offered couples two-for-one prices—a big savings. "Do you have a driver?"

"You bet," the man said. "We're not stupid."

"Well, I'm not"—the woman motioned to her T-shirt, which read I'M WITH STUPID with an arrow pointing left—"but he might be."

"Yo-o-u." He locked his arm around her neck, gave her a noogie with his knuckles, and prodded her down the path to where their driver in a Lincoln Town Car awaited.

Oh, to feel so lighthearted, I thought.

Willow and I entered Maison Rousseau. The registration desk was to the left, the valet stand to the right. In the center of the foyer near the fountain, which was situated in front of the arched portico that joined the gardens on either side of the inn, stood a pretty display of art on verdigris baker's racks. Willow had brought vases, picture frames, serving plates, and baskets. She must have supplied the baker's racks, too. I couldn't remember us having any on hand.

A dark-haired man with broad shoulders was installing the rest of the art. A tea service set for four and a cashbox rested on an antique oak table.

"Eli," Willow called as she released my arm.

The man pivoted, and I gasped. "Elijah George, is that you?"

He ran a hand through his stick-straight hair. "One and the same, though everyone calls me Eli now."

Elijah and I had gone to elementary school together. Even back then he'd had the most gorgeous brown eyes. I couldn't remember a time when they hadn't twinkled with merriment. He was trim and fit and stood well over six feet tall.

"What are you doing here?" I asked.

"What does it look like?" He gestured to the baker's racks. "Giving Willow a hand."

"He's got the day off," Willow said.

"No, I mean what are you doing in Nouvelle Vie? The last I'd heard, you and your family moved across the country. You were, what, eleven at the time?"

"Good memory." He gave me a thumbs-up. "We settled in New York. Dad worked for NBC until a month ago, when he retired. Mom continues to sell flowers. She delivers sprays to everyone with a Fifth Avenue or Park Avenue address."

"And you?" I asked. "What did you end up doing?"

"I went to NYU. Afterward, I became a chef."

"A chef?" Memories of Eli and I making mud pies at the ripe age of five sprang to mind. Was that the beginning of his future as a chef? It wasn't mine. "I thought you were going to become an astronaut or a research scientist."

"He's sort of a scientist," Willow said. "He's working at the Sonoma Health and Fitness Resort. They brought him on to make sure every meal is designed with superfoods and foods packed with antioxidants. That's where the science skills come in."

"Wow," I blinked. "I'm impressed." The all-white resort was set on a sprawling piece of property and boasted a very tony clientele. Celebrities from every walk of life stayed there.

"I knew you'd be thrilled to see him," Willow went on. "I got the lowdown about you two when he came into the shop looking for a few mirrors. I've told him all about your success. I also told him that I was helping a good cause over here at the inn, and he offered to help. What a sport, right?"

I poked her arm and said sotto voce, "What are you doing?"

"Fixing you up, *natch*. If I'm going to be in love, you might as well be."

"You're in love?"

"Maybe. My new beau and I spent a lovely night together. There was chemistry." She flicked her fingers to signify fireworks. "Hot chemistry."

"That's great, but Willow"—I leveled her with a firm look—"I'm dating Nash."

"Exclusively?" she asked.

I didn't know how to answer that. The more I thought about it, the readier I was to say *yes*. But how did he feel? We needed to talk.

When I didn't answer, she moved on. "Did I tell you Eli is an expert on which herbs and foods increase brain function?"

He reddened, endearingly.

"And no GMO," Willow continued. "Isn't that fabulous? You and he should get together sometime and compare notes."

I bobbed my head. What else could I do? "Eli, it would be nice to get caught up, but right now, I've got to get back to work. We're taste-testing the week's specials before we're slammed with diners. Sorry."

"No worries."

He smiled easily, and the memory of a dance we'd attended in seventh grade—a sock hop—flickered through my mind. He'd had braces put on his teeth the week before and had been so self-conscious. No longer.

As I turned to leave, Willow gripped my elbow and said, "I'll give him your number."

I skewered her with a scathing look, but she was already heading toward Eli.

Chapter 7

On the way to the bistro, I fumed and mumbled to myself. What was Willow up to? Did she want Nash back? Was her story about having a new *beau*—what a pretentious word—a hoax? I entered the kitchen and pushed the memory of her self-satisfied face from my mind before I pressed ahead with the meals.

The morning tasting went smoothly. Heather had picked the right wines to pair with each entrée. I liked the Grgich Hills Sauvignon Blanc, which had a nutty, citrusy flavor; it perfectly complemented the pork medallions. The lunch crowd liked the pairing, as well; we sold out of both. We ran out of crème brûlée, too. I must have torched the tops of at least forty desserts; Stefan had caramelized the others. At three PM, I declared the day a success.

Needing a walk to clear my head and craving a cup of strongly brewed coffee, I donned a sunhat, sprayed my face with sunblock, and headed out.

Down the street from Bistro Rousseau, mixed in with the other upscale eateries, jazz clubs, and high-end shops, was the café called Chocolate. I loved visiting it, with its coffee-cup-shaped chairs and walnut tables. I enjoyed standing at the white granite counter and eyeing the luscious pastries displayed on tiered cake plates, though today I wouldn't indulge. If I were going to eat anything, it would have to be protein. A pastry would send me on a sugar high which would then plummet me to a sugar low. No thanks.

"Hiya, Mimi." The owner, Irene, approached me as I arrived, the skirt of her white smocked dress swishing around her calves. She was as sweet as her café and as warmhearted as her adopted Labrador retriever. "You look beat. Are you okay, honey?" Her eyes were darker than mine, more the color of Hershey's Kisses, and she invariably wore her pink-tinted hair in a loose braid.

"I'm fine. I'm burning the candle—"

"—at both ends. I understand." She wiped her hands on the cocoa-brown apron that protected her dress and gripped my elbow. "Running a restaurant is hard enough, but to also manage the inn and have a festival on the premises to boot? I admire you."

"Admit it. You think I'm crazy."

"I know the name of a good therapist." She winked.

I chuckled.

"What'll it be?" She released me. "Your usual? Hot chocolate and a croissant?"

"A café latte to go, with an extra shot of espresso. Two-percent milk. That's all."

"Geez, you really are off your game," she said and headed toward the counter.

I followed and perched on an available stool. "Say, Irene, before you make that latte—"

"What's up?"

"On the night Renee Wells died—"

"Oh, lordy. What a shame." Irene wagged her head. "What is this world coming to? You know, Camille and I are neighbors."

"I had no idea."

"I live in the corner house with the green gables."

"I adore that house. You have a beautiful garden. I particularly love your autumn-toned chrysanthemums."

"What a pity." Irene sighed. "I had to replace all of them. My adorable Chocolate Chip tore through them and decimated them." Chocolate Chip was her rescue Labrador retriever. "But enough about the mundane. Poor Camille. I can't imagine losing a sibling, and to violence no less." Irene was an only child. She'd relocated to Napa Valley when her parents retired here. "How is she?"

"She's coping."

"If she needs anything, you tell her I'm at the ready."

"Thanks." I folded my arms on the counter. "Tell me something. Did Renee's husband come in here that night? He's got tan skin and ginger-colored hair—"

"And beady eyes." She narrowed hers in imitation.

"Yes, that's him."

Irene pursed her lips and scanned the café as if trying to picture everyone who had stopped in that evening. After a long moment, she shook her head. "I don't recall having seen him. He's been in once or twice, which is how I knew about the eyes, but he's not a regular."

"He said he came in to access the Internet."

"Let me ask around. Are you sure you're going to pass on a croissant?"

"Yep. I need protein."

"I have a homemade nut bar, packed with goodies."

"And no sugar?"

"Well, of course, there's sugar."

"I'll pass."

A minute later when Irene returned with my to-go latte, she said, "No one can vouch for that man being here. Granted, not all of the staff who were working that night are on the job right now, but a few are."

On my way back to the bistro, I couldn't stop thinking about Rusty Wells. If he had lied about his whereabouts that night, did it mean he'd lied about not killing Renee? On the other hand, if I proved he was lying and he hadn't killed his wife, then his testimony corroborating Camille's whereabouts would be in question, too.

I crossed the bistro parking lot, and a breeze kicked up. My sun hat flew off and wafted over a row of vehicles. While collecting it, I spotted a battered green truck with the license plate WELS EGS. Rusty was on the premises.

Seeing as I had a half hour before I needed to supervise the kitchen for the dinner crowd and because I was curious why Rusty claimed he had gone to Chocolate on the night of the murder when he hadn't—if Irene's employees were correct—I struck out across the lot and followed a crowd through the inn to the festivities.

I found Rusty in the Sisley Garden. The scalloped eaves of the white tents were flapping, the bells were jingling with merry abandon, and the chatter among the crowd was joyous. Rusty, on the other hand, wasn't happy. He was arguing with Allie O'Malley near the end of a line of people waiting to purchase something at TUTTI FRUTTI.

"You can't do that!" Allie shouted, her voice carrying on the wind. She threw her arms wide. "Please!" Her white tunic top was billowing over her white trousers and flapping like crazy. If she wasn't careful, I feared the breeze might catch her tunic and lift her like an umbrella.

"Leave," Rusty said, looking and sounding official. Like the other employees, he had donned a pair of crisp khaki pants and an iron-pressed khaki shirt, and his hair was combed. "You're not welcome here. I'm running this now."

"But it's mine."

"No, it's not. You sold it lock, stock, and barrel. To my wife." Rusty's face flamed beet red, and his pointy lips looked even sharper because of the way he was pursing his mouth.

"That's not true. I sold it to her with the agreement that I would earn a percentage."

"That's not what I heard."

"She also promised that I could buy it back at any time. She lied. That makes the contract invalid. A woman's word is her bond."

"Sue me."

I gazed at the festival guests. A few standing near SHAKE YOUR BOOTY were agitated. Some were even covering their children's ears. Parker Price, clad in a casual tan suit and straw fedora, was among the crowd, glad-handing a few constituents. He made eye contact with me and lifted his meaty chin, silently asking if I wanted his help. I waved him off and, taking matters into my own hands, marched to Rusty and Allie.

"Hey, you two"—I offered a solicitous smile—"can you take this discussion elsewhere?" I jutted my head in the direction of the gawking crowd.

Allie gaped, not realizing what a stir she and Rusty were causing.

Rusty scowled at me. "It's not your business."

"Yes, it is," I said. "I own the joint, remember?" *Joint?* I bit back a grin. Had I said *joint* to sound tough? What a joke. "Look around, Rusty. This isn't good for PR."

Rusty scanned the crowd and blanched. "Gosh, you're right. I—" He scratched his head. "I don't know what we were thinking. Allie, listen—"

"No, you listen," she began, trying to sound as menacing as I had, but then her façade cracked. Her lower lip started to quiver and moisture pressed at the corners of her eyes. "This"—she spread her arms wide, encompassing the festival—"is everything I dreamed of. I couldn't get it up and running, but Renee did. After she blew me off, I reconsidered. I was going to talk to her about partnering with her, learning from her, but now she's dead, and I'm stuck. Don't you see? I have nothing. I thought you would understand, Rusty. I hoped"—she scuffed the heel of her white ballerina flat against the ground, a fruitless gesture; it made no sound—"you would take pity and give me a chance. Guess I was wrong. You're . . . heartless." Tears spilled down her cheeks. She pivoted and hurried in the direction of the inn.

As she fled, I again pondered whether she had it in her to be a killer. She seemed so pathetic that I couldn't imagine her capable of committing a brutal act.

"Aw, man." Rusty rubbed his cheek then glowered at me. "What are you staring at? Why are you here?" He took a step toward me.

"Whoa!" I held up two hands, keeping him at bay. "I wanted a word with you. That's all."

"What about?"

"I was at Chocolate talking with the owner. She . . ." How could I broach this topic without making him defensive? I couldn't. His mouth was set in a grimace. I plowed ahead. "She said no one remembers you being there on the night of the murder."

He flinched but covered his reaction by lifting a defiant chin. "What were you doing, spying on me?"

"No, Irene and I were chatting and she—"

"You don't believe I'm innocent."

"I don't know what to think, Rusty. You lied about being at the café. Did you lie about everything else?"

"I didn't kill Renee." His voice cracked. His shoulders sagged.

"I swear. I think Camille did it. She must've been crazy jealous when she learned that Renee had a thing for that Donovan dude."

I raised an eyebrow. "I've been meaning to ask, how and when did you find out about Donovan?"

"The people around here have been chin-wagging like nobody's business." He opened and closed his hands like talking sock puppets. "A woman saw Renee and him together. That day. At The Bookery. She told another woman that he put his hand on Renee's lower back, and all of a sudden, everyone around here was gossiping. They were *eloping*, one person said." He mimed quotation marks around the word *eloping*. "They were going to get *married*, another claimed." More finger bracketing. "They were planning to *off the husband*—meaning me."

"People were saying that?"

"Folks love to gossip. They read all those silly rag magazines at the grocery store, and crazy ideas come into their heads. Scout's honor." He raised a hand, three fingers up, thumb anchoring his pinky. "I'll bet Camille caught wind of the brouhaha and decided she could kill Renee and lay the blame on me. She has a temper."

"Who, Camille?"

"Yeah." He aimed a finger in my direction. "You know what she did to Renee when they were teens, don't you? She ran after her with a meat cleaver."

"Give me a break."

"It's true. She flies off the handle. Renee told me so."

I knew my chef could be demanding, but would she aim a weapon? At a person? At her sister? No, not a chance. "Rusty, you told the sheriff you saw Camille at the entrance to the hiking trail that night. You gave her an alibi. Did you lie about that?"

"Maybe."

I couldn't tell whether he was yanking my chain or trying to formulate a plan to implicate Camille. His gaze was darting right and left, refusing to focus on mine. "What else did you fabricate?"

He grunted. "Look, I've heard about you and what happened a few months ago."

"Huh?"

"You're curious. You're a snoop."

"I am not."

"You solved that murder. You stopped at nothing."

"He was my benefactor and my friend. I wanted to know the truth."

He aimed a finger at his mouth. "Read my lips. I. Did. Not. Do. It. Keep your nose out of my business. The sheriff will get to the bottom of it." He turned to leave.

"Hold it, Mr. Wells." As much as I preferred the soft approach when dealing with bullies—I had encountered plenty of them during my stint in the restaurant business—I was not going to let him bulldoze me. "I can close this festival down. What then?"

"And ruin all the fun for these people? You wouldn't do that. That could hurt your standing in the community." Rusty puffed out his chest. "And, let's be honest, I don't think you or your business could suffer another blow—having a murder on the premises as well as a chef who's a murderer."

I squared my shoulders. "Are you threatening me?"

"Two can tango," he said, messing up the metaphor.

"Mimi"—Parker Price pulled alongside me, his gaze trained on Rusty—"is everything okay?"

"Fine, Councilman. Thank you."

Parker jutted a hand toward Rusty. "How are you, my man?"

Rusty stepped backward and peered up at Parker, who was a

good six inches taller. "You're Price." He didn't reciprocate the handshake.

Parker didn't react to the slight. "That's correct."

"My wife told me about you."

"Hope it was all good. If word gets around that I'm a jerk, I won't have a job." Parker knuckled Rusty on the arm—hard.

Rusty held his ground. "Renee said you were quite the talker."

"Renee was your wife?" Parker stammered. "Gee, I didn't know. Sorry for your loss. To be truthful, I didn't know her very well."

Rusty cocked his head. "That's not what I heard."

Parker bridled. "Who says differently?"

"She did."

"Man, she was pulling your leg. We shared a brief hello. That's all. She and my wife were friendly. They're the ones who had tea and exchanged recipes and the like."

"That's odd." Rusty worked his tongue inside his cheek. "Renee didn't cook."

Until that fateful night, I thought.

"That is odd." Parker scratched his chin. "Felicity told me your wife asked for a recipe."

"A recipe for what?"

"Disaster," Parker blurted, but he had the decency to blanch when he realized how improper his kneejerk response was. "Sorry. That was rude of me. Way out of line." He stroked his chin. "I believe Renee asked for a paleo cookie recipe. *Paleo*." He snuffled. "Who eats that stuff?" He directed his attention to me. "Mimi, if you're okay, I'll be moving on."

"Hold on, Councilman." Rusty's nose curled up in a snarl. "About your beautiful wife . . . She and I"—he flicked a finger between him and an imaginary Felicity—"have met. In fact, she and I got along rather well."

Parker didn't miss the lewd insinuation. His hands balled into fists. After a long, edgy moment, he forced his hands to unfurl. "My wife gets along with everyone. She doesn't play favorites." He threw Rusty a cautionary look before departing.

Rusty sniggered and headed in the opposite direction.

I let out the breath I'd been holding. What was up with the tension between those two? The sun was shining. There wasn't a cloud in the sky. I couldn't blame the friction on electricity from an impending storm. Was Rusty suggesting that Parker and Renee had hooked up? Did Parker honestly believe Felicity could have had a fling with Rusty, who was—Felicity would no doubt remind him—way beneath her social scale?

Allie appeared in the portico. She had reapplied her makeup and run a comb through her mane of hair. She drifted into the throng and smiled at each passing patron.

Rusty was also making his way among the people, chatting up the crowd. He ignored Allie as he passed her. In defiance, she lifted her chin and pressed on.

When Rusty neared the TUTTI FRUTTI tent, he swiveled his head and threw me a vile look. A split second later, he offered a tight grin. I shivered. Was he as unstable as Dr. Jekyll and Mr. Hyde? Another notion struck me. Maybe declaring eternal love for his wife earlier had been an act. Maybe he'd hated the egg farming business as much as she had. Maybe he'd killed her so he could take over this and future festivals.

Chapter 8

Even though I felt the urge to phone Tyson to tell him about Rusty's lie about Chocolate and to replay the heated encounter I'd witnessed between Rusty and Parker, I didn't have time. Duty called. Yet again, we had two seatings scheduled for dinner. *A chef's work is never done*, I thought.

I donned my chef's coat and toque and set pots of water to boil on the stove while wondering whether Jo had made any headway on finding another chef to help carry the load.

Stefan and Yukiko seemed to be getting along, which pleased me. I hated contentiousness in the kitchen. The two were rocking out to a jazzy instrumental rendition of Phil Collins's "Against All Odds." The saxophonist was phenomenal.

"I like the music," I shouted over the din.

"Glad to hear it." Stefan did a two-step toward me. "Hey, I forgot to tell you, at lunch we ran out of lamb. Yukiko and I came up with an alternative entrée. Hope that's okay."

Now they were collaborating? What next?

I said, "Sure. What is it?"

"Chicken *à la Grecque*." He followed me to the sink, where I washed my hands. "We're doing it the same way, with the sweet peppers and zucchini in the Greek citrus sauce. In addition, we'll offer *poulet dijonaise*."

"Chicken with mustard sauce," I said. "A great alternative. Perfect."

During the first seating, Heather pushed through the kitchen door. "Mimi, customers are asking for you."

I winced. "With a complaint?"

"With a compliment."

"Phew. That's what I like to hear." I dabbed my perspiring face with a clean towel and signaled Stefan. "Got this?"

He nodded. "Take a bow for me, too," he joked.

Heather guided me to a table where Tyson was dining with his mother and sister, whom he introduced as Tish. Oakley, an energetic waitress with carrot-colored hair and a winning smile, was removing their entrée dishes.

Tyson's mother, a charming goat farmer with weathered skin and finely etched wrinkles from a life of smiling, scrambled to a stand and took my hands in hers. "Mimi, my dear. Dinner is remarkable, as always."

"Thank you, Mrs. Daly."

She resumed her seat and finger-combed the short silver hair that cupped her face. "Tish, your turn. Tish works as a lawyer in San Francisco and rarely eats rich food."

"It was delicious," Tish gushed. "And just so you know, I'm the one who asked for you. 'A job well done is a job worth complimenting.' My dad used to say that."

"I say it, as well," her mother chided.

"I'm bringing my husband and children here a week from Sunday," Tish went on.

"How many children do you have?" I asked.

"Two adorable eight-year-old towheads."

Tyson snickered. "Adorable is pushing it."

His sister thwacked him on the arm.

"How do you manage kids with a career?" I asked, thinking of Jo and her concerns.

"My firm has an in-house daycare facility."

Oakley reappeared to refill their water glasses. "Coffee?" she asked.

Mrs. Daly raised her hand.

Tyson brushed my arm. "Mimi, how is everything in the kitchen without Chef C at the helm?"

"We're managing. You might have forgotten, but I've done this before, in a prior life." The restaurant in San Francisco where I'd served as executive chef had seated over a hundred people at every meal. The kitchen had been twice as big; the staff, double. "How is the investigation going?"

"Okay," he said.

His sister snickered. "How cryptic of you, little brother. Dad taught you well."

"Are you saying you're nothing like him?" Tyson dipped his fingers into his water glass and spritzed his sister with droplets.

Their mother *tsk*ed to quiet their banter. "Mimi, return to your post. We don't want to keep you."

"Tyson . . ." I paused.

He tilted his head as he dried off his hand. "What?"

"Nothing."

Now was not the time to mention the heated vibes I'd picked up between Allie and Rusty as well as between Rusty and Parker, nor was it the time to tell him what I'd discovered at Chocolate. Our fine sheriff was enjoying a night out. His family deserved his undivided attention. I would fill him in tomorrow on my observations.

* * *

When I arrived home at half past eleven, my feet were sore and my back was aching. I pressed open the front door and did my best to be quiet so I wouldn't disturb Camille.

To my surprise, she was wide awake and mopping the kitchen floor.

"What are you doing?" I asked.

"There is chicken feed on the hardwood. My fault."

"There was chicken feed in your kitchen, too."

"It is everywhere. Renee tracked it in. She used to say that the farm would not leave the soles of one's shoes." Tears pooled in Camille's eyes.

I rushed to her and threw my arms around her. The mop handle pressed into my chest. "Cry," I said. "Let it out. It's okay."

"That is the problem. I cannot stop"—she hiccupped—"crying. I have been weeping all day. Whenever I think of something she said or did, I—"

The aquarium let out a burp. Cagney and Lacey were goggling us from inside their tank. They swam off but returned and brushed their cheeks against one another. I wondered whether they wished they could hug like humans, or maybe they were thinking we looked ridiculous. Either way, I didn't care; I didn't let go of my grief-stricken chef.

"I think of all of our times together," Camille said. "I rehash things I told Renee and regret the sentiments I did not reveal. I think of funny and not-so-funny moments."

"Like the time you chased her with a meat cleaver?"

Camille pressed away from me and wiped the tears off her face. "Who told you that?"

"Rusty."

"Liar. It was the other way around. Renee chased me. She was furious that our father would pay for my schooling and not hers. 'I have no talent,' she yelled at me. 'How am I to get by?' I told her she had plenty of talent but no constancy. How furious that made her." A smile tugged at Camille's lips. "She looked so funny whenever she got mad. Her nose would scrunch up, and her eyes would grow very small, and she would snort like a piglet." She imitated the sound.

"Camille, I can't believe you're finding this humorous in the least. She ran after you with a meat cleaver."

"I was not frightened. She did not know how to use it. The sharp edge of the blade was pointing toward her. Looking back, she was always gearing for a fight. That is the phrase, yes?" Camille erupted in giggles, but suddenly, the giggles morphed into tears and she started to convulse. I attempted to comfort her, but she wouldn't let me. "No, *merci*. It will pass. It *must* pass."

I understood. I'd felt the same when people had tried to comfort me after my late husband's death.

Camille began mopping again. "*C'est la vie*."

I moseyed to the fish tank, opened a small can of fish food, and gave my pets their daily pinch of flakes. As the two vied for their fair share, I recalled Renee's heated encounters with Allie as well as with Rusty. How many enemies had she made over the years? "Camille, you said Renee was always gearing for a fight."

"Gearing, yes, but never following through. She had a fiery temper, but her passions waned. Do not let Rusty fill your head with nonsense." She sniffed, clearly not over him mixing up the meat cleaver story. Though he had a tendency to lie, maybe this story wasn't his fault. Perhaps Renee had given him the wrong account.

"Where did you see Rusty?" Camille asked.

"He's managing the festival."

She grumbled. "Someone has to, I suppose."

"Would you care for tea?"

"Yes, thank you."

I fetched my favorite Forsyth by Royal Doulton teacups—I loved the design of a thin green line next to gold—and filled them with instant hot water, one of the luxuries I'd installed in the cottage when we had revamped it. I added an English Breakfast tea bag and two tablespoons of milk to each. I knew Camille liked it that way. I set the cups, saucers, spoons, and napkins on the kitchen table and sat down.

As I let my tea steep, I offered my theory about Rusty's endgame—to get out of the egg-farming business. Camille didn't respond. She rinsed the mop and squeezed the water into the sink. Afterward, she propped the mop in the sink, handle in the air.

"Is it possible that he was the one who tracked the chicken feed into your kitchen?" I asked.

Camille joined me at the table. "I cannot believe he would kill Renee. He loved her with all his heart."

"What if he killed her in a green-eyed rage?"

"Why would he be jealous?"

"Because of Donovan."

Camille huffed. "Renee would not have left Rusty. Donovan was a passing fancy."

Using a spoon, I removed my teabag, wound the string around the spoon to press the remaining brew into the cup, and set the teabag and spoon on the saucer. "Donovan came to the bistro today."

"I do not wish to talk about him."

"But—"

"No." She ran a finger around the rim of her teacup and stopped. Her gaze met mine. "When Renee met Rusty, she fell head over heels. First love is so sweet, no?"

"But then she fell out of love with him."

"Did she?"

"She wanted a divorce. She filed papers."

Camille sighed. Her sadness was palpable.

I took a sip of tea and set the cup down. "Is it possible, prior to having a crush on Donovan, that Renee could have hooked up with someone else? Say, someone who made her want to divorce Rusty?" I thought of Parker Price but didn't mention his name. Earlier, he'd been so cagey about not knowing her well. I couldn't tell if he had been taunting Rusty or telling the truth. "She's been staying with you for a few weeks. Did she ever mention meeting another man?"

"No. Never. It did not happen." Camille stirred her tea but didn't drink it. After a long silence, she said, "I have thought of a temporary chef for you. Victor Richard." She pronounced his surname with a French accent, the *ch* sounding like *sh*. "He is very talented. His résumé is excellent. We worked together years ago. I jotted his number down for you." She pointed to a notepad on the counter. "I must go to sleep," she said, ending any further discussion. She rose from the table and settled onto the couch fully clothed.

I let her be.

* * *

I awoke at dawn the next morning, aching from the previous day's activities and desperately craving time off to recuperate. When I realized it was Tuesday, I silently cheered. Tuesday was the single day of the week that we closed the bistro.

In order not to wake Camille, I drank my morning coffee on the patio. Listening to birds twittering in the nearby vineyard and orchard revived me. When I finished my coffee, I tiptoed into the kitchen and quickly threw together an autumn-themed quiche made with ham and pumpkin. The moment I removed it from the oven, I cut myself a portion and savored it for breakfast. When I finished, I plated a slice for Camille.

At nine AM, I contacted Victor Richard, who said he was ready, willing, and able to start Wednesday. He had a pompous voice, but I tried to reserve judgment. Camille vouched for him; I needed him.

Camille awoke a half hour later and ate the quiche. We didn't talk. We didn't discuss her sorrow. I hoped that, as soon as Tyson found her sister's killer, she would start to heal and rediscover her sparkle.

Tyson. I pulled out my cell phone and texted him that I had information I wanted to share. He didn't respond. I would give him the day before I'd reach out a second time.

Midmorning, Nash sent me a text message to remind me about our date. I replied that I couldn't wait and sped into my bedroom to get dressed.

Though we had planned to go wine tasting on previous occasions, we hadn't yet done so. I was excited. Going during Crush Week would be a challenge, of course, because everyone was out and about and the roads would be packed with vehicles, but I would be with Nash, so I didn't care how long the drive would take.

As usual, he was prompt. He entered and gave me a lingering kiss.

"Was that the kiss you promised?" I asked.

"Nope. You'll get that one after the *jambon-beurre*."

"Nice pronunciation."

"I practiced." He grinned and raked me with his gaze. "You look wonderful."

The weather was going to be warm. I'd thrown on a pair of cream capris and a sleeveless cream top with aqua-green stitching around the V-neck.

"We almost match," he said. He wasn't wearing his typical jeans, white shirt, and leather jacket. He had donned a pair of tan cargo shorts and an ecru-and-turquoise plaid shirt.

"Should I put on something else?" I asked. My father and mother had never dressed in matching outfits. If either accidentally did, one or the other would hightail it to the bedroom to change.

"We're different enough," he said. "You should grab a shawl, though, in case it's cold in the winery."

"Where are we going?" I plucked an aqua shawl off the hat rack.

"It's a secret." Eyes twinkling with mischief, he moved past me to greet my goldfish and scratched the tank with a fingertip. Lacey swam to him and pressed her face against the glass, swishing this way and that. Cagney hung back. She could be a little shy.

Camille emerged from the bathroom and stopped short. Her hair was flat against her head, her face devoid of makeup. She pulled the collar of her robe around her neck.

"Morning, Chef," Nash said, acting as if seeing her in my cottage was the most normal thing in the world.

"Good morning."

"We'll be back in a few hours, Camille," I said. "Will you be okay?"

She licked her lips. "Mimi, I am going to find another place to stay."

"No. Don't—"

"Until the sheriff allows me to return to my house."

"Let's talk about this later. Please."

"I have made up my mind. Go." She shooed us with her hand. "Do not forget the picnic I packed."

Though Camille might have been working through intense emotions, she had felt the urge to cook and had prepared a number of miniature sandwiches using whatever she could find in my refrigerator. She had cooked up a fresh batch of crisp sweet potato chips, as well. Of course, a picnic by my chef would not have been complete without dessert—chocolate-dipped madeleine cookies. I had sneaked one before Nash arrived. Delectable.

Out on the road, the traffic was moving at a crawl. Nash tuned the radio to a jazz station. I didn't recognize the song that was playing. The rhythm was quite chaotic and seemed to be mimicking the thoughts about Camille that were running roughshod in my mind.

So much for taking the day off from worry. What was I going to do about her? How could I urge her to rejoin the world of the living? Was I expecting too much too soon? After Derrick died, I'd lived in an emotional cocoon for a good month. Lots of dark chocolate bonbons had been consumed.

Nash cut into my thoughts. "Where are you?" he asked gently.

"I'm here. Nice car. I love the smell of new leather."

"Me, too." Buying the GMC Acadia had been a big splurge for him. His family had never been well-to-do, living paycheck to paycheck. Throughout high school, he had worked odd jobs to save for college. "Hey, I spoke with Willow earlier. She said she ran into you."

"She did."

"She said she's showing some of her wares at the inn."

"Mm-hm." I thought of my brief encounter with Eli. He hadn't called. Maybe Willow had taken the hint and not given him my telephone number. Good. I wasn't interested. I liked Nash. A lot. But now wasn't the time to talk about our relationship. Not with Camille—

He brushed my arm. "Are you okay?"

"I'm worried about Chef C. I'm sure you could see she isn't well. Losing her sister has set her adrift, and with Tyson thinking she might be guilty of murder . . ." I twisted in my seat. "She didn't do it."

"Of course she didn't."

We passed the town of St. Helena, every shop on the thoroughfare busy with foot traffic, and continued on.

"Are we heading to Healdsburg?" I asked.

"Not quite that far. So, tell me, have you put any thought into who might have killed Renee? Do you have a suspect in mind?"

I glanced sideways at him.

"C'mon," he said. "I know you. You've got theories."

"Why would you think—"

"Because you're the most caring woman I know. Plus, you're observant, and the sister of the victim is staying in your home, not to mention that your bistro must be bedlam without her in attendance."

"I'm doing pretty well on my own."

He grinned. "That wasn't meant as a slight. You are not only the chef; you're also the chief bottle washer. Plus, need I remind you that you have a festival on the grounds? If you solve this, your life can return to normal."

I leaned back in my seat, pleased by how well he could read me. Was that a sign that we belonged together? "Okay," I said. "If I were a betting woman, I'd say Renee's husband Rusty killed her."

"Why?"

"Renee wanted out of the egg-farming business. Maybe Rusty did, too, and decided that he could helm the festivals all by his lonesome."

"He's taken charge?"

"He sure has."

"Are they a money earner?"

"They might be. I watched Rusty with the crowds yesterday. He seemed to be in his element."

"Here we are." Nash pulled to a stop near the entrance to Castello di Amorosa.

"You've got to be kidding," I said. "We're going wine tasting here?"

"I thought you could use a let-your-hair-down day." He rubbed his knuckles along my cheekbone. "You're tough, but let's face it, seeing another dead body can't have done you any emotional favors."

Castello di Amorosa featured a huge castle at the top of its hill. Though it was a favorite tourist spot, I'd never been inside. Fourth-generation vintner Dario Sattui had built the castle and had made sure that it was faithful to the architecture of the twelfth- and thirteenth-century time period. It even had a moat, a drawbridge, defense towers, and notably one of the best underground wine caves in Napa Valley. A banner welcoming Crush Week enthusiasts spanned the entrance. Streams of people were tramping up the steep driveway. Signs mentioned that the two-level parking lot was full.

Nash made a U-turn and parked on the main road like others were doing. He exited the vehicle, dashed to my side to open my door, and offered his hand.

"Why, thank you, kind sir."

"You are welcome, my lady.

"Are we going to mingle with all these people?" I stepped out of the car and brushed the seat belt wrinkles from my blouse.

"We have a private tour." With his hand resting on my lower back, he guided me up the hill. "By the way, I didn't have the heart to tell Camille, but we'll have plenty to eat."

I smiled. "The picnic will keep."

"Wait until you see the knight's chamber and the torture chamber inside the castle."

"There really is a torture chamber?"

"Yep."

"I'd heard about it but thought it was a rumor. Will I be freaked out? I've been known to jump into a date's lap at scary movies."

"You? Scared?" He wrapped an arm around my waist, guiding me over a few bumpy spots on the path. "I don't buy it."

"It happened once. The summer between my junior and senior year in high school. During a midnight showing of *The Shining* with Jack Nicholson. I was expecting a comedy. Wasn't he known for his comedies?"

Nash laughed and drew me closer. "This is going to be fun. Boo!"

I mock-scowled at him. "Is the wine any good?"

"We'll see."

Chapter 9

We roamed the exterior grounds for thirty minutes, drinking in the incredible blue sky and evergreen views of the valley and neighboring vineyards, like Sterling, Paoletti, and Frank Family, to name a few, before we headed toward the drawbridge entrance to start our tour.

For the next few hours, Nash and I tabled any discussion about Camille or the murder. The castle tour was intriguing. The details Sattui had included in the architecture were rich and authentic. The grand dining room with its tapestries was incredible. The torture chamber, complete with an Iron Maiden with spikes that would impale its victim when closed, was chilling to visit. As forewarned, Nash—the imp—poked me in the ribs numerous times to scare me. I jumped on cue.

At the end of our tour, we sat in the brick-lined tasting room, arms propped on the counter, elbows touching, and listened as our tour guide introduced us to five different wines. She paired cheese with each tasting. My favorite pairing was the Chianti with Mimolette, a nutty orange cheese originally made at the request of Louis XIV who had wanted a French cheese to replace the popular, non-French Edam. The high acidity of the Chianti made the flavors of the cheese pop.

When our tour guide excused herself for a moment, I said,

"Truth, Nash." I set my wine glass on the counter. "Why did you bring me here?"

"Besides spending time with the most beautiful woman I know?"

"I think you have an ulterior motive."

He ran a finger along my wrist. "Are you a mind reader?"

"I wish." *If only I could read the mind of Renee's killer,* I thought, and pushed the notion aside. I was with Nash. On a date. *Focus on the present,* my mother would say. "The wine is good, the tour was fun, I'm enjoying the company, but this is not what I had in mind when I said we should go wine tasting. What is it about this area that interests you? It is the *area* and not the wine—as good as it was—right?"

"Nailed." He squeezed my hand. "Yes. I'm looking to purchase a patch of land nearby on behalf of Nouvelle Vie Vineyards so we can start growing Merlot grapes."

"Hasn't Merlot wine become persona non grata, especially after the character in that *Sideways* movie panned it?"

"It's making a comeback, and I love it. It's smooth and goes with everything, including fish. It's one of the primary grapes used in making Bordeaux wines." For the next few minutes, he outlined his plan. He intended to make the Merlot using the "international style," utilizing late harvesting to get the ripest grapes, which produced inky-colored wines with velvety tannins, rich with intense fruit flavors.

I listened, enthralled, loving how he talked about wine. His eyes lit up; his smile broadened. He clearly enjoyed what he did.

"Did my mother put you up to this?" I asked.

"She approved the plan."

"And where is this prime piece of property? Next door?"

"See? You are psychic."

"Aha. That's why we roamed the exterior of the castle for a half hour before entering. You wanted to take a peek at the property from above."

"No one can fool you." He pecked my cheek.

"Did you like what you saw?"

"Indeed I did."

We sipped for a wee bit longer. Afterward, we returned to his SUV and drove to the nearby winery with the land that was for sale.

For the next hour, we hobnobbed with a delightful elderly woman who had grown tired of running a vineyard. Her boys had married and moved away. They had no interest in making wine. They were interested in making money. Only money. Over the past three years, she had allowed her land to grow fallow. By the end of the hour, Nash and the woman had a handshake agreement. Nash's realtor, who happened to be Jorianne's father, would write up a contract.

We climbed into the Acadia as the sun was disappearing over the Mayacamas Mountain Range to the west.

"How about taking our picnic to my place for dinner?" I asked.

"What about that ham sandwich you promised me?"

"I'll make it for you on our next date."

Listening to one of his favorite artists, Bobby McFerrin, we battled traffic to Nouvelle Vie. "Don't Worry, Be Happy" continued to play in my mind as we entered my cottage.

"Camille!" I called in case she was in a state of undress.

She didn't answer. I caught sight of a note lying on the kitchen table. She had written it on a sheet of my cream-and-gold stationery.

Dear Mimi,

I consulted with Jorianne, and she found me a room at the inn. I think this is best for now. Thank you for your support. I hope you understand.

- Fondly, Camille

I displayed it to Nash. "What do you think I should do?"

He shrugged. "She's an adult."

"With a stubborn streak." I grabbed my cell phone, dialed the inn, and asked for Camille's room. The receptionist said Camille had put a Do Not Disturb request on all calls. I hung up and gawked at Nash. "She asked for privacy. I should go over there and—"

"Now who's being stubborn?" He removed the cell phone from my grip and kissed me. "Let's eat. You're hungry."

"Don't handle me."

"Don't mollycoddle *her*."

The water in the fish tank burbled. I spun around. Cagney and Lacey were watching us.

I laughed. "You're right. I need food and a gallon of water. I'm parched after all the wine."

Nash set my cell phone on the counter, fetched two crystal goblets from the cupboard, and filled them with ice water while I set out green paisley mats, matching napkins, and two white bone china plates.

"Simple for a simple meal," I said. "Okay with you?"

"Anything you do is okay with me."

Chef C had created an amazing sauce for the sandwiches. It tasted like a mixture of mustard, honey, and rosemary with a hint of something else. Nutmeg, I decided. The flavors made the sliced turkey shine. I opened the door to the patio, and we sat in companionable silence, the only sounds that disturbed the moment being the crunch of the savory sweet potato chips and the waning chirruping of critters that were heading to bed for the night.

After our meal, I made tea. I carried the mugs to the kitchen table and noticed Nash staring at something to his right. "What's caught your eye?"

He swiveled in his chair and hooked one arm over the back. "That dry-erase board looks pretty darned empty."

I kept a dry-erase board on an easel in my kitchen so I could work out menus for the bistro ahead of our Monday morning tastings. I'd wiped it clean the night before, after Camille had drifted off. "What are you suggesting?"

"In June, you used it to compile a list of suspects when Bryan died. Why not do so now?"

"I told you on our drive, I don't know anything, and Tyson—"

"Will appreciate your input."

"In your dreams!" I cried. Tyson hadn't responded to my earlier message. It was too late to call him.

Nash moved to the dry-erase board and picked up the marker. "C'mon. Granted, the sheriff's department is a large, capable organization, but it's stretched thin because of Crush Week. You saw how many black-and-whites were on the road today. Drunk drivers and fender benders are keeping the authorities plenty busy." He offered the marker to me. "Go on. Jot down your thoughts and talk me through them. Start with Rusty Wells."

Goaded into action, I joined him at the board and wrote Rusty's name. Beside it I added possible motives: *angry about divorce*, *jealous about Donovan*, and *money*.

"Why would money be his motive?" Nash asked. "Did Renee have a life insurance policy?"

I reiterated the theory I'd shared on the drive to the winery—that Rusty might have wanted to get out of the egg-farming business as much as Renee had.

"Does he have an alibi?" Nash asked.

"It's bogus." I tapped the marker on the board. "But if he can't corroborate his own, then he can't confirm the one he provided for Camille, either."

"That's not good." Nash rose and slipped behind me. He lifted my hair and kissed the nape of my neck.

I shivered in a good way and said, "Don't distract me."

"You love it."

I murmured that I did and redirected my gaze to the board.

"Who else?" he asked. "Maybe someone on the festival staff was angry with her."

"You'd know better than I would on that point. You were a volunteer."

"I can't think of a soul who didn't like Renee. She was on top of things. She made sure people stayed hydrated and fed. And she was witty and funny."

"She wasn't always good-humored," I countered. "In fact, she was quite condescending to Allie O'Malley."

"You're right. I remember the two of them going at it. Write down Allie's name."

I hesitated. "I'm not sure I should."

"Why not?"

"Because the more I see her, the less I think she's capable of murder. She seems too fragile. No, that's not the word. She seems"—I wiggled the marker until I landed on—"demoralized. Beaten down."

"Sometimes the downtrodden are the first to fight."

"But even she's smart enough to know that she couldn't regain her business if Renee were dead. Not without a court battle." I paused. "Except that's not exactly true."

"It's not?"

"When she argued with Rusty, she told him Renee's word was her bond, and that made the contract invalid."

"She argued with Rusty?"

"Yes."

"Does she have an alibi?"

"I don't know." Reluctantly I wrote Allie's name on the board with her motive: *festival control*; *money*. "She's on Tyson's radar."

"Good. Who else?" He started to rub my shoulders. "Donovan Coleman is innocent. He has a solid alibi."

"Right."

I wrote Parker Price's name on the board.

"Why him?" Nash asked.

"I got a weird vibe from him yesterday. He and Rusty were exchanging barbs. Something he said made me wonder whether he'd had an affair with Renee. He said they hadn't known each other well, but that could have been a lie."

"Why would he kill her if he was having an affair with her?"

"Maybe she threatened to tell Felicity."

Nash nodded. "Go on."

"Right after that, Rusty, in true one-upmanship style, insinuated there might have been something between himself and Felicity."

"Men are pigs."

"Not you."

"Not me." He massaged my neck, working his deliciously strong thumbs along my spine.

"Come to think of it, Renee and Felicity had a tense chat the day you were volunteering. There was an undercurrent I couldn't quite put my finger on. Maybe Felicity thought Parker was cheating with Renee."

"Better write her name on the board. A woman might want to kill her competition."

I obeyed and added the possible motives. For Parker: *to end an affair or protect the secret*. For Felicity: *jealousy*.

Hookups. Affairs. Rumors. What was the truth? After I set down the marker, I spun around. "Thanks for the massage. It—"

A flurry of feelings welled up inside me as I drank in his face. Unable to help myself, I threw my arms around his neck and kissed him. He encircled me with his arms and drew me closer.

After a long time, he released me and retreated a step. "Whoa. Talk about out of the blue. Well, not entirely out of the blue. We'd talked about a kiss after the ham sandwich, but then we didn't have the ham sandwich, and I thought . . ." He scratched his head. "Maybe I should leave before we, *you know*." He waggled a finger between us. His mouth quirked up on one side. "Because I want to, but you . . ."

We hadn't *you know* yet because I wasn't ready. My husband had only been dead sixteen months. Nash had understood my struggle and was giving me space. Was I ready now? I was attracted to him, that was for sure, but, no, I wasn't ready yet. I couldn't give myself freely while worrying about Camille and her predicament.

"Soon," I said, my voice thick with unspoken emotions.

"Promise?"

"Yes, now go." I gave him a playful peck and pushed him toward the door. "Get out of here. No more thinking about murder and mayhem."

"Or kissing."

"Definitely no more thinking about kissing."

He swung open the door and stepped outside. He hesitated on the doorstep and turned back. His face grew serious. "I had a great time today, Mimi."

"Me, too."

"I love sharing Napa with you."

My cheeks warmed. Oh, man, I was toast.

"One more thing . . ." He clasped my hand and drew me out to the landing. He cupped my chin and gazed at me for a long, intense moment. "At some point, we should discuss *us*." Before I could respond, he kissed me gently and said, "G'night," and then trotted along the path toward the parking lot, waving until he was out of sight.

Dreamily I pivoted to reenter my place but froze when I heard something rustle around the side. "Raymond?" I called. Our dedicated gardener often went hunting at night for creepy-crawly things that might damage the garden plants. When he didn't answer, I said, "Nash?" thinking maybe he had skirted around the cottage to surprise me. He'd had so much fun scaring me in the torture chamber.

Silence.

My heart snagged in my chest. Dang, I hated feeling edgy. I'd been fearless when I lived in San Francisco. After the few run-ins I'd experienced in Nouvelle Vie in June, however, I wasn't as confident.

I hurried inside and started to swing the door shut. A split second before it closed, Scoundrel bounded inside.

"Girl, was it you I heard out there?" I slammed and locked the door. "No?"

She looked as frightened as I did. I raced for my cell phone and dialed Nash. He didn't answer. I called Raymond next. Nada.

Scoundrel nuzzled my ankle. Her tail, which often curled into a question mark, whisked my bare leg and sent a shiver through me. Like an alert bodyguard, she made the rounds of the cottage. She peered out the windows and the sliding glass door leading to the patio.

"Is somebody out there?" I asked her, as if expecting an answer. "What spooked you?"

She meowed.

"Not a great help, cat," I groused. Following her lead, I double-checked all the locks. I even peeked out the windows looking for a telltale sign of a prowler. Everything seemed normal.

Until something went *snap!*

Chapter 10

"What was that?" I rasped.

Scoundrel stared at me, her eyes wide.

"It was nothing," I assured her. "A critter. That's all. A rodent or a raccoon frolicking in the vineyard or the orchard."

Frolicking? Yeah, right. More like snap-crackle-popping.

I peeked out the glass door leading to the patio again and stifled a gasp. A person with a flashlight was standing in the adjacent vineyard. Who was it? Someone I knew? I swallowed hard as another thought occurred to me. Maybe Renee hadn't been the killer's intended target. Maybe Camille was. Maybe whoever was lurking outside my cottage believed Camille was still staying with me and had come to hurt her. When whoever it was realized I was home and knowing two would be harder to knock off than one, he . . . or she . . . had decided to flee through the vineyard. Except the person wasn't fleeing.

He . . . or she . . . started moving away from the cottage. Slowly. Not in a hurry. I urged myself to relax. Maybe it was a late-night workman or gardener, like Raymond, picking bugs off the vines. Or maybe it was a Crush Week fan that had gotten separated from their group. Midnight vineyard walks during Crush Week were common. People loved to drink in the aroma.

When the stranger disappeared from sight, I said to Scoundrel, "We're safe, girl."

Over the course of the next hour, I continued to repeat those words: *We're safe*. No bogeyman or ax-wielding slasher or murderer was loitering outside. No thief was trying to break in. *Safe*.

Even so, for the first time ever, I allowed Scoundrel to sleep inside. Acting like she had always been my cat, she nestled on top of my comforter and curled into a ball. Around two AM, her rhythmic breathing lulled me to sleep.

* * *

Thanks to the calming force of the cat's presence, I awoke Wednesday morning feeling rested and ready for the day . . .

Until I entered the bistro and Heather informed me that we were two waitstaff and one cook short. Red, our redheaded bartender—a woman I adored for her wine knowledge, her mixology talent, and sassy wit—was grumbling because she had to not only stock the bar but also set the rear patio tables. Oakley, who was typically effervescent, was carping that she had been assigned floor-mopping duty last week and didn't deserve it this week. Even so, she plowed ahead, her ponytail swishing right and left along with the mop. Oh, how she wanted the opportunity to do something more substantial, she told me confidentially. She even offered to serve as the concierge at the inn on her days off. We didn't have a concierge yet. I assured her I would consider the possibility, but floor mopping was the task for now.

To make matters worse, when I entered the kitchen, I met Victor Richard and realized in an instant that I'd underestimated the pomposity I'd sensed during our telephone conversation.

"*Bonjour*, Mimi." He pumped my hand. "I am Victor Richard. You may call me Chef." In a way, he reminded me of Peter Sellers in the zany, bumbling role of Inspector Clouseau, complete with the thick mustache and thicker French accent. "I look forward to commanding the kitchen."

"Um, Victor—Chef—I'll be in command. You're here to assist."

"No, no. That is not my way. I command."

"You don't know the kitchen."

"What is to know? It is tiny. Small. Less than small." He swept an arm to indicate the area. "In fact, it is cramped, but have no fear, I will manage."

I gawped at him. Was he for real? Dismissing me in front of my staff? Stefan and the others were staring at him, mouths agape.

"Let's begin," Victor said. Like a health inspector, he orbited the kitchen, checking out the countertops with his fingertip. His nose wrinkled and nostrils flared, depending on what he detected. He scrutinized the foods set on the sous-chef counter. Without donning sanitary gloves, he dipped his fingers into a plate of sesame seeds and muttered, "Chicken feed. What a mess."

When he passed by, I signaled to Stefan to toss the seeds.

I tolerated Victor Richard through lunch. Afterward, I paid him a full day's salary and asked him to leave. He blustered and protested, but in the end, he exited.

A minute later, I nestled on my stool by the farmhouse table and dug into a bowl of onion soup. The cheesy bread topping was crisp and the onions cooked al dente. In a word, it was divine.

"Thank heaven he's gone." Stefan perched on the neighboring stool. "How could Camille have recommended him?"

"She's off her game," I said. "Besides, she knew him a long time ago. Perhaps all his successes have changed him."

Stefan clucked his tongue. "Uh-uh. Wrong-o." He wiggled his cell phone. "I checked out his bio online while you were giving him the boot. He hasn't had any successes. In fact, he hasn't worked at any of the places he cited to Camille. He lied through his teeth."

"You're kidding."

"He's a fraud. A phony. He hoodwinked her. Everyone, listen up." Stefan grabbed a wooden spoon and leaped onto an upside-down milk crate. Flailing the wooden spoon like a conductor and using a snooty French accent, he regaled the staff. "This salad is pedantic." He pointed to an imaginary dish on the counter. "This is mundane." He bounded off the milk crate and toured the kitchen, his chin high, his nostrils flared. "Tedious," he shouted. "Tiresome. Monotonous. Boring."

At one point, I had wondered whether Victor had consulted a thesaurus before arriving. The fish entrée and all of the appetizers were *common*. The soufflés were *ordinary*. The crème brûlée merely *tolerable*.

"And you are all lazy!" Stefan remounted the milk crate. "We need the food served *tout de suite*. Do you hear me?"

In chorus they yelled: "We hear you!"

Stefan chortled. "As if Victor had ever used a soft voice in his life!"

Perhaps Victor thought a chef needed to bellow. He had repeatedly reminded me and everyone else that he and he alone was in command.

"Repeat after me," Stefan said. "You are lazy."

"We are lazy."

"You are ruthless swine."

"We are ruthless swine," the staff said in unison, and then, to a person, doubled over laughing.

At that moment, Heather breezed through the kitchen door, the skirt of her honey-colored chiffon dress ruffling from her brisk pace. "What the heck is going on?"

"Stefan is entertaining the troops. Okay"—I rose to my feet and clapped twice—"that's enough, you guys. I'm going to see if Jo can find us another replacement. You take a break, too." I bussed my bowl of onion soup to the sink. "See you here in one hour to prep for dinner."

Stefan bounded off the milk crate, hung his spoon *baton* on its hook, and offered Yukiko his arm. "Grab a sunhat, Twinkletoes. Let's catch some rays."

My stomach did a flip-flop. *Twinkletoes?* Was a relationship budding between the two of them? Hadn't they been at each other's throats just the other day?

Heather walked with me to the front entrance and said, "Mimi, if you see Camille while you're at the inn, please tell her we miss her."

* * *

Jo wasn't in her office. Her assistant advised me to look in the Renoir Retreat, adding that Jo had needed a breath of fresh air after speaking with her father on the telephone.

Minutes later I crossed through an archway trimmed with chili-red bougainvillea and searched for Jo among the crowd. The line at SWEETIE PIES was lengthy. I didn't see a frowning face in the bunch. The line at DONOVAN'S DELIGHTS was longer. Donovan, who looked energized, was handing out free samples. Had Rusty met him yet? I could only imagine how that encounter might have gone.

I found Jo near COLORFUL COOKIES. In her scarlet wrap dress, she blended in with the red tents, the vast array of red balloons, and the various red-themed plantings. As I drew near, I noticed her face was tear-stained. I hurried to her and slipped my arm through hers.

"Walk with me," I ordered. She didn't resist. "Is everything okay?" I asked as we meandered through the boisterous throng.

"It's Dad."

"Is he sick?"

"No. He's healthier than an ox and"—her voice snagged—"he's *dating*."

During the summer, I'd heard a rumor that her father was seeing someone. I didn't believe the buzz because, after Jo's mother had walked out, he had sworn off women. "Who?"

"The same woman."

"Same?"

Jo broke free of me and jammed a fist against her hip. "As in they're going steady."

"How long have they been dating?"

"Two months."

"Wow, that's quick."

"I know."

I knuckled her arm. "Don't you want him to be happy?"

"Yes, but . . ." She nibbled her lip.

"Look, I'll admit I was concerned when my mother started seeing Stefan's father."

"You were?"

"Don't get me wrong. I like Anthony." Anthony Alton was a former financier for the government. He had stepped down because he didn't agree with the current political climate and decided to run for Congress, where he thought he might do more good. "However, knowing my mom was seeing him on a regular basis felt like a betrayal, like she was going to forget my dad. I confronted her. She assured me she would never forget my father. He was and would always be the love of her life, but she was lonely. She didn't want to sit home all the time or simply hang out with girlfriends. I think she was starved for affection and yearned for an occasional kiss, you know?"

Jo bobbed her head.

"Meet the woman," I said. "Get to know her. Your dad deserves the best. Does your sister know?"

"What do you think? Of course she does! She knows everything before I do."

I smirked.

Jo pouted on purpose. "I sound like I'm five years old."

"Maybe six," I teased.

She shimmied her shoulders and fluffed her hair with her fingertips. "Did you need to see me about something?"

"Yes." I told her about the fiasco known as Victor Richard. I begged her to find me another temporary chef, pronto.

"On it."

"Before you go, have you seen Camille since she secured a room at the inn?"

"No. She's a hermit, but I hear she's eating. She ordered room service."

"Which room?"

Jo lifted her chin and looked disdainfully down her nose. "We at Maison Rousseau ensure that each guest's privacy is sacred."

"Give me a break."

She giggled. "Fine. West Wing, room 104. It was the only room available. We are fully booked."

"Mimi," a woman called.

Jo gave me a quick hug and hurried off as Felicity Price approached in a revealing getup, this one an emerald green cocktail dress that didn't quite fit the casual vibe of the festival.

"What a surprise to see you," I said. "Why are you attending today?"

"How could I stay away? This party is the talk of the town." She air-kissed me on both cheeks. "Parker is using the opportunity to get to know folks. He's been moving from garden to garden. A politician's glad-handing is never done. Now, where is he? I lost him a bit ago." She scanned the crowd. "There he is. See him? He's so handsome. So engaging." She wiggled a polished finger.

Parker was standing with a group of women between the tents for SUGAR BLISS CAKE BOUTIQUE and PURELY FROSTING. He was twirling a jaunty fedora on a finger and telling a story. Two of the women were nibbling oversized iced cookies. Two others were peeling the wrappers off cupcakes. All were paying rapt attention to Parker. A forty-something woman in orange joined the group. She was licking an overly long spoon that I assumed she'd purchased at the frosting booth.

A glint of concern crossed Felicity's face, but she quickly slapped on a smile and refocused on me. "It's such a shame about Renee. She would have loved to see how successful her little venture was, don't you think?"

"Yes, she would have." I cocked my head. "May I ask how well you knew her? You seemed pretty chummy."

"Chummy? Heavens, no."

"You invited her to tea."

"Darling"—Felicity peeled a loose strand of hair off her face and tucked it behind her ear—"I invite everyone with whom we do a fundraising drive to tea. Between us girls, I think Renee wanted to hobnob with me so she could brag about it in her pitches for future festivals, and who was I to call foul because"—she leaned in—"I'll admit I had an ulterior motive, too. I thought she would hold sway with the competition judges." She straightened. "It turns out she didn't."

Whoa! If it weren't so warm out, Felicity's last statement might have given me frostbite. I pictured the list of possible hookups that I'd written on the dry-erase board and wondered whether I had guessed right. What if Felicity had sensed there was something going on between her husband and Renee, despite Parker's claim that they'd barely known one another? I recalled my chat with Felicity's daughter, Philomena, who had overheard her parents arguing about love. Maybe Felicity had been accusing her husband of falling in love with Renee.

Wanting to know more—I didn't think I was imagining the hint of animosity—I said, "Come to think of it, when I saw the two of you together, you weren't all that chummy with each other. You were rather cool."

Felicity smiled, but the sparkle didn't reach her eyes. "Darling, we weren't enemies, if that's what you're insinuating. You need to know someone well to be an enemy, or you need to be vying for the same prize. As manager of the festival, she couldn't compete in the muffin competition."

Nice deflection, I mused and wondered about the tactic. I revisited the notion that Rusty and Felicity had hooked up. Had she cozied up to him to win the competition?

"How well do you know Renee's husband?" I asked.

"Scarcely at all. Why do you ask?"

"If your husband wants to win over constituents, he needs to work harder with Rusty."

"Why is that?"

"I don't think he likes him."

"Men." Felicity flicked a hand. "You can never tell which way the wind blows with them."

"Is it possible Parker thinks Rusty likes you more than he should?"

Felicity barked out a laugh. "Don't be ridiculous, darling. Rusty's a farmer. He wouldn't dream of lusting after me." She scanned the crowd, and her mouth turned downward again. The woman in orange was wiping something off Parker's cheek. The others in the group had departed.

"Who's that with Parker?" I asked.

"Whomever do you mean?" Felicity's voice glided upward in a fake way.

"The woman in orange."

"That's Louvain Cook. Haven't you met her? I could've sworn she's eaten lunch at your bistro."

I had become familiar with each of our regular customers, but we had a lot of one-time diners. It was impossible to memorize every face or name, though I was determined to try.

"Louvain and I grew up together," Felicity went on. "She relocated from Atlanta when she was a slip of a girl. We're like sisters. She's one of the finalists in the pie-baking competition. It turns out that she's quite good with pie dough." She placed a hand on her chest. "Did I know she could bake a pie, let alone crimp a perfect crust? No, I did not. Though she does have quite a gift for crimping a person's style."

"Ouch."

Felicity snorted. "It was a joke. She and I are like this." She crossed her fingers. "Tight."

I glanced at Parker and Louvain. They were still in conversation, but Louvain had stepped a respectable distance away from him.

"Louvain's never had much fashion sense," Felicity went on. "Orange is not her color. It's not mine, either, but I have the intelligence not to wear it. She should dress in jewel tones, like I do."

"Isn't orange a jewel tone?" I asked. "There are orange garnets and opals." I wasn't the most educated person when it came to gems, but Jo had taken a geology class in college and had asked me to drive from San Francisco to Berkeley to quiz her when she was preparing for the final.

"Well, yes, but they aren't truly . . ." She trailed off and wiggled her fingers. "Parker, darling. Over here."

Parker made his way toward us. Louvain had disappeared. "Hey, Mimi, it's nice to see you out and about." His grin was infectious. "People are sure enjoying themselves at the festival. Sugar and spice and everything nice. Makes for happy hearts."

"And for deep pockets, I hope," Felicity said.

"Yes, hon, I've received a lot of promises for contributions, don't worry." He gazed at me. "One can never have too much money in the coffers. Politics is a pricey business." He chortled. "*Pricey*. Ha! My last name's Price. I didn't mean to make the pun."

I would have bet he had. "Puns are the lowest form of humor," I teased.

Parker chuckled. " 'Unless you think of it first,' Oscar Wilde said."

Felicity batted his arm. "Parker, darling, I wasn't talking about political contributions. I was talking about the fundraising that the festival is achieving." She addressed me. "Education needs so much additional cash to operate nowadays."

Parker said, "By the way, Mimi, we have a reservation at your place tomorrow. I hope you have the *duck à l'orange* on the menu. It's my favorite."

Orange? I winced. *Talk about bad timing.*

Felicity seemed to agree with me. With a frosty tone, she said, "Darling, Mimi doesn't have time to talk menus. Let's go. You need to drop me by the theater." She addressed me. "Philomena's in the school play."

"So I heard. She's starring in *Cats.* She must have a voice like a nightingale."

"Aw." Felicity smiled. "You remembered what I told you about her name. How sweet of you. Do you know there are two other girls in her school with the same name? I kid you not. And not one of them has shortened her name to a nickname. Isn't it amazing when classical names become the in thing?"

"Tell her to break a leg," I said.

"Not quite yet. The musical is still in rehearsals. It'll open next week."

Parker said, "You should come see it, Mimi."

"I'll try."

"Enjoy the day," Felicity said in singsong fashion and steered her husband out of the garden.

"I will. You, too," I called after her, but I feared she wouldn't if she noticed the telltale orange lipstick on Parker's collar.

Chapter 11

I headed toward the arch leading into the inn, bent on checking on my chef, but I stopped when I spied Allie sitting on a stone bench by a grouping of red roses. She was dressed in somber black and reviewing a sheet of paper. A wad of tissue poked from her fist. She looked up as I approached. Her face was as tear-stained as Jo's had been.

"Hey, Allie." I settled beside her on the bench. "Why the tears?"

"My attorney . . . He couldn't . . ." She flailed the paper. "He couldn't do anything with this lousy contract. Oh, sugar!" She cursed genteelly. "I was stupid to believe Renee. And as deaf as a doorpost. I *heard* we would be partners. Wrong! I should get my hearing checked." She crushed the tissue into a tiny ball. "She was so nice when we first met."

I recalled how *not nice* Renee had been when Allie had confronted her with the contract. Instead of rehashing why she'd lied to Allie, I said, "How did you get into the festival business in the first place?"

"I've worked in the food industry for many years, and I've attended tons of festivals. I loved every one of them. They delight people."

"Yes, they do."

"When I'm not working, I make cookies. That's how I came up with the sweet treats theme. I understood how hotels and other sites might need extra income. It was a win-win." She unfolded her crumpled tissue and continued. "When I realized I wasn't raising enough money to get started, the *win-win* was how I pitched it to Renee."

"How did you two meet?"

"She came into the restaurant where I worked pretty often. We became friends." She rolled her eyes. "*Friends*. As if. Ooh, I wish I was the one who'd wrung her neck." She slapped a hand over her mouth, tissue and all. After a moment, she lowered her hand, her face ashen. "That was horrible of me. I shouldn't have said that. One shouldn't speak ill of the dead."

"She wasn't strangled, Allie."

"She wasn't?"

"She was clobbered with a countertop mixer."

Allie winced.

If she thought Renee had been strangled, maybe that was enough to prove she was innocent. Or maybe she had practiced that answer to cover her tracks. I groaned inwardly. Was I the most jaded person in the world?

"You probably know this," she said, "since you and Sergeant Daly are friends, but he asked me for my alibi. Guess I have a good motive." She flailed the contract.

"He's asked a number of people for their alibis, including Renee's sister."

"I suppose they have to look at everyone." She sighed.

"Um, what were you doing that night, if you don't mind my asking?"

Her eyelids fluttered. "I was home baking. That always clears my head." She snuffled and dabbed her nose with the tissue. "No witnesses, though. Not cool, right?" She sucked back a sob. "How

I wish I'd never given up on the festivals. If I'd stuck it out and tried harder to get sponsors, then maybe . . ." She sank into the bench. "I'm a quitter. I always have been."

"Don't beat yourself up."

"Who would do a better job of it?" She attempted a smile but failed.

"What restaurant did you work at?"

"You wouldn't have heard of it. The Burger Garden. I was a short-order cook."

"I remember Renee mentioning that." She had intended it as a dig.

"I was known as the burger queen," Allie said. "I was an expert at whipping out fast, tasty burgers. Renee teased me for trying to put on a festival featuring sweets when what I did best was savory. She said it was all about branding."

A lightbulb went off in my mind. "Hey, do you think you could help at the bistro for a day or two, until Camille returns?" Despite Allie being a murder suspect, I liked her. Plus, Tyson hadn't arrested her, which meant he believed her alibi, right? Was I the most naïve person in the world?

"Help how?"

"I need an assistant."

"I've never cooked French food."

"We'll keep it simple. You'll do the heavy lifting like boiling water or fetching supplies."

She splayed her hands. "I'll get in the way."

"We'll make it work."

I told her where and when to report. She brightened at the prospect, thanked me, and hurried off to freshen up. Watching her disappear, I decided not to second-guess myself. I would do what Bryan Baker would have advised and trust my gut instinct.

In the meantime, I needed to touch base with Camille. On my way to her room, someone glommed onto me.

"Hey, gorgeous." The man, who reeked of alcohol, was wearing a T-shirt with a wine-stained barefoot imprint. "Which way to the loo?"

"Sweetheart, let her go." His brunette companion was wearing a similar T-shirt. "I told you it's to the left." She said to me, "Sorry. We were at Grgich doing the *I Love Lucy* experience."

That explained why her hair was tousled and grape-splattered. During Crush Week, if someone wanted to roll up his or her pants and stomp grapes with bare feet like Lucille Ball had in that iconic television episode, they could do so at Grgich Hills Winery for a fee. When they were done, they could imprint a T-shirt, like these two had, with their grape-stained feet. No, the winery didn't make the grapes into wine later; those grapes got the old heave-ho.

The man continued to hold onto me.

"Mimi, are you okay?" another man asked.

I glanced over my shoulder and was surprised but relieved to see Elijah George, clad in a tight-fitting golf shirt, shorts, and sandals. He stared daggers at my inebriated accoster. Being a tad sunburned made Eli look that much more threatening.

The guy removed his hand. He was sober enough to realize he did not want to fight a guy who was much taller and stronger than he was.

His brunette companion ushered him away saying, "Beddy-bye for you, hotshot."

"Thank you, Eli," I said. "You're a welcome sight."

"So are you." His gaze held mine for a bit, but then he scanned the crowd.

"You look a little, um, red." I twirled a finger in the direction of his face.

"Yeah, I forgot to apply sunblock."

"Why are you here? Yesterday was your day off."

"I actually get two days off a week. Yesterday was all about helping Willow. So today . . ." He jammed a hand into the pocket of his shorts. "There's a lot of sugary goodness at this event."

"There sure is." I winked. "I'll bet you've never eaten sugar in your life."

"How quickly you've forgotten that Halloween is my favorite holiday of the year."

"That's right." I snapped my fingers. "I remember one time a group of us went trick-or-treating. You were a ghoul."

"You were Princess Leia with that funky doughnut hairdo."

"Not my best look."

"I like your hair the way you're wearing it now—up. It shows off your face."

I felt my cheeks warm.

"It sure is a hectic time in Napa," Eli continued, changing the subject. "The traffic is almost as bad as it is in New York."

"Crush Week is the culprit."

"So is the weeklong Sweet Treats Festival. What a draw."

"Eli, I can't talk right now. I have to—" I stopped myself. I didn't want to reveal where Camille was. Though Eli might not care, I couldn't help thinking about the stranger in the vineyard last night, and as the saying goes, *loose lips sink ships.* "I've got a quick errand to run before returning to the bistro to prepare dinner."

"Can I call you? Willow gave me your number. We should catch up."

"Um, that would be—"

"Do you ever go out after you close for the night?"

"That's sort of late for me."

"Late? Are you kidding me? You were a night owl when we

were little. Remember all the times we slept outdoors and counted stars? Both of our mothers were worried we'd get eaten—"

"By raccoons."

"You do remember." He let out a full belly laugh.

I joined in. "You were addicted to Cheetos."

"And you liked potato chips."

"Raccoon bait," we said in unison and clawed the air with our fingertips. I couldn't recall who had coined that phrase—him or me. Silly times. Ages old.

Though I was enjoying the walk down Memory Lane, I tapped my watch. "Eli, I really have to go. The kitchen beckons."

He kissed me on the cheek. "Speak to you soon."

The tenderness of his kiss threw my insides into confusion. What the heck? He was an old friend, nothing more. I was *not* interested in him. Had Willow given him the idea I was? I pushed the maddening notion aside and scooted out the front entrance. When I felt Eli couldn't see me, I rounded the corner and raced toward the rear of the building.

A minute later, I arrived at Camille's door. I knocked once then twice. "Camille, it's me. Open up."

I saw her eyeball appear in the peephole and heard her unlocking the chain guard. She swung the door open, but her frown told me I wasn't welcome.

"May I come in?" I asked.

"I'm fine, *Mom*." She was lying. Her hair was raggedy and her skin slack.

"I know you are, but I need a hug."

Reluctantly she allowed me to enter. She closed the door, tightened the sash on her robe, and trudged to the center of the room.

So much for that hug.

The bed, with its Provençal-style coverlet, was unmade. The door to the bathroom was open. Towels lay in a lump on the floor. The remnants of a room service meal sat on the white cedar café table. At least the drapes were partially open and sunlight was entering the room.

I said, "You had an omelet, I see."

"Made with Irish cheddar cheese and herbs. My mother always believed eating protein, not sweets, helped when one was depressed. She lavished us with eggs and meats."

"She was a wise woman." I perched on the end of the unmade bed.

"I called my daughter," Camille said. "She wants to come to California and take care of me. I told her no."

"But—"

"No." Camille held up her hand. "I am fine. I do not need her. And, Mimi, I do not want you to think I am unappreciative of what you have done for me—you were so kind to open your home to me—but all I need is time to mourn without watchful eyes upon me. Do you understand?"

"Of course, but I'm a little nervous about you staying by yourself."

"I am a grown woman. I am not under attack."

"Yes, but . . ." I thought again about Camille being the murderer's target.

"What is wrong, Mimi? You look like you have seen a ghost."

"Here's the deal. Last night I sensed somebody was watching my cottage." I paced by the foot of the bed as I explained: the sounds, Scoundrel in a panic, seeing the person in the vineyard with the flashlight. "How do we know that you weren't the murderer's target? Maybe the killer came to your home looking for you and ran into Renee instead."

"No. You are mistaken." She slumped into the ladder-back chair by the café table. "Renee had enemies. I do not."

"Okay, even if you weren't the intended victim, the murderer might think you know something. Or saw something. Or figured out something. Who better than you, the person who knew your sister best, to come up with the motive for her murder?"

Camille shook her head. "I have been trying to solve this, but I cannot. I fear I did not know her at all."

"Did she fight with anyone? Who did she cross?" Other than Rusty or Allie O'Malley, whom I'd hired moments ago. Had I lost my mind?

"Renee was not like that. She had a good soul. She was off track. Her marriage—"

The doorknob jiggled.

Camille's panicked gaze swung from the door to me. "Housekeeping has been here. I sent them away."

It sounded like the intruder in the hall was slotting something into the lock. A key or a lock pick? Due to Bryan's insistence, the inn had an old-fashioned key system to complement the quaint atmosphere. Napa, he had assured me, was a safe community. Not true, I was learning.

"Who's there?" I called.

"Room service," someone replied in a low, guttural voice. Man or woman, I couldn't tell.

"I did not ring for anyone to pick up the dishes," Camille whispered.

"We didn't order room service," I said through the door.

Footsteps beat a quick retreat, which made my insides snag. Was my theory correct? Was the killer after Camille, or did he . . . she . . . think Camille had seen something that night and hoped to silence her?

I hurried to the door and peeked through the peephole. The hallway appeared empty. Even so, I grasped the umbrella we kept in the closet for guests to use if it rained and whisked open the door.

"Who's out there?" Camille asked.

I peered down the hall. "No one."

Whoever had attempted to get in was gone.

Chapter 12

"That does it!" I lifted the receiver for the room telephone and dialed the front desk. A perky receptionist answered. I didn't recognize her voice. Jo had said she'd hired a few extra people this week. "It's Mimi Rousseau."

"Yes, Miss Rousseau. What can I do for you?"

"Can you review the security camera footage quickly and describe who was recently outside room 104? Yes, I'll hold."

Camille said, "Maybe whoever tried to break in was a thief."

The receptionist came back on the line. She believed the perpetrator was a reporter attending the festival. She recognized him because earlier he had asked her directions to the competition tent.

"How would he have known which room Camille was in?" I asked.

The receptionist wasn't sure. She'd have a security guard check. We had two security guards on payroll—a night guard and a day guard—and two extras for the duration of the festival.

I ended the call and sat down opposite Camille at the dining table. "It turns out there's a reporter here covering the festival. He must have decided the better scoop was locating you."

"It wasn't the killer?"

"Let's be safe rather than sorry. If you won't stay with me, please go to my mother's house. She could use the company. We'll keep your whereabouts under wraps."

When Camille agreed, I rang my mother.

She picked up after the first jangle. "What's up? Need a recipe?"

I often called her for creative inspiration. She was a fabulous cook. I explained the situation.

"I'm on my way," Mom said. "And don't you worry. It'll be hush-hush. No reporters—or anybody else for that matter—will get past me."

"She's in room 104. Text me when you and she arrive at your place."

"Should I call Sergeant Daly and tell him about the encounter?" she asked.

"I have no proof that anyone is after Camille."

"Let him be the judge of that."

"Okay. If you do speak to him, please tell him I need to touch base with him, too."

"What about?"

"The case. He hasn't responded to any of my messages."

Under her breath she muttered, "Amateur detective." I ignored her.

After I ended the call, I dialed the receptionist again. I asked her to send a security guard to Camille's room. When he arrived and assured me he wouldn't leave until my mother appeared, I raced to the bistro.

* * *

An hour later, as I was measuring flour into a bowl at the centermost counter in the bistro kitchen, Allie pushed through the swinging doors.

"I'm here," she announced.

Heather flew in after her. "Is it true, Mimi? You've hired *her*?" She trained her gaze on Allie, who was dressed like me in tan trousers, white shirt, and clogs. A red bandana covered her hair and her skin was scrubbed free of makeup.

"Temporarily."

"But the other day, Jo said, and then you said—"

"I've got this, Heather."

"Don't you think you should reconsider?" Worry pinched her face.

I clasped her elbow and drew her toward the exit. "What's going on?" I whispered. "Are you mother-henning me because you're tending to the kittens?"

"I'm getting vibes." She wiggled her fingers by her temples.

I had learned over the past year to trust her vibes. At first I'd thought her alien pals were mystically sending them to her; now I realized they were her own gut instincts, which were usually right.

Heather continued. "I'm concerned that you might be letting your guard down and seeing good in someone where there is none."

I gazed at Allie. Had I been wrong to hire her? Should I trust Heather's gut instincts or my own? Allie sidled to the menu board and perused it. Her mouth moved but no words came out. Was she memorizing it?

"I'll keep my eye on her, okay?" I patted Heather's shoulder. "Relax. Go to the dining room and finish preparing the new menus for the evening."

At the same time Heather exited, my mother texted me: THE EAGLE HAS LANDED SAFELY. I smiled at the spy language.

Stefan joined me, a boning knife in his hand. "Um, boss, can we talk?" He jerked his head to the left, away from Allie.

I followed him to the corner. "Problem?"

"There's gossip about Miss O'Malley, like, you know, she

might've . . ." He mimed picking up a heavy object and swinging it in a downward motion.

"I don't think she did, and she has an alibi." I didn't reveal how tenuous it was. "I'm going with my intuition, okay? Like I did when I hired you and everyone else." Bryan had encouraged me to take risks. I had reminded him that taking a risk had made me marry my late husband, but he'd said that because I'd invited Derrick into my life and because of Derrick's duplicity, I had become stronger and sharper. "We're two staff short," I went on, "so I can't draw from your pool of talent. I need someone to assist me."

"Got it." Though, from the frown that linked his eyebrows, I could tell he didn't.

A shiver of angst skittered down my spine. First Heather was wary, now Stefan.

"She'll be right next to me at all times," I said.

Stefan started whistling "Another One Bites the Dust" by Queen.

I jabbed him in the ribs. "Not funny."

He chuckled and, twirling the boning knife, returned to his station, where he began to cut up whole chickens.

"Allie, grab a chef's coat from the locker"—I hitched a thumb toward the rear of the kitchen—"and hurry back to me."

When she saluted and scurried away, I gave Stefan a reassuring look. We were in sync. This would work out. He crossed his fingers and made a U-turn.

Allie proved to be even better than I'd hoped. She reacted quickly, which was a plus in a busy kitchen. Working as a short-order cook had honed that skill. And she was keen to detail. Rather than limit her to boiling water and fetching items, as planned, I gave her the chore of plating a specialty hamburger—I'd decided a simple choice on the menu would be a great addition. The task came naturally to her. Assembling the burger with Roquefort and crisp bacon was not an easy feat. She had to set the top of the brioche bun at a tilt and make the accompanying butter lettuce, beefsteak tomato, and house dill pickles look appetizing, all of which she did with flair.

For the first seating, we plated over two hundred items. As we were gearing up for the second seating, Heather poked her head into the kitchen.

"Chef Mimi?" she called. "Do you have a minute?" She beckoned me.

I hoped no one wanted to complain about the hamburgers or anything else. Allie would be crushed. She had worked her tail off. Even Stefan, after the last table had been served, had thrown her a supportive smile. I said, "Allie, I'll be right back. Take a breather."

"Sure," she said, but she didn't look like she needed a rest. She appeared energized and glowing, as if working for me had taken her mind off losing the festival and had given her the emotional boost she'd needed.

Heather guided me through the main dining room toward the office.

"What's up?" I asked.

"A diner has come forward."

"Come forward for what?"

"To tell you what she saw on the night of the murder."

"Why talk to me? Why not contact the sheriff?"

"Because she's here now, and she loves your food, and she adores Chef C, and, well, I overheard her confiding to her dinner companion that . . ." She prodded me into the office. "You'll see."

Standing beside the shabby chic chairs was a woman in a sleek aqua sheath. I'd seen her once or twice at the bistro but hadn't yet introduced myself. I made a mental note to pay more attention in the future. She had thin but muscular arms, prominent cheekbones, and long butterscotch-blonde hair. *Runner or tennis player?* I wondered. She was somewhere in her forties, but her sun-tanned skin made her look a tad older. A couple of weeks ago, I had seen her walking her French bulldogs on one of my midafternoon strolls; she hadn't worn a visor or hat.

"Mimi"—Heather stopped inside the doorway—"this is Ursula Drake."

I extended my arm. Ursula took my hand and squeezed hard. *Tennis player*, I determined.

"It's so good to meet you," she said. "I adore Bistro Rousseau. It is fast becoming my go-to place."

I liked hearing that.

"Ursula is a caterer," Heather offered.

Aha! Maybe her toned muscles came from lifting heavy trays of food.

"We call our business Feed Your Dreams," Ursula said. "Our office is down the street. Heard of us?"

I hadn't, but I didn't know every catering company in the area.

"We've been in business for two years. We specialize in fantasy events. No dark fantasies," she added. "More like princesses and fairy tales and such. My business partner is dining with me. He and I are taking a night off from the Crush Week crowds. Boy, have we been busy!" She widened her eyes to make her point. "We've been telling everyone we know about Bistro Rousseau. We love the menu, by the way. We've pored over it to get ideas."

"Are you planning to steal a recipe?" I asked.

"What? No. We . . ." She giggled when she realized I was joking. "I've been remiss by not introducing myself to you. I'm shy that way."

I doubted Ursula had ever been shy in her life. I pegged her as a mover and shaker. In a way she reminded me of a classier version of Felicity Price. I said, "I should've introduced myself."

She fanned a hand.

"Ursula, I don't mean to be rude," I said, "but I have to hurry to the kitchen. I have a cook in training."

"Of course. You want me to get to the point. Well, you see, my partner and I were discussing Camille. She's been an inspiration to me. That's what Heather heard us talking about."

Heather shifted feet, uncomfortable at having been caught eavesdropping.

"And?" I coaxed.

"Camille is a friend," Ursula said. "We live in the same neighborhood. She's given me lots of catering ideas. She's the one who told me about your restaurant. I haven't seen her since that dreadful night. Is she all right? Did the sheriff take her into custody?"

"No, he didn't," I said. "She's fine."

"I heard she might be guilty of—"

"She's not. The sheriff hasn't allowed her to return home because it's a crime scene."

"Where is she staying?"

I hesitated. Gee, Ursula was asking a lot of questions. "With a friend." I glanced at my watch. "I really must return to—"

"Ursula"—Heather twirled a hand—"tell Mimi what you saw."

Ursula inched toward me and lowered her voice. "On the night of the murder, I spied Camille's brother-in-law driving through the neighborhood."

"Rusty Wells?" I asked.

"That's right. I'd come home after catering a party. About ten PM. I was walking my dogs. The headlights were off on his truck. At the time I figured maybe the headlights being switched off was an oversight, but now, after learning of the murder, I've got to wonder whether he was tailing his wife. I heard a rumor that she was having an affair."

"She wasn't having an affair," I stated, although I couldn't be certain. Camille had been so vague when I'd questioned her about that.

"Really?" Ursula sounded skeptical.

"Not all rumors are true."

"No, of course not, but I overheard the sheriff talking about a love letter and assumed—"

"How did you know it was Rusty in the truck?" I pressed.

"Well, I can't be certain, but his green truck with that license plate is unmistakable. Who else would be driving it? I saw lights on in the house, but Camille wasn't home yet. At least I don't think so. I didn't see her car in the driveway. It's very distinctive. She drives an Italian import that's so teeny. Me? I wouldn't be caught . . ." She balked.

Heather gasped. I did, too, knowing Ursula was about to say *caught dead*.

Ursula pressed on. "That car of hers would get crushed in an accident, you know? Anyway, I saw movement inside. That must have been Renee, right?"

Or it was the killer cleaning up, I thought. Except nothing had been cleaned up. The floor was a mess and the fixings for soufflé were assembled on the counter.

I paused. No, that wasn't true. One thing had been cleaned up—the mixer. It had been wiped free of fingerprints. Had the killer left the other things in a mess to throw off the authorities?

"Why haven't you spoken with the sheriff?" I asked.

"I called. We've been playing phone tag. They must be overrun with activity, it being Crush Week."

Perhaps that was why Tyson hadn't responded to my text.

"Boy, Crush takes its toll on the locals' patience," Ursula added.

Nash had said the same thing as we'd driven home from our wine tasting.

Ursula continued. "When Heather said you'd want to hear what I had to say, I thought now was the perfect opportunity. I'd meet you and give my account to boot. I know you have Sergeant Daly's ear. You must have him on speed dial after . . ." She sputtered.

"After what happened in June," I finished.

"Yes. I'm so sorry. Your hand in solving Mr. Baker's murder was covered in all the newspapers."

And on TV and radio chat shows. For weeks after his murder, newshounds had wanted to interview me. I'd refused them all. That hadn't stopped others from talking.

"It's okay," I said, smiling to assure her that her blunder hadn't upset me. "What did Rusty do next?"

Ursula worked a kink out of her neck. "That's the thing. He didn't stop, and he didn't park or get out of his truck, as far as I know. I took my dogs inside to get them settled, so I might have missed that. However, I do think"—she paused for effect—"he might have shown up later. On foot."

Heather smirked and eyed me pointedly, as if to say now we were getting to the good stuff.

"As I was closing my drapes for the evening," Ursula said, "I noticed a man in an earflap hat and heavy wool coat walking along the street. He seemed cagey, you know? His head was moving right and left"—she mimed the action—"as if he was trying to spot a tail."

"Did you see his face?"

"No. There are no streetlamps in our neighborhood, but the moon was bright enough that I could tell he had a noticeable limp."

"Rusty Wells doesn't limp."

Ursula bobbed her head. "Maybe he was acting injured to, you know, throw a witness like me off the scent."

"That's what I think," Heather said.

I thanked Ursula for doing her citizenly duty, told her I'd contact Sergeant Daly on her behalf, and instructed Heather to bring Ursula and her partner a glass of Prosecco on the house. Ursula gushed her appreciation and hurried to her table. Her partner waved to me. I returned the greeting.

Before I could retreat to the kitchen, Heather gripped my elbow and tugged me into the office. "Mimi, I've been getting more vibes. This time about Rusty Wells. I saw him walking across the parking lot. He was strutting and looking smug. I feel like there's something evil in him. Right here." She thumped her chest, over her heart. "You need to tell Tyson."

"Tyson won't buy into your vibes, but I'll mention it." My dear friend Sergeant Daly, like his father and grandfather before him, liked black-and-white facts.

I started to leave, but she grabbed hold of my arm again. "Also, beware of a woman in white. She might cause you trouble."

"Which woman?"

"I don't know. I saw her in a dream."

"Hmm. Sounds like an angel."

"Don't make fun." She swatted the air.

"Maybe it was one of your Glonkirks making a visit."

She threw me an exasperated look.

I pointed to the door. "Get to work. I'll keep on the alert."

Before leaving the office, I called Tyson, but he wasn't in. Where was he? With Jo? Were they hashing out their future? Was she digging in her heels about children and freedom and whatnot? Or was Tyson doing his job and trying to find Renee's killer? I left a message, putting him on alert to contact me as well as Ursula Drake, and returned to work.

After dinner, exhausted from the number of meals we had prepared but thankful that Allie had been such a capable assistant, I headed home.

When I entered the cottage, I was revved up. I greeted Cagney and Lacey with a tap on their tank and fed them. They flipped their fins: *Human home; all is right with the world.*

As I kicked off my shoes and pulled the band from my hair, I caught a glimpse of the dry-erase board. I stared at the suspects' names I'd scrawled on it: *Rusty*, *Parker*, *Allie*, and *Felicity*. I wanted to erase Allie's name. Not once during the course of preparing the evening's meals had I felt that I'd made a bad decision to hire her temporarily. And she had an alibi. But I left her name there.

I studied the motives I had written down for Rusty and Parker. They made sense. Below Felicity's name, I added a blank line for a new suspect. On the line I scribbled a question mark to represent the man Ursula Drake had seen. Had it been Rusty or someone else?

My cell phone vibrated in my pocket. I scanned the screen. My mother had texted me that Camille was tucked into bed. She added that Riesling was acting like the nursemaid dog in *Peter Pan*. He was lying on the carpet beside Camille's slippers. If an intruder attempted to break in, the vigilant Goldendoodle would sound the alert. I wrote a THANK YOU text and then scrolled through my other texts, emails, and voicemails but didn't see any message from Tyson. Drat.

My stomach growled. Oftentimes, even after a hearty meal—I'd downed one of the specialty burgers before leaving the bistro—I craved dessert, but what could I fix? I didn't want cookies. I was out of chocolate. I found oranges and eggs in the refrigerator, and my creative juices kicked into gear. Give me an orange, an egg, and sugar, and I could make soufflé. Granted, I needed a few other items, like cornstarch and a small dash of orange-flavored liqueur, but within thirty minutes, I would have my treat.

I got to work, humming as I went.

After eating the soufflé, I regretted the decision—not because it wasn't great; it was scrumptious—but the sugar rush was shocking. What had I been thinking eating sweets so late? In desperate need of a walk to clear my head and settle my jangling insides, I threw on a pair of Uggs and strode to the front door. The aquarium tank burped as I reached for the doorknob. The fish were eyeing me with a look that could only mean *our human is nuts.*

"That was not an enemy last night," I said, believing I was right. It had been a worker or Crush Week fan. And a sneaky reporter had caused today's scare outside Camille's room at the inn. "It's safe."

The moment I stepped outside, a gentle breeze nipped my nose and tousled my hair. The full moon was high in the sky. Stars glistened across the cloudless expanse. I drank in a lungful of air and let it out. At moments like these, I often felt at one with the universe. If not for Renee's death, I might even have felt joyful. Instead my mind rehashed what Ursula had said. What if Rusty had been tailing Renee? What if—

A blur of black cut across the path in front of me. My heart snagged. I stamped my foot. "Scooter, stop it! You're going to be the death of me." The moment the words left my mouth, I winced. My mother would say, *Bite your tongue.*

The cat slinked from a bush, his tail dragging behind him. The moon reflected in his sorrowful eyes. Could cats cry?

"Hey, buddy, what's wrong?"

I scooped him up. His heart was chugging like he'd been running for miles. Had something frightened him? I heard a rustle and whipped around. A hulking person was lumbering up the walkway toward me. Lumbering and limping. My pulse zipped into high gear.

I pivoted, ready to race into the cottage, when the hulk said, "Evening, Mimi." It was Raymond.

Breathing easier, I spun around.

"Are you okay? You're pretty jumpy." As Raymond drew near, I realized why I hadn't recognized him. He was wearing a raincoat and a red-and-black-checked hat, and he was carrying a small ladder over his shoulder.

"Last night I saw someone in the vineyard. It put me on edge. And now, with you creeping up on me . . ."

"I wasn't creeping."

"Why the getup?" I asked. It wasn't raining; it wasn't even cold.

"I'm removing wasp nests."

I chuckled. "Do they come out at night like snails and slugs?"

"No, they sleep. They're much easier to catch when they're snoring."

"You're one funny guy. You should take your act on the road."

He guffawed. "Is the cat okay?" He removed a heavy leather glove from his hand and scratched Scooter under the chin.

"He's spooked. By you."

"I'm pretty scary." He cooed sweet nothings to Scooter and then said to me, "Get a good sleep." He tapped the brim of his hat and headed away.

"Hey, Raymond," I called after him. "Why are you limping?"

"Old soccer injury. It acts up around this time of year. Even more so when I do a lot of ladder climbing. G'night."

I reentered the cottage and bolted the door and deliberated about the man Ursula had spotted in Camille's neighborhood. It sure as heck hadn't been Raymond; he was one of the kindest people in the world and would have had no reason to be there.

Parker Price suffered from an old football injury. Could it have been him and not Rusty in the area? The other day, I'd seen him carrying an overcoat and earflap hat. Of course, there had to be tons of people in Napa Valley who owned similar clothing and were suffering from a leg injury, but Parker had known Renee, even if he denied the extent of their relationship. I wondered again about his cagey response to Rusty. Had he and Renee had an affair? Had she threatened to ruin his marriage by revealing their affair to his wife?

I set Scooter on the floor—yes, I was getting used to having a cat in the house—and thought again about the identity of the limping man. What if Rusty Wells had worn a disguise to make people think he was Parker? He could have parked his truck around the block and stolen back.

But Parker's name kept sticking in my craw. My theory that he and Renee had been involved could be wide of the mark, but what if he'd had a beef against her for some other reason? He was a councilman. What if she'd had some dirt on him? What if she had threatened his career? Would that have been enough to drive him to murder?

Chapter 13

Every Thursday my mother and I met for an early morning catch-up session at Chocolate. I arrived before she did and secured a table by the window. I caught her eye as she bustled past and waved. She breezed into the café, the tails of her pumpkin-toned poncho kicking up behind her. She slid into her chair and signaled Irene.

"Sorry I'm late," she said to me.

"It's okay. I caught up on a few things." The email from Nash asking how I was doing had sent a thrill through me because he'd ended it with an *XO*—a kiss and a hug. I'd replied with a quick update and an impulsive *XO* of my own. I had yet to respond to the voicemail message from Eli asking me for coffee on his next day off. I wasn't quite sure how to handle the invitation. "How's Camille?" I asked.

"She's doing fine. Eating. Listening to music. Reading Agatha Christie. Riesling is excited to have her around."

Irene arrived with two mugs of hot chocolate, heavy on the whipped cream.

I took a sip of my chocolate. Excellent, as always.

"Two warm croissants coming right up," Irene added. "But before I go, did I hear you mention Camille, Ginette? Do you know where she is? I've missed her." Camille often visited Chocolate during her afternoon break. She enjoyed the chatter and clatter.

"She's staying with me"—my mother put a finger to her lips—"but it's a secret."

"Why?" Irene asked.

"Because Mimi thinks Camille might be in danger."

"I never said that, Mom."

"You didn't want her staying alone."

"Because—" I huffed, unwilling to say more.

"Camille said you saw someone lurking outside your cottage."

"I overreacted."

"And a stranger tried to wrangle his way into her hotel room."

"A journalist."

"Gracious me." Irene placed a hand on the bib of her apron. "I've always said, 'Better to be cautious.' Mum's the word. Your secret is my secret. Please give her my love." She sauntered away and cozied up to two customers seated at a nearby table.

Mom took a sip of her chocolate, hummed her approval, and set the mug down. She ran a thumb along the rim to remove a tinge of her lipstick. "Camille wants to defy the therapist. She thinks work would be good for her. She wants to return."

"That would be great, but—"

"She doesn't believe the killer is after her."

"What if she's wrong?"

"She's mumbling to herself, sweetheart. She needs to be busy. She can continue to stay at my place as long as she wants to, of course, but I believe work will stimulate her and give her a reason to move forward. You know how bad dwelling on the negative can be."

A month after Derrick died, my mother had shown up on my doorstep. Within a minute, she'd found all the candy paper cups that had once held bonbons. Thirty minutes later, she had ushered me into a therapist's office. Three hours and fifteen minutes after that, I'd moved home. My mother hadn't manhandled me; she'd shown how much she cared.

"If you say so," I murmured.

Mom twirled a finger at my outfit. "You look nice."

"Thanks." Usually I wore my work clothes to our dates, but knowing how much she hated the neutral ensemble and seeing as I had a spare in the office, I'd decided to dress up for a change. I had thrown on a pretty peach-colored knit sweater and cigarette-style ecru pants. My hair hung loosely on my shoulders. I'd even donned single-pearl, French-wire earrings.

"Nash is a good influence on you," she said.

"He had nothing to do with my choice of clothing. He and I . . . We haven't . . . We aren't—"

"TMI. Too much information." My mother batted the air. "All I can say is, despite the crisis with Camille, there is something fresh about you. Your color is good and your eyes are bright. I believe that's Nash's doing." She sipped her hot chocolate and eyed me over the rim. "Yummy."

"What's yummy? Nash?" I joked.

"I happen to think so. Don't you?"

"Yes, I do." Our kiss the other night had floored me in a good way.

"Have you two talked about . . . your future?"

"Mother, it's way too soon for that," I said, reluctant to mention that he had actually broached the subject. *We should talk about us*, he'd said. When would we do that? Our next date? Sooner?

"Talking is important. Your father and I always made time to chat. It was one of the great blessings of our relationship. Remember that."

"Here you go." Irene returned with our croissants as well as a plate of Irish butter and sashayed away.

"By the way . . ." My mother tore her croissant into two pieces, swiped soft butter on one half, and downed it in two bites. "Nash is very good at his job. He has great business sense and a terrific work ethic. I've never seen the winery run so smoothly." She propped both elbows on the table and leaned forward. "Did he tell you about the new plot of land we're purchasing?"

"For Merlot grapes."

"I'm very excited."

I loved how she was bubbling over with good energy. "If I remember correctly, a few months ago, you were talking about getting rid of the winery and selling it. To *him*."

"Yes, but now I'm thinking of making him a partner. I never knew running the winery could be so much fun. Your father didn't want to be bothered. It all fell on my shoulders. Nash is a wonder."

I smiled to hide a twinge of regret. Her partnership with Nash might complicate our relationship. What if, one day, they had a falling out? "How does Anthony feel about your revived interest?" I asked.

"He thinks it's marvelous. Because of Nash, I can travel and do whatever I please. Even get married."

Luckily I hadn't been sipping my hot chocolate or I would have spit it across the table. "Married? You're not talking about marriage, are you?"

She gave me the evil eye, the one I'd hated since I was old enough to know it meant she was the parent and my opinion had no merit. "Why shouldn't we?"

"Why *should* you is the better question? You're not going to have children. You're travel companions."

"We are way more than *that*, sweetheart."

"TMI, Mom," I blathered, my cheeks heating like a pot of boiling water.

She chuckled and winked.

I leaned back in my chair and folded my arms. Why was I so

shaken? I recalled my conversation with Jo about her father. I'd advised her to get to know the woman he was falling for, but this was different, wasn't it? *Wasn't it?* I drew in a deep breath. "Do you love him?"

Before she could answer, my cell phone vibrated on the table. I read Tyson's name on the screen. I picked up my phone and answered. "Hello, Sergeant Daly."

My mother whispered, "I never got the chance to speak with him. If he needs to talk to me—"

I motioned for her to hold that thought.

"Miss Rousseau," Tyson said.

"Cut the attitude. Are you returning my call?"

"Yours and your mother's. How many others in your posse have contacted the department?"

I pictured him grinning like a goon while stroking that goatee of his. "You're a laugh riot," I said. *Not*, I thought.

He snorted. "What's up?"

"Did you talk with Ursula Drake?"

"We connected finally. Because she sought you out, which means you weren't snooping, I won't hold it against you."

I bit back a retort. I didn't snoop. I listened. I cared. I was loyal to my friends and family, all of which were qualities I admired in my heroes. Didn't he?

"Any more sightings?" he asked.

"Sightings."

"Of people outside your cottage."

"How did you know about that?"

"I ran into Raymond this morning." Tyson and Raymond had played soccer together in high school. Tyson had played forward; Raymond, center back. Both could run like sprinters. "He said you were pretty skittish last night. You aren't the kind to be on edge, Mimi, so what's going on?"

I filled him in about the person I'd glimpsed watching the cottage and added that a reporter had attempted to wrangle Camille at the inn. I added that when I'd seen Raymond hobbling, it had made me think of Ursula Drake's testimony about seeing a limping man in her neighborhood. "My two cents, Tyson? The limping man could have been Rusty Wells pretending to be Parker Price."

"Why would he pretend to be Parker?"

"Because he doesn't like him and wanted to implicate him. Of course, the limping man could have been Parker himself."

"Because?"

"He knew Renee, and he and she might have—"

"It wasn't Parker, Mimi. He and I have spoken."

"Why did you question him?"

"Don't think any more about it." He sounded terse. "I'm on it."

"Also—"

He ended the call.

I glared at my cell phone and growled. Tyson couldn't have sounded more patronizing than if he'd said, *Don't worry your pretty little head, sweet pea*. "Dang it." I set my cell phone facedown on the table. "What does Jo see in him?"

"What everyone else does," my mother said. "A capable, intuitive man."

"He hung up before I could tell him about the argument between Rusty and Parker or about Rusty lying—"

"Calm down." My mother laid her hand on mine. "Tyson will get to the bottom of this."

"But there might be angles he isn't considering."

"I don't mean to interrupt, ladies." Irene arrived at the table and topped off our hot chocolate. "I'm sorry if I have alert ears—it's a bad habit that I've picked up in this place—but did I hear you mention Ursula and Camille in the same sentence?"

My mother said, "You did. Mimi's investigating Renee's murder."

"I am *not* investigating, Mother. C'mon." Was she trying to tick me off? When I was in high school, she and I had had a few rows. We always made up, but my friends and I often pondered whether our mothers pushed our buttons on purpose, simply to get a reaction. Would I do the same when—*if*—I had kids?

"Tell Irene what you learned," my mother said. "She and Camille are neighbors."

"So I heard."

"Ursula is quite on top of neighborhood news," Irene said. "When she's not working, she's walking those bulldogs of hers or doing something to improve her house's curb appeal. She's very handy with a hammer, a skill acquired from years of helping Habitat for Humanity."

My mother nudged my arm. "Go on, Mimi, tell her."

I cupped my mug in my hands. "On the night of the murder, Ursula saw a man with a limp in the neighborhood. She thought it might have been Renee's husband, putting on an act, but I wondered whether Parker Price might have been the man she'd seen. Parker knew Renee. Ursula couldn't make out a face."

Irene *tsk*ed. "It might have been Parker. I've seen him in the area once or twice. Come to think of it, his visits started about the time Renee moved into Camille's house."

I gasped. "If Felicity found out—"

"That would give her motive," my mother and Irene said in unison.

Irene knuckled my mother's shoulder. "Jinx."

"What's *jinx*, Irene?" Willow appeared out of nowhere—I hadn't seen her enter the café—and sidled up to Irene, a to-go cup of coffee in hand. She coiled a bare arm over Irene's shoulder and gave her a playful squeeze. They were good friends. A few months ago,

Irene had confided that they both suffered from mood swings that affected their buying habits. They had met in a doctor's office and had bonded instantly.

Irene eased from beneath Willow's arm and said, "Butt out. We're having a private chat."

"Not anymore. I'm here." Willow fetched an empty chair from a nearby table and, without asking, wedged it between my mother and me. She settled onto it, adjusted the skirt of her marmalade-colored sheath, and popped the lid on her coffee. "C'mon, let me in on the gossip."

Irene snorted. "You are incorrigible."

"Yes, I am. Now spill." Willow blew on her coffee and took a sip.

I bit back a smile. Despite the fact that Willow was trying to throw a wrench between Nash and me by reintroducing Eli into my life—I truly believed that was her aim—I liked her.

Irene said, "We were talking about Parker Price being in the neighborhood the night Camille's sister was murdered."

"Hmm." Willow took another sip of coffee. "I didn't see him, but I did catch sight of Camille that night, about the time she told the sheriff she arrived home—eleven thirty. I've met with Sergeant Daly and verified her alibi."

I gaped. "You spoke with Tyson?"

"Mm-hmm."

"Ahem, Willow." Irene cleared her throat. "My dear sweet friend, excuse me, but you don't live in the neighborhood."

"True. I don't." She took another languid sip. The corners of her mouth twitched.

Irene planted a fist on one hip. "Then might I ask how you happened to see Camille?"

"I saw her because"—Willow dragged out the word, baiting us—"I was next door."

"At Betty's house?"

Willow swiped her hand. "Other side."

"At Bennett's place?" Irene gawped. "But he's—"

"Single."

"And your junior by ten years."

"*Shh*. It's our secret. He thinks we're the same age." Willow knuckled her friend on the arm. "What he doesn't know won't hurt him."

I said, "Is he the one you were talking about the other day?"

"One and the same." She threw Irene a look. "This is not a forever thing. I don't think I will ever want a forever romance again. I had that. It's over." She eyeballed me.

I flinched. She didn't blame me for Nash leaving her, did she? I was not the reason. According to him, she spent way above her means and that capriciousness plus her other personality quirks had ended their marriage. "Willow, did you see Parker Price or someone in an earflap hat and overcoat earlier that evening?"

"I did not, but, as previously mentioned, I was otherwise occupied. The chemistry was—" She flicked her fingers as she had the other day, indicating their chemistry was explosive.

"Are you sure you saw Camille enter the house at eleven thirty?" I asked.

"I did. After Bennett and I tripped the light fantastic, I walked onto the porch to study the stars, and there she was, heading into her house, a single grocery bag in her arms. The porch light illuminated her. She had junk in her hair." Willow wriggled her fingers above her head. "I heard a rumor that she'd gone walking in the woods. I can't imagine. It was so windy that night. But if it's true, it's a good thing she did. Otherwise, she might be dead."

I doubted Camille felt the same. If she'd come straight home from work, maybe her sister would be alive.

Chapter 14

I paid for our treats and followed my mother to her house in my Jeep. I couldn't wait to see Camille and tell her the good news. She was free. Exonerated. She had a solid alibi and a witness to verify it. As I drove, I used the hands-free cell phone feature on the steering wheel and called Heather to tell her I was running late. She assured me she would get the kitchen staff cracking.

As I drove up my mother's driveway, I was struck again by how beautiful the house was. As a child, I'd never paid attention to the lines or style. I'd romped through the gardens and catapulted over the patio railing without a care. Now, the sunlight was making the cream trim glimmer around the moss green siding. Sunlight highlighted the Mr. Lincoln tea roses bordering the path to the porch. My mother loved tending her roses.

She pulled her Toyota Corolla into the garage. I parked by the roses and climbed the steps to the porch. The front door was open. The aroma of cinnamon wafted through the screen door.

"Camille must be baking," my mother said as she entered.

I trailed her.

Riesling bounded to us for hugs and kisses. Then, as if he sensed we had come to greet Camille and not him, he barked at us, made a quick U-turn, and bolted upstairs to the guest room.

"You lead," my mother said.

The door to the guest room was ajar. Camille's overnight case lay open on the bed. The vine-themed drapes hung open. The double-sash window was ajar and allowed a cool breeze into the room. I heard the shower in the guest bathroom crank off.

"Camille?" I rapped on the doorjamb.

"Come in," she trilled. "I will be out in a second."

I entered. My mother followed me. Riesling dashed past both of us and nudged the bathroom door open.

Camille emerged, wrapped in an ecru bathrobe, her feet tucked into sea-grass slippers. My mother liked her guests to feel pampered. "Did you hear the news, Mimi? Sergeant Daly called my cell phone." Her face glowed with energy as she bent to scratch Riesling under the chin. "I recognized his number, so I answered. He said Willow—"

"Exonerated you."

"Is it not wonderful? I may return to work. But first, I must go home to get fresh clothes. In a rush to pack to stay at your cottage, I did not include a white blouse or a second pair of trousers."

"You don't have to come back today if—"

"Yes. I do." As if sensing my reservations, she said, "I need to work. It is all I dream of."

"I told you," my mother said.

Camille set her travel kit in the suitcase and zipped it up. When she spun around, her eyes were misty. "It is not *all* I dream of. I hope for an end to this nightmare."

Channeling my mother's positive energy, I said, "The sheriff will solve this." *With or without my input*, I decided. I joined Camille at the bed. She smelled of Ivory soap and vanilla-scented lotion.

"Does he have any suspects?" Camille asked.

My mother said, "Let's not talk about the case right now. Let's keep positive and upbeat. Camille, did you make cinnamon rolls?"

"Better. I made cinnamon crullers."

"Let's go downstairs and have one." We hadn't finished our croissants at Chocolate. We had been too excited to get back and see Camille.

"No, Ginette, thank you. I am too wound up. I will eat later. Right now, I need to stimulate the gray cells." She tapped her temple. "Most of all, I need to honor Renee by pressing on. She would have done the same if I were the one—"

"The killer is at large," I warned. "You could be the target."

"Then let us help figure out who is the guilty party." She shooed us out of the room so she could change. "I will be down in a few minutes."

In the kitchen, I couldn't resist. I ate half a cruller and hummed with delight. "Perfection."

A few minutes passed before Camille descended the stairs. She was wearing a clean but creased blue blouse and the same slacks she had worn to my place on the night of the murder. Riesling acted as her escort to my Jeep. I opened the rear hatch, tossed in her overnight case, and slammed it shut.

We drove to her neighborhood, north of St. Helena. The yellow barrier tape was gone. She pulled a set of keys from her pocket and hurried inside to change clothes.

Hanging outside, I studied the houses on either side of hers. According to Willow, Betty lived on one side and Bennett on the other. I'd never met either person. I pictured Betty residing in the white Victorian with the white roses and Bennett in the refurbished contemporary. I could see both porches from Camille's, so that part of Willow's story rang true. I eyed Irene's house, which was kitty-corner from Camille's. The autumn-toned chrysanthemums were gone, as she had lamented; she had replanted with white ones. Which house was Ursula Drake's? Was it the blue-and-white Victorian with the Necco wafer–style roof? That would suit her.

"Ready to go." Camille pushed through the front door. She had thrown on pleated tan pants, a crisp white blouse, and clogs, and had applied a little bit of makeup.

"You look great."

Seeing her smile sent a thrill through me. Her sister might be dead, but she was going to push through the pain. She would survive.

On the drive to the bistro, Camille said, "I am not sure that I can ever erase the memory of Renee lying on my floor."

What could I say? The image of Derrick's death had shocked me and still lingered in my mind—yes, his climbing buddies had taken a photograph. Seeing Bryan Baker dead on the rear patio of the bistro still haunted me, too. "It will get easier in time."

"Yes, I suppose."

"Do you mind if I ask a question?"

"Is it about that night?"

How to broach the delicate subject? *Dive in, Mimi.* "It's about Renee."

"What do you want to know?"

"I asked you before, but you didn't want to discuss the possibility." I moistened my mouth, which had become dryer than dry. "Is it possible that Renee was having an affair? Now that you've had time to reflect—"

"With Donovan?"

"No, not him. I told you, he's yours."

"You did not tell me that."

"I didn't? I thought I had. The night you were mopping the cottage."

"No."

She was right. I hadn't because she had cut me off and allowed for no further discussion. "I'm sorry for the oversight. The other day, when he came to the bistro asking about you, he made that very clear to me. He said he is only dating you. That means you're exclusive."

Her cheeks tinged pink. Her eyes brightened.

I veered onto St. Helena Highway. Traffic was moving. "So, could Renee have been involved with anyone else? A man with a limp was seen in the neighborhood that night. He was heading toward your house; however, the witness didn't see him enter."

"Which means he could have passed by."

"Yes."

Camille's breath caught. "What if this man entered another house?"

"The witness didn't think he lived in the neighborhood."

"No, what I meant was perhaps he was having an affair with one of my married neighbors?"

"Okay," I murmured, not grasping where she was going with her theory.

She twisted in her seat, her gaze intense. "What if Renee saw him? What if he caught her watching him? What if he stole to my place and silenced her to keep his secret safe?"

"You have a suspicious mind."

"The murder of my sister has made it so. You must tell the sheriff this possibility." Camille shot a finger at me and then faced forward and folded her hands in her lap. Discussion ended.

When we entered the bistro through the front door, Heather, who was setting tables on the rear patio, shouted, "Chef C, so good to see you!"

Camille waved hello and hurried toward the kitchen. She

paused at the door and glanced at me, her eyes moist. "How I have missed this place."

"You've only been gone a few days."

"It feels like an eon. I have missed the noise and the aromas and . . ." She drew in a deep breath. "I am nervous."

"Don't be. You're in your element."

"*Oui*, I am. Let us proceed."

I pushed through the door. The staff glimpsed Camille and shouted a joyous greeting.

Allie hurried over, her hair tucked beneath a toque, her chef's jacket splattered with something green and yellow. "I'm Allie O'Malley, but that's a mouthful, so Allie will do."

Camille eyed me.

"Allie is a temporary hire," I explained. "We've been slammed with diners because of the festival, and we're a few staff short."

"I'm here to help you in any way possible." Allie gestured to the station where she had set up the ingredients for the lunch entrées. "I hope you don't mind, Chef C—" She clamped her lower lip with her teeth. "Um, may I call you Chef C?"

Camille grinned, taking to Allie as I had. "Everyone does."

"Okay, good. I hope you don't mind, but I took the initiative and put together another hamburger special for today."

"*Another*?" Chef's noise twitched.

"We served one yesterday," I said. "Hamburgers are international, not simply American. We served it with Roquefort. It was quite a hit."

"This one is made with a French flair, too," Allie said.

"Allie used to work at the Burger Garden," I explained. "She has quite a knack."

"I made a Dijon mustard sauce," Allie added. "And I included a host of spices in the burger itself."

Stefan, who was preparing lettuce for the Caesar salads, yelled, "I tasted it. *Magnifique*!"

I grinned, happy to see he was embracing Allie.

"Come see." Allie beckoned Camille and me to follow her. "I've plated one."

I drew alongside Allie and whispered, "Remember what I said yesterday." I had told her that if and when Chef C returned to work, she was not to mention Renee at all.

"Gotcha." She motioned to a beautiful plating of a thick beef burger set on a whole-wheat bun atop a ruffle of Bibb lettuce. "Here we are. Do you like it?"

The mustard-based sauce looked savory. So did the accompaniment of a mound of crisp fresh potato chips.

"It's not too humdrum, is it? I know you like to serve elaborate dishes."

"It is not at all humdrum," Camille said. "Put together enough sauce and burgers for twenty servings, and ask Heather to add it to the top of the lunch specials."

With a spring in her step, Allie hustled out of the kitchen.

Camille steered me to one side. "I like this girl."

"Don't get too attached," I joked.

"Because she might be a suspect in Renee's murder?"

"No." I sputtered. "How did you know—"

"I have ears. I know the two of them had a falling out."

"Yes, but—"

"You do not think she did it." Camille wagged a finger near my nose. "You trust her."

"I do."

"So why should I not get attached, then? She seems spirited and eager."

"Because when you feel you're back in the swing of things and the festival ends, I will let her go. I don't have the funds for an extra employee. She knows it's a temporary gig. Now"—I clapped her on the shoulder—"get to work."

"Yes, boss, and you call Sheriff Daly."

"I'm on it."

As I headed toward the exit, Allie swooped past me. She mouthed *thank you* and dashed to assist the chef.

After I changed into my work outfit, I sat at my office desk and dialed Tyson's cell phone number. He answered after one ring.

"What, Mimi?" He sounded peeved.

"Hi, Tyson," I said with forced charm. "Is that how you greet your one and only middle school pal?" Years ago, he had been gangly and bucktoothed and he had kept to himself. When I learned that he liked to read the same books I did—mysteries—I had approached him and we had become fast friends.

He exhaled. I pictured him breathing in and out, searching for a modicum of graciousness. "You're pushing it, Mimi."

"I've got some news."

"Let me guess. It has to do with Willow Hawke."

"No, although I heard you spoke with her, and she cleared my chef, who is happy to be back at work."

"Bully for her," he said, his tone deadpan. "What news do you have then?"

"Two things. The first is about Parker Price and the second is about Rusty Wells." I still hadn't told him about Rusty's not being at Chocolate on the night of the murder. With Camille exonerated, I could do so and not worry I would damage her alibi. "A witness—"

A man with thick brown hair and wide sensual lips rapped on my door. A professional digital camera hung on a strap around his neck. "Excuse me, Miss Rousseau, got a sec?" Hairy forearms jutted from his beige camp-style shirt. Over his arm, he carried a beige photographer-style jacket—the kind with lots of pockets.

"Sir." Heather tried to block him from entering, but he was determined to get past. She nabbed the collar of his shirt.

"Let go of me." He wrenched free and strode toward me.

I bounded to my feet and, despite his good looks, picked up a letter opener and aimed it at the intruder. "Sir, what the heck do you think you're doing barging into my office?"

"The name's Oscar." He threw up his hands. "I'm not here to hurt you. Honest." His voice was raspy as if he'd been talking for hours without stopping.

"Mimi, are you there?" Tyson asked, his voice crackling through the receiver. "Is everything okay?"

"Sorry, Tyson. I'll call you right back."

"I'm sorry if I scared you," the man said. "I'm a reporter."

Was he the one who had dogged Camille the other day? "What are you reporting on?"

"You."

"Me?"

Without invitation, he dropped into a chair. *Squish!* Air hissed out of the cushion. "Oops, bad me." He offered a sly grin.

I stifled a laugh—the man wasn't a danger, just eager. I shooed Heather out of the office. "It's okay. Call Henry and check on the kittens. How are they, by the way?"

"Adorable and getting so big. I've named them all."

Uh-oh. She was bonding. Would she be able to give them up at the appropriate time?

"Haven't I shown you the latest pictures?" she asked. "I've got tons on my cell phone. I can go get it." She hitched a thumb over her shoulder.

"Later. We're fine here." I lifted my chin, signaling she should leave. I was safe. As she slipped out, I eyed Oscar. "Who do you write for?"

"The *Napa Valley Neighborhood.*"

"Never heard of it.

"It's a local rag with up-to-date news for everyone in the valley. Last week I wrote a piece about the upcoming Crush Week, letting people know where to go and what to do. Didn't you see it?"

"Didn't you hear me earlier? I haven't heard—"

"You must have seen it. It's delivered to every vendor in town, including restaurants."

"Not ours." I shook my head.

"That will be rectified." Oscar whipped out a spiral pad and pencil and jotted a note. "In the meantime, I'm trying to get the scoop on you and your success. Ten minutes of your time, that's all I ask."

"Two." I held up a pair of fingers. "What would you like to know?"

"Well, for starters, you had a benefactor named Bryan Baker. Right?"

"That's correct."

"He was murdered."

My antennae twitched. They were attuned to detect poppycock. Oscar was after a lurid story. I folded my hands and stared daggers at him. "I won't address that."

"But you helped solve the crime."

"I was able to provide some information to the sheriff."

Oscar tapped his pencil on his pad. "That's not what I heard. You were there. You took the murderer down."

"Look, Mr.—"

"Orsini. Oscar Orsini. In Italian, *orsini* means hairy. The joke's on me, right?" He rubbed a meaty forearm.

"Thank you for your interest, Mr. Orsini, but I'm going to pass."

"No. Wait. Give me a chance. We don't have to talk about your benefactor. We'll discuss you. You're the star. It's your reputation for great food that is making this place soar. You're the talk of the town." He was speaking at sixty miles a minute. "I forgot my biggest selling point. We have a readership of over five hundred thousand."

I gulped, set the letter opener down, and sank into my chair. A half a million people perused his paper? I couldn't buy that kind of publicity. "You're pulling my leg."

"No, ma'am. *The Neighbor*, as we like to call our little rag, has wide circulation. All the hotels and inns get it. The tourist havens and wineries, too. And locals read it at the coffee shops. Promise." He crossed his heart with the eraser on his pencil. "We're the biggest little secret this side of the Rockies. So, c'mon, give me an insider scoop on how you did it. I heard you're a widow, by the way. Sorry for your loss."

"Thank you." Despite his brash behavior, I sort of liked Oscar. He reminded me of a chef I'd worked for in San Francisco who had steamrolled everyone in order to turn out great meals. I'd learned a lot from him, including how *not* to steamroll.

"You left home at eighteen to become a chef," he said.

In a quick minute, I told him about my young career: moving to San Francisco, working as a sous-chef, graduating to full chef at a French restaurant, and Derrick's death. "I returned to Nouvelle Vie to start over. I met Mr. Baker, and the rest is history."

"As for food reviews, your bistro has earned over twenty in a short period of time. All positive. How did you swing that?"

Our very first food critic had liked his meal so much that he had put out the good word to his buddies to give Bistro Rousseau a try. Thanks to a friend in the restaurant business, Heather had figured out the pseudonyms many critics used to make reservations. Forewarned for nearly every appearance, we had prepared our tastiest menus.

"Word of mouth," I said.

"Tell me about the festival." Oscar licked the tip of his pencil. "Did you know the woman who was killed?"

I eyed him warily. "What's your real intent, Mr. Orsini?"

"Huh?"

"Were you the reporter who was sneaking around my chef's hotel room at Maison Rousseau trying to get the lowdown on her?"

"What? No. It wasn't me!" He leaped to his feet. "If I'd known she was staying there . . ." He snapped his fingers. "Rats. Um, has she returned to work?"

Again, I regarded him. Was he lying about not being the brazen reporter? Had he followed me to my mother's house? Had he seen me fetch Camille and bring her here? Was his endgame getting an exclusive with her?

"Oho!" He aimed his pencil at me. "You cut a look in the direction of your kitchen, which means she is here. Would she like to be part of this article? I mean, it's your restaurant, but she's doing the cooking."

"She would like to be left alone and to mourn in private."

Oscar threw up a hand in defense. "Hey, I'm not an ambulance chaser. I was merely wondering." He jotted a note. "So, are you investigating this murder, too?"

"That's it. Time's up. You're full of baloney." I shooed him toward the door. "I'd like you to leave."

"Okay. I'm going. I didn't mean to offend you." In the archway of the door, he pivoted. "Just so you know, I'm not going to hold it against you that you booted me out. I got enough good stuff. I like you, Mimi. You've got pluck. You're going to be pleased with what you read. I'll give you final approval of the story, okay?" He whipped his cell phone out of his pocket. "If it's all right, I'll snap a few photos before—"

"Don't push it."

Chapter 15

On his way out of the office, Oscar bumped into Tyson Daly. "Sorry, fella." He wasn't being dismissive by calling Tyson *fella*. Our beloved sheriff wasn't in uniform. In fact, in his jeans and golf shirt, he looked like an ordinary guy ready to spend a relaxing sightseeing day in the valley.

"Who was that?" Tyson asked as Oscar slipped past.

"A reporter."

"By your tone, I take it he's not your favorite person."

"I'm not sure what he was after. If he wanted gossip about the case, he didn't get it."

"Which case would that be?" Tyson jammed his hands into his jeans pockets.

"You know which case."

"You mean *my* case, not *yours*? The one you shouldn't be commenting on? *That* case?"

If he weren't such a good friend, I'd have clocked him. "Why are you here?" I asked.

"We didn't finish our conversation."

"Right. Are you hungry? I'll get us a couple of *croque-monsieur* sandwiches."

"Not hungry, thanks. I ate with Jo. That's where I was when you called."

"Having breakfast?" I batted my eyelashes. "At her place?"

"At the inn. We *met* for breakfast. She's . . ." He heaved a sigh. "That's why I'm here. I need your advice."

"You need *my* help?" I placed my fingertips on my chest.

He scowled. "You're her best friend."

I escorted him into the office and closed the door. "I'll tell no tales."

He stood in the center of the room. "Explain why she's keeping her distance."

How to phrase it? I perched on the edge of my desk. "She doesn't want to be boxed in. She's afraid you'll want her to have children the moment you get hitched."

"Doesn't she like kids?"

"She's . . . not sure. I think she's afraid she'll do the same thing her mother did."

"Run?"

I nodded.

"Get real." He scrubbed his hair with his hands. "Her mom was a kook."

"Jo has always wondered whether wanderlust is lurking in her genes. I think she's afraid it might trigger at the age of thirty-eight or forty."

He barked out a laugh. "You're pulling my leg."

"No, I'm not." For years after her mother split, Jo and I had discussed the gene thing. We hadn't kicked the theory around lately, but that didn't mean it wasn't cycling through her overactive imagination. I said, "Give her love and plenty of kisses, and most importantly, give her space."

"Yeah, okay. You know her best."

"And you will, too. Soon. Listen, about our earlier conversation . . ."

He settled onto one of the shabby chic chairs and propped his elbows on his knees. "Your turn. Your news."

"It isn't news; it's a guess."

"About the *case*?" He stressed the word and smirked.

"Don't give me guff, Sergeant. I'm allowed to inform you if someone confides in me."

"Who confided in you this time?"

"Camille and I were chatting about the guy with the limp that Ursula Drake saw, and we theorized that maybe the guy was in the neighborhood having a clandestine affair with a married woman. Or—"

"Or he was married and the woman was single."

I slapped my thigh. "You and I"—I waggled my finger between the two of us—"think alike."

"We're nothing alike," Tyson said and twirled his hand. "Go on."

I strolled to him and perched on the chair beside his. "We wondered whether Renee saw him and he saw *her*, and maybe he was desperate to keep the affair secret, so he stole into the house and killed her."

"Pretty brutal thing to do to hide an affair."

"Parker has a limp."

"As do many people in town, and I told you, I've cleared him. Look, Mimi"—Tyson splayed a hand—"I appreciate your help. You've got a good brain and decent reasoning powers, but I'm on top of this. I've been conducting plenty of interviews. Looking at all the angles. Camille is off the hook." He stood and headed for the door. "Relax. You don't have to keep thinking it through. Neither does she. Focus on the bistro and on growing your business."

I bounded to my feet and caught up with him. "What if Parker was having an affair with Renee?"

"He wasn't. He barely knew her."

"Okay, then, is he having an affair with Louvain Cook? Does she live in the neighborhood? Irene has seen Parker in the neighborhood."

Tyson seared me with a look. "Don't go spreading rumors."

"I noticed orange lipstick on Parker's collar the other day." I remembered the conversation I'd had a few days before with Felicity and Parker's daughter. Philomena had been upset to hear her parents arguing about *love this and love that.* Had Felicity referred to Louvain as *Love*?

"Felicity wears lipstick," he countered.

"She told me she would rather die than wear the color orange. That day, I saw Parker chatting with Louvain, who loves the color orange. Does she live in Camille's neighborhood?"

He tilted his head but kept mum.

"Why did you question Parker?" I asked.

"I wanted to know about his and Felicity's involvement with Renee as fundraisers." He moved toward the exit.

"That's not all I've got to tell you," I hurried to add before he vanished. "Rusty Wells lied about going to Chocolate on the night of the murder. No one saw him there, so where was he? If he—"

"Stop. Mimi. I've questioned Rusty Wells twice—yes, since hearing he was driving in the neighborhood—but in order to get to the bottom of why he lied about being at Chocolate, I'll interview him again. Happy? In addition"—he ticked his list off on his fingertips—"I've questioned the festival's staff to see if anyone held a grudge against Renee or knew someone who held a grudge. Now, to appease you, I'll recanvass Camille's neighborhood."

"You already did?"

"Once. It bears repeating. Please. Relax. I've got this."

"I know your tech didn't find fingerprints on the murder weapon, but did she find them anywhere else? Did any of the stuff on the floor provide a clue? Are you sure Renee wrote the love letter?"

"Yes, yes, and yes. Don't underestimate me, Mimi."

"Don't dismiss me. My heart is in the right place. All I ask is that if I call you with a theory, you consider it. You're going to marry my best friend. We've got to stay friends, too."

"Do we?"

"Yes!"

"At this rate, don't get your hopes up."

* * *

On my way to the kitchen to check on Camille and see how she was faring with the lunch menu on her first day back, my cell phone rang. The screen read Jo. I stabbed ACCEPT.

"Problem in the Bazille Garden," she said before I could say hello. She sounded out of breath. "Can you help? Raymond needs you. The wind has blown all sorts of debris around. A trellis toppled. One tent's pegs came loose, and the tent soared into the air. Plus, balloons are popping, and they're frightening the festival attendees who are out in droves to see the cooking demonstrations. There's so much electricity in the air, it's scary. But the show must go on, so Raymond wants your two cents. My two cents aren't worth a plug nickel."

"Where's Rusty?"

"Out and about. We need you, boss."

"On my way."

I cornered Heather and told her where I was going. She assured me everything was hunky-dory at the restaurant. The list of customers coming in for lunch was confirmed, and she had recently visited the kitchen.

"Get this?" she added. "Chef C and Stefan are singing duets."

"Duets?"

"*Love* duets like 'You're the One That I Want' and 'I Got You Babe.' Who knew Stefan was so gifted?"

"Who knew Camille would sing along?" I elbowed her.

As I hustled toward the inn, the love song "My Heart Will Go On," from the movie *Titanic*, popped into my mind. The lyrics sent a shudder down my spine. Was thinking of the *Titanic* prophetic? Was something disastrous about to happen?

To rid my mind of the fateful tune, I mentally chanted *Rain, rain, go away—and don't come back another day.* Everything was going to be fine. So what if wind was gusting through the festival?

On my way, I clicked the weather app on my cell phone. According to online predictions, the wind was due to die down in a half hour. *Phew!*

When I arrived at the Bazille Garden, Jo and Raymond, assisted by two khaki-clad employees, were hoisting a trellis of pink roses that had collapsed. The tents in the Bazille Garden were Giverny pink to match the inn's theme colors.

"Thank heavens," Jo said. "Raymond, Mimi is here."

"I have eyes," he sniped.

Jo stood on tiptoe, her black pencil skirt clinging to her thighs, her tangerine cropped cardigan rising above her midriff. A sizable black tote bag lay at her feet.

"It looks like you have things under control," I said.

Jo threw me a baleful look.

Rusty appeared and rushed to help.

"Where have you been?" Jo cried.

"Assisting in the other gardens. They were both suffering the same fate, but we got them under control."

"Don't worry," I said. "The wind is going to stop soon." I flashed my cell phone to show them the good news about the weather. "Raymond, I'll get the festivalgoers out of the way so you can double-check all the tent pegs and clean up debris. Rusty, may I use the loudspeaker system for an announcement?"

"Sure. It's located at the information table outside the cooking demonstration tent. Edna is manning the tent. Tell her I sent you."

"And do you have a wheel of raffle tickets handy?"

"That'd be Edna, too."

I hustled to a lean, sour-faced woman in a slim khaki-colored dress standing behind the information table. She reminded me of a severe camp counselor. All rules, all the time. Although the pink tablecloth was being whipped into a frenzy, the wind didn't seem to be affecting the woman. Not one steel-gray hair on her narrow head was blowing out of place. Helmet hair, my mother would've called it.

"Hi, Edna, I'm Mimi Rousseau, the owner of the inn. Rusty said I could use the speaker system."

"Go ahead." She handed me the microphone and switched it on. "Don't yell. Speak normally."

"He said you would have raffle tickets, too." The festival was offering a Sweet Treats Basket and Wine Tasting Package to one lucky festival attendee. The Sweet Treats Basket would be filled with tasty delights baked by the twin judges. Nouvelle Vie Vineyards was supplying the wine. The raffle money would go to the education fund. That had been Renee's idea, as well. Thinking of her and how much her sister and others would miss her made me choke with emotion. *Buck up, Mimi.*

Edna reached under the table and withdrew a wheel of blue tickets.

I raised the microphone to my mouth and said, "Ladies and gentlemen." The words popped.

Edna scrunched her nose in disapproval. "You're holding it too close."

I inched the microphone away from my mouth and continued. "The weather forecast says the wind will ease up in less than an hour. Why don't you go into the demonstration tent and enjoy the baking finals for—"

"Muffins," Edna said.

"For muffins," I repeated. "Yum! Stay inside until—"

"It all blows over?" a portly man in the crowd joked.

I smiled and gave him a thumbs-up sign.

"We had the pie baking finals earlier," Edna offered. "Louvain Cook won. She's a marvel with pie crusts."

"So I heard." I addressed the crowd. "Folks, we'll be giving free raffle tickets to each of you as you enter." I flourished the wheel of tickets. "Vendors, please don't worry. Volunteers are making the rounds to ensure that all of your tent pegs hold tight. Step right up!"

I handed the microphone to Edna and positioned myself at the entrance to the demonstration tent. People passed me in an orderly fashion, their hands extended. In a matter of minutes, I delivered over one hundred raffle tickets.

When I entered the tent, I spotted Felicity Price on stage looking confident in a sapphire-blue dress with cap sleeves. She was one of three finalists. Apparently she hadn't needed Renee's help to rise in the ranks.

The competition area was divided into three sections. Each woman controlled a preparation and presentation station as well as a set of ovens. Construction paper name plates identified the contestants' entries. Overhead, slanted mirrors provided a view for the audience of each presentation station. The contest must have started over forty-five minutes ago because Felicity was pulling muffins from the oven. She placed a lime-green silicone muffin pan on the counter and, using a thin spatula, removed the muffins one by one. She set them on a wire rack to cool. A sign at her station read CHOCOLATE COMFORT. I wondered whether these were the paleo muffins she had raved about.

It was no surprise to see Oscar Orsini standing in front of Felicity's area. He stuffed a notepad and pencil into one of the pockets of his jacket and started taking photos with his digital camera. Felicity flirtatiously wiggled her fingertips at him, then faced her opponents. The middle contestant faltered and cursed as she inserted a toothpick into her DOUBLE CHOCOLATE muffins. The contestant on the far left was standing with her finished muffins. She reminded me of a Barbie doll version of Martha Stewart. The ruffled white apron that protected her simple black dress was spotless, her hair was coiffed, and she had the ideal 36–24–36 figure. Did the woman eat anything she baked? She gazed straight ahead, her radiant smile frozen in place. Her muffins were called SINFULLY CHOCOLATE. Somehow I doubted she had ever sinned in her life.

The moderator for the contest, an elderly woman who owned a bakery in Yountville, signaled thirty seconds. As Felicity and Barbie Martha began to plate their cooled muffins, the middle contestant moaned. She slapped down her muffin pan, bare-fingered the muffin out of the hot pan onto a plate, and raised her hand signaling she was done.

The moderator blew a whistle.

A pair of middle-aged twin judges, also local bakers who were clad in matching blue frocks—although one wore her brunette hair down and the other wore hers in a French twist—ascended the stage. They studied the muffins at length. They tasted the middle contestant's muffin and, as expected, dismissed her. The poor woman left the stage whimpering. The twins ambled to Barbie Martha and tasted. The one with the French twist licked her thumb and index finger. The other twin tilted her head, deliberating.

The audience, which was packed thanks to the prevailing wind outside, collectively held its breath as the judges strolled to the other end of the stage and tasted Felicity's entry. The one with the French twist pursed her lips. The other's eyes lit up. She licked her lips and took another bite.

Felicity tugged on the cap sleeves of her dress. Barbie Martha didn't blink an eye.

The judges conferred for a brief moment before moving to the center stage. The one with the French twist produced a blue scalloped first-place ribbon; the other hoisted a portable microphone. Through it, she announced, "Felicity Price, you"—she hesitated for dramatic effect—"are the winner."

The crowd applauded.

Barbie Martha's demeanor crumpled. She gazed at Felicity with outright jealousy before turning away from the audience. As fast as she could, she packed up the items at her baking station and departed.

Felicity beamed as she received her blue ribbon. "Whee!" she shouted and did a twirl, showing off the low-cut back of her dress. After she packed up her kitchenware, she pranced down the stairs with a plate of muffins in hand.

Oscar met her and smooched her on both cheeks. "Congratulations!" He took a muffin, bit into it, and moaned his delight.

Felicity spotted me and beckoned me to join her. "Mimi, taste one."

"You must," Oscar said. "They're great."

I wavered. "Are these the paleo muffins you were bragging about, Felicity?"

"Don't be a ninny!" Her laughter sounded like tittering gone awry. "I would never enter those in a contest."

"But you said—"

"I was teasing you. Paleo-schmaleo. I eat that to keep my figure. I wouldn't serve it to my worst enemy." She elbowed Oscar, who seemed enthralled by her coyness. "Oscar, darling, say hello."

He did.

"Do you know Oscar, Mimi?"

"I do."

"Then you know he's a reporter. He's doing a piece on the winner, which is me!" She wriggled with delight and thrust the muffins toward me. "C'mon, taste one. If you like it, I'll give you the recipe."

I took a muffin and bit into it. I was astonished by how scrumptious it was—sweet, moist, and definitely bakery-worthy.

Felicity leaned in. "FYI, it's Alton Brown's recipe number seven. The buttermilk and the extra chocolate chips make all the difference. The rules didn't state that the recipe had to be mine. It'll be our little secret." She winked at me. "I love secrets."

"Darling, you look cold," Oscar said.

He removed his cell phone from his pocket, and then, without asking permission, shrugged off his jacket and slung it over Felicity's shoulders, which she accepted. Why? Was she cozying up to him so he would write something sensational about her in his article? She had to be warm after baking. Over the years, I'd participated in a few contests, and I was never cold afterward. Adrenaline worked like an internal heater. Also, what was with all the *darlings* being slung around?

Oscar pressed the RECORD button on his cell phone and started in on his interview. As Felicity responded to his questions about her high school years and beyond, a niggling sensation tweaked my insides. Wrapped in Oscar's jacket, Felicity looked formidable, which made me wonder, as I had about Rusty, whether she had donned a man's coat to make herself look like Parker and gone to Camille's house. She could have faked a limp. Did she, as I'd theorized, believe her husband was having an affair with Renee? Did jealousy provoke her to commit murder?

A hiccup of laughter slipped out of me. Tyson had asked me not to theorize about Renee's murder, and yet theories were scudding through my mind.

"What's so amusing?" Felicity asked. "You don't believe I was the head cheerleader?"

"Were you? I'm sorry." I flapped a hand. "I wasn't listening to your answers. My mind was elsewhere."

"Where?"

"On tonight's menu," I lied.

Oscar glanced at his watch. "Felicity, I have a few more questions, but I've got another appointment. Why don't I call you and we'll set a time to finish up? Afterward, I'd like you to review and approve what I've written. Okay? Good." He bussed her on the cheek and rushed off.

I'll bet that isn't all he wants you to review, I thought, and another wave of giggles burbled out of me. *Bad Mimi.*

Felicity whirled on me, her gaze piercing. "Out with it. What's putting you in stitches?"

I dragged a finger up and down. "In that jacket, you look like Parker. Put on a hat and you'd be his spitting image."

She petted the lapel. "Oscar was sweet to lend it to me."

"Admit it. You weren't in the least cold."

She jutted her chin. "I wasn't flirting to get a good writeup, if that's what you're implying. I am devoted to my husband."

"Of course you are."

Her lip started to quiver. Moisture pooled in her eyes.

I sobered instantly and clasped her arm. "Felicity, what's wrong?"

She glanced over her shoulder. The crowd in the tent had dispersed. The wind had died down. Only members of the stage crew were left. She turned back to me and whispered, "I'm not sure *he* is devoted to *me*."

"Who, Parker?"

"Who else?"

"Do you think he's having an affair?"

Her lower lip trembled, revealing her concern.

"With Renee?" I asked.

"Heavens, no. Ew, Mimi." Felicity shied away from me. "She's dead."

"That's not what I meant."

"Besides, Renee loved her husband. She told me so."

"Over tea?"

"Yes, over tea. Taiwanese oolong—her favorite."

"I heard she had a crush on Donovan Coleman."

"A teensy crush." Felicity pinched two fingers together. "Nothing more. She knew the difference. She was a bright cookie." She tried to pin the blue ribbon to her dress, but Oscar's jacket kept getting in the way. "What would make you think Renee and Parker were an item?" Her eyes grew wide as realization dawned on her. "Dear me. You can't think that I had anything to do with that poor woman's death because I"—she sputtered—"was jealous."

"No, of course not." The notion had been gaining traction in my mind. "Um, who do you think Parker is involved with?"

"I don't want to fan flames."

If she didn't, then why had she brought it up?

"Ow!" She had pricked herself with the pin.

"Let me help."

She thrust the award at me and slipped off Oscar's jacket. I attempted to weave the pin through the fabric near the shoulder.

"Why are you staring at me like that?" she demanded.

"I'm not staring. I'm concentrating."

"You want to know what my alibi was that night, don't you?"

"No." I hadn't even considered asking, but if she was offering . . .

"I told the sheriff already."

"Why did he question you?" I asked, though I knew the reason. At least Tyson had divulged that much of his investigation.

"He was interviewing everyone involved with the festival—employees, fundraisers, and volunteers. I told him I was at the theater with my daughter. Philomena had rehearsal until eleven." She grunted. "These high school productions are getting way out of hand. A year or two ago, they were three weeks long, but now they last six weeks."

"You stick around and watch each rehearsal?"

"Watch? Ha! I'm busy from the moment I arrive. I do programs and costumes, or I organize treats and such. There's so much to do. I don't really mind. It's a nice way to give back. Philomena appreciates it because"—she wove her fingers together—"we get mother–daughter bonding time. She's my joy."

I closed the pin. "Mission accomplished. Your ribbon looks great with that dress."

"You don't think it blends in too much?"

"The gold filigree makes it sparkle."

"Thanks. Why, look at the time." She glimpsed her jewel-studded watch. "I've got to leave, but first I must fetch my bakeware items and return this coat to Oscar before . . ." She didn't finish before *what*. Before heading to rehearsal? No, it was too early for that. "I hope he's still on the grounds. I'll send you that muffin recipe. Ta!" She air-kissed me and hurried up the stairs to the stage. In a flash, she stuffed her things into a duffle and dashed down the rear stairs.

Odd, I thought. Was she afraid that if she hung around me any longer she might spill something vital? Like her husband's alibi? Tyson hadn't revealed what it was.

I exited the tent and spotted Jo huddling beneath an arbor of pink bougainvillea, away from the rest of the crowd. She was checking her cell phone. Two children trotted along the balcony above.

Jo peered upward. "Don't break those flowerpots, kids!" she yelled.

Various-sized terra-cotta pots filled with seasonal flowers lined the balcony. They had been set there because, as a result of faulty planning when we had redone the inn, the spaces between the single-basket balusters were designed too wide. Little kids could fall through. Our architect had come up with the fix-it idea of potted plants and paid for them himself.

The children giggled.

Jo yelled, "I'm warning you."

The children tore off.

I raced to her. "Got a sec?"

She tossed her cell phone in her tote bag. "Sure. All fires are doused for the moment. No more popping balloons. No more toppling trellises. Raymond and the staff have tamped down all the tent pegs. They even found some sandbags to anchor those that were iffy. What's up?"

Another chorus of pounding feet rang out overhead.

Jo muttered, "Hooligans."

"Kids having fun. Listen, I wanted to tell you that my earlier hunch was right."

"What hunch?"

It dawned on me that I'd posed my theory about Parker Price having an affair with Renee to Tyson but not to Jo. I pressed on because Jo seemed intrigued, and she was a good sounding board. "I was with Felicity Price. She won the muffin contest. We got to talking, and she thinks her husband is having an affair, and I wondered whether he might have been seeing Renee or someone else in Camille's neighborhood on the sly."

"Parker? Mr. Upstanding Councilman? No way."

"Virtuous people have affairs. And if he was, then he could have been the man with the limp outside Camille's house."

"Man with a limp?" Jo shook her head. "You've lost me."

"Sorry." I recapped Ursula Drake's account to bring my pal up to speed: how Ursula had seen Rusty driving with his lights out in the neighborhood and, later, had seen a man limping near Camille's house. "That guy could have been Rusty, faking a limp to implicate Parker. Or it could have been Parker, or—"

"Mimi, there are a lot of people who limp."

"Granted, it's a reach."

"Tyson knows all this?"

I bobbed my head. "He's spoken with Ursula, as well as Parker and Felicity, it turns out, but when I was talking to Felicity, I got the distinct feeling—"

"Hold it." Jo touched my forearm. "Felicity said she suspected her husband *is* having an affair. *Is* means he couldn't be fooling around with Renee Wells, since she's, um"—Jo squirmed—"dead."

"That's what Felicity said."

"Unless, of course, she's trying to mislead you."

"I wondered the same thing. I even imagined her dressing up

like Parker so she could steal into Camille's house and kill Renee out of jealousy, except she has an alibi."

"How do you know?"

"She told me as I was pinning on her blue ribbon. She thought I was staring at her oddly, so she blurted it out."

"And . . ." Jo opened her hand, begging for more. "Don't keep me waiting."

"She claimed she was at her daughter's theater rehearsal."

"*Claimed*. You don't believe her?"

"To be honest, I'm not sure. She offered it so readily."

Jo swatted my arm. "You should tell Tyson everything."

"He wants me to butt out. He says he has plenty of suspects."

She coughed into her hand and uttered a word that sounded like *bullpuckey*. "He's cranky, and yes"—she batted her eyelashes—"it's all my fault."

"What did you say to him at breakfast?"

She gaped. "You know we met for breakfast?"

"He stopped into the bistro. We chatted. About you. He wanted to know—"

Something rattled overhead.

"Kids, dang it!" Jo yelled.

I peeked out from beneath the arbor.

So did Jo. "Mimi, watch out!"

Chapter 16

A terra-cotta pot soared from above and missed me by inches. Jo gripped my shoulders and yanked me to safety. "Are you okay?"

"Y-Yes," I stuttered as my heart hammered my chest. I dared to take another gander and gasped when I saw someone fleeing from the balcony. I retreated to the safety of the arbor, my teeth chattering.

"Did you see who did it?" Jo asked.

"I saw someone in khaki-colored clothing running away. The children that were up there before were dressed in colorful T-shirts."

"Lots of people wear neutral colors."

"Oscar's jacket was tan."

"Who's Oscar?"

"A journalist. He lent his jacket to Felicity. When she and I parted, she was on her way to return it to him. What if she didn't? What if she put it back on and was overhead, listening to us? Maybe she heard me say I didn't believe her alibi."

Footsteps pounded down the nearby staircase. When Rusty emerged, I gasped. Had he flung the pot over the railing at me? He was angry that I'd checked out his alibi at Chocolate. Maybe he thought he could silence me before I told Tyson. Maybe, I shivered, he was the stranger who'd been lurking outside my house the other night.

Rusty eyed the broken pottery and scattered dirt and flowers. "What happened?"

Jo pointed. "That flowerpot nearly creamed Mimi. I think someone threw it at her on purpose."

"Let's get you checked out, Mimi," he said. "There's a medical assistance tent near the Renoir Retreat."

He reached for my hand. I shied away.

"I'm fine," I murmured. And I was. My pulse had settled down. My toes were intact. No shards had scathed me. "I need to return to the bistro."

"They can manage without you for a half hour," Jo said. "I think a cup of tea in the library is in order to get your wits about you. Thanks, Rusty." She clasped my hand and steered me into the inn.

First we stopped by the kitchen, where Jo threw together a tray of blood-orange sorbet, oolong tea, and bite-sized orange scones. She added a tub of marmalade and ushered me into the library, a room I adored. It was small but fashionable, adorned with an eclectic assortment of comfy reading chairs and lamps. Two walls were filled with books—romances, mysteries, and classics—that guests could read during their stay. We settled in at the walnut chess table. The pieces were set on their squares. Jo shuffled them to one side and set down our treats.

"So, truth," she said. "Do you think the flowerpot incident was accidental?" She poured tea into white porcelain cups and divvied the scones, two for each of us, onto matching plates.

"The shards indicated the pot might have been small. Maybe someone accidentally bumped it and it fell through the balusters. If that's the case, we should have Raymond attend to that."

"Fatter pots. Check." Jo slathered one of her mini scones with marmalade and popped it into her mouth. After she swallowed, she said, "Why were you gawking at Rusty?"

"He was dressed in tan."

"As are all the festival employees."

"Right." I picked up the king chess piece and rolled it between my fingers.

"Why would Rusty want to hurt you?"

I set the king with the other men. "I haven't been particularly unbiased when it comes to him. I told him that I know he lied about his alibi for the night Renee was killed."

"Mimi." Jo clasped my hand. "How could you? If he's dangerous—"

"A chef acts on the fly. A recipe goes wrong, a chef fixes it by improvising."

"In the kitchen," she chided. "Not out in the real world."

I wrenched free of her grasp and bit into a scone. The flavor, enhanced by orange zest, popped in my mouth. I ate the rest and wrapped my hands around my teacup. The warmth soothed me.

Jo said, "Let's refocus on Felicity. At the time of the incident, we were talking about her, not Rusty. Like you said, if she was on the balcony, she could have heard us."

"But why throw a pot? She had to know if it hit me, it wouldn't kill me."

"Maybe she hoped to knock you out so you'd get amnesia."

I gulped.

"You should check out her alibi," Jo said.

"Oh, sure, and how do I do that?" In singsong fashion I said, " 'Gee, Felicity, where were you when a flowerpot careened in my direction?' As if she'd answer." I gave my pal the stink eye. "I'll tell Tyson."

"Except he wants you to butt out." She smirked. "Speaking of him . . ." Jo spooned more sugar into her tea and stirred.

"Yeah, speaking of him, he's head over heels for you. Why aren't you ready to commit?"

"I'm not ready to be a stay-at-home mom."

"He wouldn't expect you to be."

"How can you be sure? He's an old-fashioned, by-the-book man. Look at him. He's got that Buffalo Bill Cody beard"—she stroked her chin—"and he says, 'Yes, ma'am,' and 'No, siree.'"

"I've never heard him say, 'No, siree.' Not even once!"

"He does." She crossed her heart and hoped to die.

I smacked the table. "Hey, I know, let's start a daycare for the employees at the inn and bistro. That way any of the staff that need the service can avail themselves of it. And if and when you have kids, they're in!"

Jo pushed her teacup away and propped her elbows on the table. "What about the cost of insurance?"

"It can't be that much, can it?"

"Yes, it can." She rubbed her thumb and fingers together. "Big bucks."

"Tyson's sister's law firm provides daycare for employees."

"Her firm is huge!"

"Research it. You're the money wizard. Make it happen. I want the staff happy." A bittersweet memory flitted through my mind. Bryan Baker would have said, *Your people matter. Don't skimp.* Thinking of him and how he exuded a positive attitude perked me up. I popped the rest of my scone into my mouth and polished it off in seconds. "No matter what, I'll bet Tyson will be hands-on with kids."

Jo studied me. "Are you taking his side so he'll be more open to your curious nature?"

"My what?"

"Your snooping."

"Ooh, how I hate that word. That's the word *he* uses. I don't snoop."

"You *listen*. You *care*," she chimed. Yes, she'd heard my argument before.

I took a sip of tea and set my cup down with a *clack*. "All I'm saying is that I think the two of you are a good match. You're"—I flicked my fingers like a wizard—"magic. Work it out. Thanks for the chat. Gotta go!"

On my way to the bistro, I risked wandering through the festival one last time, hoping to spy Felicity with Oscar's jacket or at the very least looking guilty. I didn't see her anywhere.

"Mimi, hold up!" a man called.

I pivoted and spotted Eli strolling toward me looking quite relaxed in a white linen shirt and slacks.

"Nice to see you again," he said.

"You, too. How were you able to get another day off?"

"Actually, my boss wanted to see the festival. She's thinking of holding one at our place. That's her, over there."

He gestured to a very tall brunette woman in mocha yoga pants and a spandex top. She was talking to Rusty and a woman in a sleek beige tennis outfit. The tennis player was holding the hand of a child in a tan Boy Scout outfit. I gawked. Had everyone gotten the brown-toned color memo today? Were there more Scouts around? Maybe one of them had sent the flowerpot sailing over the railing.

I redirected my attention to the mother. The way she was toying with her blonde ponytail made me think of Ursula Drake. I thought of how she had debunked Rusty's alibi. Rusty caught sight of me and held up a finger as if asking me to stick around so he could join me shortly.

"I hear Willow is selling out of stock," Eli said. "She's very pleased."

"I'll bet she is."

"Are you okay?" He lowered his head to peer into my eyes. "You seem distracted."

"A few minutes ago, a flowerpot almost clocked me."

"Whoa. Sorry to hear that. A flowerpot hit me once. In New York. It came from five stories above and knocked me unconscious. I had to have six stiches." He tapped the side of his head. "Luckily my hair grew back."

"Did someone hurl it at you?"

"No, a housekeeper was dusting." He put a hand on my shoulder. "Are you saying someone threw it at you on purpose? Geez. Who did you tick off?"

"I'm not sure. Maybe the councilman's wife."

"Felicity Price?"

"Do you know her?"

Eli nodded. "She bought four of Willow's pieces that first day. She's here. I saw her in the souvenir tent buying T-shirts a few minutes ago."

"Was she with anyone?"

"Nope."

"Was she wearing a beige overcoat?"

"Animal or mineral?" Eli grinned.

"Huh?"

"Why the game of twenty questions?"

"Oh, of course." I shrugged. "I guess I'm a little shaken."

"She was wearing a blue dress with a blue-and-gold ribbon pinned to it and had a duffle bag strapped over her shoulder. Listen, I have to get back to my boss." He squeezed my arm. "I meant what I said. Let's get together and catch up."

"Your voicemail message. Gosh. I'm sorry. I meant to call you back."

"No worries. I know you're busy. See you."

As Eli sauntered off, Rusty ended his conversation with the women and jogged to me. "Hey, Mimi, how are you? That must have been quite a scare." His eyes were warm. Could a killer gaze at me with such genuine caring? But suddenly he cooled and recoiled. "What's wrong? Why are you looking at me like that?"

How was I regarding him, like a judge and jury? I would have to work on my impartial stare.

"If you're worried that I lied about going to Chocolate the night Renee died, don't," Rusty said. "I fessed up to the sheriff. I saw him about twenty minutes ago. I caught up to him in the parking lot."

"I'm not worried about that."

"Then what?"

Bite your tongue, Mimi. "It's nothing."

Rusty grunted. "C'mon, level with me."

Deliberating, I worked my tongue around the inside of my mouth. "On the night Renee died, an eyewitness saw you driving around Camille's neighborhood with your headlights switched off."

Rusty lowered his chin and worked his tongue inside his cheek. "Yeah, okay."

"She thought you might have parked down the street and snuck to the house."

"What? Uh-uh. I did not!"

"She said she saw someone wearing a heavy coat and a hunter-style hat heading in that direction."

"I don't own a hat like that."

"She said the guy was limping."

"It wasn't me. My legs work perfectly fine." He kicked out one leg followed by the other and stamped them in place. "Grade A legs. Never had an injury."

A couple of festival folks drifted nearer to us. Maybe they thought Rusty was teaching me a new dance and wanted to join in the fun.

Rusty placed a hand on my lower back and ushered me to a quieter location. "What else? There's something else, isn't there? C'mon, talk to me. I can take it, whatever it is."

"Okay, the night Renee was killed, I noticed feathers and chicken feed on Camille's kitchen floor. Camille thought Renee might have tracked it in, but I believe you did. The sheriff's forensic team can probably prove that."

He jammed his hands into his pockets. "Aw, heck. Yeah, I was there. But it's not what you think. I missed Renee so much. I wanted to see her. But it wasn't me in the coat and hat. I was wearing what you saw me in that night, jeans and my baseball cap. I had my denim jacket on. That has to be where the feathers and feed came from. That junk clings to denim something fierce." He pulled his hands from his pockets and splayed one. "I went up to the front door. It was open. I saw Renee through the screen door. She was singing along with Sinatra. I knocked and entered. She whirled on me, madder than a wet hen. She said she was baking and needed to concentrate."

"She was going to learn to make soufflé."

He scrubbed his cheek with his knuckles. "She always wanted to be a better cook. Like Camille. I think she was jealous. Camille got all the talent; she had none. Heck, she could burn water." He lowered his arm. "She ordered me to leave. I said I would after we talked. She said if I loved her, I would go and we could discuss things the next day. I told her what I needed to say couldn't wait, but she didn't want to hear it. She shook her fist and started screaming that she hated me and to go, go, go!"

"How did that make you feel? Mad?"

"No, not mad. Sad. Really sad." His eyes narrowed. "I threw up my hands"—he mimed the action—"and told her as I was leaving that I would love her to my dying day."

Or hers, I thought sadly. I said, "If it's any consolation, Felicity Price told me that Renee loved you."

"Yeah, right. Felicity Price believes in fairy tales." He heaved a sigh. "Renee hated me, that was clear, and she went to her grave hating me. I'll never get over that, Mimi. Never. But I didn't kill her. Look, I lied about my alibi because I knew it was dicey seeing as I was at the house that night. It was stupid, but it's all I've got. I left fuming and drove around. When I calmed down, I came back to talk to her one more time about . . ." He studied the cuticles of his left hand.

"About what?"

"About me selling the farm and helping her with her new venture." He splayed his arms to take in the festival. "When she kicked me out, I knew I'd have to prove to her how much I loved and believed in her, so I started researching stuff on the Internet."

"Rusty, c'mon, you admitted you didn't go to Chocolate."

"No, I didn't, but I used my cell phone. I parked on some street where the reception was good."

"Which street?"

"I can't remember the name." He scuffed the ground with the heel of his shoe. "When I couldn't find squat about how to sell the farm, I started making phone calls to a bunch of attorneys. I wanted to see if any of them would handle the sale of the farm. Nobody answered."

"It was late. Did you leave messages?"

"Yeah, of course. I even decided to swing by the courthouse on the off chance some attorney might be there. No one was."

"Did you tell the sheriff the names of the law firms you called?"

"It didn't come up." He held up his left hand. "Look, I've got to get to work. Things are getting into full swing now that the wind has died down."

"You should talk to Sergeant Daly again. Give him facts and figures."

"Will do. Promise." As he ran off, he shouted, "Thanks for believing me."

I hadn't said I did.

Chapter 17

The preparations for Thursday dinner went smoothly. Allie was working out well as a support to Camille. The kitchen staff seemed to be enjoying the positive energy. I caught Stefan smiling. Maybe he was doing so because Yukiko was nearby. I wondered again whether I should nip a staff romance in the bud but decided it wasn't my business. If things cooled between them, I wouldn't fire either unless they weren't doing their jobs.

During dinner, as I toured the kitchen taste-testing and offering suggestions—the hollandaise sauce needed a bit more lemon; the sweet potato *pommes frites* were crying out for a dash of cayenne—I felt a frisson of dread crawl up my neck. I swiveled and caught Allie, who was stirring something in a large pot, gazing at me with a curious look in her eyes. Her white chef's jacket was splattered with red sauce. I shivered as I recalled Heather's warning—okay, Heather's *vibes*—that I should beware of a woman in white. Had she envisioned Allie hurting me? Did Allie have an inkling that I was trying to figure out who killed Renee and that she had, at one time, been on my suspect list?

Granted, she couldn't have hurled the flowerpot at me. At the time she would have been here in the kitchen.

I tamped down my angst and sidled up to her. "What are you making?"

"*Purée à la ratatouille*, heavy on the red pepper," she said. "Chef will set grilled halibut on top."

"Yum." I fetched a new spoon—we never used the same spoon to taste-test—and dipped it into the mixture. The texture was perfect, and the flavor on the Scoville heat scale—a determinant for spiciness—was a tad under three thousand, which I preferred for this dish. "Lovely."

Allie beamed. "I get to help her prepare the soufflés tonight, too."

"Lucky you."

Heather entered the kitchen, paused in the doorway, and hooked a finger. "Mimi."

I tossed the tasting spoon into the sink and joined her. "What's up?"

She jutted her chin toward the main dining room. Felicity and Parker were seated at one of the tables by the window. Felicity was wearing an ecru sheath with a revealing sweetheart neckline. Parker wore a sport jacket over a gray-checkered shirt. Both were sipping their water; neither was looking at the other.

Heather whispered, "They showed up without a reservation. We had a cancelation."

"I'm glad we could accommodate them."

"Ahem. Did you notice the color of her dress?"

"It's not white," I said, still worried about the unsettling feeling I'd experienced in the kitchen.

"It's close." Heather furrowed her brow. "Do you want me to do reconnaissance? I could listen in and see if they're talking about you."

I grinned. Her feisty spirit was giving me a boost of energy. "Why don't I handle it?" I strode to the hostess podium, gathered two menus, and carried them to the Prices. "Welcome." I offered my most winning smile.

Felicity's eyelids fluttered as she peered upward. She placed a hand on mine as I offered her a menu. "Heavens, Mimi. I heard about the incident at the festival. How are you?"

"What incident?" Parker asked.

"A flowerpot almost nailed Mimi when it fell through the railing."

In truth, I believed it had soared *over* a railing, which suggested an outside agency at work.

"Are you shaken up?" Felicity asked.

"I'm right as rain," I said, using my grandmother's favorite age-old expression.

Felicity shimmied in her chair and fluffed her hair as a cool breeze hit me on the back. I spun around. Oscar Orsini was entering the bistro. He slipped a notebook into the inside pocket of his brown jacket, smoothed his hair, and addressed Heather. She waved at me and held up a single finger. Didn't he have a reservation, either? Why had he shown up? Did he know Felicity was dining here? I recalled their flirtatious interlude at the cooking contest. Was his interest more than a dalliance? Had they met privately to finish the interview?

As Heather led him in our direction, a number of female diners gave him an appraising glance. When they neared the Prices' table, Felicity smiled with impish pleasure. Parker opened the menu.

Oscar stopped. "Felicity, good evening. Parker, my man." He extended his hand.

Parker offered a terse nod but didn't shake. Felicity's mouth turned down in a frown. Had she asked Oscar to stop by to make Parker jealous? If so, her ploy wasn't working.

"Parker, don't be a boor," she said. "Say hello."

"Hello."

"Oscar, darling," Felicity crooned. "When will the article be ready?"

Parker raised an eyebrow. "What article?"

Felicity ran a finger seductively along the neckline of her dress. "Oscar is doing a piece on me for the newspaper since I won the semifinal. He writes for the *Napa Valley Neighborhood*."

"Never heard of it," Parker said.

Oscar repeated the spiel he'd given me about the expanse of his audience.

"Parker"—Felicity put her hand on his—"he wants to do a sideline on you, too. It'll be great publicity for your next campaign."

"Whatever." Parker folded his menu and said, "Mimi, I'd like to order."

To his credit, Oscar didn't flinch at the curt dismissal. In a confident voice, he said, "Have a delightful dinner, you two," and moved on.

Felicity sniffed. She craned her neck to see where Heather was taking Oscar.

"Want to know the specials?" I asked.

Parker said, "Please tell me you have that *duck à l'orange* tonight. I didn't see it on the menu."

"It's listed at the bottom right corner along with the *porc à l'orange*," Felicity said with a bite. "Anything orange is hard to miss."

Parker ignored the barb and opened the menu. He searched for the item, found it, and closed his menu with a snap. "That's what I'm having."

"I'm not ready yet," Felicity said. "What are the specials, Mimi?"

"For the appetizer, *chausson du fromage chêvre*. For the salad, a mini *salade Niçoise*. For the main course, either a vegetarian *champignon parmentier au gratin*—that's a portabella mushroom topped with mashed potatoes and Gruyère cheese—plus we're offering grilled halibut topped with *purée à la ratatouille.*"

"Perfect. I'll have the first two and the halibut." Felicity closed her menu.

Parker cleared his throat. "Are you sure you want all that, hon?"

"Are you insinuating that I'm fat?"

"Of course not, but you want to save room for dessert." He gazed at me. "Make sure you reserve one of the chef's chocolate brandy soufflés for me, Mimi."

"Make that two." Felicity stared at her husband, daring him to object. When he didn't, she said with saccharine sweetness, "And I'll pass on the *chausson* whatever."

"Chausson chêvre," Parker said.

"Right." Felicity scrunched her nose in a kittenish way. "And we'll have a bottle of that tantalizing Chardonnay from your mother's winery. I had it the last time I was here because your boyfriend Nash said it was so good." She tapped my arm. "By the way, is he ever adorable. I spent time with him when he was volunteering at the festival. What a catch." She batted her eyelashes in the direction of her husband, and again I wondered whether she was trying to make him jealous. He didn't seem to be listening. He was scrolling through email on his cell phone. "Apparently my husband is attending to correspondence from his constituents. Isn't he dedicated?"

"Seems to be," I said. "Enjoy your dinner."

Around nine thirty, a table of six women who had polished off a half dozen of the specialty soufflés asked to see Chef C. As she emerged through the kitchen door, the women rose to their feet and started whooping like a band of gleeful fans. They weren't drunk in the slightest, simply enthusiastic. My crowd-shy chef recoiled. Heather and I each clutched one of her elbows and guided her toward the group.

"It's okay, Camille," I said.

She murmured, "It is only soufflé, and Allie made most of them."

"Yes, but you take the bows."

Many of the other patrons in the bistro started to applaud. I was sure some were doing so to show their support, knowing of her loss. She suffered through the praise gallantly.

When she and I returned to the kitchen, she gave me a fierce hug. "Mimi, thank you."

"You bet."

"Tomorrow morning, I want you to take it easy. Come in late. Allie is being a terrific help."

I pretended to be wounded. "You don't need me?"

"I will always need you, but you look tired"—she motioned to my eyes—"like your brain has been moving nonstop. A woman needs rest if she is to perform at her level best."

"Thanks, *Mom*," I jibed.

Later that night when I retreated to my cottage, our dutiful gardener was puttering in the vegetable garden, a flashlight in his hand.

I said, "Do you ever sleep, Raymond?"

"Rarely. I'm good with four hours."

The notion hit me that he might be hanging out to keep an eye on me. I had acted pretty jumpy Monday night after seeing the stranger in the vineyard, and again Wednesday evening after running into him when he was carrying the ladder. Plus, Jo might have alerted him to the flowerpot incident.

As I thought of the events as a whole, worry began to tick through me. Was someone trying to frighten me?

Shaking off the feeling, I entered the cottage and tossed my purse on the kitchen counter. Scoundrel and Scooter, who appeared out of nowhere, jogged inside with me and circled my ankles. I gazed at them. "Hello, you two. Are you staying?"

In response, both bounded to the bedroom. Cagney and Lacey, with their snouts pressed to the glass, reminded me of worried parents waiting up for a teenager. I fed them and told them to settle in for the night after they dined. They flipped their tails.

Close to midnight, I snuggled into bed with the cats nestled at my feet, and I opened a new mystery by Krista Davis about a posh pet hotel. I read three delightful chapters and fell asleep dreaming of vacations I wanted to take. With Nash.

* * *

Even though Camille had told me to come in late Friday morning, I awoke early. When I opened the door to the patio, the cats dashed out. I didn't worry. They would track down Heather for their breakfast. Wrapped in my robe, I sipped my first cup of coffee and listened to the birds. Then I downed a quickie breakfast of a warmed-up piece of autumn quiche and got dressed in my work clothes. I added some pink dangling earrings to go with my tourmaline necklace for a touch of sparkle.

Around nine AM, rather than heading directly to the bistro—if I showed up too early, Camille might read me the riot act—I decided to stroll through the festival. Surprisingly, even though the event was going on its sixth day, the crowds were still huge. For one day only, all the sweet-treats vendors were setting up create-your-own tables. Per the vendors' contracts, fifty percent of the proceeds would go to the education fund. Volunteers were helping out at each location.

In the Renoir Retreat, Tyson, a few of his deputies, and Jo—who looked radiant in a red-and-white ensemble—were assisting at COLORFUL COOKIES. The vendor had set up a buffet-style table draped with a red-checkered tablecloth. A flurry of parents and children surrounded the table. Nash was there, too, serving up sprinkles, chocolate chips, and cookie icing in plastic cups. Each cup cost a quarter.

"Hey, beautiful," he said as I drew near. He slipped an arm around my waist and pecked me on the cheek. "What a wonderful surprise to see you here."

A rush of desire swept through me. I kissed his cheek. "Good to see you, too."

"What are you doing? Playing hooky? Friday is your day in the kitchen."

"Chef C is so excited to be back, she told me to take the morning off."

"So she's the boss now?" He winked.

"I'm the boss, but she has a helper who's working out great. Why are you here?"

"Cookie and I go way back."

"Cookie?"

He hitched his thumb over his shoulder. "The vendor. Charles Charleston. Cookie is his nickname. His father owns The Charleston, a fine restaurant in St. Helena. Great southern food with a wine country flair." He handed a cup of sprinkles to a curly-headed girl. "How could I say no to a good cause? Want to decorate one, young lady?"

"Sure do."

Like a display model, he showed me his wares. "We have sugar cookies and chocolate cookies and all sorts of goodies to put on top."

"I'm making Oreos," a freckle-faced boy with a lisp said at full volume. "With the sprinkles on the inside. When I'm done, I'm going to dip them in a glass of milk, right, Mom?"

His equally freckly mother hushed him.

"I'm not being loud," he said.

She clucked at him. "Yes, you are." He sulked but settled down.

A woman in a lemon-yellow shift and matching hairband standing across the table with a peanut-sized girl, who was also clad in yellow, said, "Aren't kids cute?"

"Not always," the boy's mother replied.

Jo glanced at Tyson—he had wandered to the far side of the garden and was holding a cell phone to his ear—and then she whispered to me, "*Psst.*" She mouthed the word *kids* and waggled a hand in Nash's direction. What was she asking, whether he wanted children? Whether I did? Could I handle the mercurial whims of a child? Yes, of course I could, but was I too old to start trying? And how might having a child alter my career plans?

I chose not to respond and said, "What's up with Tyson?"

"Duty calls. A three-car pileup."

Tyson returned, pecked Jo on the cheek, and said, "I've got to leave. I'll speak to you later." He hustled out of the garden.

"Hey," Nash said to the freckle-faced boy, "how about adding chocolate chips to the inside of those Oreos, too?"

His mother sighed. "Don't encourage him."

"Sugar is sugar." Nash grinned. "Might as well eat it all in one rush. Besides, your donation is for a good cause."

"Yeah, the *dentist*," the mother joked and ruffled the boy's hair. "Go on. It's okay. This once."

The child squealed with delight.

As I was selecting cups of vanilla icing and pink sprinkles—my cookie might as well match my jewelry—the aroma of honey and roses wafted over my shoulder. I recognized the scent and turned. Willow was sashaying toward us in a gold, body-hugging wraparound dress and ultrahigh heels. A slight breeze whipped her hair off her face. A film star couldn't have made a more dramatic entrance. I felt immediately underdressed and unattractive.

Nash ran a finger along my neck. He must have picked up on my unease. She was not a threat, I reminded myself. He had ended his marriage; he liked *me.*

Walking alongside Willow was a lean man with a shaved head and a twinkle in his dark eyes. Though he wore a simple white short-sleeved shirt and jeans, his aqua-colored Christian Louboutin sneakers and Rolex Daytona watch gave away how wealthy he was. He looked about ten years younger than Willow. If my guess was right, this was Bennett, who lived in Camille's neighborhood.

"Mimi, how are you?" Willow gave me a cursory hug. "Let me introduce you to Bennett Jones."

"Hi." I jutted a hand in his direction.

He pumped it eagerly. "Pleasure."

Nash shook his hand as well. "So, Bennett, I hear you're in real estate."

"You might say that." He had a mellow voice and a winning smile.

"Bennett owns hotels," Willow gushed. "Lots and lots of them. In New York, London, and Singapore."

"Bennett," I said, "I heard you live near my chef, Camille Chabot."

"I do," he replied.

"It's his third home," Willow said.

"What a shame about Camille's sister," Bennett added.

"The other day a few of us were discussing something, Bennett," I said. "Maybe you could clear it up. Councilman Price has been seen in your neighborhood a few times."

"Parker? Yes, he has. Good man." Bennett glanced over his shoulder and back at us. "Can you keep a secret?"

Willow's gaze swung between him and me. "Well, don't leave us hanging. Of course we can all keep a secret."

"Parker is taking piano lessons from Betty. She said he's going to play a special song for his wife at their upcoming anniversary."

I balked. Did that prove that Parker hadn't had an affair with Renee? Was Felicity totally off-base in her assumption that he was having an affair at all? Which song? Maybe he was learning "So Long, Farewell," so he could break the news about being in love with Louvain. *Bad Mimi. Cynical Mimi.*

Willow said, "Enough about him." She gave Bennett's arm a squeeze. "Mimi, how are you holding up? Eli told me someone tossed a flowerpot at you."

Nash's eyes widened. "Who's Eli, and why did someone throw a flowerpot at you?"

"Eli's an old friend of Mimi's," Willow crooned. "Quite the charmer, if I do say so myself. He just moved back to town."

Nash eyed me.

"He was visiting the festival," I explained. "We ran into each other."

"Mimi," Willow continued, "I also heard someone was creeping around your place the other night."

Nash gazed at me again, worry in his eyes.

"That's not exactly what happened." I patted Nash on the arm to reassure him.

"It's not?" Willow gestured between herself and Bennett. "We saw Raymond on the way in. He said you were spooked."

I needed to have a chat with Raymond. My business was private. "Nothing to be concerned about." I offered a confident smile.

"I'm glad it was nothing," Willow said. "A single woman can't be too careful."

"A married woman, either," the woman in yellow said.

"Women in general," the freckle-faced mother added.

Willow nudged Bennett to move along. "Nash, could I have a word? It's about—" She twirled a finger.

Nash appeared torn, as if he wanted to grill me about the incidents—maybe even about Eli—but he obviously needed to respond to whatever Willow required first. A money matter, I imagined. He paid her alimony. "I'll touch base with you later," he said and hurried after his ex.

"Wow," the mother in yellow said. "She is a force, isn't she?"

"That she is." I grinned. "But I like her. She owns Fruit of the Vine Artworks in Yountville."

"I know it well. I've been there many times. Recently I needed to purchase a cookie platter for Felicity Price."

"As a gift?"

"Felicity's gift to another woman. I'm her personal shopper. My older daughter is in theater with Philomena."

"Is she performing in *Cats*?"

"Yes. She's loving it."

The younger daughter in yellow said, "I love my sister's costume. She has lots of sequins and ears and a tail. Mama made it. She made them all."

The mother blushed. "I'm handy with a needle. My name is Sally Somers, by the way."

"Mimi Rousseau." I brushed the vanilla icing on a sugar cookie and scattered the pink sprinkles on top.

"You own the inn and bistro."

"I do."

"They're both so lovely," she said. "I've eaten lunch at the bistro once. I adore what you've done with it. All the mirrors and that beautiful antique bar. Exquisite. And you're putting on this festival, too?" Sally pressed a hand to her chest. "How do you manage?"

"I'm not putting on the festival. The festival coordinator rented the space."

A cloud of doubt crossed Sally's face. "It's a shame what happened to her, isn't it? Does the sheriff have a suspect?"

"He's looking into it." I regarded Sally for a long moment. "If you're in charge of costumes, then you must have seen Felicity on the night of the murder. She said she was at the theater for a rehearsal."

"I did indeed. Poor thing." Sally clucked her tongue. "She was sicker than a dog and in the restroom the whole night. Must have been something she ate."

Curious, I thought. Why hadn't Felicity mentioned that she was sick? Maybe she had been embarrassed. Or maybe she'd lied to Sally to give herself an alibi and, conveniently out of sight, had slipped out.

Chapter 18

By the time I arrived at the bistro, way before we were due to open, the place was teeming with guests. Why? Because Heather had allowed a group of thirty educators to come in for an early lunch. They weren't dining yet—they were drinking iced tea—but the chatter about how the local schools were going to benefit from the festival's fundraiser was intense.

One of the female attendees, who was wearing a white togalike sheath with gold trim, clinked a glass with a spoon. As the noise died down, the woman began to sing to the tune of "Put a Little Love in Your Heart," adding her own lyrics which extolled the virtues of giving. Though her pitch was slightly off-key, nobody seemed to mind, not even Red, which surprised me. She played in a band on her days off and could be hypercritical of musicians and singers, and yet there she was behind the bar dancing to the beat as she opened bottles of wine.

"Hi, Mimi." Heather's face was aglow with good energy. "It does my soul proud to know that I had something to do with this."

"You?" I strode into the office.

"Yep." She followed while toying with the ruffled collar of her pink silk dress. "Raymond thought it would be a great idea, but he was too shy to mention it to Rusty, so I did."

"Well, I'll be."

As I flitted around the room from desk to file cabinet, checking orders and reviewing balances—why hadn't Bryan warned me how much paperwork was involved in running a business?—Heather propped herself on the corner of a chair and demurely crossed her ankles.

"By the way," she said, "Chef C is delighted that we have Allie."

"Really?"

"She's taken to her like a mother hen, and Allie seems to be soaking up the praise. I heard through the grapevine that she's an orphan. If she weren't so old, I'd adopt her myself."

"Get out of here." I pulled a check register from the desk drawer. "Do you want kids?"

Heather was in her forties. Not many women started families that late, though nowadays with all the advances in medicine, women were having babies into their fifties. I questioned my qualms regarding starting a family. I wasn't too old. Yet.

"I did. Once. But I couldn't."

"I'm sorry."

"Me, too. My sister told me I should've adopted."

"You have a sister?" I flipped the register open. It slapped the desk as if echoing my astonishment. "Does everybody have a sister except me?"

Heather giggled. "Maybe you do."

"No. I'd know if I did. My mother couldn't keep that kind of secret, and my father was as faithful as the sun." I endorsed three checks to vendors and stuffed them into the appropriate envelopes. "How would your husband feel about adopting?"

"He'd hate it since he works at home. Writers need peace and quiet."

"Boring." I mimed a yawn.

"I know!" She bounded to her feet and headed for the door. Before exiting, she pivoted and said, "Mimi, I don't know if I should say anything."

"About?"

"I'm still getting vibes."

"Come back here." I gestured for her to return. "Vibes about a woman in white?"

"Yes."

The fleeting concern I'd had about Allie in her white chef's jacket popped into my mind. I shoved it aside. "Go on."

She lowered her voice. "I went to see my hypnotherapist about it, and he put me under to see if he could dredge up anything more, you know, to help you with Camille."

"Camille is off the hook."

"Even so, she's mourning and you're still wondering who did it."

I set my pen down. "What are you, psychic?"

"I'm empathic."

"Did your therapist tell you that?"

"Hypnotherapist," she corrected. "And yes."

I groaned inwardly. Was this guy on the up-and-up? Maybe I should schedule a session with him to check him out. I worried about how impressionable my sweet assistant was. I motioned for her to continue. "Go on. What did your doctor discover?"

"He corroborated that I did have a dream about a woman in white. He said I couldn't make out her features, but she's definitely real."

"In your dreams."

Heather tittered. "I know it's not much to go on, but I'm telling you because I care about you."

Holy moly. Did I have three mothers now? What was the world

coming to? Maybe Camille and Heather were my *sisters*, or rather, sisters-in-arms. Yes, that sounded better.

Feeling frisky, I started to drum up names of women I should be careful around: my mother in command mode, Camille in worry mode, Jo in a panicked no-children-for-me mode—

"Boss?" Oakley hurried into the office and skidded to a stop. Her braids flopped forward over her shoulders. "Sorry to intrude, but we have a situation. Come quick!"

I raced from the office and tore across the dining room. Heather followed.

Oakley said over her shoulder, "The diva accidentally swallowed a lemon wedge."

"The diva?" I asked.

Oakley pointed.

The operatic wannabe was sitting in a chair, arms raised overhead. Her lips were blue and her eyes pinpoints of fear. Two of her fellow fundraisers were standing astride her looking flummoxed.

"Step aside," I said. "I'll take over."

When I was a girl, my father had saved a boy who was drowning in a lake. Four families had gone for a day picnic. My father dove in, brought the boy to the surface, and stuck his finger down the boy's throat to dislodge his tongue, which he'd swallowed. I would never forget that moment. To save a life was a powerful skill. The very next day, I'd begged my father to enroll me in a CPR class.

"Has anyone attempted the Heimlich maneuver yet?" I asked.

No one responded.

"She tried to cough it up," Oakley said.

"And sucked it further down her throat." I pointed to her two comrades. "Help her to a standing position."

They obeyed. I slipped behind the woman, wrapped my arms

around her ribcage, and, clutching my left wrist with my right hand, gave a firm abdominal thrust. The exerted pressure to the woman's diaphragm made her moan.

"I'm going to do it again, ma'am." I repeated the effort.

She heaved, and suddenly a yellow piece of fruit burst from her mouth. She gulped in air and swung around to face me. Tears streamed down her cheeks. "Thank you," she rasped.

The woman's friends helped her to her chair. The crowd breathed a sigh of relief. Crisis averted.

Oakley offered the woman some water. "Ma'am, sip slowly," she cautioned.

I said to Heather, "Maybe she was the woman in white."

Heather gawked. "You could be right. Yes! That's it! *Phew.* What a load off my mind."

Full voice, I announced, "Ladies and gentleman, the wine is on us." I signaled Red, who nodded in understanding. My cell phone buzzed in my pocket. I pulled it out and scanned the screen: Nash was calling.

Heather said, "Our next wave of customers is due any moment."

"Alert the kitchen that I'll be right there. I've got to answer this." I hurried to my office and pressed SEND. "What's up?"

Quickly he apologized for running off to chat with his ex-wife.

Willow, I mused. Maybe she was the woman in white that I had to be careful around, although she rarely wore anything pale; she adored color. I chuckled at the gall it had taken for her to mention Eli in front of Nash. Honestly!

Nash continued to explain. As I'd suspected, Willow had a money issue. She'd asked for an advance on her alimony because of a hiccup in accounting at the shop. He'd gone there to review her books, found the glitch, and the problem was solved. When he finished his tale, he said, "How are you?"

"Busy!" I told him about the choking incident.

"You're encountering one disaster after another. Tell me about the flowerpot thing and the stranger hanging outside your cottage."

"I will, soon, but I can't talk right now. We're getting slammed in about thirty seconds. Two seatings again for lunch."

"Sorry. Bad timing. I'll catch you later. Be safe. I—" He hesitated, then said, "Bye."

I could only guess what he'd wanted to say after the word *I*. I love you? I miss you? I wish I could hold you in my arms and smother you with kisses?

Yeah, a career as a romance novelist was definitely *not* in my future.

* * *

When the kitchen staff were heading out for the afternoon break and I saw Allie exiting last, for some reason the hackles on my neck rose. Why? She didn't look particularly suspicious. She wasn't wearing her white chef's jacket. She was walking normally. Maybe I sensed something was up because one of her hands was worrying an object in her pants pocket and the other was clutching the strap of her purse in a death grip.

Was I getting vibes like Heather all of a sudden? Allie was working out well in the kitchen. Everyone had warmed to her. Surely I didn't need to be fearful of her.

Even so, I grabbed my purse and discreetly followed her to the parking lot, where she slipped into a silver VW Beetle, lowered the convertible top, and sped out of the lot. I climbed into my Jeep and zipped after her, keeping a reasonable distance away. If she was simply grabbing a breath of fresh air, then I would do the same.

As we turned north onto St. Helena Highway, traffic slowed to a crawl. Throngs of people wearing Crush Week paraphernalia were strolling along the sides of the road. Many were carrying two- and four-packs of wine.

At Spring Street, Allie veered left. I made the turn and inhaled sharply. We were entering Camille's neighborhood. Two blocks farther, she veered onto Camille's street. She drove past a number of contemporary houses, a rustic barn–style house, and three Victorians. Maybe she was house hunting. Maybe she lived nearby. I hadn't paid attention to the temporary employment record she had filled out. I didn't know her address.

When she swerved onto Camille's street, however, I gulped. Her trip to the area was not a coincidence. She had come here on purpose. Why? At a snail's pace she inched past Camille's house. To prevent her from noticing me, I pulled to the side, as if I were preparing to visit someone.

After a moment, Allie continued on and I breathed easier. I put my car into gear but drew to a halt because Allie had stopped beyond the white Victorian with the white roses. She parked and exited the car. Purse clutched to her chest, she hustled to Camille's house.

I pulled over and rested my elbow on the windowsill of my car and blocked my face with my cell phone. I doubted she knew I drove a Jeep, but better safe than sorry. I hoped she would ignore me, assuming I was a stranger reviewing messages or a lost driver consulting GPS.

As she scurried up the path to the front door, I put the car in gear and swung into Irene's driveway across the street. I glimpsed over my shoulder.

Allie didn't knock on the door. She peeked through a window and my insides snagged. Maybe she had killed Renee. Maybe she'd wanted to retrieve evidence that might implicate her. The sheriff could have overlooked something. She dug into her pocket and withdrew a set of keys. Where had she gotten those? Had Camille given them to her? Had she asked Allie to fetch something for her? If so, why had Allie parked down the street and not in Camille's driveway? She opened the screen door and slotted a key into the lock.

Before pushing the door open, Allie glanced over her shoulder. I hunkered down in my seat. Should I go in after her? No, that would be risky. If she was the killer, she could grab a butcher knife before I reached the threshold to the kitchen. If she wasn't guilty and Tyson found out that I had followed her believing she was up to no good, I would never hear the end of it. Could he—*would* he—put me in jail for obstruction?

I sat tight and waited.

Minutes later, Allie exited, locked the front door, and darted down the street. Looking as guilty as all get-out, she popped into her car and tore off.

Chapter 19

When I returned to work, adrenaline was coursing through me. I pulled into the parking spot and heard a honk. Across the lot near the vegetable garden, Raymond was perched on his eco-friendly gardening cart, talking to a guest of the inn—the Crush Week woman who had done the Lucy experience at Grgich Hills Winery. He held up a finger for me to wait. He was tapping something on a cell phone. He handed the cell phone to the woman and pedaled his cart to me.

"Hi, Mimi." He dismounted. "Are you okay?"

"I'm fine."

"No sightings? No skittish kittens?"

"Errands." Far be it for me to tell him I'd recently completed a reconnaissance mission. I would keep mum. He was a blabbermouth. *Loose lips . . .* "What were you up to over there?" I nodded at the guest who was aiming her cell phone camera at plants.

"I was teaching her about a garden app: *My Garden Answers.* You point and snap a picture of a flower or plant, and the name pops up. She can then talk to a plant specialist. It's so cool. She's worried about plants in her garden that might harm her Shih Tzu. Poisons are everywhere in a garden, you know. Cyclamen, lilies, oleander." Raymond ticked the names off on his fingertips.

"Can any harm cats?"

"Sure. Cats as well as dogs. Curious pets might eat the leaves or ingest seeds. The roots of crocus are especially bad, but don't worry. I've seen your cats and they aren't vegetarians."

"My cats?"

"Scoundrel and Scooter."

"They aren't my cats."

"If they stay in your house, they're yours. That's how I got mine."

"You have cats?"

"Six. All strays." He chuckled. "Man, have you got a lot to learn. But like I said, not to worry. Neither of them is interested in plants. They like meat. They're hunters. See, cats lack taurine, and taurine is an essential building block of proteins. Without it, cats can't survive for long, so they make up for the deficiency by being carnivores. Mice are the easiest prey. You've heard the term *cornered like a mouse*, haven't you? But cats will go for birds and moles, too. Anything small and easy to catch."

"Swell," I murmured, not excited to see what gifts the cats might bring me. Over the past year, Scoundrel had brought me a bird or two. With two cats, would I be the recipient of double the pleasure?

Raymond placed a hand on my arm. "Mimi, you're fibbing."

"About?"

"You're not fine. Something has gotten under your skin. You're perspiring and your gaze is darting every which way."

I blotted my upper lip with my fingertips. "I'm hot. That's all. And parched." *Liar, liar.* "Maybe I'll go to Chocolate and pick up a cool drink before returning to work." I didn't add: *And to collect my thoughts before returning to the kitchen and Allie.*

"Okay. Take care. Drink lots of water, too. If you need to talk, I'm here."

As Raymond remounted his cart, I said, "Hey, Raymond, it's nice of you to always help the guests. I really appreciate it."

"Glad to do it. I love educating people. What better way to make them stewards who will preserve the earth, right?"

As he drove away, I hurried down the road to Chocolate, eager to get my hands on one of Irene's iced chocolate sodas.

To my surprise, Felicity was standing near the doorway, sneakily peeking through the sidelight. *Sneakily*, I believed, because she could have easily peered through the door's larger window. Parker's office was located nearby. Was he inside the café? Did she think he was bold enough to meet his lover at the café in broad daylight?

"Hi, Felicity," I said.

She whipped around. Her cheeks were tear-stained. She quickly donned a pair of chartreuse sunglasses that matched her sundress. "Mimi, it's you! You surprised me."

"Are you going inside?"

"Um"—she bit her lip, deliberating—"I'm trying to decide. Is it too hot for coffee? I think it might be too hot for coffee. What do you think? Too hot?"

"I'm going to order an iced chocolate soda."

"Ooh, that sounds good. May I join you?"

"I'm taking mine to go."

"Sit with me for a few minutes. We should get to know each other better."

"Uh, sure. I've got a few minutes." *Just a few.*

I walked through the entrance first and held the door for her. She strolled in, her gaze riveted on Parker, who was sitting at the counter. A mug of a steaming beverage sat in front of him. A guy in a red plaid shirt sat beside him. Parker was telling him a story. The guy's shoulders were shaking from laughter. To my surprise, Rusty Wells, who almost matched the décor in his tan festival outfit, was sitting beside the guy in plaid. He was staring straight ahead, finger circling the rim of his coffee cup. He must have been seated before Parker entered, and even though he clearly did not like the councilman, had decided not to cede ground.

When Parker finished, his buddy drummed a rim shot on the counter. "Ba-dum-dum. Funny one!"

"Mimi, order me an Earl Grey tea, black," Felicity said.

"I thought you wanted something cool."

"Tea. Thanks. Tell Irene to put it on my tab. I have to go to the restroom."

I gawked. She had a tab? I didn't have one, but then I liked to pay cash for everything when I could. *No debt* was one of my mottoes.

As she walked briskly down the hallway, her high heels clickety-clacking on the tile floor, I sidled up to the counter to the left of Parker.

He rotated his head to see who had encroached on his space and frowned. At me? Or at seeing his wife heading toward the restroom?

"Hello, Parker," I said.

His buddy swiveled on his chair. "Hi, Mimi, how're you doing?" He was a vintner who regularly visited the bistro.

"I'm well. How about you?"

"Super."

"Hi, Rusty," I said.

"Mimi." One word. No warmth.

"Hey, Mimi, do you want to hear a good joke?" the vintner asked. "Parker just told it to me." Mimicking Parker's tone, he said, "This country is great. It's the only place where you can borrow money for a down payment, get a first and second mortgage"—he ticked the joke beats on the countertop—"and call yourself a homeowner." He guffawed. "Isn't that hysterical?"

"And true," Parker said. "It wouldn't sound nearly as hip to call oneself a debt owner."

"Ha-ha," the vintner chuckled.

Parker leaned forward and said to Rusty, "So, who's running your farm while you're manning the festival?"

Rusty stared daggers at Parker. "My sister."

I snickered. Even Rusty had a sister?

"What's so funny, Mimi?" he snapped.

"I was wondering whether I'm the only person on the planet without a sister. I'm feeling sort of shortchanged."

"I don't have one," Parker said. "I'm an only child."

"Aw, man, that sucks," the vintner said. "I've got eleven siblings."

Irene waltzed up to the counter. "What'll it be, Mimi?"

"One Earl Grey tea, black, and an iced chocolate soda. Put the tea on Felicity Price's tab."

"My wife is here?" Parker said, trying but failing to feign surprise.

"She went to the restroom," I said.

"I didn't know you two were buddy-buddy."

"We're—" *Lie, Mimi.* "We need to get better acquainted. Ooh. I see a free table. I'm going to nab it."

Parker clutched my elbow. "Are you prying her for information? Are you trying to see if she knows anything about Renee's murder?"

"Any treats, Mimi?" Irene cut in.

Parker must have forgotten she was standing there. He released me like a hot potato.

"Two croissants." I pulled twelve dollars from my purse and handed it to her. "Keep the change." If Felicity didn't want her croissant, I'd take it to the bistro for Heather.

I excused myself and strode to the vacant table, eager to put the tense moment with Parker behind me. I tilted a chair against the table and unfolded the napkins. By the time I returned to the counter, Irene had already set the tea and soda down.

Parker said, "Irene will bring the rest of your order over in a second." He paid for his beverage, pushed the cup aside, and rose to his feet. "Take care, Mimi."

The vintner and Rusty echoed him. "Yeah, take care, Mimi."

As I was carrying the drinks to the table, Felicity emerged from the hallway. She skirted past the counter and gave Parker a peck on the cheek. When he didn't reciprocate, she flinched but recovered and strolled across the café to where I was seated. Seconds later, Parker and his pal exited.

"Fancy seeing my husband here," Felicity said as she settled into her chair and grabbed two packets of sugar-free sweetener. One went flying in my direction and skidded off the table. I bent to retrieve it. When I resituated myself, I handed the packet to her. "Thanks," she said and dumped the contents of both packets into her tea. She wiped her hands on her napkin. "Where were we?"

"You wanted to get acquainted." I took a sip of my soda. The coolness was refreshing.

Irene arrived with our croissants. "Here you go." She set them down and moved on.

"So, Mimi"—Felicity stirred her drink—"I heard you were talking to Sunny Sally about me."

"Sally Somers?"

"The theater mom who lives and breathes yellow. Yellow clothes. Yellow furniture. Yellow housewares. Heck, even her house is painted yellow and her garden palette is yellow. Hence the nickname Sunny." Felicity giggled like a schoolgirl. "Don't worry. I'm not gossiping. It's a small town. Everyone talks."

"She told me she was your personal shopper."

"On occasion. Sally also told you I was sick at the theater the night Renee died." She sipped her drink and looked over the rim of her glass. "Were you asking about me, Mimi?"

"No." Far be it for both her and her husband to think I was prying. "We were talking about her daughter performing in *Cats* with Philomena. Sally offered the rest."

Felicity bobbed her head. "The porcelain bowl and I became fast friends."

My stomach rumbled something fierce. Was I suffering sympathy pangs? I took another sip of my soda.

"Must have been something I ate," she went on. "But enough about *that* subject. *Ugh.*" She took a sip of her tea and set the mug down. "Let's talk about that new gal you have working for you."

"Yukiko?"

"No. Allie O'Malley. Like I said, everybody around town talks, and the more time I spend at the festival, the more I've learned about her feud with Renee. Allie has quite a past. She—" Felicity spanked the table daintily with her fingertips. "Stop it, Felicity." She wriggled her nose. "Heavens, I really must get control of myself. I promised Parker that I would set a good example for our daughter and not gossip. Fourteen-year-olds can be so impressionable. No. More. Gossip." She twisted an imaginary key in front of her lips. "Let's talk about *you*."

I hated to admit it, but I was dying to know what she knew about Allie and her past, especially after following Allie to Camille's.

"I'm absolutely in love with Bistro Rousseau," Felicity went on. "I don't say that about many restaurants. How can Parker and I help your business grow?"

"We're doing great. We're sold out every night this week."

"Because of the festival and Crush Week. What a boon." She smiled solicitously. "But that can't last."

I blotted my lips with a napkin. “Even before either event began, word-of-mouth was bringing in plenty of business.”

“Well, if I can’t help you, then tell me about that handsome Nash Hawke. What plans do you have for him?” She lifted her croissant and bit off the end.

“Plans?” My stomach churned. Not in a good way. I took another sip of soda.

“Ting-a-ling. Wedding bells?”

“Oh, gosh, way too soon for that.”

“He and I were chatting at the festival the other day, and he seemed very into you.”

“He did?”

“Don’t let him get the idea you aren’t interested, darling.” She shook the remainder of her croissant at me. “Think of the big picture. A man roams if he doesn’t feel he’s your be-all and end-all. That’s what Parker is to me, and he knows it.”

After hearing her teary revelation at the competition and witnessing her subsequent barb about the color orange at dinner, I figured she was trying to convince herself that everything was hunky-dory between them.

“How’s it going with Oscar?” I asked.

“Oscar?” Her voice rose in a girlish manner.

“Your interview. Did you finish it?”

“Why, yes, we did. How sweet of you to ask. He’s such a delightful man.”

Where did Oscar Orsini fit into her big picture? Flirting with him hadn’t made Parker jealous.

My stomach roiled again. My face grew hot and moist. Suddenly the room started to spin. I felt like I was going to be sick.

Quickly, I begged off with Felicity, and not wishing to carry any sort of illness to the bistro, hurried home. Did I have the flu?

No. Maybe I had eaten something tainted, but what? I hadn't taste-tested anything before the noon crowd arrived. I'd only nibbled on cheese for lunch. I hadn't taken the teensiest bite of the croissant at the café.

As I pushed through the front door of my cottage, I pictured the soda sitting on the counter at Chocolate. Had Parker or Rusty, even though he'd been sitting a couple of seats away, put something in my drink when I was securing the table for Felicity and me? Both had told me to *take care*. Had that been a warning?

I rushed to the bathroom, grabbed a bottle of ipecac from the medicine cabinet, and downed the appropriate amount. Within seconds it did its magic. Minutes later, I felt worlds better. My stomach ached, but I was no longer perspiring and my dizziness had subsided. I wasn't going to die.

Even so, I called Jo.

Chapter 20

Sitting beside me on the sofa, Jo sort of blended in, dressed in her taupe pencil skirt and pretty cream-colored blouse. She patted my hand. "Are you sure you're okay? Do you need to go to the hospital?"

"I'm fine."

"As if." *As if* was one of her favorite sayings. "Your skin is pale. Your eyes are glassy."

"I'm okay. Promise." My stomach ached and I had a slight headache, but I could return to work. I didn't have to look good to do so.

"Somebody poisoned you." When we spoke on the phone, I told her what I thought had happened.

"Maybe it was food poisoning."

"From something you ate at Chocolate? Not a chance. Like you and me, Irene is a stickler for safety. If word gets out about a food issue"—she snapped her fingers—"reputation ruined! By the way, I searched the Internet on my way over, and I'm wondering if you were poisoned with strychnine."

"C'mon. If someone dosed me with that, I'd be dead." I rubbed my abdomen.

"No matter what, if it was intentional, then it was a warning like the flowerpot and the scare you got the other night when you thought someone was creeping around your place."

I gulped.

"Maybe a few self-defense classes would be in order," Jo suggested.

"Would that have kept me from drinking a chocolate soda?"

She glowered at me.

"If you'll recall," I went on, "I took defense classes in San Francisco. I know all about attacking soft targets. I can trap a hand and create an arm bar, and I'm darned good with elbow break-and-releases." Remaining seated, I mimed a demonstration on an invisible attacker.

"Okay. Got it. Your San Francisco stalker made you a tough cookie."

I hadn't really been stalked when I'd lived in San Francisco, but creeps had followed me twice. Knowing how those types thrived on attention, I'd ignored them. Due to their overt interest, however, I'd invested in a series of six self-defense classes. Every now and then, I practiced my moves in front of my goldfish. They watched with fascination.

My cell phone rang. I slogged off the couch, fetched it from my purse, and answered.

"Mimi," Tyson said. Wind whistled through the cell phone until he closed his vehicle window. "Jo texted me. Are you sick? Were you poisoned?"

I eyed my friend.

What? she mouthed.

Are you my mother now, too?

Too?

I nodded. I was starting to lose count of how many I had.

"I'm fine, Sergeant," I replied. "Thank you for being concerned. I think it might have been something I ate."

"Bullpuckey," Jo shouted.

"Bullpuckey," Tyson echoed. "What did you do, poke a hornet's nest?"

"Tyson"—I spoke loudly enough to let him know that I wasn't a pushover, no matter how icky I was feeling—"I wasn't poking into anything. I was having a soda at Chocolate."

"Uh-huh," he muttered.

"Before that, I was running errands," I fibbed. I would not—*not*—reveal that I had tailed Allie. "I was parched when I returned, so I decided to pop into the café before returning to work. I saw Felicity Price, and she asked me to join her."

"Is it possible that she poisoned you?" he asked.

"Yes," Jo blurted and twirled a finger, signaling she wanted to be included in the conversation. I pressed the SPEAKER button on the cell phone. "Tyson," she went on. "Mimi saw Parker there, too. She thinks Felicity was spying on her husband."

"Well, well," Tyson said. "That might explain a few things."

"Like what?" I asked.

"None of your beeswax," he replied.

Jo chuckled. I threw her a punishing stare.

"Tell him about how your soda was sitting on the counter," Jo said. "And how Parker was stationed nearby."

Obediently I filled him in on the details, adding that Rusty Wells was also at the café.

"I told you, you can rule out Parker Price as a suspect," Tyson said. "He would have no reason to want to harm you."

"How can you be so sure? Just because he was taking afternoon piano lessons in Camille's neighborhood doesn't clear him from being in the area that night."

"Piano lessons?"

I explained what Bennett Jones had told us. "I wasn't snooping," I added. "The information came up in a regular conversation."

Tyson's silence irked me. After a long moment, he said, "Mimi, I pinned down Parker's alibi and verified it. It pains me to say it, but you were right. He has a lover, and he was with her."

"Who?" Jo asked.

"Louvain Cook," I said. "Right?"

"Yes," Tyson admitted.

"Does she live in Camille's neighborhood?"

"No, Louvain lives miles away in Calistoga. She has confirmed Parker's alibi, which means he couldn't have been skulking around Camille's place."

"Unless Louvain was lying," Jo cut in.

"Felicity knows," I murmured.

"If she does, then Renee wouldn't have been her target," Tyson said. "Louvain or Parker would. As for Rusty Wells, his alibi checks out, too."

"No way!" Jo cried.

"Rusty came to the precinct," Tyson continued. "He said he told you, Mimi, about his argument with Renee at the house and decided he should bring me up to speed. You've told me everything else, but you didn't think to mention this?" Tyson clicked his tongue.

"We haven't had a moment to chat, and you've sort of made me feel like I should keep my trap shut."

Tyson cleared his throat. "The rest of what he stated bears out, too. His cell phone records show he called a number of attorneys over the course of an hour, right about the time the medical examiner figures Renee died. Rusty's Internet provider also confirmed his search that evening for farm sale sites online."

Jo rolled her eyes. "He could have done all that inside Camille's house."

"Sure, he could have," Tyson agreed, "but here's the kicker. A nun saw him loitering outside the courthouse at the time of death."

"A nun?" I coughed out a laugh. "You've got to be kidding."

"She was roaming the street looking for lost souls. She greeted Rusty, but she said he was absorbed in a chat on his cell phone."

"She came forward of her own accord?"

"She read a newspaper account about Renee. The reporter had included a wedding photograph of Renee and Rusty. She recognized him."

I ran my tongue along my teeth, processing the information. "Why didn't he mention her?"

"She said he didn't give her the time of day."

A silence fell between us.

Jo said, "Back to Felicity. She has to be the one that put something in Mimi's drink. Maybe she did it when you bent to retrieve those packets of sweetener that she sent flying off the table."

Tyson snorted. "How long did that take, Mimi, five seconds? Felicity would have to be pretty deft with sleight of hand to dose your drink."

A ridiculous image of Felicity yanking off tablecloths zipped through my mind. *Focus, Mimi.* "I agree. Besides, why would she want to hurt me?"

"Because you were snooping," Jo laughed and spanked my thigh.

I scowled. "That doesn't make sense. She would only have cause to hurt me if she'd killed Renee, and seeing as Parker wasn't involved with Renee—"

"You don't know that," Jo said. "Maybe he was having two affairs."

"Then why not dose *him* with the nausea-provoking poison? Why me?" I asked. "Tyson, Felicity said you questioned her about Renee."

He exhaled. "I questioned her and Parker. I wanted their take on Renee since they were working closely with her and the festival."

"Felicity said she told you her alibi."

"Yes. She was at her daughter's theater."

"Sally Somers corroborated that. She said Felicity got sick and spent most of the evening in the high school restroom. Unless—"

"Mimi." His tone was dark.

"Sally and I were chatting while icing cookies. People talk to me, Tyson."

He huffed.

I huffed, too, and didn't add my theory that Felicity might have pulled a fast one. If Sally said Felicity was there, she probably was. Did that leave Allie as the sole suspect? Her alibi was tenuous at best. "Tyson, I should tell you that I followed—"

All I heard was dead air. He had hung up.

* * *

I gave Jo a heartfelt hug, thanked her for her support, booted her out of my cottage, and headed to the bistro. If I got busy, I would forget about my aching stomach and Tyson's snub.

When I entered the bistro's kitchen, a soulful piano and cello rendition of Chopin's "Spring Waltz" was playing through the speakers. Red was receiving crates of wine. Chef C and Allie were reviewing the prix fixe list of options with Heather so she could print insertions for the menu. Oakley was telling Yukiko and Stefan about her parents' dude ranch that featured hoedowns and hayrides. She suggested that the two of them should go, which cemented my, *um*, concern that Yukiko and Stefan were hooking up. I pushed the notion aside. I couldn't worry about them now.

All chatter quieted when word spread that I had entered.

Heather hurried to me, her energy electric. Tendrils spilled out of her trendy updo. "Did you hear who's coming to dinner tonight?"

"How would I have? I arrived a second ago. Did you send a carrier pigeon with the message?"

"You're a hoot." She batted my arm. "Well, get ready, because it's royalty night. The leaders of the ten major wineries are dining with us."

My heart skipped a beat. Yes, the bistro was becoming more and more popular, but hosting the big guns was huge for prestige. If only I could get Oscar Orsini to write about this crowd.

"And guess who's hosting them?" she went on. "Your mother and her beau."

"Wow. Really? I knew Anthony had sway, but I had no idea he could pull off something like this."

"He didn't; your mother did. Crush Week has been making all the luminaries act like social butterflies. The French Laundry has been overrun with celebrities."

The French Laundry, located in Yountville, was included in *Restaurant Magazine*'s Top 50 restaurants in the world. To be mentioned in the same sentence with them was an honor.

Heather jutted her chin. "Look at Chef C. She's bubbling with excitement."

I had to admit that the increased activity did seem to be cheering her up.

"The dinner party isn't the only reason for her delight," Heather added.

"What else?"

"Donovan called her today. For a date."

"That explains why her eyes are sparkling."

"Let's be cautious with our enthusiasm," Heather warned.

"Why?" A prickle of fear skidded up the back of my neck. "Don't tell me you're having vibes again. Is something dire going to happen at the dinner?"

"No, although those wine bigwigs can be hypercritical." She lowered her voice. "I meant let's be cautious about Donovan. He's unpredictable. A date here, a date there. Nothing steady. If he breaks Camille's heart . . ."

"Gotcha." I nudged Heather to return to work while mentally chanting *no vibes, no vibes, no vibes.*

I caught Allie eyeballing me. She averted her glance and hurried to a boiling pot of something on the stove. Did she know I'd tailed her? Had she seen me drive by Camille's place and put two and two together? She was hiding something, but what? Felicity had suggested Allie had a *past*. If she were dangerous, wouldn't Felicity have told me that at least?

"Mimi," Chef C called. "I will need your help tonight if you can spare a hand. Having a table of twelve ready all at once is such a challenge."

She was right. Most of our parties consisted of six or fewer guests. "Of course," I said and moseyed to her. "It's my night anyway."

"I figured with you feeling under the weather . . ."

I balked. Jo must have called and alerted her. I set a reassuring hand on Camille's shoulder. "I'm fine."

"May I put you in charge of the *galantine de poularde*, then?"

I smirked. "Gee, um, how is that made again?"

"It is your specialty." She threw me a sly look. "You tell me."

Chicken galantine was a dish I'd been making for years. In

essence, it was a French classic made from deboned fowl, which was then stuffed and formed into a log. The chicken's skin worked as a casing. The forcemeat, or *farce*, from the French word for stuffing, was a mixture of seasoned chicken. I liked to layer in carrots, green beans, pistachios, and such so that when we sliced the galantine, we had a beautiful presentation of colors dotting each portion. To serve, I'd drizzle it with a savory-sweet vinaigrette made with Tawny Port wine. The dish was so pretty that most customers *oohed* when they saw it. They *aahed* when they took their first bites.

Thankful for a task, I set to work.

Two hours later, as dinner service was getting under way and Stefan, Yukiko, and the rest of the staff were moving in what felt like a synchronized dance, Heather entered.

"Mimi, you're wanted out front," she said. "Your mother has arrived."

Chef C signaled that I should go. I had done all she needed.

I met my mother at the table for twelve. She radiated confidence in a slim aqua-blue sheath—new, I imagined, since it wasn't her typical Bohemian style. Her eyes glimmered with liveliness. She was circling the table for twelve and setting out seating cards. Anthony, looking as charismatic as always, was assisting her. He nudged her. She blew him a discreet kiss.

Oakley, who was lighting candles on the table, alerted my mother to my arrival.

Mom hurried to me. "Sweetheart, how are you feeling?" She grasped my upper arms and gazed at me.

I flinched. Who else had Jo told? It was my bellyache—my business.

"Were you poisoned?" my mother asked.

"I'm not sure."

"You should have gone to the emergency room. Poison is—"

"Please don't baby me." I broke free. "I'm fine." In fact, I felt great. Whatever I'd ingested had gone through my system. Drinking a gallon of water must have helped. "Better than fine," I assured her.

Mom got the hint. She, like me, was fiercely independent. She wouldn't want a soul to know if she was ailing. She took a step backward to give me space.

"Wait until you taste the *galantine de poularde*," I said, changing the subject. "I poured my heart into the dish."

"I look forward to it. By the way, I made sure Red has one selection of each vintner's wine tonight. We'll be blind-tasting them. I'm sure there will be some gamesmanship and braggadocio. They'll be talking about the aroma, the legs, and the controversy between oak barrels versus steel barrels. But, in the end, we're all proud of what we do and supportive. We should have fun. Anthony is being a sport to play along."

"No sport involved." Anthony joined us. "I like my wine as much as the next man." Whenever he spoke, I imagined him on stage crooning "Chances Are" or "Misty" into a microphone.

I extended a hand. "Good to see you, sir."

"Cut the *sir*. I've told you before."

"Some habits are hard to break."

He glanced in the direction of the kitchen. "Is Stefan working?"

"Of course."

"Would he—"

I motioned for him to hold off. "Why don't you visit him after the meal? I don't want to break his concentration. He's preparing a number of appetizers: fig and olive tapenade and warm Brie with roasted garlic, plus a few others. He would hate to be disturbed. You know what an artist he is."

"Of course." For years, Anthony and Stefan had been at odds. Now that Anthony was living in Nouvelle Vie, Stefan seemed to be warming to his father. He said his dad was more relaxed—*cooler*—now that he wasn't trying to fix the financial woes of the country. Stefan had even risked showing his father his apartment and the watercolor landscapes that he didn't think anyone would buy. I would and I'd offered. Stefan had thought I was coddling him, of course. His talent had floored his father.

The front door opened and Nash entered, looking delicious in a silk ecru sweater and caramel-colored corduroy slacks. My insides did a happy dance.

"Nash!" My mother beckoned him. "You're sitting at that end." She wiggled a finger.

"Got it," he said and approached me. He looped an arm around my waist. "Hello, beautiful."

"I see you're one of the infamous ten tonight."

"Nouvelle Vie Vineyards might not be one of the top ten in the valley yet, but we're aspiring. It didn't hurt that I knew the hostess. How are you?"

"You heard?"

"Heard what?"

My mother wagged her head—*no*—meaning she hadn't told him anything about my stomach issue.

"I'll tell you later," I said. "It's nothing."

"You know how much I hate vague references."

I pecked his cheek. "Sit."

He stroked my shoulder and took his seat.

Moments later, the leading winemakers in the valley entered—three women and six men. Anthony and my mother guided them to their places. Mom gushed about the entrées. Anthony raved about the desserts.

Oakley orbited the table, pouring olive oil infused with rosemary into the bread plate for each setting.

Red sashayed to the table with a tray filled with twelve sets of wine flight glasses, four to each set. Then she fetched four white wine bottles that she'd wrapped in brown paper so none of the guests could guess the vintage and poured two ounces into the first tasting glass.

"Cagey," said a fine-boned blonde. She swooped her hair over her shoulder and slid into her seat, which was situated next to Nash's. She leaned toward him. "I'll know which one is mine in a single sip."

"Bet you won't," he said.

"Bet I will," she countered.

Surprisingly, I didn't feel one ounce of jealousy about her flirtatious manner—a first for me, which pleased me no end. Maybe I was growing up. Maybe I was becoming more confident.

"In fact, I'm sure I will," she added. Her eyes blazed with a dare. Her voice held an edge. She bolted to her feet, pulled a hundred-dollar bill from her sparkling evening purse, and slapped it on the table. "Who's up for a little wager, ladies and gentlemen?"

"Nash?" a woman said. "I thought that was you."

I spun around.

Willow, looking incredible in a violet lace dress, had entered the bistro with Bennett and, of all people, Eli. "I'd like to introduce you to a few friends," she said. "This is Bennett—"

"We met the other day," Nash said.

Willow petted his arm. "Of course. I forgot."

"Nice to see you again, Bennett," Nash said. Did I sense relief in his eyes because his ex was not only moving on but moving on with a guy who was well-to-do?

"And this is Eli George," Willow went on. "I told you about him. He's an old friend of Mimi's."

The way she said the word *friend* made my cheeks flame. If we were anywhere else, I'd . . . I'd have what? Taken her to the mat? *Don't be ridiculous, Mimi.*

"They've known each other since the cradle," Willow added.

"Not that long," I said.

"Since we were five," Eli offered.

Nash's gaze drifted between Eli and me.

"Nice to meet you, Nash," Eli said.

"Eli's a chef at the tony Sonoma Health and Fitness Resort," Willow went on. "They brought him in to bolster its reputation. Before the move, he was a well-known chef in New York. Lots of big-name hotels have been clamoring for him to take the helm."

Was Willow touting Eli to make Nash feel bad? If so, it was working. His jaw was set and his shoulders looked tense.

"Mimi," Eli jumped into the conversation. "The place looks fabulous. I remember how much you liked mirrors as a kid." He readdressed Nash. "Not that Mimi was egotistical. She wasn't. She had this thing."

"Thing?" Nash echoed.

"She liked to aim mirrors at stuff in the garden to make it catch the sunlight, and at night, to reflect the stars." He mimed the motion, then rotated his head to take a gander at the rest of the bistro. "I'm going to have to bring my fiancée here to show her. She'll love the ambience."

"Your what?" Willow's voice skated upward.

"His fiancée," Nash repeated, his unease gone, a merry glint in his eyes.

"Eli, you're engaged?" Willow sounded stunned. "But you never said—"

"You never asked." Eli inserted his hands into his pockets. "She's also my boss, so we've been keeping the news on the down-low."

I suppressed a smile. His boss was the tall, attractive brunette who had accompanied him to the festival. They would make a good-looking couple.

Nash patted Eli on the shoulder. "Guess you didn't get the memo about no fraternizing."

Eli grinned. "We started dating two years ago, way before she relocated here to take over the resort. In June, we decided we couldn't live apart any longer. When the chef's job became available, I jumped at the chance."

I laughed to myself. When Eli had said he'd wanted to catch up with me, that was exactly what he'd wanted to do—*catch up*—not go on a date. I felt foolish but also relieved.

On the other hand, Willow was breathing high in her chest and her nose was pinched. Was she fuming because her plan to break up Nash and me had failed? I did a mental happy dance. For once, Willow was one step behind.

Chapter 21

After seating Willow and her guests, I attended to my mother's party and made sure all the meals arrived to each guest's liking. Whenever I passed by Nash, he threw me an amorous look. I had to tamp down the urge to sneak a kiss.

Two hours later, after the wine dinner ended and Nash and I made a plan for our Tuesday date to go hot air ballooning, I blazed into the kitchen looking for Allie. With all the activity, I hadn't had a moment to question her about her afternoon foray. I really wanted to, whether Tyson approved of my intentions or not. I ran full bore into Stefan.

"Success, huh?" His grin was a mile wide. "Your mom's guests loved everything."

"They didn't merely love everything. They *adored* everything."

"I heard there was a little bookmaking on the side." He mimed jotting bets on a tip sheet. "Did that woman everyone called the shark win?"

I cackled. "She lost big-time. I guess her palate isn't as fine-tuned as she thinks."

"And what was that between you and Nash?" He waggled a finger. "In the corner by the office."

"Nothing."

"Don't kid a kidder. He was ready to get down on one knee."

"No way." Before setting our date, we had discussed Willow. He'd assured me he was onto her scheme about trying to fix me up and he wouldn't let her drive a wedge between us.

"Way." Stefan flapped his left hand and crooned the opening line to Beyonce's "Single Ladies (Put a Ring on It)."

"Get out of here." I thwacked him. "Have you seen Allie?"

"Not recently."

I hitched a thumb over my shoulder. "Your dad would like to say hello."

"I'm on it. By the way, I hear he and your mother are getting tight. Should I start calling you Sis?"

"Don't you dare!"

"Don't you want your mother to be happy?"

"Yes, of course. You and I"—I pinged a finger from his chest to mine—"we'll talk."

"You bet, *Sis*." He let out one of his rollicking laughs.

I ignored him and sidled to Camille, who was removing her chef's coat. "Have you seen Allie?"

"Not for quite a while." She retreated to the rear of the kitchen, tossed her coat into a laundry bin, and joined me. "She did well, once again. She is a real find. However, I do not think she wants this job."

"Why would you say that?"

"She looks dreamy-eyed, like she has something else on her mind."

Like proving her innocence? I thought.

"I can do without her, of course. I did before. My energy is returning. You told her this was temporary, so I will leave it up to you to decide when to let her go."

"Duly noted."

I searched the walk-in refrigerator. Allie wasn't there. I checked outside the rear door. She wasn't having a smoke. I hated to admit it, but she must have noticed me in the Jeep and, driven by guilt, decided to hightail it out of Napa Valley. I would have to alert Tyson.

Oakley sauntered into the kitchen balancing a tray of dinner plates on one shoulder. Her face was moist with perspiration and her lipstick chewed off. "Mimi, the last check has been paid. Busboys are gathering the remaining glassware. There are a few people chatting on the patio, but they don't seem to need anything. Is it okay if I leave?"

"Yes. Great work tonight."

"Thanks." She headed to the dishwashing area and paused. "Say, do you know why Allie hustled across the patio earlier to the fire pit? She seemed upset, like she was crying."

"You saw her? Is she still there?"

"I think so. Maybe she needs a word of encouragement from you."

"From me?"

"You're the boss. Your praise means a lot. By the way, I like her. She's sweet."

And possibly lethal.

I helped remove the tray from Oakley's shoulder and set it by the sink. "Have you two talked or shared stories?" Oakley knew everyone's history. She was quite a whiz with social media.

"I haven't had enough time to delve yet, but"—she rubbed her hands together like an evil scientist—"give me time."

"All right, get out of here."

As I exited the kitchen to the patio, Heather caught up to me. She was holding a tray filled with empty dessert wine glasses. "Where are you going?"

"To find Allie."

"Why?" She shuddered and rasped, "The woman in white. Of course. Allie wears a chef's coat. Oh, my." She set the tray on a table and said, "I'm going with you."

I knew I couldn't dissuade her. "Fine."

We reached the end of the patio and halted. A single ray of light from an exterior fixture at the rear of the bistro illuminated a woman crouching near the fire pit. When I realized that Allie was indeed crying—her shoulders were heaving—all of my rancor vanished.

"Allie," I said and drew near.

She bolted to a stand and wiped her face with her right hand. In the other, she was holding a kitten—a black one with white paws.

"Where did you get that?" I asked.

Allie's face went blank as if she couldn't remember.

"From the storage room," Heather said. "I brought them to work. My husband had his writing critique group." Scoundrel and Scooter emerged from the darkness and orbited Allie's ankles. Heather stuck out her hands. "It's time to take the kittens home for the night."

Allie gave the kitten to her as tears dripped down her cheeks.

"What's going on, Allie?" I asked. "Why are you crying?"

"You didn't trust me. You followed me this afternoon."

I cringed. So she had seen me.

"Why?" she pleaded.

"You were acting suspicious."

Heather's gaze swung from Allie to me. "What are you talking about?"

"Allie swiped Camille's house keys and let herself into Camille's house."

Allie jutted her chin. "Camille gave me those keys."

I threw her a skeptical look.

"She did. I swear it." Her eyelids fluttered. She was lying.

"What did you want?" I asked. "Were you looking to destroy incriminating evidence?"

"Evidence?" Heather echoed.

"Of murdering Renee."

"I didn't kill her," Allie cried. "I was . . . I was . . ."

"I think you went to Camille's without permission. I could ask her." I turned to go.

"Wait." Allie reached for me; her fingertips grazed my shoulder. Realizing she'd overstepped, she retreated. "It's not what you think."

I pivoted and folded my arms. "Enlighten us."

"Mimi, what is going on?" Camille rounded the plants at the edge of the patio. Her white shirt gleamed as the exterior light hit it. To my surprise, Donovan was with her. He looked hip in a newsboy hat, striped shirt tucked into jeans, and Doc Marten boots. "We heard voices as we were heading to the parking lot." Camille pulled up short. "Allie, *chérie*, what is wrong?"

"Chef C, I'm not a thief." Allie tucked her hands beneath her armpits.

Camille addressed me. "What is she talking about?"

"On the break this afternoon, she borrowed your house keys and stole inside your house."

"Whatever for?" Camille asked.

"I think she wanted to take whatever it was that might indicate she was at the crime scene. Am I warm, Allie?"

She shook her head. "I didn't . . . I wouldn't . . . I've never been inside Camille's house until today. Honest. I—"

I held up a hand to cut her off. "Allie, I think you lied about where you were the night Renee died. Tell us the truth."

She gawked at me. "I did lie. I wasn't home baking. But please don't jump to conclusions. I wasn't at Camille's, either. I didn't kill Renee." She chewed her lower lip.

Heather said, "Sign me up for whatever acting classes she's taking."

I nudged her and whispered, "Only a day ago you wanted to adopt her."

"I was wrong," she countered.

I refocused on Allie. "Please go on."

Out of the corner of my eye, I could see Camille. Pain pinched her face. She did not want to relive that night, and yet here she was listening to yet another alibi—this time from someone she had grown fond of.

"I was spying on a cookie baker," Allie said, her voice raspy with fear.

"Who?" Camille asked.

"Yeah, who?" Donovan echoed.

"Please, everyone." I held up both hands. "Let her tell the story."

"That's what it is," Heather said. "A story." The kitten in her arms mewed. Scoundrel and Scooter roamed around her, their tails rising in question marks. "Do you see how she's blinking? It's a telltale sign that she's lying."

"Heather, c'mon," I said. "Do I have to banish you from the discussion?"

"Nope." She hugged the kitten and smirked. "I wouldn't miss this for the world."

Camille brushed Allie's shoulder. "Continue."

"I needed a recipe for snickerdoodles." Allie's face flushed. "There's this baker who notoriously bakes at night. She's one of the judges for the festival's competitions."

"I heard about her," Donovan said. "She's the one that always wears her hair up." He twirled a finger at the nape of his neck.

"That's right," Allie said. "I stole over to her house and took photographs of the process through her window."

"Sheesh," Heather said. "Snickerdoodles are easy. I'm a lousy baker, and even I can make them."

"Not like hers," Allie exclaimed. "They're amazing. See, she believes that snickerdoodles shouldn't be crisp." She mimed snapping a cookie in half. "They should be soft and chewy."

"I agree," Donovan said.

"To do this, I knew she had to add something special to them. I wanted to figure out her secret. Guess what it was? An extra egg."

"So simple," Donovan murmured.

"Plus, she doesn't use a mixer. She stirs the batter by hand. That keeps the extra air out of the dough. It was brilliant to behold. And she used a different kind of cinnamon—Vietnamese cassia."

"Exquisite," Donovan said.

Allie gasped. "You've heard of it? I hadn't. She ground it fresh."

"How do you know so much about cookies, Allie?" Camille asked.

I said, "She's baked them all her life. That's the real reason she wanted to put on the Sweet Treats Festival."

Allie nodded. "Seeing as Renee cut me out of the event, I decided to open a bakery."

Donovan shuffled feet. Was he worried about facing more competition as he embarked on his new career?

In a flurry, Allie added, "I knew I would need excellent recipes to get started. Not my family recipes. They're pedantic. I needed *super great*!" Her enthusiasm, despite her tears, was infectious.

Camille said, "So you went to my house to get the cookie recipes I boasted about."

"To steal them," I corrected.

"Chef, you . . ." Allie faltered. "You said they were so good that you kept them under lock and key."

"How many did you take?" I asked.

"Four. The cardamom madeleines, the chocolate macarons, the *langues du chat*, and—"

"What are those?" Heather asked.

"Cat's tongues," Donovan said. "They're slim cookies dipped in semisweet chocolate."

"And your French lace cookies," Allie went on. "The ones you served at lunch. With the pecans." She reached into her pants pocket and withdrew recipe cards. She offered them to Camille.

"Allie . . ." I let her name hang in the air. All attention focused on me. "I hear you have quite a past."

"Who says?"

"Felicity Parker."

Allie placed a hand over her mouth. Through split fingers, she said, "How could she know? My record is sealed."

"I would imagine her husband was able to unseal it," I said. "Did you do something illegal? Did you hurt someone?"

"No! When I was a teenager, I . . ." Allie licked her lips. "I shoplifted a few things. From a dime store. Silly stuff. Hairpins and nylons and candy. I wanted to give my mother a good Christmas gift. We didn't have any money. Hardship makes people do all sorts of stupid stuff." She faced Camille. "I understand if you don't want me in your kitchen, Chef, but please know that I did not hurt your sister. She made me mad, but I would never kill anyone. I can't even squish a spider."

I tried to determine whether Allie was lying about any part of her tale. She could have gone to Camille's hoping to remove evidence that the sheriff had overlooked and snatched the recipes to cover this story. "Allie, did you see anyone when you were spying on the baker?"

"I didn't. Someone might have seen me, but I'm not sure. I was really focused. I . . . Wait a sec. I took photographs." She rummaged in her other pocket and pulled out her cell phone. "They should be time-stamped." She swiped the screen and opened the photo album. "There, see?"

The baker—the twin with the French twist—was hard at work in her kitchen. Allie had recorded a short movie of the woman hand-mixing dough in a bowl, and she had taken photographs of trays upon trays of cookies ready for the double ovens.

"They aren't very good," Allie admitted. "I switched off the automatic flash so she wouldn't notice me."

I returned the cell phone to her.

"None of this proves I'm innocent, does it?" Allie's voice cracked. "None of it."

The word *none* sent my thoughts flying to Rusty and the *nun* who claimed she had seen him outside the courthouse. Would a nun lie? Had Rusty paid her to say he was there? Was the coroner so positive about the time of death that he could rule out Rusty as a suspect?

Tears pooled in Allie's eyes again. "Do you believe me?"

"You hated Renee," I said. "You wanted her to cede the rights to the festival back to you."

"Yes, but that was a pipe dream. We had a contract. I wasn't savvy enough to understand it. Plus, she had gotten the festival on its feet, not me. She had the know-how and flair; I didn't. And now Rusty is doing a good job. He seems to have the same pizzazz."

A very good job, I thought. *Too good*? Had he killed his wife so he could gain sole control of the business?

Camille said, "Mimi, I believe Allie. She did not kill my sister.

Let her go." She clasped Donovan's hand. Looking deflated at having been deceived, she led him away from the fire pit.

Allie blinked. "It's up to you, Mimi."

"To fire you?"

"To believe me."

"Before I do, Allie, I want to know what Renee wrote in your contract."

"Huh?"

"When you and Renee went at it last Saturday, you handed her the contract. She wrote something on it. What?"

Allie moaned. "She drew a pair of lips and told me it meant *kiss off.*"

"That was mean-spirited," Heather murmured.

Allie's mouth drew up on one side. "Renee said women had to play tough if they wanted to get ahead. She added that if she had to buck up, then I had to as well."

"Buck up about what?" I asked.

"She didn't say. Maybe someone was giving her grief. Maybe her husband or a fundraiser or a vendor or—" She blew out an exasperated breath and straightened her shoulders. "I will buck up, Mimi. I will be tough and strong, and I will find my path. Thank you for the chance. You don't need to pay me. Good-bye."

When I arrived home, I was exhausted, but not too tired to notice that the front door of my cottage was ajar.

Chapter 22

Scoundrel and Scooter, who had accompanied me home, didn't seem alarmed. They dashed through the opening and disappeared. Me? I hung back. My adrenaline was pumping so loudly I could barely hear myself think. I pulled my cell phone from my pocket. I wasn't typically a scaredy-cat, but I also wasn't stupid. I dialed Raymond, who was on the property, and explained my concern. In a matter of seconds he arrived on his gardening cart.

"Stand aside, Mimi." He grabbed a shovel from his array of tools and thwacked the door with his hand. It flew open and bounced off the interior wall.

The cats darted outside as Raymond stepped inside.

"Did you leave the television on?" he called, out of sight.

"No." Dread gripped me. Had someone entered my house? Why switch on the television? "Maybe the maid came by," I yelled. "She's scheduled to clean on Wednesdays, but she missed that day."

Raymond appeared in the doorway, the shovel resting on his shoulder. "The closets and the bathroom are all clear. I even peeked under the bed and double-checked all the windows. I think you're right; it was the maid. She turned down the bed and left some sprigs of wisteria on your bedside table."

"That was sweet." I breathed a sigh of relief. "Thanks, Raymond. What would I do without you?"

"Good question. FYI, Tyson suggested, given your propensity for investigating things that don't concern you, that you might want to hire a full-time security guard."

I smirked. Since when had he and Tyson become best buds? "You two have been talking about me?"

"He's the talker; I'm the listener."

"Tell him he can take a long walk off a short pier."

"Tell him yourself. I'm no dummy." Raymond winked and made his way to his cart.

"For the record, these *things* I look into do concern me or the people I love."

Raymond raised one hand in a don't-shoot-the-messenger gesture, then waved good-bye.

Scoundrel and Scooter hurtled inside before I closed and locked the door. After brushing my teeth, I crawled into bed with the fireplace poker by my side.

* * *

Needless to say, I tossed all night, my dreams filled with images of a tear-streaked Allie and a television gone amok. I awoke with a start Saturday morning. As I showered, I wondered whether I was wrong to have let Allie go free. I downed a mug of strong coffee and a cup of Greek yogurt and mulled over whether she had duped us with her tearful plea. I returned the fireplace poker to its usual spot and pondered whether she'd had the time to race from the fire pit to my place and switch on the TV. How would she have entered? The front door lock was intact. If not her, then who? Did the killer think I knew something and believe that scaring me would make me hold my tongue?

Cagney and Lacey gazed at me. I tapped the glass and said, "I'm okay. Don't worry." Then I signaled Scoundrel and Scooter, who were lying in their new *rightful* places on my bed, and said, "Let's go."

They bolted out the door ahead of me. I locked it and double-checked the knob to make sure I wasn't lax, and then headed to work.

Feeling safe within the bistro kitchen's walls, Chef C and I put together Saturday lunch and dinner menus. Despite her sorrow about her sister's death and losing Allie as a helper, she seemed chipper.

During a break, I sat at the farmhouse-style table and downed a slice of her French apple tart enhanced with apricot jelly. Sure, Greek yogurt was good for me, but it didn't take the place of a delectable slice of tart.

Camille took a seat beside me. "My date with Donovan went well."

"I'm glad to hear that."

"You were right. He says he is dedicated to me." Her eyes misted over. "I cannot believe it, of course. I am so blessed." She folded her hands in her lap and added, "I will be seeing him again after tonight's closing."

"Good for you."

"How about you and Nash? Are you doing okay?"

Nash? I had to admit I hadn't thought about him since the confrontation with Allie. My mind had been going a mile a minute. "We have a date on Tuesday."

"Good. Do not let life distract you from living."

* * *

Following lunch service, I experienced a desperate need to drink in fresh air and stretch my legs. I ventured over to the festival. I wanted to observe the last day's final competition featuring soufflés. I entered the tent through the west gate and stood near the rear. Among the crowd, I caught sight of Allie. She was standing along the far side of the tent. Her mane of hair was windblown, but the rest of her looked festive and upbeat. She was wearing a tomato-red romper with a lime-green T-shirt beneath, and her arms sported colorful beaded bracelets.

Rusty was standing near the east tent entrance, arms folded across his body, mouth set, shoulders hunched. He seemed to be fighting hard to keep his eyes open. Had he stayed up past his bedtime and snuck into my cottage pretending to be the maid?

"Let's get a move on," the moderator said into a microphone.

The sister judges roved in front of the three finalists on the stage. The twin with the French twist—the one who was featured in Allie's snickerdoodle movie—tapped each presentation table as she passed.

I was surprised to see the contestant I'd nicknamed Barbie Martha on stage. Yet again she sported a perfect hairdo and wore a spotless ruffled apron over a black dress. She put her utensils down and held up both hands. The sign at her station read CHOCOLATE SOUFFLÉ WITH RASPBERRY SAUCE. Next to the sign sat a beautiful soufflé, baked in a CorningWare French white round baking dish. The audience could view her masterpiece via the slanted mirrors that hung overhead. My mouth began to salivate. I loved a combination of chocolate and raspberries. Heaven!

Within seconds, the twin with the French twist stopped in front of Barbie Martha and raised a hand. Barbie Martha squealed with delight, received her ribbon, and headed down the stairs toward Oscar Orsini, who was waiting with his digital camera in hand.

Before she could reach him, however, Felicity, in a snug pearl white dress, and Louvain, wearing a flouncy orange getup, approached her. None exchanged hugs or congratulations. In fact, Felicity and Louvain faced off against Barbie Martha like she was their foe in a Western-style standoff. Nobody was packing heat, but the sparks were flying between them.

Uh-oh, I thought.

"You had no right to enter another competition," Felicity said loudly enough that I could pick up their exchange, even over the movement of the boisterous crowd snaking out of the tent.

"We were allowed to enter any and all competitions," Barbie Martha replied in a squeaky-high voice that didn't quite fit her idyllic looks. Maybe she was nervous. She was confronting two wildcat women, after all. "Didn't you read the fine print? One must always read the—"

"You did this on purpose." Louvain poked the woman just beneath her clavicle. "To make Felicity look bad."

Okay, my head was spinning. Louvain was having an affair with Felicity's husband, and yet, here she was, defending Felicity in public. Why? To cover up the affair or because she liked Felicity, who claimed they were tight?

"You've been doing this since high school, Bebe," Louvain continued. "It's always a competition for you. Always."

I stifled a snort. The woman's name was Bebe? That sounded a heck of a lot like *Barbie*. Maybe I did have ESP.

"She's right, Bebe," Felicity said. "You ran against me for class president."

"And tried to out-bake me for the home economics award," Louvain added.

"And your husband." Felicity wagged her finger. "Honestly. Why did he feel compelled to run against Parker for councilman? I'll tell you why. Because you put him up to it."

"He lost, of course." Louvain smirked.

"And let's not forget last month"—Felicity leaned in, her eyes gleaming with malicious intent—"when your daughter, as if she were your stand-in, vied against my talented Philomena for the part of Grizabella."

"We know how that worked out," Louvain said.

For a moment, I thought Bebe might cry. She was blinking rapidly. Her lower lip was quivering. But then she stood taller, lifted her chin, and offered a regal smile. "This is one contest I won't lose, ladies. You wait and see. Soufflé will reign supreme."

I smirked. An Iron Chef couldn't have announced that last line better.

"You'll have to come with your A games," Bebe added, and without another word, strutted away.

Felicity and Louvain stormed after her.

Oscar strode after them, too. "Ladies, wait!"

Rusty raced up to me. "This is horrible. Is there going to be a catfight?"

"No," I assured him. "It'll blow over."

"You think?"

"It will." Allie joined us, her face flushed with energy. "Felicity and Louvain are trying to rile Bebe to throw her off her game."

"You know them?" I asked.

"Uh-huh."

"How?"

"Because . . ." She seemed to be searching for the right words. "Because I'm the one in charge of the celebratory wine tasting today for the semifinalists and finalists."

"At the bistro," Rusty said.

At the bistro? Why hadn't I heard about this?

"Right," Allie said. "I made it a point to get to know their names."

"Who put you in charge?" I asked.

"Renee had designated Heather as the party point person, but Heather has been so busy with the crowds at the bistro that she offered me the job when I started helping out temporarily in the kitchen, and I . . ." Allie licked her lips.

Suddenly I understood why Heather had been so upset with Allie last night. As swamped as she was, the responsibility of throwing a celebratory party would now fall on her shoulders.

"Rusty said it was okay if I did it," Allie said. "It's only one event. I won't be there long. I know you don't trust me, Mimi, but if you say yes, I'll tell Rusty everything."

"Why would you have to explain anything to Rusty?" I asked.

"Because he's—"

"Hold it." Rusty's gaze swung from her to me. "What's going on?"

"I stole recipes from Chef C," Allie confessed.

"Yeah, so?"

"Recipes are proprietary."

"Big deal."

"It is a big deal because I snuck into Chef C's house without permission, and Mimi saw me, and, well"—Allie jammed her lips together and popped them open—"she thought I might have killed Renee and gone there to remove evidence. But I didn't kill her, Rusty. I swear. I could never kill anyone. I think Mimi believes me, but I'm no longer in her employ, so I don't have any references."

"References for what?" I asked.

"Rusty wants to hire me to help with the festival, and he said I could manage the party."

"I thought you wanted to open a bakery."

"I told you last night, that's a fantasy."

Rusty held up a hand and leveled me with a stare. "Mimi, where do you stand?"

"Camille forgave her."

"And you?"

"She works hard," I said judiciously, though I was still wondering about the break-in at my cottage. Had Allie stolen inside to mess with my head after we parted ways, or was leaving the television on and not closing the door merely an oversight by the maid? The bed had been turned down. I'd have to check with Jo on that.

"I don't see a problem." Rusty stuck out his hand. Allie pumped it. "You usher the three finalists to the party. I sure as heck don't want to be present, given their attitudes." He released her hand. "When that's over, escort them back and stick around. I'll need you for tonight's contest and the closing ceremony."

"Really?" Allie's face filled with hope.

"People always need a second chance," Rusty said. "Maybe even the benefit of the doubt. Didn't you feel that way a few months ago, Mimi?" He threw me a mocking look. "Yeah, I'm pretty sure you did."

He marched away without waiting for a reply.

While Allie rounded up the three contentious females, I returned to the bistro to find the rear patio decorated with blue streamers and white balloons. The multicolored vases Willow had gifted to me in June were filled with freshly cut blue asters. Red had placed wineglasses as well as opened bottles of Cabernet and Chardonnay on a buffet table. Stefan and Oakley were setting out an array of pâté and cheeses to the right of the wine.

Heather met me as I entered and advised me that the semifinal competitors who had lost their rounds had arrived. Each had been allowed to invite one or two guests. Finalists' family members were there, too, she added. No one seemed downhearted. Chatter abounded about who might win tonight.

"I wish I'd known about this soiree," I said.

"Did I forget to tell you?" Heather blanched. "Gosh, I'm sorry. We've had so much going on with the festival and Renee and last night's encounter with Allie. I've got to start making lists."

"Rusty has allowed Allie to remain in charge of this portion of the festival."

"And you didn't countermand him?"

"How could I? It's not my festival. I simply own the location. Besides goodwill breeds goodwill."

"Mimi!" Parker was standing with a dignified gentleman whom I recognized from political posters—Bebe's husband. There didn't seem to be any animosity between the two men. "Nice gig," he called. "Where's my bride?"

"On her way." *Along with your paramour*, I thought but didn't offer.

Philomena had stationed herself at a bistro table with another girl her age. By the look of her, I figured the girl was Bebe's daughter—perfect hair, cheekbones, and figure. She was a total contrast to gawky Philomena, although both girls were wearing holey jeans and pastel crop-tops. The two were sipping the bistro's specialty lemonade while engrossed in something on their iPhones.

When Louvain, Felicity, and Bebe followed Allie inside, a chesty woman with white-blonde hair wiggled a flute of champagne and shouted, "Hey, sis. You-hoo! Lovey, over here!" Louvain's sister, I determined.

"Be right there," Louvain said.

Allie guided the three women around the patio, pointing out the various food stations.

Bebe said, "Excuse me a sec." She strode to the teenagers and tapped her watch. "Fifteen minutes, ladies, and we leave for the theater."

"But what about the party?" her daughter whined.

"You'll have plenty of parties in your lifetime. We have to clean up the theater so I can get back here in time for the final bake-off. Drink up." Bebe rejoined Allie and the others. "Felicity, will you be joining us for theater cleanup?"

"Not on a bet. You'll do fine without me. It's party time." Felicity tapped Louvain on the shoulder, hooked a finger to follow her, and made a beeline for me. "Mimi, come with us." She led the way to Parker. "Darling," she said curtly.

Parker looped an arm around her waist and pecked her on the cheek. "Hey, hon," he said, and added, "Hello, Louvain."

"Parker." Her tone was sultry and rife with hidden meaning.

"How did the competition go?" Parker asked. "Who won this afternoon's round?"

"Bebe." Felicity wrinkled her nose.

Parker chuckled. "Are you peeved beyond compare?"

"Sort of."

Parker squeezed her. "It's time to end the feud, hon."

"Feud? We don't have a feud." Felicity eyed Bebe's husband. "Bebe and I are besties."

"As if," Louvain said. "You and I are BFFs."

Felicity bobbed her head. "That's true. Since high school. Speaking of which—"

"Uh-uh. Don't." Louvain swatted Felicity's arm. "I do not want to think about our wild heathen days."

"Heathen? Speak for yourself, girlfriend."

"My, my. How we partied hearty." Louvain flapped a hand in front of her face. "Why, I remember when we went to get tattoos at two in the morning."

"You have a tattoo, Louvain?" Parker asked.

"I do."

"What is it?"

"I'm not telling." She wagged her index finger.

"She won't even tell me," Felicity said.

Louvain pursed her lips. "Because it's a secret."

"C'mon, spill," Parker said.

I spluttered. Was the game he and Louvain were playing foreplay, or were they taunting Felicity and daring her to make a scene?

Felicity wriggled from her husband's grasp. "Parker, darling, I told you what Oscar Orsini is doing, didn't I? Of course I did. He's putting together a piece on some of the festival's competitors. Will you have time for your sit-down with him tomorrow morning?" She petted his cheek. "Of course you will." She smiled at Louvain. "He's doing a piece on you, too, isn't he, Lovey?"

Louvain reddened. Her jaw ticked. With all the pluck she could muster, she said, "Who needs someone to pry into one's affairs? Privacy is underrated." She hurried in haste to her sister, accepted the glass of champagne, and downed it in one gulp.

Felicity smirked.

Oh, yeah, she knew about the affair, but she held the upper hand. She was married to Parker, and I doubted she would ever grant him a divorce.

"Mimi!" Oakley burst through the door from the kitchen and raced to me. She clasped my hand. "Come quick."

Chapter 23

"It's Chef C," Oakley said.

"Is she sick? Choking?" My voice skated upward as I hurried after her. "Is it her heart? Have you called 911?"

"It's not her heart. It's . . . it's . . ." She couldn't form words.

I followed her into the kitchen and found Camille sitting on a stool, her toque resting on the counter, her shoulders hunched. She was clutching a cream-colored notecard and a mangled envelope in her hands.

"She's so sad," Oakley whispered.

"I can see that." My pulse settled down. I motioned to Oakley to return to the party. She hesitated, like she didn't want to leave Camille. I understood. It was hard to see someone you admired—someone you thought was as strong as brandy—broken. "Go on."

She departed.

"Chef," I said and drew near. "Bad news?"

Camille peered up at me. Tears brimmed in her eyes. She flourished the notecard. "*Oui.*"

"Who wrote you?" I asked. "Your daughter? Is Chantalle okay?"

"It is from Renee."

How horrible. I couldn't imagine receiving correspondence

from Derrick or my father or Bryan after their deaths, as if they were talking to me from their graves.

"It came in the bistro's mail today," she continued. "The original envelope is postmarked the day she died, but it—" Her voice caught. "It was damaged. It was delivered in a postal package."

"What does it say?" I asked.

"Here. Read it." She handed me the card. "Renee tells me how much she loves me, and she wishes we had more time."

I gasped. "This sounds like she knew she was going to die."

"*Exactement.*" Her eyelids fluttered; she heaved a sigh. "What terrible thing must she have done that someone would want to kill her? To not know is crushing me. Did she threaten someone? Did someone retaliate?"

I studied the notecard. It looked similar to the handcrafted one Felicity had given me as a thank you for putting on the Sweet Treats Festival.

"What are you staring at?" Camille asked.

"The card. Did she get it from Felicity Price?"

"Perhaps." Camille offered a bittersweet smile. "Renee was quite impressed with her. She told me Felicity had oodles to teach her. *Oodles*," she murmured. "Such a silly word. Maybe she went out and purchased some notecards of her own. She was trying to emulate Felicity in style and taste. As colorful as my sister always was, I noticed that she had started to change the way she was dressing. Her clothes were becoming a bit tighter and her hair more flamboyant."

"I tried to imitate a girl in high school." I handed the notecard back to her. "I believed if I acted like she did, I might entice more boys. Was I ever wrong."

"I did the same. We can all be beguiled, can we not?" Camille's tone was wistful. "Renee started drinking tea like Felicity, even though she preferred strong coffee."

"The day I met Renee, she was chatting with Felicity about having tea at her house. She was such a tease that day."

"How so?"

I smiled. "She knew Felicity had sworn off sweets, and yet she flaunted a homemade Oreo-style cookie in front of her nose."

"I prefer a macaron," Camille said as she inspected the notecard—front and back. "Why send this? What did she know? My curiosity will destroy me."

I rested a hand on her shoulder. "No, it won't. There's nothing you can do to change the past. It's not your fault."

"If only she had confided in me. If something was bothering her . . ." She fanned the card again and swallowed hard. "Return to the party, Mimi. I am fine. I will manage."

My cell phone jangled in my pocket. I pulled it out. There was a text message from Oscar Orsini: YOUR NEWSPAPER ARTICLE IS READY FOR APPROVAL. PLEASE HURRY. DEADLINES LOOM.

I gazed at Camille. "Are you sure you're all right?"

"Yes. Go."

"I promise you, I will do everything in my power to make sure your sister's murder is solved."

"*Merci.*" With great resolve, Camille stuffed the card and mangled envelope into her pocket, rose to her feet, and smacked her hands together. "I will make tarts for tomorrow. Busy hands heal a broken heart."

* * *

After checking with Allie and Heather to make sure they didn't need me for the party, I sped to the *Napa Valley Neighborhood* location. The workplace was so tiny and cramped that I wondered whether Oscar was a one-man operation, with him doing the writing, editing, publishing, and distribution. Piles of papers and folders stood on the various desks that were pushed up against the walls. I counted ten file cabinets, three printers, and two copy machines. A private office stood at the far end of the room. The door was ajar. Levolor blinds hung in the single window. Maybe Oscar and another journalist shared the space and duties, I decided.

Oscar, looking cool and confident in a blue blazer, white shirt, and jeans, exited the office and met me as I entered. He shook my hand. "So glad you could make it. Coffee?"

"I'll pass." The rank smell of stale coffee made my nose flare. The temperature in the room was stifling as well. "Thanks."

"Let's get to it then." He glanced over his shoulder as he led me to a table set with four computers. "Sorry about the heat. The AC broke this morning." Upon closer inspection, I realized he wasn't in the least *cool.* His face was beaded with sweat, and the collar of his shirt showed signs of perspiration. "Your story is on the second computer."

Each computer screen displayed an article. My headline read: A TASTY TREAT IN TOWN.

"Do you like the alliteration?" Oscar asked.

"It's great." What else could I say? It sounded positive.

"Sit. Read it. Take your time."

A wooden stool stood by each computer. I perched on the one by my computer and browsed the first page. A series of nicely lit photographs of Bistro Rousseau and Maison Rousseau and its gardens accompanied the article. I noted that the advertisements that would accompany the article hadn't been added yet, which made me wonder about the urgency of Oscar's message: DEADLINES LOOM.

"If you like what you read," he went on, "I need you to sign off on it. As I told you, we put out one newspaper a week, but everyone in Napa Valley will read it. Care for some water?"

"No, thanks."

"I'm going to get some. I'll be back in a bit." He slipped into the office and closed the door, leaving me alone.

By page two—there were three—I was surprised to find myself enjoying what he'd written. He had interviewed Heather, Stefan, and Jorianne, each of whom loved their jobs. He had even obtained quotes from Rusty Wells, who was thrilled to hold his festival at Maison Rousseau. I noted the reference that it was *his*, not his *wife's*. He praised my staff and commended me for my willingness to try *new things*.

When I finished reading the article in its entirety and was waiting for the signature approval page to pop up, I glanced at the articles on the other computers. The one to my left featured Crush Week festivities at six of the better-known wineries in the area. They had formed a coalition and had created what they were calling a *traveling party*. For a fee, guests could move from one vineyard to the next and taste wines paired with a selection of appetizers. Three of the vineyard owners that were mentioned in the article had dined with my mother the other night. I made a mental note to tell her about the idea so she could team up with popular vintners next year.

The computer to my right featured an article about the finalist I'd dubbed Barbie Martha—Bebe Ballantyne. The headline for Bebe's piece read: DAY IN AND DAY OUT. Four photographs depicted her as the perfect mom: with her husband dining over candlelight, with her daughter at the theater, by herself in the kitchen baking, and alone in the yard pruning award-winning roses.

The computer beyond that displayed an article about Felicity. I recalled how she'd asked Louvain if she was going to be highlighted, as well. Had she ordered Oscar to omit her *BFF*?

Felicity's title read: DREAMS FOR MY FUTURE. Intrigued to read more, I glanced toward the office into which Oscar had retreated. The door was shut and the blinds were closed. I scooted over two stools, clicked the down arrow on that computer, and scrolled through

Felicity's article. As in mine, there were a number of photographs. In one, a young Felicity stood in front of a bank. She was clad in a two-piece black suit and flaunting a fistful of money. In another, she was high school age and dressed like a reporter in a belted raincoat and fedora. She was thrusting a microphone at a blonde who had covered her face. Both photo setups looked like they had been done in jest. In the third, the current Felicity posed with her competition-winning muffins and blue ribbon. There were three blank squares set aside for other photographs. Each one was marked: INSERT PHOTO OF PARKER.

"Hey, there," Oscar said as he emerged from the office.

Dang. Caught red-handed. I didn't have time to sneak to my stool. "Hey, there," I said.

He shuffled to my side while sipping from a bottle of Perrier. "Peeking?"

"I was waiting for my authorization page to load, and—"

"Sorry." He groaned. "For some reason, those take forever. I must speak to our tech person about that."

I aimed a finger at the computer with Felicity's article and, in an effort to align us, said, "I find her fascinating, don't you?"

"She's mercurial."

"Indeed. Where did you get these pictures of her?"

"I took the photograph at the festival. The others I found in"—he pointed at an oak desk that was stacked with books—"her high school yearbook. Man, she was a star. She performed in theater. She was a cheerleader. She headlined the local radio show. She ran for office. She was hot."

"Um, isn't she hot now?"

"Well, yeah." His neck flamed lobster red. He retrieved a grey-and-burgundy burlap-covered book and strode to me. "Do you know that she dreamed of becoming First Lady? Let me show you." He flipped open the yearbook to a page filled with photographs of

Felicity in a variety of costumes. He tapped one where she had positioned herself in front of the Capitol Building in Washington, DC, clad in a Jacqueline Kennedy–style sheath. Jackie couldn't have appeared more ready for stardom. Then he tapped another where she was dressed like Marilyn Monroe in a platinum wig and revealing white gown, her back to the camera and looking coyly over her shoulder, her infinity sign tattoo already in place.

"Why does Felicity have a full-page spread? What was she, the prom queen?"

"Nah, in addition to everything else, she was the yearbook editor." He chortled.

I motioned to a photograph of Felicity and Parker—he in his football uniform and she in a form-hugging cheerleading outfit. They weren't linked arm in arm. "They don't seem very chummy here."

"They weren't. Yet." He flipped a page and indicated a photo of Parker in a tux and Louvain in a gold ball gown. "It turns out Parker and Louvain Cook were sweethearts before he fell in love with Felicity."

"Hmm. Felicity told me she and Louvain were best friends back then."

"They were."

Yet Felicity had already added the tattoo that signified her endless bond with Parker? Talk about cheeky.

Oscar flipped to another page and displayed a photo of Felicity and Louvain hugging in a home economics class. Both wore black bib aprons. Flour dusted their cheeks. "This was taken right after they won a baking competition. Their entry was chocolate peppermint iced cookies."

"So, um, how to put this delicately . . ." I licked my lips. "Are you saying Felicity stole her friend's boyfriend?"

"Heh-heh. Not exactly. On prom night"—Oscar worked his

tongue inside his cheek—"Parker caught Louvain making out with the field goal kicker."

"Ouch."

"Felicity was there to pick up the pieces of his broken heart. The rest is history." He clapped the yearbook shut and replaced it on top of the stack of books.

I gazed again at the article about Felicity. "Are you doing a piece on each of the baking competition finalists?" I asked.

"Only Felicity and Bebe."

"Why not Louvain?"

"Um . . ." He rotated his head to survey the room, reminding me of a meerkat on the alert for danger. When he refocused on me, he forced the other computer screens into sleep mode. "Felicity asked me to skip Louvain."

Aha! As I'd suspected. "So much for being best friends," I said.

He sniggered. "Felicity told me it was good-natured competition. I gather they like to prank each other. I agreed because, after snagging you, I had plenty of material for the next edition."

I tilted my head. "You like Felicity, don't you?"

"Well, sure. Who doesn't? But not like *that*. She's married. I would never . . ." He flapped his hand.

"Why did you show up at the bistro for dinner the other night? Did Felicity ask you to flirt with her so Parker would be jealous?"

"What? No." Oscar reddened.

"Did she pay you?"

"Pay me? No. I . . ." Oscar screwed up his mouth. "Okay, yeah, you found me out. I did it because Felicity said it was all in fun. I'm all about *fun*."

I'll bet, I thought, and inwardly cheered because I'd been right. His testimony reinforced my theory that Felicity knew about Parker and Louvain's affair. Did she fear that if she lost Parker to

Louvain now, all her hopes and dreams of remaining Parker's beloved wife for infinity were ruined?

A beep sounded.

"There's your approval page." Oscar pointed at my screen. "Go ahead and sign in the blank box and click that you reviewed the agreement."

I did.

"Our business is concluded."

"Thank you." I shook his hand. "Next time you come into Bistro Rousseau for lunch or dinner, dessert is on the house."

"Your delicious orange soufflé? That's my favorite."

"Of course."

On the way back to the bistro, I thought about Felicity and her mini feud with Louvain. She pretended to be warm to Louvain, but deep down, she was as cold as ice. The notion made me recall the subzero way she had treated Renee that day at the festival. Renee had teased and cajoled, but Felicity hadn't thawed. Why? Had Renee learned about Parker and Louvain's affair and threatened to reveal the news to the world, thus putting Felicity's future happiness in jeopardy? No way. Why would Renee do such a thing? Though I'd only known her for a New York minute, she hadn't seemed the meddling type . . . although I supposed she could be considered vindictive after what she'd done to Allie. On the other hand, wouldn't Felicity have safeguarded her future better if she'd knocked off Louvain?

I recalled the yearbook photograph of Felicity in reporter garb and Ursula Drake's account of seeing a limping man sneaking into Camille's neighborhood. Could the shambling person have been Felicity posing as her husband? No. If Felicity had donned Parker's overcoat, it would have dragged on the ground. Plus, she had an alibi. Sally Somers had said she was at the theater that night.

But was she really?

Chapter 24

St. Mary's High School was a private co-ed school south of Yountville. It boasted a well-maintained Mission Revival–style campus with low-pitched adobe tile roofs and an enclosed courtyard. The azaleas were no longer in bloom, but the red tea roses were. The afternoon sun made the school's green-and-gold WELCOME sign shimmer.

I cut across the campus following signs to the theater complex. I paused in front of the building to admire the grassy expanse. It was so green that I wondered whether Raymond might have tutored the groundskeeper.

Inside the theater, I blinked to help my eyes adjust to the dark.

"Lights!" a woman ordered.

Suddenly, all the lights popped on, making it possible to take in the plush loge seats and what looked like a state-of-the-art control booth. St. Mary's donors had done a bang-up job.

Bebe, who had changed from her competition clothing into jeans, fashionable plaid shirt, tennis shoes, and a bandanna to protect her hair, stood center stage. She clapped her hands. "Okay, everybody, let's get a move on. Cleanup time. Hop to it."

Moans were heard from people offstage.

"Grab those brooms and put on those happy faces," Bebe said. A television preschool hostess couldn't have acted cheerier.

A troupe of teenagers and a gaggle of older women—the actors' mothers, I assumed; Felicity was not in the mix—marched onto the stage. Each manned a broom. A cloud of confetti whooshed into the air.

Bebe caught sight of me and raised a hand to shield her eyes from the bright lights. "Mimi? Is that you? C'mon up." She beckoned me.

I strolled down an aisle and climbed the stairs at the right of the orchestra pit to the stage.

"What are you doing here?" Bebe asked. "Have you come to help? We could use it."

"Sure." I knew how to win friends and influence people.

"Swell." Bebe thrust an extra broom in my direction.

I accepted it and started sweeping.

A few of the teens picked up piles of confetti and hurled it at each other.

"Cut it out," Bebe ordered.

The giggling stopped; somber sweeping resumed.

"Tech week is a bear." Bebe grinned at me. "This is what the stage will look like at the end of every performance. Ugh!" She lowered her voice. "This was last night's rehearsal mess, but I simply couldn't make the kids clean up on a Friday night, you know? Between you and me, the director is nuts for coming up with this finale. How on earth could he expect the actors to help out when they're exhausted? But surprise, surprise. They're rallying."

"Is Felicity here?" I pushed my broom in one direction and tried not to cough from the dust it was kicking up.

"Are you kidding? Didn't you hear her at the bistro? She's in party celebration mode. La-di-da." The bite in Bebe's voice was unmistakable. "You two"—she singled out a pair of twin boys—"bring out the trash cans. Philomena, distribute dustpans and please tell my daughter to put in an appearance. Where is she? Texting?"

"Doing math homework in the green room," Philomena said.

"Tell her math can wait."

"Yes, ma'am." Philomena scurried offstage.

"Do you think Felicity will win the bake-off?" I asked as I pushed confetti to the right.

"Not a chance. I might not rival *you* in the dessert department, but my soufflé is pretty darned terrific." She winked like we were old friends. "By the way, I love your crème brûlée. Do you use a culinary torch or the good old-fashioned warehouse special?"

"The latter."

"Me, too."

I stopped sweeping and propped an arm on the broomstick. "Bebe, before coming here, I was at the *Napa Valley Neighborhood* office. I saw the articles on you and Felicity."

"What a farce. Felicity arranged that to tick off Louvain. She—"

Philomena and Bebe's daughter emerged from the wings.

"About time, ladies," Bebe said. "Grab dustpans." She refocused on me.

"I was wondering about something," I said. "On the night Renee Wells died, Felicity said she was here volunteering." *Clumsy segue*, I thought, but continued. "Sally Somers confirmed that, but she said Felicity was sick and hung out in the bathroom all night."

Bebe rolled her eyes. "How like Felicity, convincing everyone she was present and then wheedling her way out of helping by hiding in the restroom. In the privacy of a stall, she could check stock prices on her cell phone." She mimed swiping her finger on a digital device. "But Sally's mistaken. I saw Felicity leave the theater with a bunch of costume pieces she said she was going to repair. She preferred to use her own sewing machine."

"Wait a sec. Isn't Sally the wardrobe coordinator for the theater?"

"She is, but we're overwhelmed at this point with last-minute touchups. I'd bet Felicity didn't tell Sally what she was doing because she wanted to make sure her daughter's costume was the best of the bunch."

As I pushed my pile of debris toward Philomena, I pondered whether Felicity had taken more than the costumes for *Cats*—like an overcoat and earflap hat.

Bebe swept her pile of confetti toward mine. "Philomena, help us out."

The girl squatted and set her dustpan near my broom. "Go ahead, Miss Rousseau."

"Call me Mimi." I pushed the pile into the pan.

Bebe followed suit. When she finished, she collected my broom. "Dump that, Philomena. Mimi, thanks for the help."

She headed across the stage, and I couldn't help wondering why Sally had believed Felicity had been sick in the restroom. *Get real, Mimi.* Maybe it was a simple case of Felicity telling her it was so and Sally being too busy to notice Felicity had hoodwinked her.

On the other hand, Bebe could be lying. She had pivoted away from me. Was she avoiding making eye contact because she'd meant to implicate Felicity? There was clearly no love lost between them. The notion that Felicity had left with costumes in hand, however, had the ring of truth.

"Bebe, do you have a wardrobe room filled with costumes, or do you make or rent new ones for each production?"

"Sorry"—she pivoted, her finger rummaging in her eye—"got a

blast of dust." That explained why she'd turned away from me. "Costumes? We're overflowing with them. People are always donating. St. Mary's is known for high-quality shows. The locals like to support that."

I pictured Felicity finding an overcoat and earflap-style hat in the mix of costumes. Not necessarily that night. It could have been any night. But that was when the idea must have come to her. Under the guise of taking the costumes home for repair, she could sneak to Camille's neighborhood, pretending to be her husband, limp and all. By doing so, she could implicate him in Renee's murder. That would jeopardize his future, of course, but Parker had said she was wicked smart. Maybe Felicity had realized that she, the aggrieved wife of a murderer and adulterer, could move up the political ladder without him.

But why kill Renee? Did she truly believe Parker was having an affair with her as well as Louvain? What if Renee had hinted as much to Felicity when she'd gone to her house for tea? Had that pushed Felicity over the edge?

* * *

Driving to the bistro, I telephoned Tyson. He was out and couldn't be reached. I left a voicemail message about Felicity's iffy alibi and possible motive and dialed Jo.

"Phew," she said. "You got my text."

"No, I didn't. What's wrong?" I glanced at my cell phone screen. Blank.

"Rusty is in the hospital. He fell off a ladder. No one was around. A volunteer found him lying in the Sisley Garden, out cold. She was distraught and couldn't rouse him. She called 911 and rode with him in the ambulance. She contacted me from the hospital."

A chill ran up the nape of my neck. I said, "Where was Allie?"

"Allie?"

"Yes, Allie."

I scrapped my meanderings about Felicity and refocused on Allie. Was she innocent of Renee's murder, as everyone—including me—wanted to believe, or had she killed Renee and was now muscling her way into the festival circuit by putting Rusty out of commission, too?

"She's at the bistro." Jo could see the rear patio from her office window. "She's standing with Heather. The party is spirited. Why?"

I explained my suspicion.

Jo *tsk*ed. "Allie had nothing to do with his accident. I'm sure of it. Come back to work and we'll talk. Where have you been?"

I told her about my visit to the newspaper office and how that had raised my suspicions about Felicity's alibi, which had led me to St. Mary's High School, but added that I couldn't nail down her motive. Jealousy was all I could come up with.

"Might I remind you"—Jo cleared her throat on purpose—"that Felicity was in the vicinity when the flowerpot careened toward you, and she was present when you ingested that poison."

"I'm not sure it was poison."

"It was toxic. Don't quibble. Did you call Tyson and tell him your concerns?"

"Right before calling you. He was out. I left a message."

"I'll track him down. You get back to the bistro and detain Felicity. When Tyson gets there, he'll make sense of the mess."

The mess!

"Jo," I blurted as an image scudded through my mind. "The mess on the floor at Camille's. I thought Renee had tried to draw a heart in the flour."

"What flour?"

"From the canister. I told you about the flour on the floor.

There were snippets of paper and feathers and seed and . . ." I waved a hand. "It doesn't matter. What matters is . . . what if she wasn't drawing a heart but she was drawing the beginning of an infinity sign? Felicity has a tattoo on her back."

"Which would mean Renee was implicating her."

"Exactly."

"Hurry."

Traffic was a bear going north. Crush Week crowds were out in force. I arrived at the bistro twenty minutes later. Taking the last turn too fast, my wheels skidded on the pavement. I hit the brakes and came to a screeching halt. I bolted from the car and raced to the rear patio.

Oakley was setting platters of dessert on each table. Red was pouring champagne. Parker and Bebe's husband were sitting at one table having a heated tête-à-tête. Louvain was cackling at something her sister had said. Across the room, two blurs of white caught my eye. Felicity was at the buffet table dodging Stefan. He was doing his best to remove serving dishes.

Felicity was talking into her cell phone. When she caught sight of me, she frowned. Loudly enough for all to hear, she said to whoever was on the line, "Oh, yes, I'll win the finals. You can bet on it. I've got my game face on." The conversation sounded forced, like she was trying to prove she was talking to a fan, but when she stared daggers at me, I knew something was wonky. Was she talking to Oscar? Was he telling her about my interest in her photo spread? Or maybe Bebe was Felicity's friend after all and had alerted her that, *oops*, she had contradicted Felicity's alibi for the night Renee was killed.

Someone tapped me on the shoulder. I whipped around.

Allie blinked and retreated a pace, arms raised. "Sorry. I didn't mean to scare you."

"You didn't. Actually, yes you did, but—"

"Did you hear about Rusty?" She lowered her arms and tugged her tomato-colored romper down around her hips.

"Poor guy. I hope he's going to be all right."

"Me, too. We were working so well together."

I shot her a curious look.

"Not in that way." Allie flapped her hands like Oscar had, denying any hint of scandal. "I'm not into guys. Hey"—she pointed toward the floor—"what's that on your shoe, toilet paper?"

I glanced down. I had tracked in a strip of confetti from the theater. I bent to remove it and stopped as I thought again of the mess at the crime scene. Little snippets of paper had been mixed in with the chicken feed and feathers on Camille's kitchen floor. Camille had thought Renee had tracked in the scraps from the festival or from her visit to The Bookery, seeing as they had been having a celebration. But what if Felicity had tracked in the confetti? Even though the student actors cleaned up after every performance, bits of confetti would have lingered. Had some stuck to her shoes? Tyson's technicians would have logged in the evidence they'd found at the crime scene. Maybe he could locate a piece of confetti and match it to the stuff used at the theater.

Felicity ended her call, hoisted her tote higher on her shoulder, and stomped to the exit. "Parker, I'm leaving."

Oh, no, she wasn't. I raced after her.

Chapter 25

I reached the door first because Felicity had paused by her husband's table.

"On your feet, Parker," she said. "It's time to go."

"Not now, hon," Parker said. "We're just getting to the good stuff."

Heather entered the patio from the main dining room and joined me. "What's going on? Why are you out of breath?"

I pointed to Felicity. "I can't let her leave."

"Now, Parker," Felicity said.

"Uh-uh. You know how I like these little tarts." He lifted a plate of cookies, mini fruit tarts, and ramekins of vanilla soufflé. Camille had gone all out with the dessert choices. "If you'll be kind enough to get me some milk for my tea."

"Milk? Why you . . ." Felicity growled. "Get it yourself. Or better yet, have your *tart* Louvain get it for you."

Parker blanched. Louvain cringed.

"Yes," Felicity said, her voice rising in intensity, "I know about you and Louvain and your matching football tattoos."

"F-football tattoo?" Louvain sputtered. "I don't—"

"Do you think I'm blind, Lovey?" Felicity shouted as she kept her focus on her husband. "Are you leaving me for her, Parker? Is that the plan? Well, if it is, get ready, darling, because she's going to milk you for all you're worth. She's after you for your money. Capital M-O-N-E-Y."

"That's not true," Louvain blurted. "I love him."

Bebe's husband and the others on the patio froze, as if immobilized in a tableau.

As Felicity continued her rant about Parker being weak and Louvain being easy, the word *money* went *pow* in my brain, and the conversation I'd witnessed between Renee and Felicity started to make sense. Renee had praised Felicity and Parker for being adept at fundraising for education. Right afterward, Renee had taunted her with the cookie. Felicity had demurred, claiming she didn't eat sweets. Renee countered that she knew Felicity enjoyed dipping cookies into skim milk, and added, "We've got to watch our figures, don't we?" At the time, I hadn't picked up on the underlying meaning. Sure, Renee had punctuated a few of the words, but, not knowing her well, I'd thought it was her cadence. Looking back, the words *skim milk* and *figures* stood out. She had gone on to say that she had received quite an *education* after viewing Felicity's book collection. She hadn't meant literature books; she'd meant *accounting* books. Had Renee discovered that Felicity's husband was skimming money from their fundraising? Had she been baiting Felicity to confess Parker's guilt, or had she, in front of me and the rest of the festivalgoers, been blackmailing Felicity?

The telephone at the hostess desk jangled. I hoped it was Jo calling to say Tyson was en route. I was convinced Felicity had killed Renee not out of jealousy but out of self-preservation, and she was ready to flee the scene.

"Felicity," I said.

She didn't respond. She was still raving at her wayward husband for being spineless.

I recalled another moment when Allie had told me what Renee had said after drawing lips on their contract—she'd had to buck up and be *tougher* than most. Tougher in what way? Had Renee extorted Felicity in order to fund future festival plans? Had she told Felicity that she would expose her husband's skimming operation and not simply ruin Felicity's standing in the community but destroy Parker's political career, as well? Parker had shown up at that moment and guided Felicity away from Renee. Had Felicity mentioned the issue with Renee to him? Had Parker, knowing he was leaving Felicity for Louvain, sloughed it off? Maybe that was why Felicity had decided to implicate Parker in Renee's murder. She could kill two birds with one stone.

My breathing heightened as I stepped toward Parker's table. I had to ask. I had to know the truth. I said, "Sir."

"What?" Parker snapped, then quickly looked relieved to be facing someone other than his outraged wife. "Sorry, Mimi. Call me Parker."

"Pardon my bluntness, sir, but um . . ." I hesitated.

"How dare you butt in." Felicity's lip turned up in a snarl.

"Back off, hon. She wants to ask me a question. Go on, Mimi."

"Sir, were you skimming from the education fundraising accounts?"

"What?" He scrambled to his feet. His face blazed red. "I can't believe you would ask such a thing. I am as honest"—he thumped his chest—"as the day is long."

Felicity snorted. "Except when it comes to matters of the heart."

Parker recoiled. Louvain wheezed and turned pale.

"Then it was you, Felicity," I said.

She raised her chin. "I don't know what you're talking about."

"You skimmed funds and juggled the books. Renee found out. She threatened to reveal what you did."

"Don't be ridiculous."

"If she told the world that Parker was having an affair, big deal. That wouldn't hamper his or even your future if you decided to enter politics. But larceny would."

Parker grabbed hold of Felicity's arm. "What is Mimi talking about? What did you do?"

Felicity hissed. "She has no proof."

"Has no proof? Did you do it?" His gaze grew dark. "Did you? Answer me."

She blinked.

He thrust her away. "You disgust me."

"Don't get all high and mighty with me, darling," she said as she smoothed the skirt of her pearl-white dress.

Heather's warning, *Beware of a woman in white*, zipped through my mind.

"How did you think we were affording all our trips?" Felicity went on. "And our lifestyle and the private school for Philomena? Not on your meager salary."

"But I thought . . ." Parker wagged his head. "You said you were good with a budget. Math was always your forte."

"You were wearing blinders."

I said, "Renee saw evidence at your house when you invited her for tea, didn't she, Felicity?"

She looked down her nose at me. "There I was being all nice and sweet to her, making her favorite tea, and what did she do? Snooped. The gall."

"She taunted you at the festival in front of me, but I didn't catch the threat at the time."

"She was quite good at a double entendre."

"You went to Camille's house that night to confront her."

"You can't prove that."

"You dressed up as Parker."

Felicity pursed her lips.

"I'm guessing you'd been following him frequently to confirm he was having an affair with Louvain and quickly realized he was also going to my chef's neighborhood on a regular basis. At first, you probably suspected him of carrying on two affairs, but you soon learned he was taking piano lessons."

She clucked her tongue, but she didn't deny it.

"That fit right into your plan," I continued. "People had seen him there, so on the night of the murder, to implicate him, you put on an overcoat and earflap hat and limped through the neighborhood."

"That's crazy. His coat would hang down to my ankles."

"Not *his* coat. A coat you borrowed from the high school theater's costume closet."

"Speaking of high school"—she dumped her cell phone into her tote and folded her arms—"need I remind you that I have an alibi? I was at the theater until the end of rehearsal. Sally Somers will corroborate that."

"She did. She said you were sicker than a dog."

"That's right."

"Except Bebe saw you leaving with costumes. Was there an overcoat in the mix, I wonder?"

Felicity cocked a hip. "Bebe hates me. Sally will confirm—"

"I think you fooled Sally. You left the theater, drove to Camille's neighborhood, and waited for Renee to enter her sister's house—"

"I did not."

"And then you hobbled along the street. When you arrived, to your delight, you found the door unlocked. Renee was expecting her sister to come home from work. You entered and explained that you wanted to settle accounts. Did you offer her hush money?"

"Hush money?" Her mouth grew thin and cruel. "Mimi, for heaven's sake. What dime-store novel have you been reading?"

"You told her you would pay for her silence, but she turned you down," I continued, undeterred. "Did she laugh? Did she insult you? Was that what enraged you so much that you slammed her in the head with the mixer? Before she died, she tried to draw an infinity sign in the flour on the floor. A sign like the tattoo on your back."

"That's it. I've heard enough lies. Parker"—Felicity glowered at her husband—"you are a poor excuse of a man. Why aren't you standing up for me? Why aren't you defending me, the love of your life? And why, for heaven's sake, were you taking those stupid piano lessons?"

Parker's mouth opened but no words came out.

"Because I asked him to." Louvain pressed a hand on her chest. "He did it for *me*. We intend to play duets together."

Aha. Parker had lied to Betty about his reason for needing lessons.

Felicity huffed. "You never appreciated what I did for you, Parker. I helped you get through college. I negotiated your football contract. I planned your future. *Our* future. You weren't going to stay a councilman forever. You were going to become governor and then president. It was simply a matter of time. Well, guess what, you idiot? You jumped into another bed and lost that chance." She stomped toward the exit.

"Wait!" I hurried after her and grabbed her arm. She had yet to admit anything.

"Give it up, Mimi." She tugged free. Her tote plummeted to the floor. Out of it spilled her cell phone, a multitude of makeup, and a packet of wisteria seeds with its top rolled over as if it had been opened.

Seeing the seeds made me recall my conversation with Raymond when he had warned that cats could get sick by ingesting a number of garden plants. That memory brought another discussion to mind, when I'd been seven and walking through the family vineyard with my grandmother. She had told me how toxic wisteria was. At the time, it was growing at the ends of the rows of grapes to keep birds and pests away. The seeds were lethal, she'd said. If eaten, they would cause nausea, dizziness, and worse.

Felicity tried to gather her things.

I nabbed the packet of seeds before she could and flaunted them in her face. "Why do you have these?"

"I've been planting. I told you how wonderful my garden is."

"You poisoned me."

"What on earth are you talking about?"

"You put these seeds in my soda at Chocolate."

"Don't be ridiculous."

"You pushed sweetener packets off the table, and as I bent to fetch the packets, you dosed my drink."

"You're insane."

"You've been going after me ever since I asked you whether Parker was having an affair with Renee."

Parker shouted, "I was not!"

"I told her you weren't," Felicity huffed.

"That's true," I said. "You did. But immediately following that, you divulged your alibi. Why? I hadn't asked for it. I had no reason to. You had no motive to kill Renee." I splayed a hand. "But you were feeling guilty, weren't you? When we met at Chocolate, you tried to make me think Allie had killed Renee. You said she had a past."

"I didn't kill her," Allie said.

Heather put a comforting arm around her shoulder. "*Shh.*"

"On Tuesday night, Felicity, you came by my place," I said. "You were worried that I'd remember your exchange with Renee at the festival, put two and two together, and realize why you'd want her dead."

"Get real."

"You didn't knock. You didn't confront me. Maybe you had second thoughts and that's why you retreated through the vineyard."

"I have no idea where you live. I couldn't find your cottage if you drew me a map."

"And yet you know I live in a cottage."

Felicity sniffed.

"The other day," I went on, "after you won your semifinal, someone wearing tan clothing hurled a large flowerpot over the railing and nearly hit me. I think, after revealing your alibi to me, you were terrified that I might figure out the truth, so you put on Oscar's jacket and stole to the balcony above where Jo and I were chatting."

"You're nuts." She faced the others. "I went straight to the theater that day."

"No, you didn't."

"Yes, I—"

"A friend saw you at the souvenir tent buying T-shirts."

She sputtered.

"You tried to poison me at Chocolate because you missed hitting me with the flowerpot."

"I didn't mean to poison *you* at all. I—" She clapped a hand over her mouth.

Chapter 26

Everyone on the patio went quiet.

"Who did you mean to poison, Felicity?" I asked. "Your husband?"

She cut a look in his direction.

"You were hovering outside Chocolate when I arrived," I said. "Were you spying on him? Did you think he was meeting Louvain?"

"I . . ." She worked her upper lip between her teeth. "I wanted to make him sick. I wanted him to need me to nurse him back to health. I've always been the one to look after him."

"Did you put seeds in his mug?"

"Yes, but he didn't drink a drop of his coffee. He left, and I . . ." She moaned. "I still had some in my hands." She splayed her hands as if showing me the offending seeds. "I had to get rid of them. I didn't mean to hurt you. Yes, I wanted to scare you. I thought you'd stop asking questions if you believed you were in danger."

"Is that why you broke into my cottage and left sprigs of wisteria on my bedside table, as a follow-up warning?"

"Ooh," she moaned as an admission and covered her face with both hands.

The door to the patio squeaked open. Jo raced in.

"Where's Tyson?" I asked.

"A minute away. Why is Felicity crying?"

"I think she wants to confess to killing Renee."

"What?" Felicity dropped her hands. Her eyes were dry. "No!"

I quickly told Jo my theory about Felicity skimming from the education funds and Renee finding out and holding it over Felicity. Pretending to be Parker, Felicity had gone to Camille's neighborhood so she could confront Renee.

"That's all I did," Felicity cut in. "Confront her."

"But Renee was defiant, wasn't she?" I said, baiting her.

"Yes."

"Uppity."

"Yes. Yes. That's it! Oh, Mimi, you understand. She told me how she was going to destroy my husband." She glanced at Parker, pleading with her eyes. "I couldn't let her do that, darling. I love you so much." She lowered her chin. Her lower lip started to quiver. "So much."

Was her daughter this good an actress? I wondered. "Did Renee blackmail you?" I asked.

"She railed at me and called me names. Horrible, horrible names."

"That's when you grabbed the mixer," I said.

"Yes!"

"And struck her."

Felicity inhaled and held her breath.

At that exact second, Tyson entered the patio and took in the scene. Everyone was staring at Felicity in unabashed shock.

"What's going on?" Tyson asked.

Jo slipped her hand around his elbow and whispered what had transpired. After a long moment, Tyson hissed through his nose. "Mrs. Price, I'm afraid I'll need you to come to the station with me."

"But it was self-defense," she cried. "Any judge in America will realize that."

Parker scoffed. "You don't murder someone for calling you names, Felicity. Otherwise, I'd have done you in years ago."

Tyson recited Felicity's Miranda rights. When he finished, I mentioned the confetti and the infinity drawing in the flour. He murmured that he'd get to me in the next day or two, and then he escorted Felicity out of the bistro. Parker, who looked shaken by the ordeal, went with them.

Given the circumstances, Allie, who was officially in charge of the festival until Rusty was released from the hospital, announced that the best way to end the festival competition was to declare it a tie. She contacted Bebe by telephone and informed her. Supposedly, Bebe was delighted to learn she was a co-winner, though I'd have wagered she would continue to assert that her soufflé would have won the competition hands down. Louvain, with her humiliated husband in tow, clutched her sister's hand and disappeared from the bistro. I imagined she would touch base with Parker after an appropriate amount of time had passed.

Allie also took it upon herself to arrange Renee's memorial. She said it was the least she could do for Rusty. She corralled Heather and Jo and steered the two of them to the hostess podium so they could pin down the best day for it.

After the rest of the contestants and guests departed and Allie left to take command of the festival's closing ceremony, we set up the bistro for dinner. Camille and I worked side by side in the kitchen. Although she was thrilled to know the truth, she was glum. She promised she would rally.

When we closed for the night, the staff pleaded with Camille and me to party with them. They were going to the jazz club down the street. Stefan and Yukiko were leading the pack and walking hand in hand. Camille said no; she was exhausted. I begged off, too, and headed home.

The moment I entered the cottage, with Scoundrel and Scooter trailing me inside, my cell phone rang. It was Nash. He asked if he could come over. He'd heard what had happened with Felicity and needed to see me.

When he arrived, looking delicious in a cream camp shirt and coffee-colored corduroy trousers, I threw my arms around his neck and drank in his musky scent.

As I was ushering him inside, Raymond showed up in a beekeeper's-type outfit. He rapped on the doorjamb. "Is everything okay, Mimi?" He trained the beam from his flashlight at Nash. "Is this guy bothering you?"

Nash said, "Very funny."

Raymond grinned, pleased with himself.

"I'm safe," I said. "Go deal with the bees."

"Wasps," he corrected. "And I'm done for the night. It's time for a beer, a pizza, and some ESPN." He gave me a small salute and headed off, the glow of his flashlight lighting the path.

I led Nash inside. He encircled me with his arms and drew me to him. For a long while, he just held me and stroked my back in a soothing rhythm. After a long moment, our mouths met. We kissed for a very long time.

When we came up for air, he said, "Wow. Was it something I said?"

"It's your cologne."

"Soap?"

"That's the ticket. And the hug. The hug was . . . incredible."

He caressed my hair and kissed my forehead. "You're okay?"

"Never better, now that you're here."

He surveyed the living room. "You wiped off the dry-erase board."

I nodded. "Case closed."

"Care to give me a recap?"

I took his hand and ushered him to the sofa. "Let me pour you a glass of wine. This might take time to explain. Maybe all night."

"I'm game." He offered a sexy grin.

* * *

On Tuesday afternoon, Camille and my mother showed up on my doorstep. My mother was wearing one of her Bohemian outfits. Camille was dressed in clothes I'd never seen her wearing—jeans and a plaid shirt.

"Camille invited me to lunch at her house as a thank you for my hospitality and, well,"—my mother pushed past me into the cottage—"there's something you need to see."

She stopped short when she caught sight of Nash sitting on the sofa.

Camille bumped into her. "Oh, my."

"We're sorry to intrude," my mother said. "We had no idea. We—"

"It's not a problem, Mother. We—"

"Just returned from hot air ballooning," Nash said. "It was fabulous."

She eyed us knowingly. "Is that why your faces look flushed?"

That and a little necking, I mused as even more heat rushed into my cheeks.

The fish tank burped as if Cagney and Lacey meant to give us away.

I giggled. "What's up?"

Camille was holding an envelope in her hand—a mangled cream-colored enveloped. "You will not believe what we have discovered." She waggled the envelope. "Renee sent this to me."

"You showed it to me before."

"Yes, but I overlooked something."

Scooter and Scoundrel emerged from the bedroom. The

excitement in Camille's voice must have wakened them. In the past few days, they had become couch potatoes. They had even let me—not Heather—feed them. I was getting the hang of it.

"Look at this." Camille pulled a sheet of stationery from the envelope. "I did not know this existed until today. I was showing your mother the notecard and the damaged envelope that had come in the postal package, and she discovered this other letter. In my haste—"

"It had stuck to the folds of the original envelope," my mother said, reassuring Camille. "They're the same color, and given the state of the envelope—" My mother waved her hand. "In it, Renee spells out everything that Felicity was doing. It took a full page of stationery, which was why she hadn't written more on the notecard."

"Let me see," I said.

Camille handed me the letter. I unfolded it and browsed the first paragraph. Indeed, Renee had laid out every detail of her encounter with Felicity—seeing the accounting books and figuring out that she was skimming.

"Renee always understood numbers," Camille said. "She wrote the letter as insurance."

I added, "She must have swiped a notecard from Felicity's collection thinking that would somehow verify her claim."

"*Oui.*" Camille's voice cracked. "If only she had told me in person."

"No doubt she was embarrassed to admit she intended to blackmail Felicity."

"But she didn't," my mother said. "She didn't want to blackmail her at all. Read everything, sweetheart. Down to the bottom."

Renee continued, explaining how she intended to protect ten percent of the festival's proceeds that were tagged for the education fund. She warned Felicity to keep her hands out of the till. She didn't threaten Felicity's life, and she wasn't blackmailing her. She wasn't going to tell the world, either. She simply wanted proceeds for the festival to be on the up-and-up. She hoped the warning would make Felicity rethink her illicit activities and cease and desist.

I thought about Felicity's confession. When I'd asked her whether Renee had blackmailed her, she hadn't said *yes.* She'd simply tried to build a case of self-defense.

I put an arm around Camille and gave her a squeeze. "You must feel great."

"It exonerates her." She sniffed. "That is enough."

Nash said, "This calls for a celebration. Tea, everyone?" He strolled into the kitchen and fetched a tin of green tea from a cupboard.

My mother said, "He knows where your tea is?"

"It's not like it's rocket science, Mom. Small kitchen. Four cupboards."

"First try." She bumped me with her hip.

My cheeks warmed. Nash and I had spent three straight nights together and realized we were both head over heels for each other. As for our future? Oh, yeah, we had discussed that.

"By the way," Nash said, "I heard Rusty sold his farm and is going to continue to run the festivals. Are you okay with that, Camille?"

"Yes, of course. He is innocent. He loved Renee. He wants to do what made her happy."

"Allie will be helping out," I said. "They make a great team."

"She is not going to open a bakery?" Camille asked.

"I think she realized that if she had to, um, *borrow* recipes, then perhaps it wasn't the right business for her. Speaking of bakeries, how are things going with you and Donovan?"

"Very well. He wants to take me fly-fishing."

I snickered. I couldn't picture Camille dressed in waders and knee-high boots. Jo, on the other hand, loved to go fly-fishing.

"I am open to new experiences," Camille said. "That is what Renee would want for me. Besides, if I catch enough trout, we could serve trout almandine on the menu."

I high-fived her. "That's the spirit!"

Someone knocked on my door. I opened it. Jo sauntered inside.

"Speak of the devil," I said.

"I'm the devil?" she joked.

"I was making a mental note to call you." I tapped my temple.

"What's going on?" She unbuttoned the single button of her blazer and placed one hand on her hip. "Are you having a party and you didn't invite me?"

"It's impromptu," I said. "Why are you here?"

Her cheeks were rosy. Her eyes were glittering with excitement. "We did it."

"We, who?"

"Tyson and I."

"Did what? You'd better not have eloped. I've never been a bridesmaid."

She thwacked my arm. "We got engaged." She flashed her hand at me. The princess-style diamond on her fourth finger glistened.

"Wow, wow, wow." I threw my arms around her. "It's about time. I'm so happy for you. When's the big day?"

"I haven't a clue."

My mother said, "Better question: when are you going to start a family?"

Jo and I exchanged looks and burst into hysterics. When we finally brought ourselves under control, we sang in unison, "Mom."

Recipes Included

Autumn Quiche (with deep-dish pastry shell recipes, gluten-free and regular)
Beef Bourguignon
Brochette d'Agneau à la Grecque (Lamb with Greek sauce)
Camille's Special Sauce
Champignon Parmentier au Gratin (Mushrooms parmentier with cheese)
Côte de Porc (Pork chops with cornichons)
Crème Anglaise
Lobster Bisque
Porc à l'Orange (Pork in orange sauce)
Poulet Dijonaise (Chicken with mustard sauce)
Soufflé à l'Orange
Soufflé au Chocolat (with brandy sauce)
Soufflé Salted Caramel
Vanilla Bean Sugar Cookies (gluten-free and regular)

Autumn Quiche

From Mimi:
One of my favorite dishes is quiche. I can eat it for breakfast, lunch, or dinner. And it's easy to prepare. There are only a few ingredients in this recipe. I love the combination of ham with pumpkin. So savory. I often premake pie shells and freeze them so I have one on hand. There are also plenty of good pie shells that you can buy at the grocery store if you want this recipe to be, *ahem*, as "easy as pie."

(serves 8)

3 large eggs
1 can (15 ounces) solid-pack pumpkin
1 small can (5 ounces) evaporated milk
½ pound ham of your choice, diced fine (you may use Canadian bacon)
½ cup finely chopped onion
½ cup + 2 tablespoons grated Parmesan cheese
1 tablespoon cornstarch
1 teaspoon fresh ground pepper
1 deep-dish pie shell (may use frozen; use gluten-free if necessary)

Preheat the oven to 375 degrees F.

In a large bowl, whisk the eggs, pumpkin, and evaporated milk until blended. Stir in the diced ham and onion.

In a small bowl, toss the Parmesan cheese with the cornstarch and pepper. Add the cheese mixture to the egg mixture. Stir well.

Pour the mixture into the pie shell.

Bake on a lower oven rack for 50–60 minutes or until a toothpick inserted into the center comes out clean.

Remove from the oven and let stand 15 minutes before serving.

Deep-Dish Pastry Dough, Gluten-Free Version

(makes 1 deep-dish pie shell)

1 ½ cups sifted gluten-free flour*
¾ teaspoon xanthan gum
1 teaspoon salt
7 tablespoons butter or shortening
3–5 tablespoons water

Put the gluten-free flour, xanthan gum, and salt into a food processor fitted with a blade. Cut in 3 tablespoons of butter or shortening and pulse 30 seconds. Cut in another 4 tablespoons of butter or shortening. Pulse again for 30 seconds. Sprinkle with 3–5 tablespoons water and pulse a third time for 30 seconds.

Remove the dough from the food processor and form into a ball using your hands. Wrap with wax paper or plastic wrap. Chill the dough for 30 minutes.

Remove the dough from the refrigerator and remove the covering. Place a large piece of parchment paper on a countertop. (Sprinkle parchment paper with 2–4 tablespoons gluten-free flour.) Place the dough on top of the parchment paper. Cover with another

* I use a combination of sweet rice flour and tapioca starch; you can use store-bought ingredients like Bob's Red Mill or King Arthur gluten-free flour.

large piece of parchment paper. This prevents the dough from sticking to the rolling pin. Roll out dough so it is ¼-inch thick and large enough to fit into a 9-inch deep-dish pie plate, with at least a ½-inch border along the edge.

Spray the deep-dish pie plate with nonstick spray or rub with butter or shortening.

Remove the top parchment paper. Place the pie plate upside down on the dough. Flip the dough and pie plate. Remove the parchment paper. Press the dough into the pie plate. Crimp the edges. Note: Why flip the dough and pie plate? Because gluten-free pastry dough, unlike regular pastry dough, doesn't roll into a tube or fold well and has a tendency to break. This flip technique works best for me. If your dough does break, don't worry. Use a little water and fingertips to press any breakage back together. Nobody will see the bottom of the quiche. Also, here's a quickie tip for gluten-free pastry. If you run a knife between the pastry and the dish before filling with mixture, the pastry will not stick to the pie plate.

Deep-Dish Pastry Dough, Regular Version

(makes 1 deep-dish pie shell)

1 ½ cups sifted flour
1 teaspoon salt
7 tablespoons butter or shortening
3–5 tablespoons water

Put flour and salt into a food processor fitted with a blade. Cut in 3 tablespoons of butter or shortening and pulse for 30 seconds. Cut in another 4 tablespoons of butter or shortening. Pulse again for 30 seconds. Sprinkle with 3–5 tablespoons water and pulse a third time for 30 seconds.

Remove the dough from the food processor and form into a ball using your hands. Wrap with wax paper or plastic wrap. Chill the dough for 30 minutes.

Remove the dough from the refrigerator and remove the covering. Place a large piece of parchment paper on a countertop. (Sprinkle parchment paper with 2–4 tablespoons flour.) Place the dough on top of the parchment paper. Cover with another large piece of parchment paper. This prevents the dough from sticking to the rolling pin. Roll out dough so it is ¼-inch thick and large enough to fit into 9-inch deep-dish pie plate, with at least a ½-inch border along the edge.

Remove the top parchment paper. Gently roll the dough into a tube, removing the bottom layer of parchment paper, and then place the tube of dough into the pie plate. Unfurl the dough. Press the dough into the pie plate. Crimp the edges.

Beef Bourguignon

From Mimi:
There is nothing quite like a good stew to warm the heart and soul. The most wonderful thing about Beef Bourguignon is the mixture of flavors. Yes, there is a lot of wine in this recipe, but it enhances every other flavor. The French love their wine. And the aromas in your kitchen? To die for! If you like, serve this with a thick slice of sourdough bread rubbed with a clove of garlic. Yum!

(serves 8)

8 ounces bacon, diced
2 ½ pounds chuck beef, cut into 1-inch cubes
1 pound carrots, sliced into 1-inch chunks
2 sweet onions, sliced
2 cloves garlic, diced
1 pound fresh mushrooms, thickly sliced, stems discarded
1 tablespoon olive oil
kosher salt, 1 teaspoon plus 1 tablespoon, divided
freshly ground black pepper, 1 teaspoon plus 2 teaspoons, divided
½ cup cognac
1 bottle decent dry red wine, like a Burgundy or Pinot Noir
2–3 cups beef broth (gluten-free if necessary)
1 tablespoon tomato paste
1 teaspoon fresh thyme leaves (or ½ teaspoon dried)
3–5 whole cloves

4 tablespoons unsalted butter, divided
3 tablespoons cornstarch

Preheat the oven to 250 degrees F.

On a cutting board, cut all the ingredients that require it: bacon, chuck beef, carrots, sweet onions, garlic, and mushrooms. Set aside.

Heat the olive oil over medium heat in a large oven-safe baking pan that can be used on the stovetop. I use my Le Creuset. Add the diced bacon and cook over medium heat for about 8–10 minutes, stirring occasionally. The bacon should become lightly browned. Remove the bacon and reserve on a large plate.

Sprinkle the beef cubes with 1 teaspoon salt and 1 teaspoon freshly ground pepper. In batches—using single layers—sear the beef in the oil for 3–5 minutes, turning often, using tongs, so the beef browns on all sides. Remove the beef to the plate with the bacon and continue to cook all the beef cubes. Set aside.

Toss the carrots, sliced onions, 1 tablespoon of salt, and 2 teaspoons of pepper in the oil/fat in the pan and cook for 10–15 minutes, stirring occasionally, until the onions are lightly browned.

Add the garlic and cook for 1 more minute.

Add the cognac and—*get ready; stand back*—light the cognac with a match or kitchen torch to burn off the alcohol. *Whoosh!* Return the meat and bacon to the pot. Add a bottle of wine—yes, an entire bottle—plus enough beef broth to cover the meat. Add the tomato paste, thyme, and cloves. Bring the mixture to a simmer.

Cover with a lid and put the pot in the oven for 1 hour to 1 hour and 15 minutes, or until the meat and vegetables are really tender. Remove and set on the stovetop.

In a small cup, combine 2 tablespoons of butter and cornstarch with a fork. Add the mixture to the stew. Stir well.

In a separate pan, sauté the mushrooms in 2 tablespoons of butter for 4–6 minutes until lightly browned. Add to the stew.

Bring the stew to a boil on top of the stove and then cover, lower the heat, and simmer for 15 minutes. If desired, season with more salt and pepper to taste. Serve hot.

Brochette D'Agneau à la Grecque (Lamb with Greek sauce)

From Mimi:
The sauce for these kebabs is so flavorful. I'm not sure if it's because of the lime juice or the grapefruit juice or the Greek yogurt, but it really tenderizes the meat and offers a lovely Mediterranean flavor to the dish. I might use this sauce on chicken or fish, as well. Salmon in particular. Enjoy.

(serves 2)

For the kebab

1 pound lamb meat
1 yellow pepper, cut into squares
1 zucchini, cut into 8 thick slices
1 red onion, quartered

For the sauce

2 tablespoons freshly squeezed orange juice
2 tablespoons freshly squeezed lime juice
2 tablespoons grapefruit juice
2 tablespoons honey

½ cup plain Greek yogurt
2 tablespoons olive oil
½ teaspoon salt
½ teaspoon ground pepper
1 teaspoon fresh rosemary, crushed (stems removed)
Pam or olive oil for grill

For the sauce, in a small bowl, mix the orange juice, lime juice, grapefruit juice, honey, Greek yogurt, olive oil, salt, pepper, and rosemary. Stir well.

Cut the lamb into cubes, about 1 ½ inches in size. If they're too big, they won't cook evenly on the grill. Tenderize the lamb meat by pounding with a meat tenderizer mallet. Set the lamb in a 13×9–inch pan. Pour the marinade over the lamb, coating on all sides. Wrap and chill for 2 hours.

When ready to barbecue, skewer the kebab using lamb, pepper, zucchini, and onion. Repeat. (You might want to break the onion into smaller parts.) Brush the kebab on all sides with remaining marinade.

Heat a barbecue grill to medium high (about 400 degrees F). Spray the grill with olive-oil Pam or baste with olive oil.

Set the kebabs on the grill and cook for 3 minutes. Turn. Cook another 3 minutes. Turn. Cook another 3 minutes.

For medium rare, cook a total of 9–10 minutes. For medium, cook a total of 11–12 minutes. For medium well, cook a total of 13–14 minutes.

Remove from heat.

Present the dish either on the skewer or slide it off the skewer and plate accordingly.

Camille's Special Sauce

From Camille:
This is a very easy recipe to put together, and though it works on a sandwich, it is also an excellent sauce for fish, poultry, and pork. Enjoy the subtle flavor of nutmeg. All of your guests will be trying to guess what the secret ingredient is.

(makes ½ cup)

¼ cup mustard
2 tablespoons olive oil
3 tablespoons honey
½ teaspoon dried rosemary
⅛ teaspoon nutmeg

In a small bowl, mix all the ingredients. Cover and reserve until needed.

Champignon Parmentier au Gratin (Mushrooms parmentier with cheese)

(Vegetarian)

From Mimi:
This is one of my favorite vegetarian recipes. It serves beautifully as an entrée or as a side dish and is rich with cheese. Savory-loving foodies will adore it. Make sure you have everything on the counter and ready to go before you start. There are a lot of little steps, each taking a minute or so, but in an hour, you'll be happy you made this. FYI: What does *parmentier* mean in French? Well, it's actually a man's name. Antoine Augustin Parmentier was a chemist who focused on agronomy and nutrition. He was the one who convinced the Faculty of Medicine in Paris, way back in 1772, that the potato was a useful source of carbohydrates. Hence, his name might be used in recipes that feature potatoes, as this one does.

(serves 2 as an entrée or 6 as a side dish)

For the mushroom base

2 large portabella mushrooms
1 tablespoon plus 1 teaspoon butter
1 tablespoon olive oil, more as needed
½ large red onion, chopped

2 cloves garlic
¼ cup red wine (dry Burgundy, Pinot Noir, or Cabernet)
¼ cup vegetable stock
1 teaspoon thyme (or 3 tablespoons fresh thyme)
1 teaspoon kosher salt
½ teaspoon ground black pepper (6 grinds)
1 ½ teaspoons cornstarch
1 tablespoon chopped chives

For the cheese potato topping

2 tablespoons milk
2 tablespoons butter
½ teaspoon kosher salt
½ teaspoon ground pepper (6 grinds)
2 ounces Gruyère cheese, cut into small squares
2 tablespoons grated Parmesan, more if desired

In a medium saucepan, pour 1 inch of water. Set the potatoes in the water and bring the water to a boil. Turn down the heat to medium, cover the pot, and steam the potatoes for 30 minutes. Pour off the water. Set aside.

For the mushroom base: Clean and quarter the mushrooms. Remove the stems. Heat 1 tablespoon of the butter with 1 ½ teaspoons olive oil. Sauté the mushrooms until cooked and golden; flip once. Remove the mushrooms and set aside. Add another teaspoon of olive oil and the onions. Sauté the onions until soft, about 1 minute. Add the garlic and sauté for another minute.

Deglaze with the wine and reduce the liquid to no more than a spoonful, about 1 minute. Add the stock, thyme, and mushrooms and season with salt and pepper. Cook until the stock has reduced, about 1–2 minutes.

Mix the cornstarch with the remaining 1 teaspoon of butter and stir it into the onion mixture. Cook until the sauce has thickened, about 1 minute. Stir in the chives. Spoon the mixture into a 16-ounce gratin or baking dish.

For the cheese potato topping: Heat the oven to 425 degrees F.

In the saucepan containing the potatoes, mash the potatoes with the milk and butter until smooth. Add more milk if necessary. You want them creamy. Season with salt and pepper. Stir in the Gruyère cheese cubes. Spoon the potato mixture over the mushroom mixture. Smooth with your spoon. Sprinkle with Parmesan.

Bake the gratin until bubbling hot and golden on top, about 15–18 minutes.

Côte de Porc
(Pork chops with cornichons)

From Mimi:
This is one of the simplest dishes to make—very few ingredients—and it is packed with flavor. It's a bit messy because of the pork and oil, but it's so worth it. By the way, I adore white pepper. It creates a dish that is a tad spicier than if you were to use regular pepper.

(serves 6)

6 (6-ounce) pork chops (about ½ inch thick; you may use bone-in chops)
½ teaspoon kosher salt, divided
½ teaspoon white pepper, divided
1 tablespoon olive oil, divided
½ cup diced shallots
⅔ cup vegetable or chicken broth
⅔ cup white wine
1 teaspoon Dijon mustard
¼ cup thinly sliced cornichons
¼ cup chopped fresh chives

Sprinkle the pork chops with ¼ teaspoon salt and ¼ teaspoon white pepper. Heat 2 teaspoons of olive oil in a large nonstick skillet over medium-high heat. Add the pork chops. Cover! This mixture will spit. Cook 8 minutes, turning after 4 minutes, until the chops are golden brown. Remove pork from the pan and set on a plate; keep warm by covering with foil.

Meanwhile, add 1 more teaspoon of oil and shallots to the pan. Cook for 1 minute, stirring constantly. Stir in the broth and wine, scraping the pan to loosen browned bits. Bring the onions to a boil. Cook until the liquid is reduced (about 8 minutes). Stir in ¼ teaspoon salt, ¼ teaspoon white pepper, and Dijon mustard. Remove the pan from heat. Stir in the cornichons.

Arrange the pork on individual plates. Pour the sauce over the pork, distributing the cornichons evenly. Sprinkle with chopped fresh chives.

Crème Anglaise

From Mimi:
This is an easy, delicious, decadent sauce that enhances so many desserts. I simply had to share it with you. Serve over fresh fruit, pound cake, or other desserts, including soufflé.

(makes 1 ½ cups)

2 large egg yolks
1 cup heavy cream
⅓ cup white sugar
1 tablespoon brandy-based orange liqueur such as Grand Marnier
¼ teaspoon vanilla extract

Whisk egg yolks, cream, sugar, orange liqueur, and vanilla in a small saucepan until smooth.

Set saucepan over medium-low heat and cook, stirring constantly, using your rubber spatula to scrape the bottom, until the mixture is hot and thickens slightly. A candy thermometer should reach 180 degrees F. This takes about 8–10 minutes.

Remove the pan from the heat and strain the sauce into a bowl to remove any large lumps. (Hopefully there are none.)

Allow sauce to cool.

Lobster Bisque (Gluten-free)

From Mimi:
This lobster bisque recipe is my grandmother's. She was a fabulous cook. Of course, when I was growing up, I didn't realize how good she was. I was in the *ew, carrots* stage. But after my mother helped me fall in love with food and find my passion in the kitchen, I started practicing with family recipes. I miss my grandmother, but memories of her are firmly implanted in my psyche.

(serves 6)

2 lobster tails
4 cups water
2 cups dry white wine
2 cups chicken broth (gluten-free)
½ cup butter
1 cup onions, finely diced
½ cup carrots, finely diced
½ cup celery, finely diced
2 garlic cloves, diced
½ cup tapioca starch or other gluten-free flour or cornstarch
¼ cup brandy
1 ½ cups tomatoes, diced (you may use canned, liquid strained)
1 teaspoon paprika
1 teaspoon thyme

1 tablespoon salt
2 cups heavy cream

Chop the vegetables and set aside.

Put water, wine, and chicken stock in an 8–10-quart stock pot and bring to a boil. Place lobster tails in the broth. Reduce heat to medium and cook uncovered for 6 minutes. Remove lobster from broth and set to the side. When cool, remove the back shell and dice the lobster meat into tiny cubes.

Meanwhile, strain the broth through a sieve into a bowl and set aside.

Return pot to the stove and add the butter. Melt. Add the carrots, celery, onion, and garlic. Heat for 3 minutes on medium. Stir. Add the brandy. Stir. Add the gluten-free flour. Stir until all flour is incorporated.

Add the tomatoes, paprika, thyme, and salt. Stir well. Add the reserved broth. Stir and bring to a boil. Cook for 25–30 minutes on medium-low heat.

Remove from the heat and puree the mixture in small batches. Return to the pot. Add the lobster and cream. Heat about 3–5 minutes and serve.

Porc à l'Orange (Pork in orange sauce)

From Mimi:
I thoroughly enjoy this recipe. It has so many wonderful flavors. My particular favorite is the allspice, which gives the dish a kick. Think of it as stroganoff with an orange twist. There are a lot of ingredients but not too many steps, so don't panic. It's easy to make. I've noted a few substitutions if you need to eat gluten-free.

(serves 6)

¼ cup flour (for gluten-free, substitute potato starch)
1 teaspoon salt
½ teaspoon paprika
¼ teaspoon white pepper
¼ teaspoon allspice
1 pound pork tenderloin, sliced into 12 rounds and slightly flattened
2 tablespoons safflower oil
¼ cup chicken stock (for gluten-free, make sure stock is gluten-free)
½ cup sour cream
2 tablespoons orange juice
1 tablespoon orange rind, grated
¼ teaspoon salt
½ teaspoon Worcestershire sauce
2 tablespoons orange liqueur

wild rice or Arborio rice, 6 portions (cook ahead or
simultaneously)
parsley
orange slices

In a small bowl, combine flour (or gluten-free potato starch), salt, white pepper, paprika, and allspice. Coat the rounds of tenderloin with the flour (or gluten-free) mixture.

In a heavy skillet, heat the safflower oil over medium-high heat. When it's hot, lay the pork medallions in the oil and brown the pork well, about 4–5 minutes a side. This will spit!

Add the chicken stock (or gluten-free chicken stock), cover, and simmer for 30 minutes.

Meanwhile, in a small pan, combine the sour cream, orange juice, orange rind, salt, Worcestershire sauce, and orange liqueur. By the way, orange rind is hard to measure. Figure about a half an orange for one tablespoon of rind. Over medium heat, bring the mixture to a low bubble but **do not boil**. Cook for 2–3 minutes. Turn off heat and set aside.

Turn off the pork and serve 2 slices of the pork over each portion of wild rice or Arborio rice. Drizzle 2–4 tablespoons of the orange sauce over the pork. Garnish with parsley and orange slices.

Poulet Dijonaise (Chicken with mustard sauce)

From Mimi:

Okay, Poulet Dijonaise is just a fancy way of saying chicken with mustard sauce. Let's face it. All names of recipes written in another language make them sound fancy. But in case you didn't know, Dijon mustard is a traditional mustard of France. It is named after the town of Dijon, which is situated in the Burgundy region. As it so happens, Dijon was the center of mustard making in the early Middle Ages. So if you want something really French, think Dijon mustard . . . and Brie cheese . . . and Roquefort cheese . . . and . . .

(serves 4)

4 chicken breasts, approximately 6 ounces each and about ½ inch thick
1 tablespoon unsalted butter
⅓ cup dry white wine, more if needed
1 tablespoon Dijon mustard
1 teaspoon lemon juice
¼ teaspoon dried thyme
1 teaspoon cornstarch
1–2 tablespoons heavy cream

On a cutting board, pound the chicken breasts so they are thin and tender. In a large skillet over medium heat, melt the butter. When the butter is hot but not brown, put the chicken breasts in the skillet and cook until browned (about 12 minutes). Turn the chicken once or twice during cooking. You'll want to cover the pan as the chicken and butter might spit. When done, remove the chicken and set aside on a plate. Cover in foil to keep warm.

Meanwhile, keeping the pan on medium heat, pour the white wine into the skillet to deglaze the pan. Stir to make sure to get all the crunchy bits that have stuck to the skillet. Add the Dijon mustard, lemon juice, thyme, cornstarch, and heavy cream. (I prefer 2 tablespoons.) Whisk until the sauce holds together and thickens, about 1–2 minutes.

Serve chicken breasts on plates and spoon sauce over the top. This is delicious with white rice seasoned with onions. You could also serve the dish with roasted potatoes.

Soufflé à l'Orange

From Mimi:
Give me an orange, eggs, and sugar, and I can whip up a soufflé in minutes. That's why I love this particular soufflé. So easy. So quick. So delicious. I use triple sec in this recipe, but you could use any of your favorite orange-flavored liqueurs.

(serves 1–2)

1 teaspoon butter, for ramekins
1 teaspoon sugar, for ramekins
1 orange for 1 teaspoon orange zest and 2 tablespoons orange juice
1 egg yolk
2 egg whites
2 tablespoons sugar
1 tablespoon cornstarch
1 teaspoon triple sec
powdered sugar

Preheat the oven to 400 degrees F.

Brush 2 (4-ounce) ramekins or 1 (8-ounce) ramekin with 1 teaspoon soft butter, then coat with ½ teaspoon sugar each or 1 teaspoon for the larger ramekin. Pour out extra sugar. Set ramekins aside. Using a grater, grate the zest from the rind of an orange and reserve.

Separate the 2 eggs and toss out one of the yolks so you have

1 egg yolk in a bowl and 2 egg whites in another bowl. Whisk the egg yolk with 2 tablespoons sugar and the cornstarch until smooth. Whisk in the 2 tablespoons orange juice.

Place the mixture in a saucepan and heat over medium heat, stirring constantly until it thickens, about 2 minutes. Remove from heat and add the orange zest and triple sec. Let this mixture cool.

Meanwhile, in a small bowl, whisk the egg whites until they form soft peaks. Gradually add 2 teaspoons sugar and keep whisking until they form stiff peaks. Fold the egg whites into the orange mixture and then pour the mixture into the prepared ramekin(s).

Bake small ramekins for 15–17 minutes or bake the larger ramekin for 20–22 minutes, until the soufflés are golden on top. Remove from the oven and sprinkle with powdered sugar. Serve immediately.

Soufflé au Chocolat (with brandy sauce)

From Mimi:

There are many ways to make chocolate soufflé. Some have a few ingredients. A few have a lot of ingredients. You will find recipes including coffee, lemon, and so much more. The most important thing to remember is the ratio of eggs to chocolate. The more egg whites, the fluffier the soufflé. By the way, your egg whites will keep longer if use sugar as well as an acid, such as lemon juice, vinegar, or cream of tartar. Also, what is the difference between stiff and dry egg whites? To me, the dry stage is when the egg whites look like they are starting to break down again. You want them to be glossy and hold a peak. Enjoy!

(makes 4–5 small portions)

2 tablespoons unsalted butter, plus 1 tablespoon for preparing the ramekins
2 tablespoons sugar, plus ¼ cup sugar, plus 2 ½ teaspoons for preparing the ramekins
3 ½ ounces finely chopped bittersweet or semisweet chocolate
¾ teaspoon pure vanilla extract
2 large egg yolks
1 ½ tablespoons warm water
4 large egg whites, room temperature
¼ teaspoon fresh lemon juice
confectioners' sugar for garnish

Brush 5 (4-ounce) ramekins with 1 tablespoon soft butter, then coat with about ½ teaspoon sugar each. Pour out the extra sugar. Set ramekins aside. Set an oven rack in the lower third of the oven and preheat the oven to 400 degrees F.

Put the chocolate and 2 tablespoons unsalted butter in a small saucepan. Bring a larger saucepan filled with an inch of water to a slow simmer. Set the small saucepan over, *but not touching*, the water. Stir the chocolate and butter occasionally until melted and smooth, about 1–2 minutes. Remove from the heat and lift the saucepan out of the larger saucepan. Stir the vanilla extract into the chocolate mixture. Set aside.

In a large bowl or the bowl of a countertop mixer, combine the egg yolks and warm water. Beat until frothy. Add 2 tablespoons sugar and continue beating until frothy and the mixture thickens, about 5 minutes. Very gently fold the yolks into the chocolate mixture. Set aside.

In a large bowl, mix the egg whites and lemon juice. Beat on medium until frothy. Gradually add the ¼ cup of sugar and increase speed to high. Beat until the whites hold a stiff but not dry peak.

Fold about a third of the egg whites into the chocolate mixture to lighten. It will look like melted vanilla-chocolate swirl ice cream. Then fold in the remaining whites until blended.

Gently spoon the soufflé mixture into the ramekins—they will be very full—and place the ramekins on a baking sheet.

Bake the soufflés for 15–17 minutes. They should rise about 1 to 1 ½ inches from the top. When a toothpick comes out slightly moist, they are done. Remove them from the oven and dust with confectioners' sugar. Serve immediately (with brandy sauce, if desired).

Brandy Sauce

(makes about ¾ cup)

3 tablespoons unsalted butter, cut into small pieces
½ cup tightly packed dark brown sugar
3 tablespoons granulated sugar
⅓ cup heavy cream
2 tablespoons brandy

Combine the butter, brown sugar, granulated sugar, and cream in a medium, heavy-bottomed saucepan. Stir the mixture over low heat until the sugar dissolves, then increase the heat to medium and bring the sauce to a gentle boil. Stir often.

Cook 5 more minutes. Remove the saucepan from the heat and stir in the brandy.

Serve immediately, or cool to room temperature, then cover and refrigerate until needed. To rewarm, microwave the uncovered sauce on low for about 1 minute.

Soufflé Salted Caramel

From Mimi:
I have to tell you that I am a huge fan of caramel. I like it as a candy, and I love it on ice cream. And now, this soufflé might be my favorite dessert. It's decadent. It's creamy. It's packed with caramel flavor. The pinch of sea salt gives it a delicious kick. Soufflé is easy to make, but it does sink quickly. Do not despair. Simply enjoy the flavor of whatever result you get.

(makes 2)

For caramel

6 tablespoons water
¼ cup sugar
1 tablespoon crème fraiche

For soufflé

½ tablespoon butter
3 tablespoons plus 2 teaspoons sugar
3 egg yolks
1 ½ tablespoons cornstarch
1 cup warm milk

1 egg white
¼ teaspoon white wine vinegar

For salted caramel sauce

6 tablespoons brown sugar
¼ cup butter
3 tablespoons heavy cream
⅛ teaspoon vanilla
pinch of sea salt

First, make the caramel. In a sauté pan, over medium heat, bring water and sugar to a boil. Stir until it is a dark golden color, about 5–7 minutes, then add the crème fraiche and stir on low heat until smooth. Set aside.

Preheat the oven to 400 degrees F. Brush two 3-inch-wide ceramic dishes (5–6 ounces) with ½ tablespoon melted butter. Dust each with 1 teaspoon sugar. Shake off the excess.

In a medium saucepan (off the heat), whisk together the egg yolks, 3 tablespoons sugar, and cornstarch, then slowly add the warm milk. *Note: I heat the milk in the microwave oven for 45 seconds on high.* Whisk to incorporate. Cook the mixture on medium heat, whisking constantly, until thick. Then stir in the caramel, which will be sticky. Set the mixture aside and allow to cool slightly, whisking occasionally to prevent a skin from forming.

In a small bowl, whisk the egg white with the vinegar until stiff peaks form. Gently fold the egg whites into the caramel-egg mixture. Pour mixture into the two prepared baking dishes.

Bake for 25–35 minutes until golden. There will be a slight

wobble in the center. Remove ramekins from the oven. Let cool 15 minutes. They might sink a bit.

Meanwhile, make the salted caramel sauce. Put the brown sugar, butter, heavy cream, vanilla, and sea salt in a saucepan. Bring to a boil. Let bubble for 1–2 minutes until glossy, stirring constantly.

Serve the soufflé with a side of the salted caramel sauce.

PS: The salted caramel sauce is terrific over vanilla ice cream!

Vanilla Bean Sugar Cookies, Gluten-Free

From Mimi:
These are the most delicious sugar cookies ever, and they are so easy to make. Just a few ingredients. I'm offering you both the gluten-free and the regular flour versions so you can decide which you want. If you have children around, make sure you have some decorations ready.

(makes 20–24 cookies)

1 stick unsalted butter
½ cup plus 1 ½ tablespoons sugar
1 egg
1 vanilla bean
½ cup sweet rice flour
½ cup white rice flour
1 teaspoon cream of tartar
½ teaspoon xanthan gum

In a medium-sized bowl, cream butter, sugar, egg, and the insides of one vanilla bean. How do you remove the insides? Lay the bean on a cutting board and slice lengthwise. Peel open and scrape the beans out with the tip of a knife. Add the beans to the mixture and stir well.

Add the sweet rice flour, white rice flour, cream of tartar, and xanthan gum. Mix well.

Drop by walnut-sized spoonfuls onto a cookie sheet covered with parchment paper. Press the spoonfuls with the back of a spoon to a silver dollar–sized shape. You might need to wet the spoon with hot water. Shake the water off the spoon before pressing the dough.

Bake cookies at 375 degrees F for 10–12 minutes maximum. They will be really thin and should be lightly brown around the edges. Let cool 1 minute, then remove from the tray with a spatula and set on racks to cool. These get very crisp.

If you like, these may be decorated with colored sprinkles, powdered sugar, or nuts. Decorate while warm. Store in an airtight box or freeze. These are great freezer cookies!

Also, you may want to freeze a small portion of the mixture so you can make fresh cookies whenever you have a craving. Put the amount of batter for approximately 3–4 cookies in a freezer-safe container. When ready, remove the container from the freezer, let the mixture come to room temperature, and bake the cookies as above.

Vanilla Bean Sugar Cookies, Regular

(makes 24 cookies)

1 stick unsalted butter
½ cup plus 1 ½ tablespoons sugar
1 egg
1 vanilla bean
1 cup regular flour, sifted
1 teaspoon cream of tartar

In a medium-sized bowl, cream butter, sugar, egg, and the insides of one vanilla bean. How do you remove the insides? Lay the bean on a cutting board and slice lengthwise. Peel open and scrape the beans out with the tip of a knife. Add the beans to the mixture and stir well. Add the flour and cream of tartar. Mix well.

Drop by walnut-sized spoonfuls onto a cookie sheet covered with parchment paper. Press the spoonfuls with the back of a spoon to a silver dollar–sized shape. You might need to wet the spoon with hot water. Shake the water off the spoon before pressing the dough.

Bake cookies at 375 degrees F for 10–12 minutes maximum. They will be thin and should be lightly brown around the edges. Let cool 1 minute, then remove from the tray with a spatula and set on racks to cool. These get very crisp.

If you like, these may be decorated with colored sprinkles, powdered sugar, or nuts. Decorate while warm. Store in an airtight box.

Note: These are great cookies to store in the freezer and eat right from the freezer!

Also, you might consider freezing a small portion of the mixture so you can make fresh cookies whenever you'd like. Put the amount of batter for approximately 3–4 cookies in a freezer-safe container. When ready, remove the container from the freezer, let the mixture come to room temperature, and bake the cookies as above.

Acknowledgments

> Cooking is great, love is grand, but soufflés fall and lovers come and go. But you can always depend on a book.
>
> —Claudia Christian

Thank you to my family and friends for all your support. I am so blessed to have you in my life.

Thank you to all of my friends and consultants who helped me learn more about French cooking. It is not easy, but it is delicious.

Thank you to my talented author friends, Krista Davis and Hannah Dennison, for your words of wisdom and calm. Thank you to my brainstormers at Plothatchers: Krista, Janet K, Janet B, Kaye, Marilyn, and Peg. Thanks to my blog mates on Mystery Lovers Kitchen: Cleo, Krista, Sheila, Leslie, Mary Jane/Victoria, Roberta/Lucy, and Linda/Erika. As always, it is a delight to cook up "crime" with you. Thank you to my Crooked Lane fellow authors. It's been a pleasure getting to know you.

Thanks to those who have helped make *A French Bistro Mystery* series fun to write and a delight to promote: my fabulous editor, Faith Black; my keen-eyed copy editor, Jenny Chen, and Rachel Keith. Thanks to my talented cover artist, Teresa Fasolino, who always captures the right tone. Thanks to my agent, John Talbot, for believing in me. Thanks to Sheridan Stancliff. You are an Internet and creative marvel and make my life so much easier.

Thank you to my street team, The Cake and Dagger Club.

Thank you to all the cozy mystery lovers in the Delicious Mysteries group, the Save our Cozies group, the Cozy Experience group, and beyond. I cherish your enthusiasm.

Thanks to Donovan Coleman and Selma Mann for allowing me to use Donovan's name in this work of fiction. I hope you like how Donovan turned out. He was fun to write.

I've said it before and it bears repeating: thank you librarians, teachers, booksellers, and readers for eagerly jumping into a new series. I hope you will continue to embrace Mimi Rousseau and her family and friends as you have embraced my other casts of characters.

Last but not least, my heart goes out to all of the people in California's wine country who suffered such horrible loss in the wildfires of 2017. I can't imagine your heartbreak. I hope that my mysteries might entertain you and give you some comfort and *hope*.

Savor the mystery.